SHADOW LEGENDS

SERIES BY NELLIE H. STEELE

Cate Kensie Mysteries

Shadow Slayers Stories

Lily & Cassie by the Sea Mysteries

Pearl Party Mysteries

Middle Age is Murder Cozy Mysteries

Duchess of Blackmoore Mysteries

Maggie Edwards Adventures

Clif & Ri on the Sea Adventures

Whispers of Witchcraft

snapped her gaze to him with a sniffle. "No. It's my
ot a hairball."
I, I mean…sure, your mom isn't doing so hot but
orking on that. But that weird feeling in your gut
e a hairball. I mean…you are part cat now."
heaved a sigh, climbing to her oddly jointed cat-like
gs and pacing the floor at the foot of the bed. "Yes, I
Iow is progress going on getting me back to being
Paige?"
Il, there's good news and bad news on that front."
e me the bad news first."
esn't work that way," Dewey said with a shake of his
Iere's the good news. I *can* make you non-feline."
at's great! I can't wait to not be part cat."
e bad news is…you'd be part dog."
e screwed up her face as she stared at him. "What?"
h. The reversal serum I created will strip away the
arts, but instead of putting back the human ones, it'll
them with dog."
e slid her eyes closed as she crossed her arms and
er head. "You're joking."
not. Now, there is a little more good news."
at is it? That you're close to creating the serum that'll
work?"
, but if you don't want to be a dog, I can easily swap
werewolf, harpy, or mermaid."
ose are all worse."
bobbed his head up and down. "I thought so, too,
s why I went for dog. The thing is…no more hairballs,
downside is…you can't eat chocolate. Or grapes."
on't want to be part dog."
vey held his paws in the air. "Okay, okay. I'll keep at it
f I can find one that'll just reverse the cat stuff."
ase. I'm getting sick of being part cat, too."

SHADOW LEGENDS

A MAGICAL LIBRARY CONTEMPORARY FANTASY NOVEL

SHELVING MAGIC
BOOK EIGHT

NELLIE H. STEELE

Cover designed by Alex Calder.

❀ Created with Vellum

CHAPTER

*P*aige Turner tried to pres
face in a desperate attem
had fallen. She slid a paw onto her mc
perched on the edge of the hospital be

A variety of machines beeped, pro
mother remained alive…barely.

It had been days since she'd found
life under the Mexican ruins. And i
progress had been made. Instead, s
bedside as research had been performe
Twilight Trance.

A magically induced coma of sort
mechanisms for reversal.

Paige shook her head at the idea. Sh
all of this to watch her mother die in fro

Dewey fluttered into the room, a co
his teal features as he buzzed toward
don't look so good."

"I don't feel so good," she said with a
He pressed his lips together. "Is it a h

She
mom. I
"We
we're
could l
She
back le
know.
human
"We
"Gi
"Dc
head. "
"Th
"Th
Pai
"Ye
feline
replac
Pai
shook
"I'n
"W
actuall
"N
out fo
"Tl
He
which
but th
"I
Do
to see
"P

1

"Is it the hairballs?"

"Stop talking about hairballs." She shook her head. "That's only part of the stuff I hate. Last night, Devon came by to sit with me."

"Okay? What does that have to do with anything."

Paige's feline features turned stony. "He scratched my ears, and I started purring."

"Whoa. Hey, now, this is a PG conversation. I don't need to hear anymore."

Paige narrowed her eyes. "Really? Says the dragon writing steamy paranormal romance involving me and Devon."

"That's different."

Paige shook her head. "Whatever. Just...please find a cure. I want to be ready to roll if they find something to help my mom."

"Technically, you are ready to roll. I mean...you're actually readier to roll than you were before."

"Readier? That's not even a word, is it?"

Dewey shrugged. "Who cares. The point is...you are faster and more agile than a human Paige. So, technically, you're in better shape to track down an asset as cat Paige than human Paige."

"I don't want to be a cat while I track down an asset. Too many things could go wrong."

"To be fair, a lot could go wrong with human Paige, too. I mean...if history serves as any reminder, you're pretty accident-prone as a straight human."

She clenched her jaw tightly, her words sliding through clenched teeth. "Just fix this."

Dewey held his paws in the air again. "Okay, okay. I'm on it."

He flicked his gaze to the woman in the bed. "Any changes?"

3

Paige sank onto the edge of the mattress again. "None. She's just...inching closer to death with every breath."

The words made her burst into tears again, and she hid her face in her paws.

Dewey patted her on the head. "Paige, we'll find an answer. Drucinda is tracking every possible lead. We'll find something. We didn't come all this way just to give up."

"I should be helping," Paige cried. "But how can I? I can't even type with these stupid paws."

"Being part cat shouldn't be stopping you from doing anything, Paige. You'll have to find a way to work around it. Maybe type-to-text or something?"

Paige's features crinkled. "Right. You're right. I can't cry every time something weird happens to me. Around here, it happens like twice a week, so I'd just constantly be crying."

"You sort of are."

"What?" She snapped her gaze to him, her claws popping out.

"I said...that's bizarre."

She narrowed her eyes, certain that wasn't what he'd said but willing to let it slide. The door to the hospital room burst open, and Devon strode in.

"Hey, babe, how's Mom?"

Paige stared at him for a moment, her paws curling into fists. "*My* mom is no different."

"Well, technically, she's also my mom."

"Mother-in-law," Paige reminded him.

"Oh, yeah," Dewey answered with a nod. "I'd forgotten. We need to wake Reed up so she can meet her new son-in-law. Wow. I bet she's going to be so proud of you becoming a princess, Paige."

"Oh, I'm certain," Paige said with a bob of her furry head. "She's going to wake up and pet my furry little head and be so happy that I married a vampire."

SHADOW LEGENDS

A MAGICAL LIBRARY CONTEMPORARY FANTASY NOVEL

SHELVING MAGIC
BOOK EIGHT

NELLIE H. STEELE

CHAPTER 1

*P*aige Turner tried to press a tissue to her furry face in a desperate attempt to dry the tears that had fallen. She slid a paw onto her mother's pale form as she perched on the edge of the hospital bed.

A variety of machines beeped, providing proof that her mother remained alive...barely.

It had been days since she'd found her mother clinging to life under the Mexican ruins. And in those days, no real progress had been made. Instead, she'd sat vigil at her bedside as research had been performed on her condition.

Twilight Trance.

A magically induced coma of sorts that had no known mechanisms for reversal.

Paige shook her head at the idea. She hadn't gone through all of this to watch her mother die in front of her.

Dewey fluttered into the room, a consoling expression on his teal features as he buzzed toward her. "Hey, Paige. You don't look so good."

"I don't feel so good," she said with a shake of her head.

He pressed his lips together. "Is it a hairball?"

1

She snapped her gaze to him with a sniffle. "No. It's my mom. Not a hairball."

"Well, I mean…sure, your mom isn't doing so hot but we're working on that. But that weird feeling in your gut could be a hairball. I mean…you are part cat now."

She heaved a sigh, climbing to her oddly jointed cat-like back legs and pacing the floor at the foot of the bed. "Yes, I know. How is progress going on getting me back to being human Paige?"

"Well, there's good news and bad news on that front."

"Give me the bad news first."

"Doesn't work that way," Dewey said with a shake of his head. "Here's the good news. I *can* make you non-feline."

"That's great! I can't wait to not be part cat."

"The bad news is…you'd be part dog."

Paige screwed up her face as she stared at him. "What?"

"Yeah. The reversal serum I created will strip away the feline parts, but instead of putting back the human ones, it'll replace them with dog."

Paige slid her eyes closed as she crossed her arms and shook her head. "You're joking."

"I'm not. Now, there is a little more good news."

"What is it? That you're close to creating the serum that'll actually work?"

"No, but if you don't want to be a dog, I can easily swap out for werewolf, harpy, or mermaid."

"Those are all worse."

He bobbed his head up and down. "I thought so, too, which is why I went for dog. The thing is…no more hairballs, but the downside is…you can't eat chocolate. Or grapes."

"I don't want to be part dog."

Dewey held his paws in the air. "Okay, okay. I'll keep at it to see if I can find one that'll just reverse the cat stuff."

"Please. I'm getting sick of being part cat, too."

"Who is going to be happy that you married a vampire?" Drucinda asked.

"Reed," Dewey answered her. "Paige is royalty now. I bet she's going to be thrilled. Her little baby, all grown up and a princess."

"I doubt it," Drucinda answered with a shake of her head as she marched to the monitors to read them. "She'll likely be horrified."

"Really?" Dewey rubbed his chin as he pondered it.

"Remember, she disappeared thirty years ago. We have no idea how much of the current world she knows. But if she hasn't kept up with things, she'll likely still see Dominic Durand as an enemy."

"Yeah," Devon answered as he nodded. "She wasn't happy when you brought me on board. In fact, she was pretty upset."

Drucinda flicked her gaze to him. "Correct. Although, she had a soft spot for you after you delivered little baby Paige."

"Not much of one. She probably thought we were both involved in that threat against her."

Dewey's eyes went wide as he stared into space. "Oh, she probably thinks this was your endgame all along! Now, you've won. You waited over thirty years for Paige to grow up so you could marry her and ruin Reed's life."

"But I didn't," Devon said with a shake of his head. "Didn't the note say they'd do something terrible to Paige?"

"It really depends on your view of marriage whether or not you'd fall into that category," Dewey answered.

"Like awful terrible. Like kidnap her or kill her."

"Oh, well, you almost killed her. Remember when you went all beast mode and marked her?"

Devon threw his hands in the air. "I'm never going to live that down, am I?"

"It was pretty crappy, Devon," Paige said. "I mean...I

nearly died. And Dewey had to save me, and he messed up the serum, and I turned purple."

"I never meant to hurt you," Devon answered.

"What did you think would happen when you sliced me open?" Paige demanded.

Dewey fluttered over to land on her shoulder, his eyebrows raised, and his arms crossed. "Yeah, Beefcake, explain."

"I...I..." He pressed his lips together and shook his head. "I...slipped on the bathroom tile and accidentally sliced her, okay? I didn't mean to do it. And I was totally going to fix it, but then you got all weird."

Paige's eyes went wide. "All weird? Maybe because I was poisoned and scared."

"I'm sorry, okay? Those stupid penny tiles are super slick. I was trying to find you, and then bam, I was falling. I grabbed onto the shower curtain, but with my weight, it crumpled, and I scratched you."

"Those tiles are really difficult to navigate with that smooth vampire skin. Poor thing," Drucinda said with a pat of his shoulder.

"Yeah." Devon bobbed his head as he stared at his friend. "Very slick."

Paige heaved a sigh. "Fine, okay, you didn't mean to kill me. But still, I'm not sure my mom is going to love you."

"Well, I'm going to try my best to make a good impression. I think helping to save her life is a good start."

Drucinda rubbed his arm. "It is, darling. I'll tell her, don't worry."

"What do you mean, you'll tell her? I'm her daughter. I'll talk to her first."

"A daughter she may not even know. We have no idea how long she's been like this or what she knows of the world. She may recognize me, but she may not know you at all."

Paige's stomach twisted into a knot as Drucinda's words sliced her. Her mother had only seen her as a baby. She may not recognize Paige or feel close to her.

The idea brought tears to her eyes again.

"Well, actually, we know she wasn't in a coma while at the French Chateau. Paige's stony Golem friend said he knew Reed. He called her Mama, and said she took care of him."

Drucinda crossed her arms as she stared at the woman in the bed. "Yes, she couldn't have been in this Twilight Trance for longer than a week or so, or she'd be dead already. But that doesn't mean she's kept tabs on the outside world."

"Fine," Paige said with a sigh despite it twisting her insides into knots, "when she wakes up, you can talk to her first."

"We can both talk to her," Drucinda offered. "Let's just take things one step at a time."

"If she wakes up," Paige lamented, hanging her head.

Drucinda crossed to the monitor, eyeing it again. "I think she will. We have a promising lead."

Paige's heart leapt at the words, her pulse racing as adrenaline coursed through her veins. "You do? What is it?"

"It isn't much, but...I may have stumbled upon something that will undo the trance."

"What?" Dewey questioned.

Devon's features crinkled. "Yeah, there's nothing in this world that I know of that'll reverse this. I asked my dad, and he said the same."

Drucinda held a finger in the air as she stalked closer to them. "Ah, but there is the trick. There is nothing in this world. No one said there was nothing in any world."

"So, there is something?" Paige asked, her voice breathy with hope.

"A serum. Tricky to find and not in this world. But not impossible once one opens the horizon to other realms."

"Other realms?" Paige asked. "So, we just need one of those Realm Wrangler things, and we can grab this stuff, right?"

"Not quite. There is something else you'll need. But I've worked out where you can get this particular serum. Though it'll take some work."

"What's the serum?" Dewey asked. "Can I whip up a batch here?"

"And risk turning my mom into a mushroom? Umm, no," Paige said with a shake of her head.

"Uh, Paige, at no time were you in danger of turning into a fungus. Please. I know what I'm doing."

"Right, that's why you have turned me purple, puny, into a puddle, plastered– "

"Okay, okay, I get it. I've done a few...less than perfect things, but I've *never* come close to making you a fungus."

Drucinda set her hands on her hips. "Will you two please stop babbling and pay attention?"

"Fine," Paige said, crossing her arms. "What's the serum?"

"Eclipsarum Elixir," Drucinda answered.

Dewey burst into laughter. "Are you joking? That's a myth. It's not real. It's like...saying goldfish have a three-second memory."

"That's true," Paige answered.

Dewey rolled his eyes. "Paige, goldfish have memories that can span centuries."

"They don't live centuries."

Dewey shook his head at her. "Sometimes, Paige, sometimes."

"Never mind. It does exist, I have found it. But...you will have to do some traveling to get it."

"Where to?" Dewey asked. "Realm of Eternal Frost? Enchanted Forest? Underworld Abyss?"

"None of those," Drucinda said with a shake of her head. "Have you ever heard of a place called…Bucksville?"

CHAPTER 2

$\mathcal{P}$aige wrinkled her nose and shook her head. "Bucksville? No, should I have?"

"No way," Devon said, his eyes wide. "Oh, can I go? I'll go get the stuff."

Paige glanced at him. "You've heard of it."

"Everyone's heard of it," Dewey answered.

"And you should have, too. It's the place your mother went after drinking from the Magician's Teapot."

Heat washed over her body as she flicked her gaze to her ailing mother in the hospital bed. "While she was pregnant with me."

"Yes," Drucinda answered with a nod. "She went into the last book she read. She went to Bucksville."

"And that's where this…elixir is?" Paige questioned.

"Yes, I believe so. Or in a similar realm. But the Slayers can help you find it if they don't have immediate access."

"Slayers?" Paige asked, her lips tugging into a wince.

"The Shadow Slayers," Devon said with a nod. "Celine, Damien, Michael, Gray, Alexander, and my personal favorite, Marcus."

"Of course you'd like the bad guy," Dewey said with a shake of his head.

"Marcus was misunderstood."

"Says the vampire."

"Sounds like you didn't read the whole series."

"I did so...ish," Dewey shot back.

"Stop," Drucinda said with a shake of her head. "Paige will go. *After* you've fixed her. She can't go like that."

"I still don't get it. So, I'll have to go into...what realm? The Shadow Slayers realm? I'm still not clear on what happened to my mom."

Dewey fluttered into the air in front of her. "Your mom went into a fictional realm."

"Oh, like the fractured fairy tale we were in?"

"Sort of, yes," Dewey said with a nod. "But this time... we're going to a *really* messed up place."

Paige screwed up her face. "Really messed up?"

Dewey nodded. "We're going to the realm of...Nellie H. Steele." He arched an eyebrow as he let the words hang in the air.

Paige slid her eyes side to side. "Okay...sounds reasonable."

"Are you joking? Have you read her books?"

"No," Paige said, her voice tentative.

Devon clicked his tongue and shook his head as Dewey flung his paws in the air. "Well, there you go. You have no idea the type of chaos she can inflict."

"He's right," Devon said. "Creatures that are just frightening, crazy people..."

"Explosions, car accidents, amnesia, kidnapping," Dewey outlined.

"Those were the romances, that's a different realm," Drucinda said.

"There were explosions in romance books?"

"I told you she was crazy. And now we've got to immerse ourselves into this madness." Dewey slapped his paws over his face.

"Can't be that bad. No crazier than what we're dealing with right now," Paige said.

"Remember that when you're being chased by a Serpede," Devon answered, a shiver shaking him. "I still have nightmares about those."

Paige grimaced as she tried to determine what a Serpede might be. "Okay, so...how do we get into this...Nellie's realm?"

"Please don't say we have to use that teapot," Dewey said, clutching his paws together as he pleaded with Drucinda. "We have no idea how to get back. We could be stuck in that maniac's world forever."

"I would prefer you didn't as it seems that teapot doesn't allow for control. No, instead, I think we should use a Chapter Gate."

"Ohhh," Dewey said with a nod. "Yeah, that'll work. Where's the nearest?"

"Enchanted Realm Park."

"The fairy-tale themed amusement park over in Germany?"

Drucinda bobbed her head. "That's the one."

"All right. Should we head there? Oh, wait," Dewey said with a shake of his head. "I need to fix Paige."

"Yes, you do, little man. She can't go there looking like that."

"No. Well, she could...but probably not best."

"You'd better get cracking," Drucinda answered before she shifted her gaze to Paige. "And you had better get reading. You need to be prepared for the types of surprises you may encounter."

"Prepared? I mean...it's a book..."

"You have no idea what kind of psycho we're dealing with here, Paige. She is responsible for the creation of Dominique, a character so vile, so crazy, there just aren't words."

"Don't forget Crazy Kyle," Drucinda answered.

"Ugh, don't get me started on him," Dewey said with a shake of his head. "The destruction in that series...for romance? Puhleeze."

"Fine, all right. I love books. I love to read. I'll grab my e-reader and hang out with my mom and read her books."

"Good, you do your research, Dewey will cure you, and I will work on travel arrangements to the Enchanted Realm Park."

"Sounds like a plan," Paige said as she crossed to her bag and dug into it for her reader. "I hope I have a cord to charge this. I usually carry it."

"If not, I can run out and grab you one," Devon said. "And also...I'd like to go with you."

"So you can meet Mark or whoever?"

"Marcus, and no. I'm...worried about you, Paigey."

"What did I say about calling me Paigey?"

Devon lifted a shoulder. "But I like it. It's cute. And we are married, so I feel like a pet name is in order."

Paige heaved a sigh as she let her gaze fall to the floor. "You have a point. Fine, call me Paigey."

"Thanks, Paigey." He grinned at her.

"Well, with that settled," Dewey said, "I'm heading in to work on turning you into a human, you sit down and read a little of the Slayers. Actually...would you mind reading in the lab so I can have you there for experimentation?"

"That sounds frightening, but sure. As long as someone can sit with my mom? I don't want her alone."

Drucinda bobbed her head. "I'll stay. I can make the travel arrangements from here."

"I'll keep you company, Dru," Devon said as he eased into an armchair.

"Thanks," Paige said to them before, with e-reader in hand, she followed Dewey from the room.

They made their way to the hospital's lab, and she plopped onto a stool. "Okay, so what book do I start with?"

"Shadows of the Past," Dewey said as he fluttered around the room collecting ingredients.

Paige pulled up the book and dove in.

Dewey buzzed past her tapping a wooden spoon on a metal bowl.

"Will you stop that? I'm trying to read."

"Sorry," he answered before he let it clatter down on the counter and zipped across the room to retrieve more ingredients.

Paige tried to concentrate on the words on the page as her mind stretched in a thousand different directions.

While she tried to study the world she'd soon be entering, she found her mind drifting to her mother's condition, Dewey's frantic work, and whether or not they'd be able to save Reed.

She found herself skimming the text before she stared into space again.

"How far did you get?" Dewey asked as he stirred something.

He twisted to face her, holding the bowl in one hand as he stirred with the other. Before she could answer, the bottom of the bowl dropped out as smoke rose from the concoction.

His eyes went wide as he wrinkled his nose. "Whoops."

"Yeah, I'm not putting that in my body. Nothing even remotely close to that is going in my body."

"Just calm down. I accidentally added too much Magnimum."

"What?"

"Never mind," Dewey said as he twisted away from her. "How far did you get?"

"Josie is having nightmares. I feel like I'm living her life."

"Just wait...her life is way worse than yours. Although, she also has a hot husband, so...some similarities."

"Is her husband a vampire?" Paige returned her gaze her reader.

"No, warlock."

Paige sucked in a breath, continuing to the next chapter as Dewey restarted his potion-making. She eyed him as she flicked her page. He bobbed his head as he measured a glowing powder into a measuring spoon and poured it in.

She smiled at his hard work before she continued reading. A second later, a whooshing noise sounded as smoke curled from the pipette Dewey held.

"Dang it," he grumbled.

"Maybe don't use the Magnimum," Paige said with a shrug.

"Really? Did you pass Potion-Making with flying colors? Do you want to stay part-cat?"

She slouched lower in her chair. "Proceed."

"That's what I thought. Don't question my potion-making skills."

"Well, I'm sorry, but I've been turned purple and turned into a panther, and so on, so...just...making some suggestions."

"Well, don't. You're lucky you're alive, Paige. I mean... purple or dead? Those were your choices."

"When you put it that way, purple."

"Exactly. So, keep reading," he wiggled his fingers at her, "and I'll keep working to save your life."

"Right." She curled her legs under her as she continued to read. When she looked up again, Dewey hovered in front of her, grinning.

"How far did you get?"

"This guy, Gray, is her husband. Color me shocked."

"Well, I'm about to color you human," Dewey said with an arch of his eyebrow.

Paige stared at the glowing pearl substance floating in the bowl. "Are you sure?"

His grin faded. "Yes, I'm sure."

"Like sure sure? Like one hundred percent sure?"

Dewey narrowed his eyes. "Drink the potion, Paige, or you can stay a cat."

She waved the bowl closer. "Give it here."

Dewey shoved it forward into her hands. She set her reader aside before she lapped up the potion.

"How was the flavor?" Dewey asked. "I made it bubble gum."

"It was good. A little sweet, but decent. Good job on the flavor." She licked her chops before she licked a paw and raked it over her face.

"You're welcome," he answered as he collected the. bowl.

"How long do you think this'll take to work?"

"Oh, I'd say in an hour we'll know."

"An hour? Ugh," she groaned. "That's so long to wait."

"Sorry. I erred on the side of slow, but safe."

Paige sucked in a breath. "I guess I can understand that. I'd rather be human in an hour than be turning into something else in two minutes."

She picked up her reader to continue the story, but she found herself eyeing her furry paws every few seconds.

After fifteen minutes, a tingly sensation started to pulsate within her. "Hey, Dewey?"

"Yeah?" he answered as he cleaned up his workstation.

"I'm starting to tingle."

He buzzed over and studied her. "No physical changes yet, but that's a good sign."

"I think so. Does my fur look…less furry?"

"Nah, I think you're pushing it. Give it some time."

She sucked in a deep breath as she stared at her paws, hoping they soon changed to hands. She set the e-reader down, no longer able to concentrate as she waited for her transformation.

"Come on, come on," she whispered.

"Talking to yourself, Paige?" Dewey asked.

"Yeah, I'm trying to encourage this serum to work."

"Now, your fur is looking sparse," Dewey said as he studied her.

"Really?" Her heart skipped a beat as her lips curled into a grin.

"Yeah…" His voice stopped as his fleshy eyebrows pinched together.

"What? What is it?" She glanced down at her paws again.

"Nothing," Dewey said with a shake of his head. "Totally fine."

"Dewey! I'm going to find out sooner or later."

Dewey tugged his lips back in a wince. "Well, it's just… your nose."

"What's wrong with my nose? Get me a mirror."

Dewey zipped across the room in search of one as Paige patted her nose with a paw. "It's kind of…beak-like."

"Beak-like?" Paige snatched the mirror from him and held it up, her eyes going wide. "No! What have you done?"

She stared at the yellow beak poking from her face as her eyes started to morph into dark beads. "What's happening?"

"Ohhh, your fur…it's…changed to feathers."

"What?" she screeched as she rose.

Dewey gasped. "Paige! You're a penguin!"

CHAPTER 3

"*I*'m a what?" Paige tried to take a step forward, but she found her legs odd to use. Instead, she waddled on webbed feet as the thick feathers continued to spread across her body. "This isn't funny."

"Wait, wait, the feathers...they're getting sparse. You're changing again."

Paige held the mirror up as green spikes poked from her head. "What are those?"

"Looks like...leaves..." Dewey flew back a foot from her. "Oh, you're a pineapple."

Paige frowned at him as her hands disappeared and the mirror clattered to the floor. "This isn't funny."

"Uh-oh, you broke the mirror. Now you'll have bad luck."

"*Now*, I'll have bad luck? Are you joking?"

"Think of it this way...you're easier to carry now. And if I get hungry– "

"Don't say another word," Paige warned before another set of tingles shot through her. "Something else is happening."

"Yeah...you're...getting kind of flat. You've gone from

18

Panther Paige to Penguin Paige to Pineapple Paige and now…ohhhh, that makes sense." Dewey nodded as he rubbed his chin.

"What?"

"Pancake Paige. You're a pancake."

She heaved a sigh as her flattened body fell to the floor, and she stared up at the ceiling. "This is just perfect."

"Well, not really. I'd have preferred the pineapple, but– "

"Shut up, Dewey," she snapped.

"Sorry. Oh, wait, something's happening again. Wait…oh, Paige."

"What now? A pumpkin? A pearl? A pomegranate? Parrot?"

"Nope." Dewey grinned at her as he collected a shard of glass from the floor and held it up over her head.

She crinkled her brow as she shifted to stare into it, her heart stopping. "OMG!"

"Yep," Dewey said with a nod. "You're back. Normal, human Paige is back. I did it."

Paige grabbed the glass, careful of the sharp edges as she stared at herself, one hand rubbing her cheek. "I'm me again. I'm normal Paige again."

"Yep. See, I told you I could do it."

"Good, now, let's go check on the travel arrangements. I want to get going on getting this serum right away."

She climbed to her feet and reached for her reader, tripping over the leg of the stool and sprawling across the floor.

"Yep, you're back," Dewey said as he hovered over top of her.

"You couldn't have gotten rid of that part of me?"

"I could try but…"

She held a hand up. "No, don't. I'll probably turn into a peach or a pinecone."

"Your choice. But we probably should save your mom's life first."

"Right, let's go," Paige answered.

Dewey landed on her shoulder, and they left the lab behind to return to her mother's hospital bed.

As she strode into the room, Devon grinned at her, leaping from his seat. "Paige! You're back."

He reached for her, his lips puckering for a kiss. She blocked it with her hand as she focused on Drucinda. "How is she?"

"Holding her own still, but she weakens by the minute. If you are recovered, we should go as soon as possible."

"I'm ready," Paige said with a nod.

"She isn't," Dewey answered, "but time is of the essence, so we'll have to send her in cold."

"Send me in cold?" Paige crinkled her nose. "Aren't you coming with me?"

"I'm not certain sending a dragon into this environment is wise," Drucinda answered.

"You said Nellie Steele's realm is filled with crazy stuff. Surely, she has dragons."

"Nope. No dragons. Not a dragon in sight. Dragon-like creatures, but not dragons. She even jokes that dragons don't exist."

"But…"

"Look, if you want to take him, fine, but take the carrier and perhaps the ring that changes you into a human."

"Noooo," Dewey whined. "Not that. I hate that thing. It gives me headaches."

"And it stops working after a while," Paige said. "Wait! I got a shapeshifter thing at my bridal shower. Take that!"

"Earrings. Shapeshifting earrings. I don't want to wear earrings," Dewey wrinkled his nose.

"You got shapeshifting earrings at the shower? Why didn't you tell me?" Devon asked.

"Uhhh," Paige answered with a shake of her head. "Anyway…take your pick, Dewey, but hurry up. I don't want to go there alone, and you probably should have something so you don't have to stay stuffed in the carrier."

"Ummm," Dewey rubbed his chin, "I'll take the ring."

"Coming right up, little man. I'll grab it along with the carrier, and we'll meet at the car."

Paige approached her mother's bedside, taking the woman's hand in hers. "Mom, I'm going to get something to help you. Please keep fighting, okay?"

Silence stretched until Dewey spoke. "Uh, Paige, not to be a pain, but I don't think she's doing any fighting at all. She's just lying there–"

"Dude…come on," Devon said with a shake of his head.

"I'm just…okay, fine." Dewey raised his paws in the air. "Yep."

Devon rubbed Paige's shoulder. "I'll take good care of her while you're gone, Paigey. Don't worry, babe."

"Thanks," Paige said, trying to find comfort in his words. At the end of the day, Devon had turned out to be a good friend. And he was trying to be a nice husband.

Paige heaved a sigh, patting her thighs. "Well, I guess we should go."

"You want me to come with you to the park?" Devon asked. "I haven't been there since I was a kid."

"Umm, I mean, that's sweet and all, but…I want someone to stay with my mom."

"I can do that," Ronnie answered from the door. "You two go."

"Thanks, Ronnie," Devon said with a grin before he flicked his gaze to Paige. "So, can I go?"

"I mean, yes. You're an adult, so if you want to go to the

park...you can go to the park." She shrugged, wincing as Dewey smacked her in the back of the head.

"Idiot...he's trying to be supportive."

Paige shifted her weight as she wrinkled her nose. "Yes, I'd like it if you went."

"Sometimes, Paige, sometimes," Dewey murmured.

"Awesome. I'd like to wish you luck before you leave. I also want to ride the Blood Rush." His eyes widened. "Oh, hey, we should ride it together. You know, like a honeymoon trip."

"Right, sure. Yes. We can do that."

"Yeah!" Devon said, pumping a fist in the air. "I can't wait. Oh, and you, too, buddy."

He poked a finger at Dewey. "In human form, of course."

"Sure, right, just make me get on those stilts, and then put me on the world's worst roller coaster."

Devon grinned and nodded at his comment. "Let's go."

"Paige, don't let him put me on the roller coaster," Dewey said as they left her mother's room behind after receiving well-wishes from Ronnie.

They made the short trip to the amusement park. Paige eyed the large fairy-tale castle that greeted them on the way in before she shifted her eyes to the myriad of rides. Dewey slipped on the ring before they left the car, morphing into human form.

With their admission paid, they strolled through the park, riding a few rides before they finally approached an enclosed boat ride through a haunted castle.

"This ride will take us to the Chapter Gate. We'll need to jump off of it mid-way."

"Won't we get in trouble?" Paige asked.

"No, people do it all the time," Drucinda answered as they shuffled forward in the line. "Anyway, it doesn't matter. You two won't be here."

"Right," Paige said, her stomach clenching. "We'll be in Bucksville."

"Ah, the rocky coast of Maine," Dewey said. "It would be a nice trip if we didn't have to deal with the Slayers."

"I thought they seemed nice in the book," Paige said with a shrug. "I liked Damien."

Dewey shook his head. "You would."

Devon shoved his hands in his pockets. "Like…liked him a lot or…as a friend?"

"Relax, Devon, I'm not going to fall in love with a fictional character."

"It's just that…a fictional character almost killed me to win your hand in marriage."

Paige scowled. "Good point. Okay, fine, liked him as a friend."

"No one is falling in love while we're there. It's going to be a nightmare. We'll be too busy trying to stay alive." Dewey shuffled forward to the turnstile leading to the next boat.

The attendant waved them over, and they pushed through, climbing into the bobbing boat and settling onto the seats for the ride to begin.

Paige's stomach fluttered as they floated into the first chamber. "When do we hop off? I'm nervous. The sign clearly said keep your hands inside the ride at all times."

Drucinda rolled her eyes at her. "Third chamber. The werewolf one. That's where we take our leave."

"Right," Paige said, staring up at a swaying vampire above their heads.

"They really typecast vampires here," Devon said with a wrinkled nose as he stared at the white-faced vampires holding goblets of blood in their hands in the next chamber.

"Yeah, you don't look anything like these guys. Although, they do look like the Transylvanians."

23

"Yeah, everyone thinks the Transylvanians are the only vampires on the earth." Devon heaved a sigh.

"Get ready," Drucinda warned. "Exiting on the left as soon as we enter the next chamber."

Paige nodded, her stomach twisting into a tight knot. As they passed from one room to the other, Devon rose and scrambled from the boat, pulling Paige along with him.

Drucinda wrangled Dewey onto the side, too, allowing the boat to continue on without them.

She pushed through a door marked STAFF ONLY into a dark passage. "Follow me."

They crept forward a few feet before Drucinda pressed a stone on the wall. A panel slid away, and she ducked inside.

Paige followed behind her into the darkness, lit only be a glow ahead of them.

"Is that the Chapter Gate?"

"Yes," Drucinda answered. "That's it up ahead."

They continued toward it, finding a large arch decorated in runes. Paige sucked in a breath as her eyes rose to the top. "Uhh, suddenly, this seems like a horrible idea."

"Buck up, Paige, at least we'll be able to save your mom."

Devon stopped her as they entered the room housing the gate. "Paige, be safe. Come back to me. I love you."

"Uhh, thanks. Yeah, I, uh…I will be and…I…you're…"

"Just say it, Paige," Dewey groaned.

"I'm…really glad you're on my side," she managed.

"Me too," he answered before he hugged her tightly.

"I've brought the book you'll need to carry to enter." Drucinda thrust a paperback forward.

Paige stared down at the red-clad woman on the cover, her features morphing with a sudden fear.

"Just walk straight through until you're there, got it?"

Paige nodded as she patted the book. Dewey linked his arm through hers.

With a deep breath in, they shared a glance and a nod before she stepped forward. She gnawed on her lower lip as they crept closer.

A strange power vibrated from the arch, making her tremble all over. She tightened her grip on the paperback, her knuckles turning white.

"Good luck," Drucinda called.

"Get 'em, babe!" Devon encouraged.

After one final glance over her shoulder, they stepped into the portal. Thoughts swirled in her mind about what they'd find on the other end as blackness surrounded them.

CHAPTER 4

*P*aige's heart thudded against her ribs and blood rushed into her ears as she continued through the darkness.

"Sure is dark in here," Dewey said, his voice echoing.

"Y-yeah," she stammered. "I'm glad I'm not alone."

"Me too," Dewey answered.

"We should have asked how long this would take. I keep walking and walking but there's no end in sight."

"Tell me about it. If it's going to be a while, I'd like to take this ring off so I can fly. Walking is for the birds."

"Actually, birds can fly, too, so– "

"Oh-ho-ho-ho-ho," Dewey said, his sarcastic laughter echoing. "So funny. Not. It's not funny, Paige."

"Sorry. I'm just trying to make conversation. Do you think something went wrong?"

"Went wrong?" Dewey asked.

"Yeah. I mean…if it was going to take this long, you'd think Drucinda would have warned us."

"Well, no. I mean, it would never occur to her to warn us. She thinks people are as knowledgeable as she is."

"So, we'd just naturally know it takes forever to get through a Chapter Gate?"

"Yeah."

"Does it?" Paige asked, her eyebrows crinkling as she continued forward in the blackness.

"How would I know? I spent ten years trapped in the archives."

"I thought maybe you read about it or something."

"Nope. I had no cause to read about it. None."

Paige heaved a sigh. "Well, I guess, we just keep–wait...I hear something."

"What?"

Paige strained, turning her ear toward the noise. "The ocean."

"Oh, that would make sense. The Slayers live on the rocky coast of Maine."

"Maybe we're almost there. Come on!" Paige blindly reached for Dewey, finding it strange to touch his human hand rather than this scaly paw. She tugged him forward, quickening her pace.

"Wait, wait."

Paige's heart skipped a beat. "What is it?"

"I can't go that fast. I'm...still getting used to these stupid legs."

"Okay, sorry." Paige slowed her pace. "Although, if these people are as bad as you say they are, maybe you should practice running."

"It's not *them* who are bad. It's their enemies."

"Whatever. You should know how to run," Paige said as light finally struck them, dancing as a pinpoint in the distance.

"Light!" Dewey exclaimed.

"I know." A smile spread across Paige's features as she continued toward it. Dampness surrounded them, and the scent of salty air filled her nostrils. "Smells like the sea."

"And feels like a cave. Ugh. I hate the cold. Why did they have to live in Maine?"

"I think it'll be nice to see. I've never been to Maine."

"Oh, yeah, it'll be real nice. When you're not almost being killed."

Paige pressed her lips into a thin line and shook her head as the light grew larger and larger. She made out the rocky insides of a cave.

A rocky beach lay beyond it. She grinned, hurrying forward when she tripped over something and sprawled forward.

"Whoa!" Dewey called behind her. "You almost pulled me down."

"Sorry. I fell over something." She twisted to glance behind her as what had sent her splatting onto the ground. Her eyes went wide, and she scrambled away from the massive lump. "What the hell is that?"

Dewey circled around it, rubbing his chin. "Dracopire. Nellie loves inventing creatures."

"A what?"

"Dragon-line vampire from another realm. These bad boys can breathe fire and suck blood."

"What are they doing in Maine?"

"War," Dewey said with a nod.

"War?" Paige asked as she collected the book she'd dropped and rose to stand.

"Yeah. Dominique brought them to war against the Slayers. Nasty things, these guys. Figures we'd walk into the middle of their war." Dewey shook his head. "At least, we came across a dead one instead of a live one."

Paige grimaced as she stared at the scaly dragon-like creature's body. "Yeah. Good thing– "

"Hello?"

Her heart skipped a beat at the unknown male voice. "We should hide!"

"Why?" Dewey asked. "We have to figure out who has the Eclipsarum Elixir. Why not ask this fellow?"

"Hello!" the voice called again. "Is someone in there?"

"Uh, yeah," Paige called back. "It's, uh…wait, who are you?"

"Damien. Who are you?"

"Damien?" Paige mouthed.

"Didn't you read the book at all? Her cousin…duh."

"I know who he is…I'm just…this is weird," Paige said before she raised her voice. "Uh, hi, Damien. I'm… Paige…Turner."

A laugh escaped him. "Right. Yeah, I bet. Listen, come out here and tell me who you really are, or I'm going to tell Celine. This is private property, you know?"

Paige swallowed hard as she stepped forward. "Yeah, I know. But that's really my name."

"Tell him we need his help," Dewey whispered.

Paige waved the comment away with a wrinkle of her nose as she stepped into the cloudy Maine day. A tall, lanky blond stood in front of her. "Wow, he looks just like I expected."

"Right? I think Nellie based him off of– "

"Nellie?" Damien said before Dewey finished his statement. "Oh, no. Please, not another set of people telling us we aren't real."

Paige licked her lips as she shared a glance with Dewey. "Uhh, well…the thing is…"

Damien flicked his eyebrows up as he waited for an answer.

Paige grinned at him, hoping it broke the ice. Before she

could continue, a pretty blonde picked her way across the rocks toward them. "Hey, D, who are your friends?"

"Ohh, wow, it's Celine." Dewey's eyes went wide. "She's one of my favorites."

Damien glanced over his shoulder before he focused again on Paige and Dewey, rolling his eyes. "She says her name is Paige Turner."

Celine stopped for a second, her brow furrowing as she studied Paige. "Wait a minute...are you...related to Reed Moore?"

Paige's heart stopped for a second before it pounded against her ribs. "Yes. Reed is my mother."

Damien flung a hand in the air. "Right. Why didn't I know that? Obviously Reed Moore is the mother of Paige Turner." He twisted to face Celine as she sidled up to them. "And they're yammering on about that Nellie person again. You know the one who– "

"Yeah, I know. Created us. I remember. What are you doing here? Where did you come from?"

Paige tugged her lips into a grimace. "Uhh, we came from– "

"Mars?" Damien ventured. "Oh, no, wait...what did Reed say? 'The real world.'" He put air quotes around the last phrase.

"Easy, D." Celine patted his shoulder before she focused on Paige and Dewey.

"Michael is going to lose it."

"Michael...Michael Carlyle. Billionaire, rogue, in love with Celine, but willing to settle for Celeste," Dewey answered.

"Maybe we shouldn't comment on their lives," Paige suggested.

"Great idea," Damien answered.

"Look, I'm with Damien. I don't know what you're doing

here, but the last time your mother was here, she was nearly killed a number of times," Celine said. "In fact…I think she was killed."

Paige shook her head. "No. The entire time she was here she was in a coma. But when she got 'killed', she woke up from the coma."

"Wait, wait, wait." Damien waved his hands in the air, his features pinched. "This makes no sense. You're Reed's daughter. But Reed wasn't here all *that* long ago. What are you? Thirty, at least?"

"Hey!" Paige exclaimed.

"She's thirty-four, not a day over," Dewey said, poking a finger at him.

"Okay, well, I guessed lower so there's no reason to get snarky with me."

"Snark is the best thing I do," Dewey shot back.

"How can you possibly think we're the fake ones and you're the real ones?" Damien scratched his head as he glanced at Celine.

"Damien makes a good point. You are thirty-four, but we saw Reed a matter of weeks ago, and she was pregnant with you."

"So, you saw my mom when she was pregnant with me," Paige said, her lips tugging into a frown. They'd seen her before she'd been kidnapped, before she'd spent thirty years being kept from her daughter, and before she was dying.

"Yep," Celine said with a bob of her head as another man approached in the distance.

"Everything all right here?" he called in a British accent.

Paige glanced at Dewey. "Is that him?"

"Nah, that's Alexander. Alex, buddy. I know you anywhere. You know you're one of my fav– "

"Oh, no," the man said with a shake of his head. "Another set of them who believes we are story characters."

Celine crossed her arms as she bobbed her head. "Yep. I don't know what you're doing here, but I would suggest you leave before– "

"Wait, wait. We need your help. Desperately," Paige answered, her features pleading.

"You need our help?" Damien asked. "How can we help you? We're fake, remember?"

"Yes, but…it's a long story and…wow, it's really damp here. Can we go inside somewhere and talk about it?"

Celine and Alexander exchanged a glance. "Why not?" she answered. "Follow me. Be careful, the rocks are slippery."

They picked their way across the beach, following the others. Paige wobbled on a few rocks, making her best attempt to hang on to Dewey who struggled to move at all.

"What's wrong with him?"

"He's not used to his legs," Paige said.

Damien offered her a wide-eyed stare before he continued on without answering.

"Nice going, Paige. Why don't you just tell them I'm a dragon?"

"I'm planning on it," she hissed. "We need them to trust us. And we can't do that by lying to them. Plus, then you can take that ring off and fly."

"Oh, good plan," he said with a bob of his head before he raised his voice. "Hey, are we going to the main house or Alexander's? Would really like to see both while I'm here."

"Yeah, of course. We'll give you the grand tour," Damien answered. "Do you want to see the town, too?"

"I mean, if you're offering, I'd love to see it."

Damien rolled his eyes and shook his head.

"Stop asking for stuff. We're annoying them, and we need them," Paige whispered.

"Sorry. But it's sort of cool. I've read them since I was a little baby dragon. I loved the Shadow Slayers."

They climbed to the top of the rocky coast, the scent of pine filling the air as they passed through the thick trees, leaving the coast behind.

As the pines thinned, a sprawling gothic house appeared in a clearing. Paige stared up at it, her jaw unhinged. "Wow. That's some house."

They crossed the lawn and entered the house. Her eyes swept upward in the dark foyer, taking in the high ceilings, the massive staircase, and the intricate details on the architecture. "Oh, wow."

"Wow is right," Dewey answered with a nod. "This place looks just like what I expected."

A man with sandy blonde hair bounced down the stairs, eyeing them. "Hey, guys, what's– "

"Michael!" Dewey exclaimed, his eyes going wide.

"Oh, no," Michael answered. "No, no, no, no, no. Not again. No. Please tell me these people are not here to tell us we only exist in a book."

"Sorry, bud," Damien said as he clapped a hand on to Michael's shoulder. "They *are,* in fact, telling us that."

He waved a hand toward Paige. "Meet Paige Turner. Daughter of Reed Moore."

Michael stared at her for a moment before he burst into laughter. "You're kidding me. This a joke, right?"

"No," Paige said with a shake of her head. "It's not."

"How in the world do you possibly expect us to believe we're the fictional characters and you're real with a name like that?"

She set her jaw, already unimpressed with the crew who insisted she was fictional.

"But...how can you not accept it?" Dewey asked.

"And who are you again?" Michael asked.

"Dewey."

A grin spread across Michael's face again. "Let me guess.

Dewey Decimal."

"No!" Dewey exclaimed, heat entering his voice. "It's Deci*mael*. I'm French."

Michael and Damien exchanged a glance, both still chuckling. "Yeah, okay, buddy. And you think we're the fake ones."

"Okay, look– "

Dewey ripped the book from Paige's hands before she could finish her statement and tossed it in front of them. "Explain that, then!"

All eyes fell to the book on the floor. The words *Hellscape* were emblazoned across the top and a hooded woman in a red cloak twisted to stare at what looked like a passage leading straight to the depths of Hell.

"What is this?" Michael asked.

"Hellscape," Damien read as he collected the book from the ground.

"Open it," Dewey snapped. "Go on."

Damien flipped the book over, scanning it before he pulled open the front cover.

"There's that author they keep bringing up." Michael poked a finger at the title page.

"Yeah." Damien turned to the first chapter.

"Read it."

"Look, we don't have time to– "

"Read," Dewey growled.

Damien shifted his weight from one foot to the other as he cleared this throat.

"Odd sights have plagued some Mainers near the coastal town of Bucksville in the Down East region. Channel Four has obtained this footage posted on social media that appear to show fireballs descending from the skies over the small town."

The screen flashed to a grainy video showing red splotches falling from the sky before it shifted to a Bucksville resident.

"I didn't know what it was, man, but it looked like fire just raining down from the skies."

The newscaster reappeared on the screen and nodded. "Indeed, it does," she said with a glance toward her colleague.

"Yes, it does, Sarah, but Channel Four has learned that this phenomenon was merely the result of a meteor burning up upon entry into the atmosphere. Local government officials say no one on the ground was hurt, and the meteor pieces never reached the ground."

"Scary, but thank goodness," the perfectly-coiffed blonde said with a grin. "And now on to the week's weather. We go over to—"

Celine clicked off the screen and tossed the remote onto the couch cushion before she sank onto it and dropped her head into her hands. "Ugh, this is not good at all."

"Nothing about Dominique ever is," Gray said, waving a brandy in front of her before he sipped his own.

She grabbed it and took a long swallow, barely tasting the hints of caramel that floated across her tongue. "And what the hell is she doing with these injections?"

Celine crossed to him and yanked the book from his hands. "Injections?"

She fanned through the pages. "Does it say what she's doing with the injections?"

"Not in that book," Dewey said with a shake of his head. "Sorry, kid."

Celine's shoulders slumped. "I was hoping to gain some sort of advantage over her."

"I can't believe you believe this," Michael said with a shake of his head. "I mean, so what...they brought a book with our names in it. That proves nothing. Maybe someone is chronicling our lives. Or maybe they made this up just to ensure our cooperation."

"I found something interesting, actually," Alexander interjected. "It may not explain anything, but it could...even the playing field."

"What's that supposed to mean?" Paige asked.

Alexander poked a finger in the air before he motioned for them to follow him.

They snaked through a back hall and into a large library. Paige inhaled the comforting smell of aging leather and well-worn pages.

"I found this after your mother was here." Alexander crossed to a shelf, scanned it, then tugged a book from the middle. He thrust it toward them. "You're turn...read."

Paige stared down at the colorful image of a redhead sporting black glasses in front of a library shelf. A small teal dragon perched on her shoulder. A sinking sensation filled her as she suddenly felt her head swimming. This couldn't be what she thought it was. Was she about to find out her entire life was...fictional?

CHAPTER 5

*P*aige's heart hammered against her ribs as she stared down at what she assumed was a likeness of herself. "What is this?"

"Read it," Michael said, crossing his arms.

"Okay." Paige flicked open the book as Dewey peered over her shoulder. She cleared her throat and launched into the story.

Paige Turner frantically scrubbed at the wet stains dotting her turquoise blouse. The cheap paper towel wadded into a clump, doing little to remove any of the muddy marks. Instead of lifting the spots, her blouse now sported flecks of damp paper towel.

Paige's shoulders slumped as she fought the losing battle in the tiny bathroom stall. She glanced down her ruined outfit. She couldn't show up to her interview looking like this.

Her nose wrinkled. "What is this?"

"I would wager that is your life story," Alexander said. "A disastrous interview but the job secured by a mysterious bracelet. A missing mother. A magical library filled with artifacts. Is any of that familiar?"

Heat rose in her cheeks as she scanned a few more

pages. The first chapter perfectly outlined what had happened the day she's landed her job at the Shadow Harbor Library.

"No, this can't be right."

Michael crossed his arms, a smarmy smile on his handsome features. "Now who's the fictional character, *Paige Turner?*"

"No...no, I'm real. I'm...real. I have...real feelings and thoughts and dreams and hopes."

"Uh-huh. Same thing we said. And then your mother said noooo. You're not real. You're just characters in a book." Michael offered her a haughty glance.

"May I ask a question?" Alexander ventured.

Paige swallowed hard, trying to wrap her mind around what she'd just read. "Uhhh, maybe?"

"Are there really dragons where you're from?"

Paige's eyes flicked to Dewey next to her. "Welllllll, about that."

"No," Damien said, his eyes wide, "seriously? Aw, why didn't you bring the tiny dragon?"

"Teacup," Alexander corrected. "He's a teacup, and he's quite sensitive about his size."

"I am not," Dewey shouted back, his fingers curled into fists.

"Wait," Alexander said, his eyes focusing on Dewey. "Dewey...you're Dewey. But you're not a dragon."

"Think again, pal." Dewey yanked the ring off his finger, transforming back into his teacup dragon form. "There, happy?"

Jaws dropped as Dewey fluttered around the room. "Yes, I'm tiny. Keep staring. Why don't you take a picture, it'll last longer?"

Damien lifted his phone to snap one, and Dewey knocked it from his hands. "I was joking."

Paige shook her head. "Stop. This is...insane. We can't all be fictional characters. That makes zero sense."

"Stinks, huh?" Michael asked. "Having someone tell you you're not real. That you're just a figment of someone's imagination. Every action you take, every word you say...all scripted by some maniac who apparently loves to create chaos and wreak havoc at every turn."

Paige shifted her weight. "Yeah, it kind of does. But...how do these books exist?"

"Why don't we just forget about the books for now?" Celine asked. "If we're fictional, then...I guess it will work out, eventually, but if we're not– "

"We have to make sure things work out because no one is going to write us out of the trouble we're in," Paige finished.

Celine nodded. "Right. So, we need to handle our own problems." She set her crystal-blue eyes on Paige. "I still don't understand why you're here, though. Is it related to why your mother was here?"

"Oh, my mom accidentally got sucked into this realm when she used a Magician's Teapot."

"That's right...the magical teapot," Michael said with a snap of his fingers. "Celine, how could you forget that?"

Paige offered him an unimpressed stare before she continued. "I'm here for a different reason."

"Which is?" Alexander prodded.

Before she could answer, the doors open, and a handsome man strolled in.

"You must be Gray," Dewey said.

Gray froze, staring at the tiny dragon floating in the air. "Does someone want to tell me why there's a small dragon floating around the library?"

"This is Dewey, a friend of Paige's," Celine said. "They're...from the same place Reed Moore was from."

"Oh, no," Gray said with a shake of his head. "Not another

set of people who think we're fake. And please, don't tell me you're a fan of Marcus Northcott."

"Actually, I haven't read much of the book, but– "

"Marcus is my favorite," Dewey answered before he poked a finger at Paige. "And Devon, her husband's, too. Marcus has a fan-club. Especially after the whole thing with Cate."

Gray shook his head. "I don't understand it."

Dewey fluttered back and forth as he spoke. "I think it's really that whole bad-boy-turned-good trope that's so popular with the ladies. He really– "

"Enough," Gray interrupted. "I don't want to hear anymore. Why are you here?"

Celine shoved her hands into the pockets of her hoodie. "Paige was just about to tell us."

"We need your help."

"Why don't you ask Northcott if you love him so much?" Gray shot back.

"Actually, that's probably a good idea," Dewey said. "I'm convinced he'll know where this serum is that we need."

"What serum?" Alexander asked.

"Eclipsarum Elixir," Paige answered.

Gray crossed his arms. "Never heard of it."

Dewey landed on Paige's shoulder. "I'll bet Marcus has. We should ask him. Point us in the direction of the house by the sea."

The Slayers exchanged glances.

"So, you basically want to just plow into Marcus's place unannounced and ask for his help?" Damien asked.

"Yeah, I'm still not convinced you actually read these books because if you had, you'd know that's not going to work," Michael added.

Celine nodded. "They have a point. Marcus isn't exactly the most helpful individual in the world."

"Well, that's why we need your help," Paige said. "Maybe you could…introduce us and…foster a relationship."

Michael doubled over with laughter. "Foster a relationship? With Marcus Northcott? Are you joking?"

"Maybe the better approach would be for me to ask Marcus about this Elixir and gauge if he knows anything about it," Celine offered.

"Right. Good idea, Celine. And then we," Dewey said, waving his finger in the air to encompass the rest of them, "will go to Alexander's to do research on it using his extensive library of references."

Alexander shifted his weight from foot to foot, shooting a glance at his fellow Slayers. "It is rather alarming that they know so much about our habits."

"Well, if you read that book, you know about ours, too," Paige pointed out.

"Some of them, yes," Alexander answered. "Although, I hadn't gotten to the part where you married Devon. Thanks for the spoiler."

"Sorry," Dewey said with a shrug. "But we all knew where this was going, didn't we?"

"I didn't." Paige shook her head. "I didn't know. I hadn't expected to marry him."

"Well, anyway," Dewey said as he fluttered into the air and landed on Alexander's shoulder. "Let's go! We have a lot of work to do."

"Wait, before we break up this little party, why are you looking for this stuff?"

"Oh," Paige said, her gaze falling to the floor. "It's for my mom. She'd been missing for– "

"Thirty years, yes. I read that," Alexander answered. "But she's alive?"

"Yes, but not doing well. She's in a magical trance. We need the elixir to save her life. She's dying."

"Oh, how terrible," he answered. "I'm so sorry."

Celine pressed her lips together into a thin line. "Sorry, Paige. Okay. I'll see what Marcus knows." She flicked her gaze to Alexander. "Meet at your place?"

"Apparently."

"Onward, Al!" Dewey said with a raised fist. "I can't wait to see this place. Looks like the old homestead in England, huh?"

They shuffled from the room with Celine setting off in a different direction while the others took the path leading to Alexander's house.

Paige sucked in the pine-scented air as they strolled through the trees, her mind fixed on the fact that her mother had likely walked this path while here.

She wondered how she was doing now, if there had been any change. Her stomach twisted into a tight knot as she hoped finding the elixir would be simple. Maybe they'd be able to get back to them by nightfall.

Get back…Her heart stopped. How did they get back? Drucinda hadn't told her. Did they just go back to the cave and keep walking? Was there a Chapter Gate inside? She hadn't seen anything glowing there. Was there some other way?

"Dewey!" she called in a loud whisper. "Dewey."

"Smell that pine," Dewey said as he rode along on Alexander's shoulder, sucking in a big breath. "Wow. Look at these trees."

"Many of them are very old," Alexander answered. "Particularly on this estate."

"I'll bet, Al. Beautiful property. Just like it's described in the bo–" Dewey tugged his teal lips back in a wince. "Oh, sorry. Didn't mean to bring up a sore subject."

"Quite all right. I think we can all agree this may be some…fluke, and we are all, indeed, very real."

"If we're not, it's a pretty sick joke," Gray said.

"Well, writers do usually add quite a bit of drama into their plots, so it would explain some things," Dewey answered. "I, myself, am a writer. I'm writing a paranormal romance about Paige and Devon."

Michael shook his head at the dragon. "I can't believe this."

"I can't believe you told us there were no such things as dragons, and here we are looking at a dragon," Damien said to Celine.

Michael shrugged. "Celine said there are no such things… here on this Earth. I guess on their Earth there is."

"I want to live on their Earth," Damien lamented. "It sounds cooler."

"Uh, it's not," Paige answered with a shake of her head. "I've been nearly killed like a dozen times in less than a year. There are werewolves, and vampires, and other stuff…all kinds of other stuff. And they're all horrible."

"But there are cute little dragons," Damien shot back.

"Hey," Dewey retorted with a wag of his finger, "I'm just little. Not cute. I can bite, you know? I can do some damage."

Damien held up his hands before he twisted to Paige, his voice lowered to a whisper. "So, are there big dragons, too?"

"I heard that," Dewey answered. "Yes, there are. My entire family is normal sized. Only I got the teacup gene. But size doesn't matter."

"Sure it doesn't, buddy," Michael said with a nod and a fake smile.

Dewey grimaced at him as the trees cleared and Alexander's house came into view. "Wow, this place looks great. I bet you've got secret passage and everything."

"I have a few," Alexander answered. "Though I haven't used them in years."

"No? Well, let's starting using them, Al. I want to try it

out." Dewey raised his eyes to the house again. "Oh, you even have a cool gargoyle. Neat."

Damien stopped walking mid-stride, freezing as he wrinkled his nose. "Uh, that's not a gargoyle."

"Then what is– "

The so-called gargoyle shifted before it leapt from the rooftop and strutted toward them. Paige stared at a woman identical to Celine in every way except her hair color.

Dewey fluttered off of Alexander's shoulder and retreated to sit on Paige's. "Uh-oh."

"Uh-oh, what?" she asked. "She's related to Celine, right?"

"Yeah, her cousin. But she's completely crazy. Totally nuts. Also, she's really evil."

"Seriously?" Paige asked as she glanced forward at the leather-clad woman who cocked a hip and set her hands on her waist, grinning at them. "Okay, yeah that fits."

"Totally nuts. She killed one of her own just to prove a point," Dewey answered.

"Well, well, well, are we entertaining? Looks like we picked up a few new friends. Another redhead and...some sort of strange bird."

"Hey, lady, I'm a dragon!" Dewey shouted back.

"There are no such thing as dragons," she answered before she poked a finger at Paige. "But I am interested in you."

"I'm no one important. I'm just here...accidentally. And they are...taking me to the house to wait for the police to come and arrest me because I am a criminal."

Dominique's eyebrows rose, an amused expression playing on her pretty features. "Really? Well, then you and me should talk, Red. I love criminals. I'm one myself."

"I told you she was nuts," Dewey whispered.

The smile slid from Dominique's features. "Hey, Dragon, I heard that."

"Oh, yeah?" Dewey asked. "What are you going to do about it, Cupcake?"

"Dude, I would not do that if I was you," Michael hissed. "She'll literally kill you and feed your body to the birds."

"What am I going to do about it? I'm going rip you limb from limb."

"No, you won't, Sugar Plum. Paige would never let that happen?"

"Huh?" Paige asked, her features twisting. "Dewey, why do you keep saying things like that?"

"I don't know. It's like I don't have control over my own words. Like…I'm being scripted."

Her forehead crinkled. "Well, get unscripted."

Dominique laced her fingers together and stretched before she rolled her neck back and forth. "All right, Red. You wanna play? Let's play."

Her features devolved into an angry glare as purple-red orbs exploded from her hands, hovering in the air above her with a white-hot energy.

Paige's eyes went wide as her heart hammered against her ribs. She could never defeat Dominique. The woman would squash her like a bug. She'd never save her mother, because she was staring into the eyes of death.

CHAPTER 6

*P*aige's features melted with fear, her lips tugging back into a grimace. "Holy shi– "

Her words were cut off as Dominique hurled a fireball her way, causing her to dive to the side to avoid being singed by it.

It hit a tree, charring it as it exploded.

A smaller blue fireball sailed toward the woman, discharged from Gray.

Dominique chuckled before she deflected it and took another step toward Paige. "Nice try, Gray. You always were useless, though. Come on, Red, let's see what you've got."

"Wait…" she tried, but no more words came.

"For?" Dominique asked. "Your dragon buddy told me you had skills. Let's see them."

"I have…wait!" A grin slid over Paige's face. "I do. Haha! I do."

She raised her arm, dangling her charm bracelet in the air. With an arch of her eyebrow, she shouted, "Stop, you foul beast!"

Dominique stood motionless before her eyebrows pinched together. "What the hell was that?"

"Oh, crap," Paige groaned. "Was really hoping that would work."

"Has it ever worked?" Dominique asked.

"Yeah, plenty of times," Dewey chimed in. "On all sorts of beasts."

The brunette chuckled as she shook her head. "Well, not on this one. And now, you're going to pay for that."

"Uh…" Paige's eyes darted from side to side as she tried to work out a way to escape her current situation.

Another few fireballs rained down on Dominique, but she dodged them easily, undeterred from her attack on Paige.

"Listen, there's something really important you need to know."

"Oh, yeah? Tell me," Dominique answered as she whipped up another red-hot fireball and flung it toward Paige.

Paige dove to the ground, wincing as her cheek picked up dirt and pine needles as she landed. "There's…a way bigger threat than me out there."

Dominique laughed again. "Red, you're not a threat. I'm just having some fun here. Although, I'm starting to think the dragon was lying about your skills."

"The thing is," Paige said, puffing for breath as she scrambled to her feet, "you…could be killed at any moment. Probably by some weird thing."

Dominique screwed up her face. "What are saying? I'm not in that much danger."

"Aren't you? Because…like some random thing is going to come up probably that'll kill you. Or…like your cousin, Celine, will suddenly find a way. During an epic battle, her powers will increase or something."

"Yeah, that's not going to happen. Nice try, though."

"Well, I know it's going to happen because...I'm...from the future."

"Okay, Marty McFly, how am I going to die?"

"Okay, actually, I'm not from the future-future, I'm like from another place where...you are...fictional."

Dominique tilted her head at the words, her eyebrows pinching. Paige waited for her reaction. If she was crazy, maybe she'd have a breakdown or something.

"You know, the last nutty redhead I met said the same thing. And do you know what I did to her?"

"No?" Paige questioned. Dominique and her mother must have spoken. Too bad she didn't know what happened.

"I tossed her out to sea," Dominique answered.

Paige's eyes went wide as her feet left the ground. "Whoa. Hey, put me down!"

"If we're fictional, who cares, right?" She lifted her eyebrows. "Oh, hey, maybe by some weird plot twist, you'll live."

"Put me down! Put me down!" Paige cried. "Okay, wait, I have more."

"Better hurry up," Dominique said.

"I can be useful. I know how your story goes. I can tell you the end so you can...change it."

Dominique offered her a questioning glance, prodding her to continue.

Before she could, Damien smashed into Dominique's side, driving her into one of the trees and knocking her to the ground. Paige smacked into the ground below.

Hands grabbed her and lifted her to her feet. "Run!"

She twisted to find Michael tugging her along. Dewey buzzed in front of her, racing toward Alexander's house. Damien scrambled to his feet, following them.

He took a fireball to the back, knocking him to the

ground, but he leapt up and continued forward as though he wasn't hurt.

They reached the house and barreled inside.

Paige gasped for breath as she waited for Damien to appear. The moment he slid through the door, Alexander closed it and locked it behind them. "She really is a problem."

"Thank you," Paige said to Damien. "You saved my life."

"No problem. Next time, though, maybe don't taunt her."

"Sorry," Dewey said as he landed on Paige's shoulder. "Sometimes, I can't stop myself. And I figured...when am I ever going to meet someone like Dominique again. She's just so...explosive."

"Yeah, she almost exploded me, Dewey. We can die here, you know?"

"I guess. Well, anyway, we're no worse for wear. Lead the way to the library, Al."

Alexander clicked his tongue and shook his head. "This way."

"Place is great, Al," Dewey said as he floated into the room. "Really love the old-world charm. So, where would we find info on this elixir? Any ideas?"

"Not really. But I suppose we can start with some of the more general guides to serums and the like and go from there."

"Okay," Dewey answered as he fluttered to the shelves. "Just point me in the right direction, and I'll start pulling them."

"Dewey's great at research," Paige said with a nod.

"Thanks, Paige. I appreciate that," Dewey answered. "Oh, found one. Stirling's Guide to Potions, Serums, and Elixirs."

He wrangled the thick leather tome from the shelf, dropping in the air as it came free and delivered it to Paige. "We'll start with this one."

Paige dusted off cover and tugged it open.

"Look for anything even close to this elixir," Dewey said. "Or conditions that involve magical sleep."

"I'm not seeing anything," Paige said, her frustration building already with the check of one reference. She had hoped these people would be more knowledgeable. Or just have some of the elixir on them. "What about this?"

"Sleeping serum? That's probably to put people to sleep, but we'll check it."

Paige paged through to the entry, her shoulders slumping. "Yep…how to put people to sleep. Dang it."

"This likely won't be easy," Alexander answered as he poured over another volume at the desk. "None of us have heard of this."

"Which makes me wonder if it actually exists," Paige said with a sigh.

"I thought you knew it existed?" Michael asked.

"Well, we think it exists…here. We think. A friend of ours did the research. At first, we thought this elixir was just a legend, but then we realized it just existed in another realm."

"What made you think it was in this realm?"

"Drucinda tracked that all down. And she doesn't make mistakes."

"Let's hope for your sake, she's right, and we find it soon. Before Dominique kills you," Damien answered, tugging a book from the shelf.

"And for my mom," Paige said.

"You said she's in some sort of trance?"

Paige nodded, her features pinching. "She's dying. I found her after over three decades, and she's dying."

Damien tugged another book from the shelf. "Not if we can help it."

Paige pressed her lips together into a partial smile.

"Uh-oh. Really glad Devon isn't here," Dewey said.

Paige snapped her gaze to him. "Why?"

"Because he'd be pretty jealous about your book boyfriend over there."

"What? I don't have a book boyfriend."

Dewey flicked his eyebrows up as he studied the paper in their book before flipping to another. "I think you do. Kind of looks like you're making eyes at Damien."

"What about me?" Damien asked.

"Nothing," Paige said with a shake of her head. "Absolutely nothing. Just wondering if you found anything in your book yet."

"Nope, sorry. Nothing here. Maybe Celine will have better luck."

"Let's hope so," Paige answered.

A chilly breeze floated past her, and she shivered, rubbing her arms to rid herself of goosebumps.

A second later, Dewey's eyes went wide, and he dumped the heavy book on her lap with a thud before he buzzed across the room. "Ohhhh, boy! Marcus Northcott. I'd recognize you anywhere. I'm so honored to be in your evil presence, sir."

Dewey bowed his head in reverence.

The dark-haired, dark-eyed man arched an eyebrow at the dragon, his features unimpressed.

Dewey raised his gaze to Marcus. "You're my favorite. Absolutely favorite. You're bad but not in like a crazy way like Dominique. In super smart way, but also, you're not terrible. Just…morally gray, basically."

"You must be Dewey, the dragon," he answered, his British accent crisp and his voice betraying just how unimpressed he really was.

"That's me. Dewey the dragon. Yep. At your service. Seriously, if you need anything…I'm your guy."

"I still say you people haven't actually read the books," Gray answered from an armchair.

"What's the matter, Buckley? Don't have an adoring fan club? I'm not surprised."

"Ohhh, there's the zinger." Dewey twisted to eye Paige. "I love this guy."

"I'll love him more if he knows where the elixir is," Paige said as she climbed to her feet and dumped the book on the coffee table. "So, do you?"

"Marcus doesn't know of any offhand in this realm," Celine answered.

"No, but there may be a location…however, we would need several things to access it, and it may be a false lead."

"I'll try anything," Paige said, her voice breathless. "Anything. Just tell me what I need to do."

"There is something called the Aroostook Enigma. Hidden in a cave, a mystical safe with keys scattered across several realms. It supposedly contains a number of magical objects, one of which it was rumored would be sought by those from another realm."

Paige chewed her lower lip. "Well, I'm from another realm, so maybe that's it."

"How sure are you that this is what she's looking for?" Gray asked.

"Not at all certain, though, it's worth a try," Marcus shot back.

"Says you. What happens when we don't find it."

"Have you a better idea, Buckley?"

"Bet he doesn't," Dewey said with a shake of his head, clapping Marcus on the shoulder. "Marc, I think you're onto something here."

The man arched a dark eyebrow, staring down at the paw on him. "I'm so pleased you agree."

Paige winced as the man sounded anything but pleased. "So, where are these keys? Oh, please not another Super Mario realm or anything weird."

"There's a Super Mario realm?" Damien asked.

Paige nodded. "Yeah. It was horrible, too. You don't want to get stuck there."

"I have never heard of such a thing. And I don't know the exact locations. We must research, and once you have them, I will assist you in reaching them."

Paige's lips parted before she grinned. "Wow, thank you. That's so nice of you."

"Don't give him too much credit," Celine answered with a shake of her head.

"Catherine made me do it," he added.

"Catherine?" Paige asked.

Dewey grinned, his eyes sparkling. "Cate Kensie is here?"

"No," Marcus shot back. "Catherine Northcott is here."

"Riiiiight," Dewey said with a nod. "Cause you married her and became slightly less morally gray."

The man stared at him, his nose wrinkling.

"Well, I'll start pulling references on this Aroostook Enigma," Alexander said. "And we will see what we can learn. We haven't found any references to the elixir so far."

Paige crossed to the bookshelf to take a load of books from Damien, who had already begun to find references. "Why was this never found before?"

"You've never been to Aroostook County," Gray answered. "This is rural Maine. Nothing around for miles."

"Oh, well, that makes sense then," Paige answered with a nod. "Come on, Dewey. Let's get searching."

"Oh, uh… I was wondering if I could go with Marcus. I want to meet Cate."

"No, you may not," Marcus answered.

"Aw, man. Maybe another time, huh?"

"Or not," the man shot back before he turned to Celine. "Contact me if you manage to find anything. I won't hold my breath."

Paige crinkled her nose at the comment. "Wow, he's kind of rude."

"He's worse than that," Damien answered as he plopped down next to her.

Michael leaned over the back of the couch, propping his elbow on the cushion as he studied Damien's book. "Yeah, you caught him on a good day. The marriage to Cate really made him bearable."

"I'm going to have to read all of these books when I get back," Paige answered before she dove into her text. "So, what are the chances there will just be like a list of these?"

Damien burst into laughter, glancing at her with a grin before he sobered and cleared this throat. "Zero chance."

"He is correct," Alexander answered. "We'll likely need to piece together several bits of information."

"It'll take all of us," Celine answered, grabbing another book and collapsing into a chair.

"Wow, I'm super glad I don't live here. We get all our information from a computer."

"I got the impression magic was hidden in your world, too," Alexander said from his desk.

"It is," Paige answered, "but the library has a system with all the information compiled in it. Sometimes, we still have to use books, though."

"Nothing like that exists here," Celine answered. "Everything is word of mouth."

"So, we may never find this," Paige said, her shoulders slumping.

"We'll find it," Michael answered. "We've never failed yet."

Paige bobbed her head, offering him a tight-lipped smile.

Dewey landed on her shoulder, whispering in her ear. "Ohhh, he's a good book boyfriend, too."

"Stop it," she snapped. "I don't have a book boyfriend. I don't even have a real boyfriend. I have a fake husband."

"Uh-huh. Tell that to D-boy himself. He really believes in your marriage. And you're going to look like the jerk when you leave him."

"I'm not...look, let's just worry about that when we're not in a realm of crazy people and my mom's not dying."

"I'm just saying. Never too early to start planning how you're *not* getting a divorce."

"Yeah, well, I'm not going to turn into a vampire either, so, there's that."

"Do you two always talk this much when you're researching?" Michael asked.

Paige winced. "Sorry, we're a little...yes. We do. I just... we'll be quiet now."

Michael offered her a smile and a nod before returning to his book.

"Boy, somebody's uptight, huh?" Dewey hissed.

"Stop it, you're going to get us in trouble again."

Dewey waved his paw at her. "So what? We'll never see them again. They're not even real!"

Paige snapped her book shut. "Nothing in this one."

"I may have found something," Damien announced. Celine set her book aside to peer into his. "This book is talking about the Aroostook Enigma and recounts clues to each of the four key piece locations."

Paige shifted closer on the couch to peer into the book. "What are they?"

Damien read the first aloud. "Within wall that whisper secrets of old, where spirits roam and tales are told, seek a room with treasure deep, where shadows dance and secrets sleep."

"What the heck does that mean? It's random and vague," Paige answered.

"What are the others. Maybe once we hear them all we can cobble something together," Michael said.

"Uhh," Damien began, poking a finger at the page, "where whispers of the forest carry tales untold, in a place where secrets breathe and stories unfold, seek where nature's voice breaks the silence's thrall, there lies the key piece where creatures heed the call."

"Nope," Michael said with a shake of his head, "that didn't help at all."

"Okay, here are the last two," Damien said. "Where waters gleam with a lustrous hue, in a mansion where secrets accrue, search where opulence meets mystery's lore, and the key piece may be found at the core."

"These are all bogus," Dewey said with a shake of his head. "Totally. It's just made up rhymes."

"What is the last one?" Alexander asked.

"In a town where shadows dance and secrets keep, in the hollow where midnight spirits creep, seek where darkness reigns and stories follow, there lies the key beneath the midnight's swallow."

Dewey flung his paws in the air. "Useless."

"I agree," Michael said as he pushed back in the chair. "It's totally vague. We need more information."

They spent another few hours pouring over books, but Damien's find remained their top clue. As night crept over the great estate, Paige yawned, her eyes starting to slide shut.

Her book toppled to the floor, startling her awake again. "Sorry. Sorry."

"It's okay. Maybe you two should try to get some sleep," Celine answered.

Dewey stretched and yawned. "Yes, please. I'm beat."

"Sure. We'll get you set up in a few bedrooms upstairs."

"None of you are going to sleep?"

Celine grinned at her as they followed her from the library. "We're all immortals. We don't need sleep."

Paige rubbed at her sore neck as they climbed the stairs. "Right. That's handy."

"We'll find answers, Paige," Celine promised as she led her into a bedroom. "And through that door is a bathroom that leads to another bedroom."

"Thanks," Paige said with a nod as Celine pulled the door closed, wishing them a good night.

"Mind if I bunk with you?" Dewey asked, already pulling back the blanket on her bed.

"No. I'd rather not be alone here. This place is weird."

"Tell me about it. I like reading about the Slayers, but living with them is kind of messed up."

Paige crawled between the sheets, stretching out as her head hit the pillow. "I should have read more of their books. Maybe there are clues in them about those stupid locations."

"Nah," Dewey said, his arm flung over his eyes, "I read them all. Nary a clue in any of them."

Paige heaved a sigh as her eyes slid closed. "Great. We're doomed."

CHAPTER 7

a frantic pounding awakened her. She groaned as she glanced at the clock.

"What time is it?" Dewey asked.

"It's like six in the morning."

"Why don't these people sleep?" Dewey moaned.

"Coming!" Paige answered as she dragged herself from the bed and shuffled to the door.

She tugged it open to find a breathless Damien waiting on the other side. He grinned at her. "We found something."

Her heart ramped up as adrenaline seeped into her veins, awakening her. "You did?"

"Yeah. Meet me downstairs. We have breakfast, too."

"Somebody say breakfast?" Dewey asked as he appeared at the door. "What kind?"

"Eggs, bacon, pancakes– "

Dewey buzzed past him into the hall. "Lead the way, my good man. You had me at bacon."

"Awesome. And the blueberry scones are good, too."

Dewey rubbed his paws together as they made their way down the hall. "I can't wait to try them. All the food, really."

"He loves food. So, what did you find on the other front?" Paige asked.

"Can you let us eat first?" Dewey asked.

"How about if we talk about it while we eat?" Damien suggested.

"Good plan," Dewey answered with a nod as they descended the stairs.

They made their way to a formal dining room. The scent of food lingered in the air, and Dewey buzzed straight to the sideboard loaded with a variety of eats. "Oh, boy, Al, you really put on a spread."

He loaded his plate with everything, including the blueberry scones, and buzzed to the table, hovering there for a moment with a frown. "You don't happen to have a booster seat, do you?"

"Just a second," Damien said, disappearing from the room.

He returned with a few throw cushions and tossed them on a chair. "There you go."

"Thanks," Dewey said as he perched on the pillows and dug into his meal.

Paige slid into the seat next to him with a full plate. "Thank you for breakfast and your help. So, you found something?"

"I think so," Damien said. "Celine's running it by Marcus this morning to see what he thinks, but it makes sense."

Michael sipped his orange juice. "Ish. It makes sense-ish."

"What does that mean?" Paige pushed the eggs around on her plate as she eyed him.

"It makes about as good sense as it's going to make. I mean…it's completely crazy."

Damien bobbed his head as he set his juice on the table. "Which falls perfectly in line with anything happening here."

"So, what is it?" Paige asked.

Damien raised a finger in the air before he gathered a few

59

items from below his chair, balancing them on his lap. "Well, I plugged all of these riddles into a search engine one by one and it didn't yield much, but when I stuck them in all at once..."

"Yeah?" Paige leaned forward, the corners of her lips turning upward. "You got answers?"

"We think," Michael said.

"It makes some semblance of sense given our discussion yesterday," Alexander said.

"Yes, and because each clue says something about stores or tales or mysteries." Damien poked his finger against whatever sat in his lap.

"Okay, which means what?"

Damien lifted a stack of books in the air. "Books. The key is found in a bunch of books."

Paige wrinkled her nose. "Like in a hollowed out book? I don't understand."

Michael shook his head. "I don't think it's going to be that easy. I think you have to go inside the book to get it."

"Ohhh, like fractured fairy tales," Dewey said as he shoveled more eggs onto his fork.

"Oh, great. I hope we don't pick up anymore 'friends' to bring back. So, how are we supposed to know which books to find these in? The clues were really vague."

"Individually, yes. But on their own...no. There is one author who has locations that fit every single clue." Damien grinned at her.

"Let me guess. That maniac, Nellie Steele." Dewey poked a piece of bacon at Damien to punctuate his statement.

"One and the same," Michael said. "The supposed author of Shadow Slayers and Shelving Magic, an epic tale about a woman named Paige Turner and her teacup dragon sidekick, Dewey."

"Hey!" Dewey shouted with a mouthful of scone, "I'm not a sidekick! I'm a main!"

Michael shrugged. "That's not what the internet says."

"Well, the internet is wrong," Dewey answered.

"Umm, okay, can we get back to the subject at hand? What books do we need to go into do you think and why?"

"Okay, first clue was whispering secrets and spirts and talks about a treasure within." Damien lifted a book with a Victorian House on the front. "*Ghosts, Lore and a House by the Shore* has a house named Whispering Manor that is supposedly haunted *and* houses a pirate treasure."

"Okay, that fits. What about the next one?" Paige questioned. "Something about forests and nature's voice."

Damien shuffled the books, waving another one in the air.

Paige leaned closer to read the title. "*Moving is Murder?*"

"A book where a woman moves to Salem Falls only to learn the animals can talk."

Paige shifted in her seat. "Okay, that could fit the bill."

"The next one talks about waters gleaming and a mansion with a mystery." Damien brandished another book. "*Murder of Pearl.* Set at what will become Pearl Pond Estate in a sprawling mansion."

He continued, lifting a final book in the air. "And last but not least, midnight spirits, shadows and secrets. *Ghostly Gossip* takes place in a town called Midnight Hollow. It all fits. The keys are scattered in these fictional worlds."

"Or nonfictional worlds," Michael said with a wave of his hand, "because I'm still not convinced I'm just a figment of someone's imagination."

"Yeah, maybe this person...is like a biographer."

"Nellie?" Damien asked. "So, she's...documenting our lives?"

Paige shrugged. "It could be. I mean…we're all real, right?"

"Right. Which means these people are probably real, too," Damien said with a nod. "Lily and Cassie, Ellie, Carly and Althea, and Kelly and Jodi."

"You probably should study up on them, you may encounter them when you go to retrieve the key," Alexander added.

"Right. I could try to read a few chapters in each…" Paige suggested.

"I actually did a little reading last night and created some notes based on what I found from other readers and my own perusal of these books." Damien produced a notepad filled with scribble. "You can review these until we determine a way to send you to each of these places."

"Gee, thanks," Paige said as she accepted the tablet and scanned it. "This will really help."

"Looks like all of these people love mysteries, so you could appeal to their sense of adventure to help you solve this case," Michael added.

Paige bobbed her head. "Right. Well, maybe I can get in and get out without them ever knowing."

"Uhhh, I'd plan on running into a few of them. You'll likely need to get into each of their houses to find these keys."

Paige's eyes went wide. "Oh, no. Okay, umm, well, we're decent at making friends in a pinch."

"And enemies," Dewey pointed out before biting into a scone. "We're good at getting people really mad at us."

"Yeah, that's probably not something you want to do," Michael answered.

"Actually," Damien said, "I'd be happy to go with you. I'd love to see some of these places."

"Oh, uh…" Paige furrowed her brow. Would it be helpful to take him or not?

"If you're trying to figure out if you'd be better off without Damien, the answer is no," Michael said. "In a quick pinch, he can figure out the best way to get you out of trouble. Sounds like you two get into trouble quite a bit."

"We're pretty good at it, yeah," Dewey said with a bob of his head. "There was this one time when we– "

"Okay, maybe we'll save stories for another time," Paige said as she tossed her napkin onto the table. "I think we should dive into these notes and start making a plan."

"Hopefully, Celine will be back soon," Damien said. "Then we can figure out a good way to tackle this."

"Feel free to use the library or the sitting room," Alexander chimed in. "Make yourself comfortable."

"Thanks." Dewey fluttered into the air and palmed a few more scones before he landed on Paige's shoulder. "Mmm, these are good."

Paige wandered from the dining room down the hall in search of the library. Her stomach twisted into a tight knot. How would they find all these keys?

She crossed the foyer and pushed into the library.

"What do we got?" Dewey asked as he settled into the couch's cushions.

"I guess we'll start with Lily and Cassie. Let's see…" Paige scanned the notes. "Mother-daughter duo who moved to the small town of Hideaway Bay after losing both their husbands. Wow."

"Nellie's a real monster, huh?" Dewey said. "Okay, keep going."

Paige tapped the paper where she'd left off. "Moved into a supposedly haunted house– "

"Ha!" Dewey barked. "Haunted houses. As if those exist. Okay, go on."

"Uh, Damien seems to think they do…at least in this book, they do. He says they have a ghost named Ri who haunts the house. And they've found a pirate treasure there. They own a shop called Buy the Sea–oh, that's clever–and they enjoy tea."

"Maybe we can buy them a nice set of exotic teas to bribe our way into the house," Dewey suggested.

"Maybe."

"Okay, who's up next?"

Paige flipped the paper over to find the next set of notes. "Ellie. Ellie is a recent divorcee who inherited her aunt's bed and breakfast after the woman was murdered. She can talk to animals, specifically, she talks to her miniature bulldog, Lola, and her sassy cat, Cleo."

"Talking pets, huh? That's too far for me."

"Says the talking dragon. Okay, next up, sisters Kelly and Jodi who own a pearl-shucking business. They inherit a mansion unexpectedly along with a fortune."

"Wow, they sound like they're having the best time."

"Well, not so much since dead bodies constantly turn up anywhere they go," Paige answered.

Dewey cringed. "Ugh, okay, let's not spend too much time with them."

"Right, get in, get out, and get on to Carly and Althea. Carly is a teen who lost her parents and moved to live with her enigmatic grandmother, Althea, who is a psychic witch helping spirits on their journey to another world."

"More ghosts. She has a real thing with ghosts."

"Yeah. Lots of ghosts. Wait, no ghosts in Kelly and Jodi or Ellie, though."

"There are no such things as ghosts," Dewey repeated. "So, a few of these trips will be ridiculous. We'll have to play along though, I guess."

"Yeah," Paige answered. "I hope they're all friendly. I wonder if we can just explain that we need their help, and they'll help us?"

"Are you insane? Do you think they're just going to give us the key?"

"Well, if we frame it like they're helping us solve a mystery, maybe. They like mysteries."

Dewey flicked his fleshy eyebrows up. "Oh, I get it. Like… The Case of the Missing Key."

"Right. Only less Nancy Drewish and more…well, Nancy Drew is fine."

"Yep. We'll go all Nancy Drew on their butts." Dewey poked a finger at her.

"That'll do it!" Paige agreed and they attempted to high five, missing again. "Dang it. Okay, I guess we're ready. Hopefully, Celine will get the information we need to move on this."

"I have the information," Celine said as she wandered into the room with Damien and Marcus.

"You know how to get us to these places?"

"Yes. There is a chapter gate in the sea cave. Once you are in the book, you'll need to find a way back, of course, so recall the spot you arrive in."

"And we'll send Damien with you to help," Celine said.

"Spot we arrived in. Right. Okay, well…can we go right away? I'm not sure how long it will take to get these keys but every second counts for my mom."

"Sure, I'm ready to go when you are," Damien answered.

Paige rose from her seat, and Dewey landed on her shoulder.

"Ahhh, the dragon's not going, right?"

"Yes, the dragon is going," Dewey snapped. "The dragon is the snarky side kick, remember?"

"But…none of these people have seen a dragon."

Dewey rolled his eyes. "Oh, right. They've seen ghosts, talking animals, and all of that, but no dragons."

He waved a hand in the air as he shook his head and

retrieved his ring from under a scale. He hopped off Paige's shoulder and slipped it onto his finger, transforming into his human self. "There. Happy now, D-boy?"

Damien frowned at him and shrugged. "Well, you couldn't go as a dragon."

"Okay, well, he's human now so, we can go. I'm not leaving Dewey behind."

Damien sucked in a deep breath and nodded. "I get it. We're kind of the same way. Slayers stick together."

"I really wish you'd stop calling us Slayers...it sounds like we're gang of serial killers," Michael said as he strode into the room.

"I like it. Plus, it was the name of the series on your book. Shadow Slayers. It sounds cool, like you're a...way cooler version of the ghostbusters," Paige said.

Michael offered her a less-than-amused smile. "Yeah, that's us. Cooler versions of the ghostbusters."

"I'm really not sure," Damien said. "The Ghostbusters were pretty cool. Well, anyway, did you want to get moving on this?"

Paige bobbed her head. "Yes, definitely. I'd really like to get started. Did you have a world you wanted to start with?"

"I mean...let's just start at the top and knock them out one by one."

Paige nodded as she scanned the note sheet again. "Lily and Cassie it is!"

The group made their way back to the sea cave Paige and Dewey had arrived in. "So, I didn't see anything glowing in here. The Chapter Gate in our world glows."

Marcus glanced at her before rolling his eyes. "Humans."

He gathered sandy dirt from the cave's floor and blew it in the air. It sparkled as it settled on the Chapter Gate, illuminating it.

"Oh," Paige said. "Nice. Okay, well, I guess here we go."

"Just a second," Dewey said as he shifted around, wincing.

"What's the problem?"

"I hate this body. It's awful. These arms." He flung them around in the air. "And these stupid legs."

"Well, you can't be a dragon. You have to be in human form."

"I know, I know. I'm just…preparing." After a few more fidgets, he blew out a long breath. "Okay, I'm ready."

Marcus clicked his tongue and heaved a sigh. "Enter through the gate with the book in your hand. When you want to return, walk back through the gate without. Simple, even you three should be able to handle it."

Paige wrinkled her nose at the statement. "Hey– "

"Ignore him," Damien said as he brandished the book. "Let's see if we can find a key."

Paige nodded, and the trio crept forward, passing under the Chapter Gate's arch. They continued through the darkness until dim light surrounded them. Paige's heart thudded hard against her ribs as she wondered if this would lead to anything or be another false lead.

CHAPTER 8

The scent of sea salt and dampness swept through Paige's nostrils again. "Another place by the sea."

"Yep," Damien said, "didn't you read all the notes? The series is Lily and Cassie by the Sea."

"Ugh, there's sand. I'm so sick of sand," Dewey complained. "It's hard to walk in. And it sticks to everything."

"Well, with any luck, we can be out of here soon. Come on, let's take a look around."

They left the confines of the cave behind, exiting onto the beach.

"Wow, these houses are nice," Paige said. "I'd like to live here."

"You can, Paige," Dewey informed her. "You have a rich husband, remember?"

"Yeah, but where is this quaint little seaside town in our world? Does it exist? Can I find a nice little walkable town with beautiful homes that sit by the sea?"

"There's Lily and Cassie's house," Damien said, pointing ahead at a rambling Victorian.

"Oh, yeah, I recognize it from the book cover," Paige said with a nod. "Do you think anyone's home?"

"I don't know, but I don't think we should just go in."

Paige wrinkled her nose.

"You think we should?" Damien asked.

Paige tugged her lips back into a half-wince. "Well, I mean…is it *really* wrong?"

Damien stared at her with an incredulous expression. "Yeah. I mean, it's breaking and entering."

"Look, first of all, D," Dewey said, "these people in this town don't look like they lock their doors, so it's only entering. And second, I think what Paige is getting at is…can you actually commit a crime in a cozy mystery?"

"I don't even understand the logic behind that question. First of all, cozy mysteries are based on a crime, usually murder but sometimes others, to start with, so yes, you *can* commit a crime in a cozy mystery."

"Noted," Dewey answered, "but let me riddle you this. We are in a fictional world, so this is hardly going to follow us back to the real world. Is a fictional crime really a crime? And on that note, in cozy mysteries, the amateur sleuths themselves often commit crimes to solve the crimes."

"I…don't know what to say," Damien answered with a crinkle of his forehead. "I'm…not breaking into Lily and Cassie's house even if it is fictional."

Dewey heaved a sigh. "Goody-goody. Come on, Paige, we'll break in."

"Well, let's have a closer look, at least. I don't want to break in if someone's home."

"Obviously. I have no desire to spend time in a fictional jail."

"Oh, so you think you can't commit a fictional crime, but you believe in fictional jails?" Damien asked.

"Obviously, there are fictional jails where they put

fictional criminals. But I'm not fictional, so I'm not a fictional criminal, but I could spend time in a fictional jail anyway, which I'd like to avoid," Dewey said.

"If the jail is fictional, and we're not could it hold us? We normally escape jails…even non-fictional jails. But fictional ones…" Paige paused as she tried to sort through the logic.

"Let's not find out. But the house looks quiet, so maybe we can do a little snooping." Dewey closed in on the deck at the rear of the house and narrowed his eyes at the sliding door. "I don't see anyone."

"Let's circle around front and see if there's any movement," Paige suggested.

Dewey nodded as Damien trailed behind them. "I'm not participating in this criminal activity," he called.

Dewey waved his comment away as they rounded the house, studying the wide porch that wrapped around the corner.

Paige winced. "Car is in the drive."

"Yeah, but do they have two cars?"

"I don't know. I didn't read the book. Maybe Damien knows." Paige took a few steps back toward him. "Hey, do you know if both Lily *and* Cassie have cars?"

Damien dug a paper from his pocket and unfolded it. "Umm, yes. Lily has a Mercedes SUV while Cassie has a Jeep Wrangler, pink."

"The Wrangler isn't here!" Dewey said. "Let's go inside and find this key."

Dewey twisted toward the porch, slipping in the sand that surrounded the house. "Stupid legs. I ought to take this ring– "

"Don't," Paige warned. "Because we could run into someone at any time."

"Fine," Dewey said as she yanked him up to stand. "I'll keep the stupid legs."

"Just deal with it, Dewey," Paige grumbled as she helped him up the stairs. "I wonder how easy this'll be."

Damien peered through the railing on the porch at them. "I don't think they'll leave this thing lying around. If they even know what it is."

"I looked at the illustration from the book you found the riddles in," Paige answered. "They may not know what it is. It's just a wedge with some scrollwork on it."

"Okay, well, good luck."

"Are you seriously not coming inside?"

"I'll be the lookout," Damien said with a salute.

"If you see anything, make a bird noise. We'll know exactly what that means," Dewey answered as he tried the door. "Locked. What kind of people lock their doors in a town like this?"

"Apparently, Lily and Cassie."

"They've had multiple break-ins related to the treasure and more," Damien called from the edge of the porch. "They lock their doors and have an alarm system, although they don't always use it because it's a hassle."

"At least one of us read the book," Dewey said as he glanced at the window. "Do you think we could get in one of those?"

Paige shrugged as she crossed to it and tried to push it open. "Nope. Won't budge. Uh, do you know how to pick a lock?"

"Why would I know that?" Dewey asked. "I'm a dragon who has spent a decade living underground. How many locks do you think I picked in my time?"

"I don't know. Maybe it's a skill you learned as a hobby or something," Paige answered as she continued around the house in search of another opening.

She rounded another corner, finding the back door. With

a twist of the knob, the door popped open. "Oops, someone forgot to lock the back door."

It creaked on its hinges as she shoved it inside.

"No alarm blaring either," Dewey said. "Should we go for it?"

"We have to. We need this key. Come on." Paige stepped inside the kitchen, scanning the space. "Looks like the kitchen."

"Wow, you should be an amateur sleuth in a cozy mystery next, Paige. You're really quick."

She shot him an annoyed glance before she shook her head. "Come on."

"Where do you think they'd keep this thing if they have it?" Dewey murmured.

"If I was a key– "

"Oh, please don't start with that again," Dewey grumbled as they stepped into the hall. "You *can't* be a key. A vampire, sure."

"I was just a panther. I lived life as a half-cat for like a week. I could be a key if I wanted," Paige shot back. "Just... look over there for this key."

"Hey, here's a big library. Maybe it'll be in the desk drawer or something." Dewey wandered into the room and tugged open a drawer.

"Good idea. You check the desk, I'll check these cupboards below the bookshelves. Maybe we'll get lucky."

Paige crouched as she pulled open the two doors and peered inside.

"Stop!" an odd voice shouted.

Paige froze, color rising into her cheeks as her heart began to hammer against her ribs. They'd been caught. Someone was home. Would they be friendly?

She plastered a smile on her face as she slowly started to twist toward the voice.

"Uh, Paige?" Dewey questioned.

She slid her eyes toward him, spotting his raised hands and the confused expression on his face. Her gaze flicked to the figure hovering in the doorway. Her muscles relaxed, and she rose to her feet. "Is that…"

"Yep," Dewey said with a nod. "A doll."

Paige inched closer, staring at the face. "That's…weird. How did it get here?"

"Voices. Check. Intruder." The doll raised its arms in the air. "Call police."

"Police?" Paige gasped. "No, we're not…intruders. We're friends of Lily and Cassie, and they told us to come here and find a key."

"No!" the doll shouted.

"Uh, Paige," Dewey murmured, "you're arguing with a doll."

"Well, the doll is…OMG, I'm arguing with a doll. How is this happening?"

"No," the doll said again. "Ri."

"Ri?" Paige wrinkled her nose as she stared at the Victorian figure with the odd white eyes.

"What?" Dewey asked. "What's a Ri?"

"Ri. Pirate. Ghost. Friend."

"This doll's a nut job," Dewey said with a shake of his head.

The doll's hand flung forward and smacked him in the head. "Nitwit."

"Whoa," Paige said as Dewey winched.

"Ow, watch it, you stupid piece of plastic."

"No! Ri!" The doll waved her hands in the air.

"Dewey, you're making her mad. She's not plastic. She's a…I don't know what she is but stop calling her plastic."

"Ri help."

Paige sucked in a breath and bobbed her head. "Oh,

perfect. Yes, we would love your help. We're a looking for a key of sorts. It's– "

The doll karate chopped Paige before she shoved her to the floor. "Ow, hey!"

She did the same to Dewey, knocking him off the legs he wobbled on to begin with. "This doll is a real bi– "

Wind swirled around the room, cutting off his words and two chairs slid from the table to the center, the backs pressed together. "Sit," the doll insisted.

"Pass, doll," Dewey grumbled. "We're not taking orders from you."

The doll raised her hand in the air again, and Dewey scrambled to the chair to take his seat. Paige joined him, sliding onto the seat behind his. The doll raised her arms in the air again and rope wrapped around them. "Ri help Lily and Cassie."

"I can't believe this," Paige cried. "We've been trapped by a doll."

A cat wandered into the room, eyeing them with his solitary eye before it rubbed against the doll.

Dewey sucked in gasp. "The one-eyed cat!"

"I see it. He's cute. I love cats. Hi, buddy," Paige said with a grin.

"Stop talking to the stupid cat. We need to get out of here!"

Paige wriggled under the tight ropes, unable to free herself. "Maybe he can chew through the ropes."

"Okay, you keep trying that angle while I actually think. Wait, wait, I may have an idea."

"What is it? Can you get loose of the ropes?"

"Maybe." He grunted with effort as the bindings tightened around her.

"What are you doing?"

"Trying to get this…ring off," he groaned. "If I can get it off– "

"You'll be a tiny dragon and probably can fly free of the ropes."

"Right. But the stupid thing is stuck on this ridiculously puffy knuckle I've got. These fingers are stupid."

"Hey, they're slimmer than your normal ones."

"Are you saying I have fat fingers?"

"No, just…fleshy." Paige winced as he tugged tighter against her, the rope tugging her chest hard.

"I'm sorry my fat little fingers aren't up to your standard, Paige." He heaved a sigh. "It's no use. I can't get the stupid thing off. Hey, doll, come over and pull my ring off, would you?"

"No," the doll answered in her strange robotic voice.

"I don't think she's going to help us escape, Dewey. She's pretty insistent on keeping us captured for Lily and Cassie."

"Well, that's just perfect. I can't believe we've been caught by a doll."

"Pirate," the doll answered.

"Why does she keep saying that?" Dewey asked. "She's a Victorian doll, she's not a pirate."

"Ri, pirate. Captain Ri."

Paige scrunched her forehead. "Wait…didn't they find a pirate treasure here? I wonder if…

Dewey burst into laughter. "A female pirate captain? Come on, Paige."

The doll raced across the room and smacked him in the head.

"Ow, stop smacking me, Ri."

"Ri, pirate captain."

Dewey sighed. "Okay, fine. You were a pirate captain. Sure." He twisted to peer at Paige over his shoulder. "I think she's nuts."

Another crack sounded behind Paige followed by a cry of pain.

"Stop it, Dewey. You're making her mad. So, uh, Ri, was it? You were a pirate captain?"

"Yes. *Grandmistress.*"

"Was the *Grandmistress* your ship?"

"Yes."

"That's kind of cool, Ri," Paige said with a smile at the doll. "A female pirate captain. You were a woman before your time. A real feminist."

"Gee, Paige, why don't you just ask her for drinks and if you two can be besties?"

"I'm trying to get her to be nicer to us and help us out," Paige said through clenched teeth.

"Do you really think a pirate captain is going to be nice to us and let us go?"

"Well, she's obviously nice to Lily and Cassie. She's tied us up here for them to find because they are friends."

"This is a stupid plan. Maybe we can get Damien's attention somehow."

"Should we just yell for help?" Paige asked. "I don't know if he'll hear us or come in, but…"

"Worth a shot. We're not getting anywhere on our own," Dewey said.

"Okay, on three…one, two– "

"Wait, wait. Do we yell on three or after three?"

"After three. One, two, three, yell."

"Okay," Dewey answered.

Paige sucked in a breath. Okay, one, two– "

"Wait," Dewey interrupted.

"What now?"

"What do we yell? Help? Damien? Help us, Damien? What?"

Paige chewed her lower lip. "Uhh, maybe…help. Let's yell help."

"Got it. Yell help after three."

"Okay, here we go. One, two, three, HELP!"

They shouted at the same time before they waited.

Paige strained to listen for any answer. "Do you think he heard us?"

"I don't hear anything. Maybe he didn't. Want to try again?"

"Okay," Paige said with a nod.

After another count, they shouted for help a second time.

"I still don't hear anything," Dewey said. "This is ridiculous. Is he deaf?"

"Maybe we're too far away. He was at the corner of the house."

"Well, there's not much we can do about that."

Paige's forehead creased as she worked through scenarios. "Okay, maybe we can like…hop over closer to the door."

"Hop?"

"Yeah, like…let's…just…" Paige shifted around in the seat. "Just lift up and shift over. We'll try to move the chairs."

"Fine," Dewey grumbled.

Together, they tried to shift the chairs toward the door. They wobbled back and forth making no progress.

"Wait, we need to do this together. Like shimmy at the same time."

Dewey blew out an aggravated sigh. "Fine. On three."

After a countdown, they tried again, shifting an inch. "Okay, that worked. Again."

They continued to work their way over until Dewey shifted on three instead of after three. The movement sent them teetering.

"Oh shoot," Paige said as she leaned hard toward the side, trying to stop them from falling.

It didn't work. A second later, they crashed to the floor on their sides, still strapped firmly into the chairs.

"Dang it," Paige grumbled. "Now, look what you did."

"What I did?" Dewey said, his voice sharp. "I didn't do it."

"Yes, you did. You went on three instead of after and now we're stuck on the stupid floor."

"Maybe we can get up."

"How?" Paige asked, her voice incredulous.

"Ask your bestie, the pirate ghost. Maybe she can drag us back up to sit."

The ghost rolled over to them on her wheeled base. "Nitwits."

"I don't think that's going to happen. We're stuck here and– "

A bird call sounded from outside followed by the crunch of gravel. Paige's heart hammered against her ribs. "Oh, no."

"Oh, yes. I think we're about to get caught."

CHAPTER 9

rakes squealed outside as Paige desperately tried to free herself from the ropes that bound her to the chair. "Oh, come on!"

"Not going to happen, Paige. Face it. We're done."

"We can't be done. No. I don't accept that. We've fought our way out of worse spots," Paige said as she wriggled under the rope.

"Paige…we're goners. We're– "

Voices outside the house floated to them, followed by the sound of a key sliding into a lock.

"Quick, try to take your ring off again!" Paige hissed.

"I'm trying, I'm trying, but that may be worse. We don't want them coming inside to see a dragon flying around," Dewey answered.

A second later, the door swung open, and two blondes plowed into the room.

The doll raced toward them. "Ri. Intruder. Capture."

The older of the two furrowed her brow as she stared at the doll.

"Another intruder?" the younger blonde asked.

"Library. Tie up."

"Wow, they talk to her like she's real," Dewey whispered.

The women's gazes shifted from the doll to Paige and Dewey, tied to the knocked-over chairs. Their eyes went wide.

"I'm calling Wyatt," the younger one said.

"Hi there," Paige answered with a grin. "I'm Paige. Uh, no need to call to anyone. We were just...accidentally inside your house."

The older woman crossed her arms. "There is no treasure here, anymore. We gave it all away."

"Uh, yeah, we're not...we're not treasure hunters, per se. We're, ummm, we need your help. We've come from...a land far, far away."

"Paige, try to not sound crazy."

"Shut up, I'm doing my best here."

The older woman shuffled a few steps closer, her eyes narrowing. "You need our help?"

"Mom, don't encourage them," the younger one said as she pressed her phone to her ear.

"Please don't call the police," Paige said as she wriggled under the ropes. "We won't hurt you. We do need help. Please. My mom's really sick. And I'm trying to save her life."

"By breaking into our house?" the younger woman asked.

"Yes. You...there's supposed to be a key here that opens a lock that has a serum that will save her life. Look, it's a long story, and it probably sounds crazy, but I'm just trying to help my mom." Paige let her head thunk to the floor below as she frowned.

"Hey, Wyatt, it's Cassie...Yeah, we have another problem...If you wouldn't mind, thanks." She ended the call as Paige's heart sank. "He said he'll be over in five."

A few minutes later, the shrill wail of a police siren cut through the tense silence.

"Great," Paige lamented.

"Well, you wouldn't listen. You had to blab everything, and now we'll probably get the book thrown at us."

Cassie pulled the door open and a man in a sheriff's uniform stepped inside, his eyes falling on them.

"Wow," he said, his nose wrinkling. "How'd you manage to get them tied up?" He flicked his gaze to Lily. "Did you use your bat?"

"No, this is one time I didn't use my trusty bat. Ri did it."

The man frowned. "Oh, uh…right. I didn't realize the perps were still on the scene. I'll call for backup, and we'll have them out of your hair in no time. Of course, you'll have to file a report, but…"

"Actually, they mentioned needing help. I'd like to hear them out," Lily answered. "I just…didn't want to do that without someone here with a gun." She glanced at Paige and Dewey still on the floor. "He has a gun, you see? Don't do anything stupid."

"We promise," Paige answered. "Thank you for the chance."

"What about your buddy here?" Lily asked with her arms crossed.

"Dewey. That's my friend, Dewey. And he promises, too. Right, Dewey?"

He didn't answer, and Paige shimmied around in her chair. "Right, Dewey?" she growled between clenched teeth.

"Yeah, yeah, totally. I'd never do anything stupid."

"Okay, untie them."

"Mom!" Cassie said with a huff. "We can't untie them."

"Wyatt's here…with a gun."

"What if they have a gun?"

"I do not have a gun. I promise," Paige said with a shake of her head. "I don't even know how to use a gun."

"Like I'm going to believe you," Cassie said with an incredulous glance.

"Look, okay, don't untie me. I already told you. I'm looking for a piece of a key. I need it to open a safe that contains a serum that will save my mother's life."

"Yeah, I heard your story the first time," Cassie answered. "But that makes no sense. Why would we have a piece of this key? And what kind of magical serum is hidden in a locked safe?"

"Look, lady, we don't make the rules," Dewey said, "we're just playing by them trying to save Paige's mom."

"Yes," Paige said with a nod. "I don't know why it's here, but there are four pieces. The clue for the first piece led here."

"Where are the others?" Lily asked.

"A place called Salem Falls—"

The two women exchanged a glance.

"Do you know it?"

"We've heard of it, yes," Lily answered. "Keep talking. Where else?"

"Uhh, Pearl Pond Estate."

Lily arched an eyebrow as she stared at her daughter. "And the last one?"

"Midnight Hollow."

Lily scoffed. "Really? Do you expect us to believe this?"

Paige swallowed hard, butterflies filling her stomach as she wondered if she'd soon be carted off to jail. "Yes? I mean...it's true. I–I didn't make the names of the towns."

"It's just that..." Lily settled her arms across her chest.

"Yeah?" Paige asked.

"We know all of these places."

Paige's heart skipped a beat as her eyes went wide. "Really? You do? Do you think you could help us find all of the key pieces? I don't want to have to keep breaking into people's houses."

"No," Cassie answered. "Why would we help you with what sounds like a completely bogus, made-up quest?"

"Because we need help, and it's not made up. I swear," Paige said, her features pinched. "I know it sounds…weird, but I swear it's legit."

Lily sucked in a breath, shooting a glance at her daughter.

Cassie's features pinched as she shot her mother a questioning glance. "If you want to help them…I guess it's another mystery."

"Yes, yes, a mystery. And you love mysteries. Right? You are quite the pair of amateur sleuths."

"Stop trying to butter us up," Cassie answered, shooting her an unimpressed glance.

"Well, I mean…you've solved a case with a pirate treasure. Look how smart you are."

"She said stop pandering, Paige. Look, Lily, can you get us untied here? We've been through enough at the hands of your crazy ghost."

"No!" Ri shouted.

"She's not crazy," Lily answered as she patted the doll on the shoulder. "She's a very nice ghost. She helps us a lot."

"Yeah, she may be able to help us find the key," Cassie added. "She knows a lot."

"We'll take all the help we can get. Now, if you'll untie us…I have a sketch of the key in my pocket."

"Okay, untie 'em, Cass." Lily tilted her head toward them.

"Why do I have to do it? If they're up to no good, I'll be the one who gets it."

"We're not up to no good," Paige insisted. "Please, please. Let me prove it."

"Ri, can you untie them?" Cassie asked.

"Yes," the ghost answered.

Cassie backed away as the doll waved her hands in the air, and the ropes magically fell away.

With a wince, Paige climbed to her feet along with Dewey. "Thanks."

Lily lifted her chin, her arms crossed. "Show us this key."

Paige dug into her pocket and pulled out the folded sketch. "Here, see?"

She held it forward with a shaky hand.

Cassie reached forward and snatched it, studying the drawing before she showed it to her mother and Wyatt. "Have either of you ever seen anything like this?"

"No, I haven't. Ri?" Lily asked

"Key. Hidden. Panel."

Paige's heart skipped a beat as the ghost spoke. "What panel? Where?"

Lily held up a hand, waving at her to stop. "Just a minute. This will take a little bit. She's not good at communicating."

"She's pretty good at tying people up," Dewey snapped.

"Yes, she is. But speaking is hard for her. So, you have seen this?" Lily asked.

"Secret. Key. Keep. Protect. Panel."

"There are hidden panels all over this house," Cassie answered. "Some of which we may not even know about. We're going to need Ri's help to find it."

Paige puffed out her cheeks as she ran her fingers through her hair. "Oh, man. Can we do anything to make her talk more? Like a seance or something?"

"No, sorry. Sometimes, though, she'll have a little break-through if we feed her," Lily answered.

"She eats?"

"Oh, yeah," Wyatt answered. "She eats. And eats. And eats. Although, I wouldn't mind eating."

"Tacos," the ghost answered.

"She eats tacos?"

"Who doesn't eat tacos? Everyone loves tacos," Lily answered.

"I could go for tacos," Dewey said with a shrug.

"Okay, that's…fine. But…we had a friend…he's outside. Can we get him?"

"Sure. The more the merrier." Lily shrugged. "So, that's seven orders of tacos?"

"Better get two extra-large pitchers of margaritas. We're going to need it," Wyatt added. "And don't forget the churros."

"Aren't you on duty?" Paige asked.

His forehead crinkled as he glanced at her. "So what?"

"So…you're…never mind. No problem at all. I'll just get Damien."

She skirted around the others as Cassie pressed her cell phone to her ear and pulled the front door open. She glanced outside, searching the area for Damien.

"Damien? Damien!" she called, but he did not respond. "Damien, you can come out. It's okay. They're going to help us."

A figure emerged from behind a pine tree. "You got caught?"

"Yeah, by the ghost. But it's okay. They're going to help us find this key *and* all the others."

Damien's eyes went wide as he crossed toward her. "Really? Oh, that'll be a help."

"Yeah, and we're getting tacos," Paige answered. "Come on."

He climbed the stairs and ducked into the foyer, eyeing the others warily.

"Lily, Cassie, this is our friend, Damien."

He waved as he offered them a tight-lipped grin. "Thanks for helping. This will make things so much easier."

"Apparently, the first key is somewhere in this house.

Where, we don't know, but maybe with some tacos, Ri will power up and show us," Cassie answered.

"Why don't we head into the kitchen and sit down?" Lily suggested. "The food should be here in twenty minutes."

"Great. Wow," Damien said as his eyes raised upward. "This house is really nice. And right by the sea."

"We love it," Cassie said with a smile.

"I live by the sea, too. Right on the coast of Maine."

"Oh, that's a beautiful state," Lily answered as she led them back to the kitchen.

They settled around the table, and Paige drummed her fingers against it, nervous energy filling her. They passed out the tacos and started into their meal.

As Damien shifted in his chair, a book toppled to the floor from one of his pockets.

"Oops," Cassie said as she bent to pick it up. Her brow furrowed as she stared down at the image on the cover. "What is this?"

Lily peered over her shoulder. "Ghosts, Lore and a House by the Shore?"

"Why is there a picture of our house on it?"

"Uhhh," Paige began before shooting a worried glance at Dewey.

"Might as well tell them. It can't get much worse."

"Tell us what?" Cassie asked.

Paige shifted in her seat. "We've all recently discovered that…we're characters in a specific author's books. We aren't sure what that means but…it seems like…we're fictional."

"What?" Cassie cried.

Wyatt's forehead crinkled as his gaze floated around the room. "Mind blown."

"Right?" Damien said. "When I first heard it…I was stunned. I mean, I feel real."

Wyatt pinched himself. "Ouch. Me too. Although…"

"What?" Paige asked.

"It would explain a lot of things. Mayor Thompson, for example. Her behavior is…"

"Over-the-top. Like it's scripted," Lily answered.

Silence stretched amongst the group until a loud burp emerged from Ri.

The doll raised her hands in the air. "Sorry."

Paige furrowed her brows as she stared at the doll. "Did she seriously just– "

Cassie polished off the last of her taco. "She was a pirate. It comes with the territory. Anyway, I don't think we should dwell on this…wrinkle."

"I agree," Lily answered. "I feel real. I walk and talk and make decisions independently. Let's just… work to find all the pieces of this key you need."

Paige bobbed her head as she sipped the sour margarita, her lips puckering. "Yes, that's…a good idea. Stop thinking about how weird it is that we're not real– "

"We're real," Lily insisted. "I'm real. You seem real. Your friend is real."

"Yes, I am. Thank you, Lily," Dewey answered. "I like you."

Lily smiled at him. "Thanks. Now, let's eat our dessert, then search for this key."

Wyatt dunked his churro into the chocolate sauce before taking a bite.

"You're not about to double dip that, are you?" Dewey asked with narrowed eyes.

He froze mid-chew, his eyes sliding to Lily. "I mean…no."

Dewey poked a finger at him. "Right answer, Sheriff."

Wyatt frowned down at his plate for a minute until Lily spooned chocolate sauce onto it. "Double dip as much as you'd like, Wyatt."

"Thanks, Lil. So, do you ladies have any idea where this key could be? What if it was among the treasure you found?"

Cassie lifted her shoulders. "It could have been. Clif and Ri amassed quite a fortune along with several interesting objects used to open other treasure hoards."

"No," Ri answered. "Key here."

Paige's heart leapt at the words. "It's here? Are you sure?"

"Here."

Cassie raised her eyebrows. "If she says it's here, it's here. We just need to figure out where."

Lily wiped her fingers on her napkin before she rose. "Ri, any chance you can lead us to where it is?"

"Ri help." The doll rolled from the room.

The group hurried from their seats to follow her. She reached the stairs and stopped.

Paige waited for someone to carry her up, but the ghost lifted herself off the floor and floated up to the next level.

"Whoa," Dewey whispered, his voice filled with awe.

"Right? That's creepy."

"No!" Ri yelled from the top of the stairs.

"Don't say stuff like that. She really takes exception," Cassie whispered to her. "She likes to be treated like a real person."

"But...she's a doll."

"She's actually the spirit of a woman who used to live in this house, then became a pirate captain. She just inhabits the doll for a form."

"How do you live like this?" Paige asked as they ascended the stairs.

"How do you live in a world where you need four pieces of a strange key to open a safe that contains a serum that will save your mother's life?"

Paige wrinkled her nose as she stared at Cassie. "Okay, fair. There are a lot of other weird things, too, so I'll give you that."

"I guess we each have our strange things in life. At least we can help each other out. I hope we find all your keys."

In front of them, the doll zipped around the banister and down the hall. They followed her into a bedroom.

"The key is in my room?" Cassie asked.

"Hidden. Floor."

Their gazes all fell to the floor.

"Where?" Cassie asked.

"Floor. Floor. Floor. Floor." The ghost raced back and forth chanting the word over and over.

"Are there any creaks you're aware of?" Lily asked. "Maybe there's a loose board we can pry up."

"Umm…" Cassie scratched her head. "Yeah. A few. One is here."

She stalked toward an ensuite bathroom and pressed against a creaky board.

The sheriff pulled a pocketknife from his belt and flicked it open. "Nothing."

Cassie crossed to another spot. "Here."

They tried again but weren't able to pull anything up.

Paige's heart sank as she wondered if this was a false lead.

Cassie moved to a new spot by her window seat and tromped on a board. "Here."

Wyatt followed her, sticking his knife into the groove between the boards. One of them popped up a second later. He grabbed it with his fingertips and tugged, wincing with effort. It shifted out of the way, revealing a cubby.

Cassie dropped to her knees, toggling on her cell phone flashlight.

"Is there anything in there?"

"Yes," Cassie answered as she reached into the hole.

Paige held her breath, waiting to see what emerged. Would they finally find the first part of the key?

CHAPTER 10

*P*aige held her breath as Cassie dug around under the floor.

"Almost got it," she said before she finally pulled out a scrap of fabric.

"Is there anything inside?" Paige asked.

"Yes," Cassie said.

She laid it on the floor and carefully unwrapped it. Paige hurried over, staring down at the object. Her heart skipped a beat as she caught sight of something that looked just like the sketch. "That's it! That's part of the key."

"We did it!" Cassie said with a grin. "Thanks, Ri."

"Yes, thank you...Ri," Paige stammered, finding it odd to thank a ghost.

"One down, three to go," Dewey said.

"Yes. Oh, I feel so much better knowing we found one, at least. I hope the others are just as easy."

As Wyatt replaced the floorboard, and Cassie rose to her feet, dusting herself off, Lily pulled her cell phone from her pocket. "We can probably make it to Pearl Pond estate before nightfall. It's the closest. Should we head up there and talk to Kelly and Jodi?"

"Sure," Cassie said with a nod. "Oh, uh…do you three have a car?"

"No, we don't. But I can drive, so maybe I could rent one?"

"Okay. Then you can follow us. We won't fit otherwise," Cassie said.

Damien furrowed his brows. "We could fit. I mean…we could squeeze in the back. We'd be okay. Unless it's like an eight-hour drive or something?"

"Well, no, there are six of us," Cassie answered.

"Oh, I didn't know the sheriff was going," Damien answered.

Cassie straightened, confusion on her face. "Oh, then there would be seven of us."

Paige scanned the group, trying to count them again. Where was she coming up with the seventh person? "Umm…"

"Oh, I don't need to go," Wyatt answered. "You ladies probably have this well in hand."

"So, we're back to five," Damien answered.

"Six," Cassie said. "You three, Mom, me, Ri."

Paige's jaw dropped open. "The ghost is going?"

"Ri go."

"She doesn't like to stay at home alone," Cassie answered. "We can split between my Wrangler and Mom's car. Wyatt, can you check on Willy if we end up staying overnight?"

"Absolutely. No problem."

"Staying overnight?" Paige asked as she shifted her weight. "I really hoped to kind of grab these four keys in a day."

Lily offered her a consoling smile. "I think you may need to manage your expectations. We do need to drive to these places. Salem Falls isn't very far, but far enough that it'll take the better part of a day."

Her heart sank at the words. "Oh. Right."

"You don't have a car, but did you want me to drive you into town to pick up your luggage?"

"We don't have that either," Paige answered. "We just... when we got this lead...we...came here without really thinking ahead, I guess. I..."

"Oh, well, that's okay. I could lend you a few things," Cassie said to Paige.

"Yeah, I could drop some stuff by for Dewey and Damien," the sheriff added.

"Oh, wow, thanks," Damien said. "That's very nice of you."

"No problem. I'll run home now and throw some things into a duffel and drop it off. Give me thirty minutes or so."

"Sounds good. We'll pack a few things and be ready to head out soon." Lily waved her phone in the air. "I'll text Kelly and let her know we're coming."

"Thank you so much for your help," Paige said, her heart melting with appreciation over the help they were giving her. Maybe they really could save her mom, after all.

"Is there anything we can do to help?"

"Why don't you three take a stroll into town to buy some road trip snacks?" Cassie suggested.

"Oh, uh, sure. We can– "

"You don't have money, do you?" Lily asked.

"I have...two dollars," Paige answered, tugging the wrinkled bills from her pocket.

Lily held a finger in the air before she strode from the room. She returned a minute later with a few bills. "Here's fifty. That should be enough. Buy whatever you'd like. We're not picky."

"Gosh, thank you so much. You've been so kind. My mom will really appreciate this, too."

"No problem. Now, get going. There's a snack shop on Main Street right by the bakery. They'd be the best place for premium snacks that aren't filled with preservatives," Lily said.

They parted ways with Damien, Dewey, and Paige heading toward town as Lily and Cassie worked on packing and readying for the impromptu trip.

"Wow, this is really small-town USA, huh?" Paige said as the buildings filled in around them.

"Yeah. It's like a perfect television town," Dewey answered as he stared at the quaint shops. "It's weird."

"I think it's nice."

"It's bigger than Bucksville, but still quaint and small. I wonder if Nellie likes small towns."

"She put me in a city…no…" Paige shook her head. "No, we're not doing this again. I am not subscribing to the idea that I live in a city because Nellie made me. I live there because I moved there when I was younger because it offered more."

"Right," Damien answered. "I moved to Bucksville for Celine. And Celine lived there because Gray's family founded it."

"I live in the city because it was the only job I could get as a tiny dragon," Dewey added as they found the snack shop.

After making their purchases, they carried their bags back to the bustling Main Street and made their way back to Whispering Manor.

"Did you get good stuff?" Cassie asked with a grin as she loaded two bags into the back of her mother's car.

"I think so. Dewey loves food, so he spent all your money."

Dewey tossed a few pieces of trail mix into his mouth before he crumpled the bag closed. "Sorry. They had really good stuff."

"I know. They're the best. Mom and I always stock up from there before a road trip." She slammed the trunk closed. "Well, I think we're all set. Wyatt dropped by some things for Dewey and Damien, and I packed you a bag with some clothes and pajamas. Ready?"

"Yep," Paige said with a nod.

"Great. I'll just grab Ri. Oh, and I guess Mom and Ri will go in her car, and I'll drive mine. Then you three can split however you'd like."

"Uh, I'll go with Cassie," Damien said. "And you two can go with Lily and...the ghost."

"Shotgun!" Dewey called as he strode toward the car.

"Of course, leave me in the back with the ghost."

"Yep," Dewey answered. "I'm not sitting with her."

Paige climbed into the backseat as Lily emerged from the house, locking it and closing the gap between them.

Within a few minutes, they were underway, heading for Pearl Pond Estate.

"I heard from Kelly," Lily said from the driver seat. "They're preparing rooms for us. They didn't know anything about the key, but they're making a list of places to look."

"Oh, great," Paige answered from behind her. "Thank you so much."

"Of course. It's a fun little mystery to solve. Cassie and I do like to solve puzzles."

"Glad we could help out, Lily," Dewey answered, his hand digging into his snack bag again. "Mmm, these gourmet snacks are delish."

"Glad you like them. Wait until you see this place. Pearl Pond Estate is really something."

Paige plastered a smile onto her face, less interested in what the estate looked like and more interested in retrieving the keys. Every second that passed was one step closer to her mother dying.

With no way to communicate with her world, she had no idea how quickly things were progressing. Instead of enjoyable, the long ride irritated her.

Maybe they should have gone back through the chapter gate and straight to Kelly and Jodi's. Was this a waste of their time.

She shifted in her seat, blowing out a long breath as she grabbed at the seat belt that felt like it was choking her.

Lily glanced as her through the rear-view mirror. "You worried about your mom, honey?"

"Yeah," Paige said with a nod, her features pinching.

"Don't worry, Paige. We're doing the best we can," Dewey answered. "Drucinda will make sure she's okay."

"Is Drucinda a friend or family?" Lily asked.

"A friend. She was my mom's best friend. She's staying with her while we try to find these keys." Paige glanced out at the rolling hills passing by their window.

"I see. Well, I'm sure she'll take good care of your mom until you get back with the keys. And we'll definitely find them. Cassie and I haven't let a good mystery beat us yet."

Paige forced another smile at her.

"It's okay, honey," Lily said. "It's a lot when our parents get sick."

Lily grabbed her purse and passed it back to Paige. "There are tissues in the front pouch."

The sentiment alone made her tear up. She dug into the pocket to find the pack, yanking a tissue free. "Thanks," she sobbed. "I may use the entire pack."

"That's okay. I have plenty more."

"Aw, Paige, it'll be okay. We didn't come this far to fail now," Dewey answered. "I mean...that would really stink if we were doing all this work, and your mom just died."

Lily furrowed her brow as she side eyed Dewey.

"Right, and if we're just fictional," Paige said between

sobs, "she'll awake at the last second, and we'll all live happily ever after."

"Yeah, and you'll be rich because you married a–oops." Dewey winced as he shot a glance at Paige. "Well, you know who you married."

Lily focused on the road, her eyelashes fluttering at the odd conversation.

"Sorry," Paige said. "We have a weird dynamic."

"It's okay. Whatever gets you through." She poked a finger at the GPS embedded in her dash. "And it passed the time. We're nearly there."

Paige blew out a shaky breath, pleased with the development. "I wonder if they'll know where the key is."

"I'm not sure, but with any luck, we can all put our heads together and find it."

"Thank you so much for your help." Paige's features pinched again as she glanced at Lily. "I'd like to think my mom will be like you. You know, once she wakes up."

"Did you not know her at all?"

"She disappeared when I was just a few days old, so no. We just found her now, and she's really sick."

"That's a shame. Well, we'll do what we can to help you. And I'd love to keep in touch if we can. I'm not sure how that works if we're all fictional, but I'm trying not to think about that."

"Me too," Paige said with a chuckle. "And I'm really sorry you and your daughter had to split up, and you're stuck with us."

"And Ri," the ghost chimed in from next to Paige.

"Right, and the ghost."

"It's okay. It seems Cassie and Damien are having a nice time back there. I think they're having a singalong."

"Weirdos," Dewey grumbled as he fidgeted in his seat.

As they rounded a bend, a glowing beacon appeared on

the crest of a hill. Paige ducked to stare at it from the back seat. "Is that Pearl Pond Estate?"

"Yep," Lily said.

"Wow, it's huge." It was going to take forever to search that entire place. Her mother may be a decade older by the time they finished here.

"When we get there, I'll send a message to Ellie in Salem Falls and let her know what's going on. She can start looking around her place, too."

"Thank you so much for your help with this."

The car's engine revved as Lily urged it up the steep hill toward the mansion at the top.

"This place reminds me of the were…" Dewey froze, wincing again. "Oh, where…where was it? Do you remember the place I'm talking about, Paige?"

"Yep. That creepy mansion with the little old lady who made us drink tea."

"Riiiiight," Dewey said with a nod. "That's the one."

Paige recalled the werewolf mansion all too well. She hoped this wasn't a repeat performance, but by the looks of the weeping woman fountain out front, it just may be.

"Wow, that fountain is creepy," Dewey said.

"Tell me about it."

"Yeah, Kelly hates it too, but her sister doesn't mind it. Anyway," Lily said as she threw the shifter into park and turned off the engine, "we're here."

Paige unbuckled her seat belt and slid from the car, craning her neck to stare up at the sprawling house. Light appeared at the doorway and a blonde wrapped in a shawl stepped out, grinning at them.

"Hey, Lily, you made it."

"We did. And these are our new friends, Paige, Dewey, and Damien. They're the ones looking for the key."

"Right." The woman bobbed her head as she stuck her

hand out. "I'm Kelly. My sister, Jodi, is inside. Come on in. We're always happy to help out a few friends."

"This place is amazing!" Paige exclaimed as she stepped inside. "Wow, those lions are…fierce."

"Aren't they great?" Another blonde strode from a back hall with a grin. "Hi, I'm Jodi."

"They are kind of…scary, but wow, the craftsmanship."

"Wait until you see some of the other things in the house," Cassie said with a grin. "I'm sure we'll get to see them all while we're searching for this key. Unless you've found it."

Kelly clicked her tongue and shook her head. "Not so far. But there are plenty of places to look. You said you found one in Whispering Manor?"

"We did," Lily answered. "Under a floorboard in Cassie's room."

"Any markings on it or anything? This place is huge, but maybe if we had an idea of a symbol or carved initials or something, we could figure out the best place to start."

"There was nothing. We honestly found it through a creaky floorboard."

Kelly winced, shooting a glance at her sister. "Ugh, well, good luck with all the creaks and groans in this house."

Paige's shoulders slumped at the words. If they didn't have any idea of where to look, would they actually find the thing? It would take forever to comb through this mansion.

She glanced around at the vast foyer. Even this room would take forever to search.

Tears brimmed again as she realized she may never find the rest of the keys. Her failure would sentence her own mother to death.

CHAPTER 11

*A*s Paige's gaze fell to the floor below, a warm hand slipped around her shoulder. She glanced up, surprised to find Lily offering her support.

"Well, you ladies know a few of the hiding spots. Maybe we can start with those. And the rest of us can explore the other parts of the house for others. Sorry to treat your house like a hidden object game, but…"

"Don't worry about that," Kelly said with a dismissive wave of her hand. "We don't mind. And there are plenty of hidden spots. I was just hoping to narrow it down a little."

"If I may," Damien chimed in, "the clue we found said to search where opulence meets mystery's lore, and the key piece may be found at the core."

"Core," Kelly answered, her brows furrowing. "Like at the core of the house?"

"Maybe," he answered with a shrug. "Does it actually mean the core of the house, or does it just mean it's somewhere in the house? I'm not sure, but it's worth a shot to start at the house's core. Does that ring any bells?"

"Well, yes." Kelly exchanged a glance with her sister.

"There is a scary set of halls under the house. We explored it a little on another…case."

"Don't ask," Jodi said with a shake of her head. "But we could start there."

"Sounds good. How do we want to do this? Are we all needed down there or should some of us stay topside and look around here?"

"Uh, why don't we split up? We know the halls down there, so whoever wants to go with us, let's grab some flashlights and go."

"Why don't you take Paige and Dewey with you," Lily suggested. "Cassie and I know the house since we've been here. We can poke around up here with Damien."

"Sure, that sounds perfect. I'll grab the flashlights, and then we'll head to the carousel room."

"Carousel room?" Paige asked.

"Yes. You have to access the basement level through the carousel room. It's…odd, but anyway…"

"Wait, you have a carousel in your house?"

Kelly grinned, wiggling her eyebrows. "We do. And it's my favorite thing about this creepy old place."

"Can we ride it?" Paige asked.

"Absolutely. We'll take a ride on it before we head into the dungeon."

"It really is fun," Jodi said with a nod as she motioned for them to follow her down the hall.

"Have fun exploring the rest of the house," Kelly said to Lily before they departed.

"This place is really amazing," Paige said to the sisters as they continued down the hall past a large dining room.

"Thanks. I think it's sort of creepy, but Jodi likes it," Kelly said.

Paige crinkled her brows. "Oh, did Jodi design it?"

"No," Kelly said with a chuckle, "we inherited it accidentally. Totally unexpected."

"Ah, the unexpected inheritance trope. I know it well," Dewey answered.

"Huh?" Kelly crinkled her nose at the words.

Paige elbowed him and shook her head.

"Oh, nothing," Dewey said.

Kelly pulled open a door in the hallway and rummaged around in the large closet, pulling flashlights from a shelf at the top.

"Thanks for helping us," Paige said as she accepted a boxy flashlight. "I really appreciate it. Sorry for the trouble."

"No trouble at all. We're kind of getting used to solving mysteries. It seems everywhere we go, a dead body turns up."

"Amateur sleuth trope," Dewey whispered.

Paige shot him an annoyed glance.

"Well, hopefully no one ends up dead here." Paige grinned, suddenly wondering if that wasn't the right thing to say.

"Right?" Kelly shot back, seeming to let the comment roll off of her easily. "Okay, let's head to the carousel."

They continued down the hall and through another hallway that had a babbling brook with stepping stones leading through it.

"What the hell kind of house is this?" Dewey asked as he carefully hopped from stone to stone. "This would be so much easier if I could fly."

"Shh, will you stop saying ridiculous things before you get us caught?"

"Sorry, Paige, I can't help it. I have that headache again. I feel awful. Wearing this ring is taking a toll."

"Well, when we get into the privacy of our rooms, you can take it off, until then just…buck up."

"Something wrong?" Kelly asked.

"Nope," Paige answered with a shake of her head. "Just discussing some of the interesting architecture in the house. That stream was something else."

"Yeah," Kelly said before she stopped in front of a massive set of bronze doors emblazoned with a set of carousel horses. "Check this out."

She and Jodi tugged the doors backward, triggering a hidden mechanism that whirred to life. Music spilled from the room as lights flickered to life, illuminating a massive spinning carousel.

Paige's jaw dropped open as she watched the horses bobbing up and down as they circled around and around in the room. "Wow! This is like…a real carousel."

"Yep," Kelly said with a grin and a nod. "It's my favorite thing in the house. Jodi and I ride it all the time. I love it in here. Come on."

She waved a hand, motioning for them to enter.

"Just be careful stepping onto the platform," Jodi warned as each sister carefully made her way onto the revolving floor.

Within a minute, they all whirled around in circles. Paige hurried to a horse and climbed on, grinning as she rode it up and down.

Dewey tried twice to climb up before he successfully mounted one. "Hey, this is sort of fun."

"Yeah," Paige answered with a nod as they continued their ride.

"I told you," Kelly said.

They rode for another few minutes before Paige twisted in her saddle and glanced at Kelly. "So, how do we get to this basement area?"

Kelly held up a finger before she climbed down off her horse. Her sister did the same, and together they wandered to the doors to pull them shut. The carousel slowed to a grinding halt, plunging them into silent darkness.

Paige's heart skipped a beat as she hurried to toggle on her flashlight to beat back the blackness. "Yikes, it sure is dark in here."

"Yep. Careful when you get down," Kelly said as they picked their way across the floor to a specific horse. With a few twists of the pole through its back, a panel slid away in the floor, leading to a black hole.

"How are we supposed to get down there?" Paige questioned, her voice rising an octave. Surely, they weren't going to jump.

"There's a ladder under here," Kelly answered as she dropped to her knees and blindly reached into the hole.

A metal ladder swung forward and unfolded, creating a new path to the floor.

"Wow, that looks rickety," Dewey said.

"Right? But it held us the last time, so we should be okay," Kelly answered as she swung her legs over the edge and stepped onto the first step.

After a few minutes, they'd all made their way down into the damp, dark basement. Paige shivered as the cooler air swirled around them.

"Creepy, right?" Kelly asked.

"We've seen worse," Dewey answered.

"Where should we start?" Paige questioned.

"Well, this place is like a maze. There are hallways everywhere. Do you feel comfortable splitting into teams of two or would you prefer to stick together?" Kelly asked.

Paige and Dewey exchanged a glance. "We're okay going off on our own. Just...don't leave us down here."

"Wouldn't dream of it. Okay. We'll take the hall to the left at the next intersection, and you can head right. Once you've checked everything out on your side, we'll regroup and head forward together."

"Sounds good." Paige nodded and raised her flashlight. "Oh, if we find anything, we'll try to give you a shout."

"Same," Kelly said with a nod as they moved forward to the first intersection of halls.

Paige and Dewey veered off to the right, their flashlight beams sweeping back and forth as they crept down the hall.

"So," Dewey said after shooting a glance over his shoulder, "do you think those two are like witches or something?"

Paige screwed up her face. "What? No. They seem like normal people."

"Do they? I mean they have a carousel in their house and some pretty large lions guarding the stairs."

"They're carved."

"That's what we think. What happens when the sun goes down?"

"The sun is down. And they're still wooden."

"Fine," Dewey shot back. "What happens when the sun goes down and the magic words are said? My guess? Those suckers come to life and stalk around the house eating people."

Paige's footsteps faltered as she wrinkled her nose. "What? No."

Dewey shrugged. "Hopefully, we won't find out the hard way, but…I'd sleep with one eye open and my shoes on. Well, not me. I'm going back into dragon mode the second I can. This headache is killing me."

"I'd tell you to pop it off now, but if Kelly and Jodi appear…"

"Yeah, they'll probably kill me and use my parts in their potions."

Paige shook her head as they reached another intersection and veered right. "They're not witches."

"Werewolves?"

"I doubt it. I think they're normal people."

"What kind of normal people accidentally inherit a house like this? I mean, come on, Paige. Use your brain."

"Unexpected inheritance is a pretty common cozy mystery trope."

"As an author, of course, I know that. But this is like unexpected, unexpected. Because they probably hexed someone."

Paige clicked her tongue. "They didn't hex anyone. Now, concentrate, would you? We need to find this key."

"I haven't seen anything so far."

"It could be anywhere. I mean, any of these blocks could be hiding it."

Dewey patted one. "Should we be trying them all?"

"Dewey, we will be a year older by the time we've done that."

"Good point. Maybe there's a way to tell just by looking at them."

"Maybe there will be something obvious. Like a cupboard or something."

"Why would there be a cupboard down here?" Dewey snorted a laugh as he shook his head.

They hit a dead end, and Paige's shoulders slumped. "I don't know. It's just wishful thinking. Come on, let's go back the other way."

She twisted on a heel and retraced her steps to the intersection, continuing down the hall in the other direction. Dewey followed behind her, hobbling.

"What's wrong with you?" Paige asked as she waited for him to catch up.

"My legs, my hips, my back. You name it. Walk, walk, walk. It's too much."

"Do you want to take a break?"

"No," Dewey said with a sigh as he shook his head. "Keep going. If I sit down, I'll never get up."

Paige crinkled her nose as she slowly continued down the hall. "Wow, it's like your eighty."

"Try three-hundred-and-eighty," Dewey said. "Dragons are different, remember?"

"Yeah, but...you're like my age in human years. And I'm not complaining about my back and my hips."

"I guess you're just so wonderful and fit," Dewey snapped.

She offered him a coy smile. "I guess so."

"Don't read too much into it. In my dragon form, I'm pretty fit, too."

"Yeah, although I think the flying is really a lot less work."

Dewey screwed up his face. "How do you figure that? I've got to keep my wings beating a pretty good clip constantly."

"Just seems...faster. Like not as much effort to get from point A to point B."

"Well, it's not, okay? It's deceptively easier. That's it."

Paige bobbed her head as she rounded the corner and froze.

"What? Are you going to complain that walking is, in fact, harder?" Dewey spread his arms to the sides.

"No, look! A cupboard." A smile spread across Paige's features as her light beam illuminated it.

Dewey shifted his gaze to the end of the corridor, his jaw dropping open. "I can't believe it."

Paige's heart lifted as a smile formed on her lips. "Let's hope we're in luck and the key's in there."

"Yeah," Dewey said matching her expression. "That would be something, huh? We could move on to the next spot. We'll bang out these keys in no time and be back to save your mom."

She wiggled her eyebrows at him. "Yep. It'll be almost too easy."

"Haha." Dewey clapped his hands together and rubbed them. "Race you."

"Race–"

Paige's eyes went wide as he took off before she could finish the statement. She scrambled to catch up with him, both of them slamming into the cupboard at the same time.

"I won!" Dewey exclaimed.

"You did not," she answered. "I was here at the same time."

"Believe whatever you want, I know I won."

"Come on, let's just open this and get the key."

He bobbed his head.

With her heart hammering against her ribs, Paige grabbed hold of the wooden knob, her fingers lingering on it before she pulled the door open. Would they find the next key?

CHAPTER 12

"Come on, open it!" Dewey said as Paige hesitated.

"I know, I know, I just...it's like that whole Schrodinger's cat thing, right?"

"Huh? Whose cat?"

"The cat that's both alive and dead until you open the box."

Dewey shook his head. "Not following you."

Paige let go of the. handle. "You know, there's a cat in a box with some sort of mechanism that might kill it, but until you observe the state of the cat, the cat is both alive and dead at the same time."

Dewey stared blankly at her for a breath. "So, you think there's a dead cat in the cupboard?"

"No," she said with a shake of her head. "Until I open the door, the key is both there and not there."

Dewey narrowed his eyes. "Have you been drinking?"

"No, I'm not drinking. How have you never heard of this?"

"It sounds ridiculous. Listen, the key is either in there or it's not. It's not both. I can't be both."

"In quantum physics, it can be. It is. Until we open this door, it's both there and not there. Until we open this door…we have hope." Her shoulders slumped as she said the words.

"Oh, that's what you're babbling about. Yeah, well, if you're going to get kicked in the gut, better to do it earlier and waste less time, now come on and open the door."

"I guess," she mumbled as she grabbed the door pull again and whipped it open, keeping her eyes closed. "Is it there?"

"No, but there's a dead cat."

Paige snapped her eyes open, her features twisting. "Really?"

"No, I just wanted you to open your eyes. Nothing here but dust." Dewey blew at the empty shelves before he coughed, waving a hand in the air.

Paige stamped a foot on the floor. "Dang it. If we never would have opened it…"

Dewey shot her a sharp glance. "Don't say that ridiculous thing. It's like when you say…if I were a key…you can't be a key. And that quantum physics stuff is nonsense. Come on, let's finish looking around."

"You're right," she said with a deep sigh as they left the cupboard behind and retraced their steps.

They made their way back to the intersection where they'd split from the sisters and waited for them to arrive.

"Find anything?" Kelly asked as her light bobbled toward them.

"No, you?"

"Nothing. Let's try this way." She slid her beam toward the only remaining hall left to explore.

"Gosh, I hope it's down here. This certainly does fit the core of the house line."

"Yeah, though, I wouldn't get my hopes up. Jodi and I were down here when we were being held hostage– "

"What?" Paige scrunched her nose as she snapped her gaze to the women.

"Yeah, it's a long story involving a Faberge egg and the Russian mob, don't ask. Anyway, there wasn't a key that we saw, but maybe we missed it."

Paige's forehead creased as she tried to imagine the wild tale while they continued down the hall until it spilled into a large chamber.

Kelly and Jodi crossed to a covered area on the floor and shoved the wooden platform aside. "Here is where the egg was. But no key."

"Any other hiding spots in the room?" Dewey asked.

"You're welcome to look around, but we haven't found any."

They spent another few minutes poking around the large room before they gave up.

Paige let her hand slap her thigh. "Nothing here."

Kelly offered her a consoling glance. "I'm really sorry."

"It's okay. It's not your fault. Maybe the others had more luck."

"We'll find it," Kelly said with a hopeful smile. "We won't let it beat us."

"Yeah," Jodi answered. "We haven't met a mystery we couldn't solve yet."

Kelly nodded. "Usually, we just stumble upon the solution, but we get it."

"Yeah, us, too," Paige said, a genuine grin crossing her features as they made their way back to the ladder. "We always come through though."

"Nellie really likes bumbling heroes," Dewey whispered.

Paige gave him a smack on the chest and shook her head.

"Oh, right, we're not supposed to talk about that."

They climbed back into the carousel room before Kelly slid the panel shut. The mechanism sprang to life again as the sisters pushed the doors open. Carefully, they leapt off the moving platform into the hall.

Paige heaved a sigh as they shuffled down the hall toward the foyer. "I wonder where Lily and Cassie are. Maybe they had more luck."

"Let's hope," Kelly said as they neared the foyer.

Excited voices floated to them as they approached. Paige quickened her steps, hoping they'd had more luck.

"Anything?" she asked as she spilled into the expansive space.

"Maybe," Cassie said as she sat on the massive staircase leading upstairs.

"Yeah," Damien answered with a nod. "We found a split here in the stairs, and we're wondering if it leads to a secret passage or panel."

"So far," Lily added, "no luck opening it, though."

Kelly climbed up to take a closer look. "Oh, yeah, I see the seam."

"Could it just be a seam and nothing more?" Jodi asked.

"No," Cassie said with a shake of her head. "It only exists on part of the stair, not across the whole thing. We just need to find a way to trigger it."

With a grimace, she pressed hard against the step. "Not spring-loaded, as you can see."

"Maybe we should grab some tools and pry it apart," Kelly suggested.

Lily wrinkled her nose. "Oh, I'd hate to tear your stairs apart and ruin your house, especially if it's a dead end."

Kelly pressed her lips together. "I know, but I hate to waste time and hold you back from moving on."

"We'll find it," Cassie said with a shake of her head. "We have lots of these in Whispering Manor. We just need to figure out what triggers the panel."

Kelly glanced around at all the woodwork on the stairway. "It could be anything."

"Yes," Damien agreed, "but with seven of us working on this, we should find it, right?"

Jodi let out a harsh laugh. "Seventy of us may have been better with all the woodwork in this house."

"Well, it's usually close to the panel," Cassie said. "So, let's start with everything close to it and spread out from there. We've already tried sliding, pulling, pushing. Now we're going to move on to search for triggers elsewhere."

Kelly climbed a few steps past them, tugging at the spindles before she tried to twist a few. "The carousel panel is triggered by twisting one of the horse's poles. I wonder if it's the same here."

Paige and Dewey climbed closer, working on the railing on the opposite side of the stairs. They spent thirty minutes poking and prodding every piece of wood available but found no way to open the panel.

Kelly plopped onto a stair, wiping at her brow. "Okay, I need a break. And maybe a snack."

"Snacks?" Dewey asked. "Are there snacks? I love snacks."

"Yeah, I think a snack is in order," Jodi agreed. "We'll go grab a few things from the pantry. Why don't you all take a break."

With a sigh, Paige eased herself to the stair below her, a frown forming on her lips.

"Don't give up, Paige," Cassie said. "We'll figure it out. Right, Mom?"

At the foot of the stairs, Lily rubbed her chin, staring at one of the lions.

"Mom?" Cassie called again.

"Yeah, we'll get," she said with a fleeting smile before she returned her eyes to the lion's snarling mouth.

"Got an idea?" Cassie asked.

Lily furrowed her brow. "Maybe. This lion's tooth is different from the other ones."

"Different how?" Damien asked.

"It's twisted. Just slightly, but definitely twisted."

Damien scurried down the stairs, his eyes flicking between the two lions. "Oh, yeah, I see it."

Lily rubbed a finger against the tooth. "I wonder if it's just a defect, or if it has some meaning."

"Have you tried pulling it?" Cassie questioned.

"Not yet. Let me give it a go," Lily answered.

She reached forward and wrapped her fingers around the large wooden tooth, giving it a tug. It didn't budge.

Paige's heart sank again as nothing happened. They'd never solve this, and they were probably wasting time here. Maybe she and Dewey should move to a new location.

Lily grunted as she wiggled the tooth to no avail. "Darn thing."

She crossed her arms, staring at it for a moment before she reached toward it and tugged straight up. The tooth popped skyward and the panel on the stairs clicked open.

"Mom! You did it!" Cassie exclaimed.

Paige's heart raced as she scrambled across the wide stair toward the panel. "Is there anything inside?"

"A wooden box. I wonder if there's anything in it." Cassie withdrew the carved item, blowing dust off of it before she wrinkled her nose.

She thrust it forward toward Paige. "Here. Open it."

"You sure? You found it."

"Just open it," Cassie said with a smile.

Paige balanced the box on her lap, her heart pounding against her ribs. She lifted the top, searching the inside for the key. Her stomach twisted as she spotted a piece of fabric. With shaky hands, she lifted it from the box and unwrapped it.

A grin spread across her features. "The key!"

"We found it!" Dewey exclaimed.

"We did!" Paige said with a pump of her fist. "Two down, two to go!"

Lily, Cassie, and Damien applauded as Kelly and Jodi returned with a large bowl of popcorn.

"What happened?" Kelly asked.

"That's celebration popcorn now," Lily said. "We found the key. And if you ever need to know, the lion's tooth opens the panel."

Kelly grinned at them as Jodi stepped forward to study the lion. "I knew these lions were cool."

"Well, at least they have a purpose other than being creepy," Kelly said. "Aw, I'm so glad that you found it. That's great."

Paige sat back, beaming at the key. With any luck, they would find the other two keys just as quickly and return to Buckville for the serum.

"You're not rushing off, are you?"

"No, I think we'd better stay the night," Lily said. "Salem Falls is a pretty good drive. We'll get an early start tomorrow morning."

Paige's heart plummeted at the words even though she understood the delay.

"Great. Well let's have our celebration before we head off to bed. Come into the living room." Kelly motioned for them to follow her.

Paige carefully placed the key back in its box and closed the lid.

"Halfway, Paige," Dewey said as they descended the staircase.

"I know. I can't wait to find the others. I hope they're all this easy."

"You and me both. I can't wait to go back home where I

can be me."

"Don't worry," she said, clapping a hand onto his shoulder. "We won't stay long, then you can take a break."

"I can't wait. Although, that popcorn smelled delicious."

They entered the living room, spending some time with their newfound friends before they retired to their respective bedrooms.

After a few minutes alone, a knock sounded at her door. Paige pulled it open to find Dewey in human form. "Mind if I bunk with you? There are creepy cherub carvings all over my room."

"Sure," Paige said as she motioned for him to enter.

He stepped inside. The moment she closed the door, he tugged off his magical ring, popping back into his dragon form. "Ahhh, that feels better."

"Nice to see you again, buddy."

"Nice to be me again, Paige. I hate my human form."

"You know," she said as she crawled between the sheets. "I kind of don't like it either."

Dewey wrinkled his nose at her. "Thanks, Paige. You're so mean."

"I'm serious. I like your dragon form. It's…cute and fun. Your human form is…stuffy."

"I'm not stuffy." He landed on the bed and adjusted the covers over him.

"You are as a human. It's like you're not having any fun at all." She switched off the light.

"I'm not," he answered in the darkness, "I have a killer headache almost all the time."

"That stinks. Well, try to get some rest. Tomorrow's a new day and a new headache."

"Yeah. I can't wait until this is over." Dewey yawned and within seconds, his breathing turned rhythmic.

Paige tossed and turned most of the night despite her

exhaustion as worry coursed through her. What if they couldn't find the keys?

She hoped they'd go back to Shadow Harbor triumphant, but she prepared herself for disappointment.

When the sun peeked through the curtains, the next morning, she opened her eyes, weary and miserable. "Ugh," she groaned, smashing a pillow over her face.

"Rise and shine, Paige," Dewey said to her. "We've got a full day of finding keys ahead of us…*after* a five-hour car trip."

She pulled the pillow away with a grimace. "I barely slept."

"Drink some extra coffee," Dewey said. "We've got to get a move on. I want to get home."

Paige flung the covers back and nodded. "Me too. I just want to save my mom. I'm so nervous we won't find one of these keys."

"Yeah, I know." Dewey landed on the bed next to her and patted her shoulder. "But we'll keep trying until we do, Paige. That's all we can do."

"Thanks, buddy. Well, I guess I should get changed and head down to start this day."

Dewey rolled his eyes. "Don't remind me. Five hours cramped in the car with those stupid legs. Ugh."

"Well, take solace in the fact that I, too, have a blinding headache from lack of sleep. So, we'll be a pair."

"Do you think Lily and Cassie would lose it if they saw me in dragon form?"

"Yes. I think they would. Don't do that. We don't need to introduce dragons to another realm."

"Why not? I mean, if this realm is fictional, which I know we said not to assume, but just if," Dewey said as he buzzed into the air, "would it really hurt?"

"It would probably lead to chaos," Paige answered as she tugged on the borrowed tunic from Cassie.

"Nellie seems to like chaos. Look at Dominique."

Paige raised her eyebrows. "Hmm, look at our lives. Complete chaos."

"Right, so maybe I could– "

"No," Paige said with a shake of her head. "Don't reveal your dragon form. Not cool. Even if any of this is real about the worlds being fictional, let's not take a chance. What if someone captures you and keeps you for experiments or something."

"Good point. Okay, guess I'll play human again." He slid the ring onto his finger with a shake of his head. "There, happy?"

"Very. Let's go." Paige slung her bag over her shoulder.

They collected Dewey's things from his room before they made their way downstairs, finding three bags waiting at the bottom.

"Looks like everyone else is up," Paige said as she dumped her duffel next to the others.

"Yeah, and I smell food." Dewey hurried down the hall toward the dining room they'd spotted last night.

Chatter and laughter flowed from within as they entered.

"Ah, there you are," Lily said with a grin. "Come in and get some breakfast before we hit the road."

Paige and Dewey crossed to the server and grabbed plates. "Sorry," she said, "I had trouble sleeping, then slept in."

"No problem. We'll get on the road whenever you've eaten. I've already spoken with Ellie in Salem Falls, and she's ready for us."

Paige settled into a seat at the dining room table. "Any chance she's seen the key?"

"No," Lily said with a shake of her head. "But her bed and

breakfast has a lot of hidden spots and secrets, so we'll be solving another mystery."

Paige's shoulders slumped at the words. "I'd like just one of these to just be sitting out on someone's mantel."

Lily chuckled at the words. "Don't worry, we'll find it."

"Got a long drive, huh?" Dewey asked as he stabbed at his eggs.

"About five hours."

Dewey whistled as he shook his head. "That's a long drive."

"It's not too bad. Cassie and I like to travel, so we're used to drives. And the scenery is lovely."

Paige pushed the food around on her plate as she nodded.

"Don't sweat it, honey," Lily said with a consoling smile. "We'll get there."

Paige forced a smile onto her lips as she nodded. "Yeah, thanks. I'm just…anxious."

"Of course, you are," Cassie answered. "It's your mom. But we'll find it."

Paige shifted in her seat. "Do you think we should split up. Maybe some of us go to Salem Falls and some of us go to Midnight Hollow?"

Lily and Cassie exchanged a glance.

"I don't mind doing that," Cassie answered, "but sometimes it takes all of us to figure it out."

"You're right. I'm sorry. I know you're both trying to help us, and I'm just being a huge pain."

"You're not. It's fine," Lily said. "I think we'll head out to load the car while you two finish your breakfast."

"Okay," Paige said with a nod. "Thanks. We won't be long."

"Speak for yourself, Paige. I'm going back for seconds."

The women and Damien disappeared from the room to load up the luggage while Paige shoved her plate away.

Dewey sat down with a fully loaded second helping and dug in.

"Ugh, how can you eat that much?"

"I can't help it. The food is good. And we have five hours in the car."

"With snacks," Paige reminded him.

He shrugged. "So?"

Cassie appeared in the doorway, her features twisted into a frown. "Hey, just wanted to tell you to take your time. We won't be leaving right away. We've got a little problem."

Paige's heart sank at the words. What was the problem and how long was it going to hold them up?"

CHAPTER 13

*P*aige held her breath, her stomach twisting into a
tight knot. "Problem? What problem?"

"Flat tire," Cassie said with a wrinkled nose.

"Really? Like...sabotaged?"

Cassie shook her head. "No, just flat. I just need to change
it. I've got a full-sized spare. Actually, Damien is changing it.
I should get back out there to help him, but I just wanted to
let you know not to rush."

Paige sucked in a breath and nodded. "Thanks, Cassie."

"Flat tire, huh?" Dewey said with a shake of his head as he
bit into another piece of bacon. "That stinks. How random."

"Typical with our luck."

"Yeah. Oh well, seems like we'll be on our way in no time."
Dewey guzzled down a glass of orange juice.

"Stop drinking so much. We'll be stopping for a bathroom
break two minutes into our drive."

"Will you stop policing me? This is an adventure. I'm in a
mansion and enjoying a lovely breakfast. Calm down, Paige."

"I can't calm down." She leapt from her seat, her fingers
curling into fists. "We are only halfway through finding these

keys. Then we need to go into the wilds of Maine to use them. And then we need to get back with the serum."

"And we will."

"But how much time will have passed? My mom was in Bucksville for a really short amount of time but like six months passed in the real world." She plopped into her seat. "Dewey, what if we don't make it in time?"

Dewey heaved a sigh, finally pushing his plate away. "Paige, we're doing the best we can. We're working hard to find these keys, and that's all we can do."

"But what if it's not enough."

Dewey rubbed her shoulder, his expression turning serious. "If our best is not enough, then that's the way it is. I know this is hard, but twisting yourself into a pretzel over it isn't helping. It's just going to drive you crazy."

A tear fell to her cheek, and she flicked it away with a sniffle. "Wrong answer."

"No, it's not the wrong answer. The answer is you need to think positive. We're doing the best we can do. You need to believe that we'll make it."

"Do you think we will?"

"Heck yeah!" Dewey answered. "Look what happened with my parents. We randomly got stuck in the jungle just when they needed us the most. And we saved them."

Paige bobbed her head, sniffling again. "Right. We can do this."

"Yes, we can. We'll find these keys and save your mom."

Paige pressed her lips together as she continued to nod. "Yes. We can do this. We will do this."

"That's it. That's the positive thinking we need."

"We've beaten werewolves, vampires– "

The smash of a cup on the floor startled her and stopped her words. She glanced up to find Kelly, mouth open in a wide O, staring at her. "You've beaten what?"

121

Heat washed over Paige as she shot a panicked glance at Dewey.

"Vampires and werewolves," Dewey answered. "In a game, of course. We play a role-playing game. Paige and I don't always like to admit it because it's a little dorky, but..."

"Oh," Kelly answered, a smile crossing her face as she pressed a hand to her chest. "Good thing. For a second there I thought we were about to get another shock."

She bent down to pick up some of the larger pieces of the smashed mug. "Can you imagine? Vampires and werewolves?"

She chuckled, and Paige and Dewey joined in with her laughter.

"That's insane," Paige answered, still nervously chuckling.

"Right? I mean, I know we inherited a mansion by pure chance, but...that goes too far."

Paige continued her nervous chuckling. "Right, totally."

Cassie shuffled into the room, and Paige leapt from her seat. "Ready? Are we ready?"

"Yep. Tires all changed. Damien's washing his hands, and then we'll be ready to roll."

Kelly crossed to her and pulled her into a hug. "Aw, this was too short of a visit. I hope you and your mom can come back again soon."

"Hey, I didn't even get to ride the carousel, so, we will definitely be back."

Kelly grinned at her before they exchanged a hug.

"Ready?" Cassie asked Paige with a grin.

"Yep." Paige glanced over her shoulder at Dewey who shoved another strip of bacon into his mouth as he crossed the room.

"Ready," he murmured.

"Sorry to pull you away from the bacon," Cassie said with a chuckle.

"It's okay. I hope the bed and breakfast has good bacon."

Cassie nodded. "Ellie makes a mean breakfast."

Dewey stopped, his features crinkling. "What about dinners?"

Cassie laughed as they stepped into the hall. "She does pretty good with that, too, but given our short notice, we may just head to the diner. You'll love it. Great burgers and shakes."

"That sounds promising. I love a good burger," Dewey answered as they reached the foyer.

Lily and Damen waited for them, and after a set of good-byes that left Paige antsy, they finally headed out the door.

Paige eagerly climbed into the backseat of Lily's SUV and clicked on her seat belt. She slid her eyes sideways to the doll propped in the seat next to her. "Did she spend the night in the car?"

Lily glanced in the rear-view mirror as she swung around the weeping woman fountain. "No, Cassie snuck her in last night and out this morning."

"Sleep, bed," the ghost said.

"Oh, that's good," Paige answered. "So, about a five-hour drive?"

"Yep." Lily patted Dewey's arm. "Don't worry, we'll stop for lunch."

"Oh good," Dewey answered. "I was wondering about that."

Lily chuckled as the mansion faded behind them, and they headed for the highway with Cassie trailing behind them. "My husband was the same way. We wouldn't be finished with one meal before he was asking about the next."

"That's Dewey," Paige said with a chuckle.

They spent the next few hours chatting on and off. Anxiety rose in Paige as the time ticked by. She tried to study the scenery, but she felt anything but relaxed. Her mind continuously wandered to her mother. How was she faring? Would they make it in time?

The stop for lunch proved tedious, with Paige tense and shoveling her food down in her best effort to get back on the road.

"Hey, you okay?" Damien asked as they waited outside of the bathrooms for Lily and Cassie.

Paige shifted the takeout container in her hands. "Yeah, just...anxious to get going. With every second that passes, I just feel like...we're going to be too late."

Damien pressed his lips together in a consoling half-smile. "Yeah, I get it. But we're going as fast as we can. And we've got some pretty great help."

"Yeah," Paige said with a nod. "Yeah, they're pretty nice. I mean...they dropped everything to chauffeur us around and make sure we find these keys."

"Cassie's pretty fun. It's a shame she's had so much tragedy."

"Uh-oh, do you like Cassie?"

Damien chuckled. "I do...as a friend. Believe me, we don't need to go further than that with the life I lead."

"Yeah, well, her mother is carting around a ghost in her backseat, so...her life is pretty weird, too."

"Not as weird as mine," Damien answered with a chuckle. "Or yours, apparently."

"Okay," Lily said with a deep breath in as she emerged from the bathroom. "We're ready."

"Great." They made their way to the car and climbed back in to continue the last bit of their journey. Paige sat with the foam container on her lap, staring down at it. "Uh, what should I do with the food?"

"Just open the container and put it on Ri's lap. She'll handle the rest."

Paige wrinkled her nose as she popped open the top and glanced at the ghost.

"Eat," Ri said.

Paige set the food on the doll's dress before she flicked her gaze out the window again.

A few minutes later, she glanced back, finding the container half-empty. "Oh, she's eating it."

"Yep. Just like the tacos. She's a good eater."

"That's…"

"Weird," Lily said with a chuckle as she pulled off the highway. "Cassie thinks so, too. And don't even get me started on how Wyatt feels about it."

Paige's heart thumped a little faster against her ribs as the highway turned to homes. "Is this Salem Falls?"

"Close," Lily said. "It's just ahead. We'll pass through it on the way to the B&B."

As the buildings filled in around her, Paige studied the beginnings of the quaint small town. They continued down Main Street past shops and restaurants.

The town fell away just as quickly as it popped up, and the road turned curvy. After another minute, Lily flicked on her turn signal and pulled onto a gravel driveway. The car bumped along until a rambling Victorian became visible through the trees.

"Oh, wow," Paige said as she ducked to view it. "Looks nice."

"It's really great," Lily answered with a smile as she brought the car to a stop. They climbed out as the front door popped open. A dog bounded from inside, howling at the top of her lungs.

"Whoa," Dewey said, leaning back against the car. "Down, boy."

"She's a girl, and Lola's bark is worse than her bite," a

woman said as she descended the few stairs to the ground. "Hi, I'm Ellie."

"Nice to see you again, Ellie," Lily said with a smile before making introductions. "Thanks for accommodating us on such short notice."

"No problem," Ellie answered with a smile as she shoved her hands into her pockets. "I'm always glad to help. Come on in."

They grabbed their bags from the back of the car and lugged them up the stairs into the grand old Victorian.

Paige's eyes raised up the ornate staircase before she glanced at the grandfather clock ticking the time away, mentally cataloging a place where the key could be.

"So, I haven't seen this key before, but there are some pretty secretive hiding spots in this old place. I'll bet if we put our heads together, we'll be able to find it," Ellie said as she shuffled in behind them.

The dog bounded behind her, her nubby tail wagging as she sniffed Dewey. "Ellie, he smells weird."

Paige's eyes went wide as she glanced up at Dewey.

"Sorry," Ellie said with a grin, "Lola is very friendly, she just barks a lot. You can pet her if you'd like."

"Ellie, no, he smells like an animal, not a human."

"Who smells like an animal?" a sassy voice asked.

Paige scanned the room in search of another human but didn't find any. Instead, a black cat slinked down the stairs, peering through the banister.

"This one," Lola answered, staring up at Dewey. "He smells funny."

The cat sniffed in the air. "Ew, he does. What kind of animal is that? Smells like a reptile."

Ellie grinned as if nothing was happening. "Why don't we get you settled in your rooms?"

Paige crinkled her nose, wondering if the woman heard them talking or not.

"Ew, Ellie, don't put that reptile in here. If he stays, I go." The cat arched her back in the air, hissing at Dewey.

"Stop that, Cleo," Ellie said with a nervous chuckle. "She's friendly, too…once you get to know her. Follow me."

They mounted the stairs, climbing up to the second level. Ellie showed them each their rooms. Paige shuffled into hers and dumped her bag on the luggage rack with a sigh. At least this place wasn't bigger than the last one, but where would they even start?

A knock sounded at her door, and she pulled it open, finding Dewey on the other side.

He pushed inside, and she slid the door closed.

"Ugh," he groaned, tugging the ring off, "I need a second to be me."

"Did you hear the pets talking or have I officially lost it?"

"No, I could hear them, but no one else was reacting, so I just didn't say anything. Especially after that dang cat accused me of being a reptile." Dewey smashed a fist against his paw as he floated in the air.

"Well…you kind of are."

"Dragons are…okay, we're reptiles, but she didn't have to say it like that. I didn't say, 'Ew, Paige, it's a feline.'" Dewey rolled his eyes.

"No, but you like cats. And this cat…she doesn't seem to like anybody."

"No, she's a real sass-mouth, that one. The dog seems nice, though."

"Yeah," Paige agreed with a nod. "I wonder if they can help us find the key."

Dewey opened his mouth to answer when a shriek sliced through the air, startling them both. Paige's heart stopped as she wondered what had just happened to elicit the blood-curdling exclamation.

With wide eyes, she glanced at Dewey, afraid to move.

CHAPTER 14

"*W*hat the hell was that?" Paige whispered.

Dewey winced, jabbing a claw at the door. "Uh-oh."

Paige twisted to find Cleo hovering in a slit in the door, her mouth hanging open. "It's a dragon! Dragon! There's a dragon in the house! Help! Help! Somebody! Somebody do something!"

"Crap," Paige said with a wrinkled nose before she turned her voice sickly sweet. "Hey, Kitty. Come in here. Here, Kitty. Come in here."

"No way, uh-huh. You aren't going to pull that 'Here, Kitty' stuff on me. I'm smart. I'm not falling for this."

"Okay," Paige said, her hands held in the air as she stared at the cat. Could she grab the cat before it scurried away? "Got it. Well, if you're smart, then you should know there's nothing to be afraid of. Dewey is a nice dragon."

"No such thing as a nice dragon. Do you breathe fire?"

"Yes," Dewey snapped. "And I am a nice dragon. I'm a pretty nice guy. I've got a lot of friends."

"Sure, you do, dragon," Cleo answered. "You fire-breathing bas– "

"Where's a dragon?" Lola asked before Cleo could finish the insult.

"There, look!" Cleo shouted, thrusting a claw in Dewey's direction.

"Whoa," Lola answered as she pushed the door further open. "I've never seen a dragon before."

"No kidding. Dragons aren't supposed to exist."

"Then how did you know what it was?" Lola asked.

"I read and watch television. Didn't you watch Lord of the Rings? It has a dragon. Way bigger than him, though. He's a shrimp."

"Hey," Dewey cried, his paws on his hips. "I'm a teacup, not a shrimp."

"Whatever, dragon," Cleo answered. "I know what you are. That dragon in Lord of the Rings destroyed cities, and nearly killed Bilbo."

"I'm not responsible for the crimes Smaug has committed. That's like holding you responsible for lion attacks."

"If the shoe fits," Cleo answered.

Dewey wrinkled his nose. "Are you saying you *want* to be held responsible for lion attacks?"

"Maybe I am responsible. Cats are excellent hunters. I could kill you in your sleep and rip you scale from scale."

"Whoa," Paige said, tugging her chin back to her chest. "That's a little harsh."

Cleo set her green eyes on Paige. "Yep."

"You're mean," Dewey shouted at the cat. "You mean old cat. Don't they feed you enough?"

"Not nearly," Cleo answered, "and I had Salmon Dinner tonight."

"So?" Dewey asked.

"I had Salmon Dinner last night. And I hate Salmon Dinner. I prefer Sea Captain's choice."

"Sorry to hear that," Paige answered. "But listen, you can't say anything about this to anyone. No one can know that Dewey is a dragon."

Cleo narrowed her eyes at Paige. "And what are you going to give me to keep me quiet?"

"Uhhh…" Paige winced, her brow furrowing as she slid her gaze sideways, her mind desperately searching for an offer. "Treats?"

"Yeah!" Lola said, her tail wagging furiously.

"What kind and how many?" Cleo asked.

"What's your favorite kind of treat?" Paige asked.

"Vanilla milkshake, extra whipped cream," Cleo answered.

Lola's tail wagged more, shaking her entire rear end. "Burger."

"What?" Paige cried. "No. I'm not…I'm not getting you a burger and a shake. That's crazy."

Cleo twisted her head to the side. "Hey, Ellie!"

"Stop, stop stop," Paige said.

"Okay, wait, how do we even know you can actually tell Ellie anything," Dewey chimed in. "Because all the humans in the room seemed not to be able to hear you."

"Ellie can hear us," Lola said. "Ellie talks to us all the time. No one else can hear us. Well, until you."

"Sure, she can. Maybe that's your scam. You say Ellie can hear you, but she really can't. You shake us down for a milkshake and a burger when, in reality, there's no way you can possibly tell a single living soul about me." Dewey crossed his arms.

Cleo narrowed her eyes at him. "You wanna test it, dragon?"

"We don't," Paige said with a shake of her head. "We really don't. Look, fine. I'll get you the dang burger and shake."

"Extra whipped cream."

"Right, right, fine. Extra whipped cream. Where I'm going to get this, I don't know." Paige pressed a hand to her forehead.

"Cookin' with Gas," Cleo said. "Go toward town, hang a left at the first street."

"Are you…" Paige pressed her lips together, shaking her head. "Never mind. Okay. I'll grab it as soon as I can."

"You'll grab it when you go to dinner. Ellie said she's taking you there tonight. Get a to-go." Cleo shook her head. "I can't believe I have to explain this to you."

"Oh, shut up," Paige said with a shake of her head. "Just… go…take a nap or something. I'll get it."

"Fine. But if you don't– "

"Don't worry, I'll get it," Paige shot back before the cat could finish.

"Fine. Come on, Lola, let's go take our pre-dinner nap."

"And don't say anything!" Dewey shouted after her.

Paige raced across the room and pushed the door closed, leaning against it.

"Nice going, Paige. Next time make sure the door is *closed.*"

Paige glared at him. "I didn't know the door wasn't fully latched, okay? You're the one who took off the stupid ring."

"I can't help it. I have a headache. I just wanted a minute to breathe."

"Breathe later," Paige said through clenched teeth.

"Oh, come on, it didn't turn out *that* bad at least. All we have to do is grab a milkshake and a burger."

"How am I going to explain that takeout order?"

"Tell them you often crave midnight snacks," Dewey said.

"You tell them that," Paige answered. "You do it."

Dewey heaved a sigh. "Fine. I'll handle it all."

"Well, it's your fault." She stalked across the room, her

hands on her head. "I can't believe we got shaken down by a cat."

"I don't know...that cat seems pretty savvy. I'll bet she's shaken down a lot of people in the past to be honest. She didn't bat an eyelash."

Paige collapsed on the edge of the bed. "Just put that ring back on so we don't get caught again. I wonder when they plan on searching for the key?"

Dewey floated to the bed and landed, plopping down next to Paige. "I don't know. Let's hope we find it soon. That stupid cat will have us bringing her all sorts of treats before long."

"I know. Once you cave to the pressure, there's no stopping it. The blackmail is just going to continue."

"Right. Until we leave."

Paige curled her fingers into a fist. "We have to find that key quickly."

"Agree. Well, maybe we'll do some poking around tonight when everyone is asleep."

"Okay," Paige said with a nod as a knock sounded at her door.

"Put that ring on," she hissed as she rose.

Dewey wrinkled his nose as he slid it onto his finger, turning back into his human form. Paige pulled open the door, finding Lily on the other side.

"All settled in?" Lily asked with a grin.

"Yep, we are. We were just talking about searching for this key."

"Well, first, I'm sure you're both hungry. We were going to head to the diner to grab some dinner, and we can discuss a search strategy there."

"Okay, that sounds good. Oh, uh...I was wondering if I could trouble you for another twenty dollars. I wanted to grab some takeout for Dewey later…sometimes he gets hungry overnight."

"Sure…just put your to-go on our tab."

"Thanks, and sorry. I…feel really bad about this. You're paying for us to eat and sleep and…"

"Honey, it's okay," Lily said, wrapping an arm around her. "You need it. And we're happy to help."

Paige wrinkled her brow, tears welling in her eyes. "I'm really glad we ran into the two nicest people in the world."

"I doubt that we're the two nicest people in the world," Lily said with a chuckle, "but I'm glad we can help. Now, let's go get some good grub."

Paige sniffled and blinked away her tears. "Okay. So, is this diner pretty good, then? Everyone seems to be raving about it."

"Everyone?" Lily asked as they stepped into the hall.

Paige winced, realizing she'd heard it from the cat. "Oh, uh, online. I checked out the reviews online. And they are all good."

"Oh, right. Well, it's a cute little place. 50s themed, good old-fashioned diner food, and really good shakes."

"I'll have to try one."

"We'll all be getting them," Lily said as they descended the stairs, finding the rest of the group at the bottom.

Ellie grinned at them. "So, we can either drive or walk… it's not far and it's a nice night."

"Well, we've been in the car all day, so why not walk?" Paige suggested.

"Good idea. These old legs could use the exercise," Lily added.

"Old legs?" Ellie swung her purse over her shoulder as she pulled open the front door. "Lily, you're not that old."

"Older than you. But living in Hideaway Bay has been good for my health."

"All that sea air?" Ellie asked as they descended the stairs and headed down the driveway.

"More like all the walking. It's nice to live somewhere where I can walk to things."

"I don't agree," Dewey whispered to Paige. "Why did you choose walking?"

Paige shook her head at him. "It's not that bad. You need to get exercise."

"I don't like walking. It's inconvenient and takes too much work."

"The way you eat, you need it. I feel so bad adding the stuff for pets on Lily's tab."

Dewey shrugged as their feet slapped the pavement. "There's not much choice here. That danged cat will ruin everything if she opens her big mouth to Ellie."

"I wonder if Dickens can talk."

"Probably. I mean, if he lived here, I bet he could."

"That could be useful," Paige murmured.

"Seems like a pain to me. Dickens tried to kill us once," Dewey reminded her.

Paige bobbed her head with a wrinkled nose. "Yeah. Well, I'm pretty certain if Cleo was bigger, she'd try to kill us, too."

They turned onto another street, spotting the old-fashioned diner ahead.

"Mmm, wow, that food smells good. Oh, I'm going to eat one of everything," Dewey said, rubbing his stomach.

Within a few minutes, they were inside the restaurant and seated at a long table. They placed their orders and sat back to wait for their food.

Paige shifted on the shiny red seat. "So, uh, not to feel like I'm rushing you, but…any ideas on where this key may be?"

"Well, I haven't seen anything like it around the B&B, but there are some pretty elaborate hiding spots. I'm thinking we could start with the attic and work our way down," Ellie suggested. "I haven't spent a lot of time up there, so it's entirely possible it's just sitting around somewhere collecting dust."

Paige's heart leapt with hope. "Oh, wow, sure."

"I hope it is," Cassie answered, "although, the first two were hidden."

Lily nodded. "She's right. One under the floorboards of Whispering Manor, and the other under the stairs at Pearl Pond estate."

Ellie rubbed her chin. "Hmm. Sounds like floors are a real theme here. I wonder if there's a hidden compartment in the staircase?"

"We could always check it out," Cassie said. "Mom and I are getting really good at finding hidden things in staircases."

They shared a laugh over their amateur sleuthing skills as their meal was delivered.

"Oh," Dewey groaned after biting into his burger. "This burger is so good."

"Yeah, really good," Paige agreed, popping a fry into her mouth.

The waitress buzzed back over with a grin. "Glad you like it. We pride ourselves on the food." She twisted toward Ellie. "Hey, I got your notes on the speakeasy, and I'm planning to get you some numbers next week."

"Great. I think it's a great idea."

Lily grinned as she sipped her milkshake. "Oh, you're going through with it?"

"Think so," the waitress answered. "It think it'll be fun."

"You're opening a speakeasy?" Paige asked.

"Sort of. It'll be a nightclub slash bar. But there used to be one under the diner a hundred years ago," the woman answered.

"No kidding," Paige said with a grin. "Wow, I'd love to see that."

"We'll show you before you leave."

Paige bobbed her head. "Awesome. I can't wait to see it."

They polished off their meal and placed the to-go order. Paige held back rolling her eyes as she ordered extra whipped cream on the milkshake for the cat.

"Come on back," the waitress, who had been introduced as Val, as with a wave. "We'll show you the space."

"I'll pass and eat the order of onion rings I got," Dewey said. "You go ahead."

"I want to take a second look, too," Ellie said as she rose.

They followed the pink-uniformed diner owner back toward the bathrooms. She stepped sideways toward a tiny coat closet. With a smack of her fist against the panel in the back, it popped open.

Val pushed it back, widening the space and motioning for them to follow her. They ducked into the dark passage. A bare bulb bloomed to life, illuminating stairs leading down.

"Wow," Paige said with a grin as they descended them and spilled into the old-fashioned bar. "This is really neat."

"Yep," Val said with a grin. "We're going to keep it old-fashioned like this. Just like it was in the twenties."

"I can't wait to get started in here."

"It'll really add to the town, Val," Ellie said with a grin.

"Well, I'll let you look around for a bit. I'd better run back up there and check on my orders."

"Thanks," Paige said as she shuffled toward the bar, swiping a hand over it.

"I wonder what it would have been like back in the twenties?" Her nose wrinkled as she recalled her brief time in the twenties when she time traveled. Maybe it wouldn't go great.

"Oh, I'll bet this place was hopping," Ellie said. "All those guys and dolls."

Paige offered a nervous chuckle, recalling her own experience with the mob. "Yeah. I'll bet."

She wrapped her knuckles on the bar. "Will be really nice this time around without the criminals."

Ellie offered her a chuckle. "Yeah. The legal part is important. Though, I'd bet this place has some tales to tell."

"I wonder if there's anything still hidden down here?"

"Like what?" Paige asked.

"I don't know. Al Capone's gun or something?" Ellie shoved her hands into her pockets and shrugged.

Paige glanced around the dusty space. "Where?"

"What about in the kegs?" Ellie poked a finger toward the large stand holding several of the round barrels.

Paige lifted a shoulder as she studied them. "Do they still have booze in them?"

"I'm not sure." Ellie approached them and knocked. "Want to forget it?"

Paige shuffled closer. "No, I'm game if you are."

Ellie reached around the rim of the barrel, tugging at the metal ring. "Hmm, we're going to need a tool to get this off."

"I doubt there's anything around here, but I'll take a look." Paige toggled on her phone's flashlight and shined the light around the space. She ducked behind the bar, stooping to search for anything that could be used to open the keg. "Not seeing much."

Ellie crouched to study the underside of the barrel before she rose and crossed to a door. "Maybe in here."

She twisted the knob and pushed on the door, but it wouldn't budge. After ramming it with her shoulder, it creaked open. "Storage closet."

"Maybe there will be something in there," Paige said as she rose, swatting at a cobweb that tickled her forehead.

"Got something!" Ellie exclaimed as she appeared in the room with grin and a hammer and chisel. "Let's see what's in this keg."

Paige aimed the light at the barrel as Ellie set the chisel in place. "I hope your friend doesn't get mad about this. Especially if there's beer or wine in there."

"Ah, this place needs a good cleaning anyway, it won't hurt anything." Ellie tapped on the chisel, shifting its location a few times until it loosened. "Here we go. It's coming loose."

"Yeah, it's–"A loud crack interrupted Paige's statement before the wooden barrel shifted and collapsed, bits of rotted wood splintering everywhere.

"Whoa," Ellie said with a wince as she darted back a few steps. A dribble of red wine trickled from within across the floor. "That was unexpected."

"Yep. And it looks like it wasn't filled very much, so maybe it's just an old, empty keg."

Ellie stepped forward, pulling a few of the intact pieces of the barrel. "No gun, but there is something in here."

"What?" Paige asked, craning her neck to peer over Ellie's shoulder.

"I don't know. It's something wrapped up."

Paige's heart skipped a beat. Could they have stumbled onto something big?

CHAPTER 15

*P*aige held her breath as Ellie shifted more of the wood pieces away, revealing a small, rusty metal box. Her heart thudded hard against her ribs as Ellie freed it from the remains of the keg.

She glanced up at Paige with a grin. "Wow, do you think there are some long-lost mob secrets in here?"

"Open it and let's find out."

"Yeah, I don't think this is going to pop open. It's pretty rusted. I'll have to pry it open with the chisel.

Ellie set the box on the table and wedged the chisel under the lid. With a few taps on the hammer, the top popped open.

Paige shined her flashlight inside, finding an object wrapped in blue fabric.

"Doesn't look like a gun," Ellie answered as she extracted it.

She unraveled the fabric, exposing the object inside. Paige's jaw dropped open as she gasped. "It's the key piece."

Ellie snapped her gaze to Paige. "Really? The one you were searching for?"

"Yep," Paige said, her heart racing as she grinned at it. "That's it. It's the key. Oh, I can't believe we found it."

"Me either, but boy, am I glad we came down here. What luck, huh?"

Paige nodded, her smile broadening. "Yeah. At least we won't have to tear your house apart to find it."

"Oh, I don't mind about that," Ellie said with a dismissive wave as she wrapped the object in the fabric again. "And at the very least, you get to stay at a nice B&B right?"

"The place is great," Paige said with a bob of her head. "Thank you so much for accommodating us on short notice."

"Oh, anything for friends." Ellie smiled at her as she poked a finger at the wrapped key. "Let's go give everyone the good news."

Paige waved it in the air with a nod. "Yes."

They left the speakeasy behind, climbing the stairs to the diner and crossing to the table.

"You'll never guess what happened down there," Ellie said as she plopped into her seat.

"You time traveled to 1920 and saw a gangster?" Lily asked.

"Close," Ellie answered before she flicked her gaze to Paige. "Show 'em."

Paige waved the fabric in the air. "We found the key inside an old keg down there."

Lily's jaw dropped open as Paige unwrapped it for the table to see. "Wow, that's amazing."

"Yeah, and now we won't need to rip apart Ellie's home to find it." Paige wrapped the object up again before attempting a high five with Dewey that missed its mark.

"On to Midnight Hollow!" Dewey exclaimed.

"After some sleep, if you don't mind," Lily answered as she rose.

"I don't…I'm ready to pass out for a few hours after that

meal," Dewey said, patting his belly. "Then we'll hit the road fresh in the morning."

Val flitted over with a bag of to-go food, handing it to Ellie.

"Oh, that's mine," Paige said with a wince as she grabbed it. "Thanks."

She gave Ellie a nervous grin as Ellie nodded, and they left the diner behind. The warm summer air broadened Paige's smile. They'd found three of the keys. They only needed one more to unlock the serum they needed to save her mother.

"Well, one more to go," Cassie said as she ambled along next to her.

"I know. I'm...excited. I hope we find it quickly. Not that I want to get away from you. You and your mom have been great, but..."

"You want to save your mom. I get it," Cassie said with a nod. "With any luck, Althea will know what you're talking about, and you can move on with the next steps soon."

"My fingers are crossed," Paige answered as they turned onto Ellie's street.

They returned to the house with Ellie telling them they were welcome to store their goodies in the refrigerator.

"Thanks," Paige said with a nod as she stuffed the bag inside before they climbed up to their rooms.

After changing, Dewey banged at her door before letting himself in. "Good going finding that key, Paige. We'll be out of this place in no time."

"I sure hope so...although..." Paige eased onto the edge of the mattress with a sigh.

"Yeah?"

"I'll miss these people. Lily and Cassie have been really nice."

Before Dewey could answer a hissing sound drew their attention to the door.

A black paw slid under the door. "Hey, open up."

Paige dragged herself from the bed, crossing the room to open the door. The cat and dog paraded in.

Cleo narrowed her eyes at Paige. "You got the stuff?"

"Yeah, I got the stuff. Hold on, I'll go get it."

She left the bedroom behind, sneaking downstairs to grab the hamburger and milkshake. She returned upstairs and eased the door closed behind her before she withdrew the items from the bag.

"Put it down and back away," Cleo said.

Paige wrinkled her nose. "Seriously? Back away?"

"I don't trust you. Do you know many times humans lure pets with treats? Next thing you know, you're manhandled into a carrier and tossed into a car. You scream and yell for help, but all that happens is some idiot pulls you out and tells you how nice of a kitty you are then proceeds to assault you and stab you with a needle."

"That's the vet. They're only doing it for your own good." Paige popped open the plain burger's container and set it down before she removed the lid from the milkshake cup and set it on the floor. She slowly backed away.

"Own good, my foot. I don't need those shots."

Paige returned to her seat on the edge of the bed next to Dewey. "You do. You don't want to get sick, do you?"

Cleo licked at the whipped cream before pausing to speak. "When I see Ellie thrown into a cage and forcibly held down and jabbed so she doesn't get sick, I'll buy into this."

Paige shot Dewey a glance as she lifted a shoulder.

Lola polished off the burger and raced over to Paige. "Mmm, that was good. Thank you."

Paige ruffled her ears. "You're welcome."

"She didn't do it out of the goodness of her heart, dummy.

It was a shake down." Cleo licked her chops before diving back into the milkshake.

"What's a shake down?" Lola asked.

"Never mind," Paige said. "I'm glad you enjoyed the burger."

"Ohhhh," the cat cried from across the room, stumbling around.

Paige's heart stopped as she leapt from her seat. "What's wrong?"

If she had killed someone's cat by bringing them a restricted treat, she'd never forgive herself.

"Ohhh." The cat flopped onto the floor, panting a little.

Paige raced toward the furry creature and dropped to her knees. "What is it? Are you sick? What's wrong?"

"Brain freeze," Cleo answered. "Wooo, that hurts."

Paige's shoulders slumped. "Are you joking? I thought something was seriously wrong."

"It is. Have you ever had brain freeze? Probably not, Ginger."

"Hey, there's no need for name-calling."

Dewey chuckled, slapping his thighs. "Hahaha, Paige, she's making fun of your red hair."

"I wouldn't laugh, dragon. You're so tiny, I could eat you as a snack."

The amusement left his face as he glared at her. "I'm not that small."

"Small enough that I could easily pop a claw in your a– "

"Okay, okay, that's enough," Paige interrupted. "Look, here's the thing, no one needs to make fun of anyone."

"Actually," Cleo said with a thump of her tail, "I do. It's a requirement of being a cat."

"It's not. It's so not. I was part cat once, so I know."

"What?" Cleo stared at Paige, her brow furrowing.

Paige slid her eyes closed and shook her head. "Never mind."

"No, I want to hear this," Cleo insisted.

"Dewey accidentally turned me into a half-panther, half-human while curing me of a werepanther scratch. I was not mean when I was a cat."

"You must have not gotten that part since you were only half. I assure you, whole cats must make fun of others."

"Okay, whatever. Could you just finish the milkshake and go take a nap? I'd like to get some sleep before we have to find the next key." Paige rose and crossed to the bed.

"Oh, yeah. Funny, you finding that key in the speakeasy. You know, my great-great-great-great-great...how many greats was that? Never mind. My ancestor used to hang around that speakeasy back in the day. Of course, she was the cat of a gangster, so that's why."

"Wow," Dewey said, "you're descended from a gangster's cat?"

Cleo raised her chin. "Why do you think I'm so good at shake downs?"

"I thought that was inherent to being a cat, too," Paige answered.

"Anyway, Ellie said you have one more to find. In Midnight Hollow," the cat said. "I knew a cat who knew cat who knew a cat from there. Lived with a lady named Althea."

"Okay?" Paige crinkled her brow.

"She said find the pixie, find the key."

"Find the pixie, find the key?" Paige repeated.

"That's what she said. Maybe it'll help you, maybe it won't. Doesn't matter to me," Cleo answered. "But I thought I'd pass it along."

"Thanks," Paige answered with a nod.

Cleo stared down at the vanilla ice cream in the cup. With

a shake of her paw, she stalked away. "I don't want anymore. Get rid of it."

"Right," Paige said with a sigh as the dog and cat scurried from the room. "Well, at least that's over with, and we have a clue."

"Yeah. A pixie. That ought to be easy to find," Dewey said as Paige retrieved the containers from the floor.

"I'll get rid of these, and then we can get some sleep."

Paige cleared the clutter, dumping it in the kitchen trash before she climbed upstairs to crawl between the covers. With the door safely locked, Dewey returned to dragon form.

She spent most of the night tossing and turning, wondering how quickly they could find the pixie. When she did sleep, she dreamt of a house, shifting in shape and size as they raced through the halls in search of a pixie.

She awoke before they ever found it, her stomach twisted into a knot. What if they fell short after finding three of the four keys?

Dewey flopped onto his back, his eyes fluttering open. He stretched and yawned, sliding his gaze to her. "Oh, you're up already."

"I couldn't sleep anymore," she said with a groan. "I barely could sleep at all."

"Too excited to sleep, huh?"

"Something like that," she said as she swung her legs over the bed and hung her head.

Dewey climbed to his feet and buzzed into the air. "Don't be depressed, Paige. We have one more to find."

"But what if we can't find it. It doesn't matter if we found three of the four. It only matters if we find four of the four."

"We'll find it. That cat gave us the clue."

"Yeah, I wonder about that. We'll probably be running all over the house looking for a pixie while she's here laughing about how we'll never find the key because it has nothing to do with the pixie."

Dewey narrowed his eyes. "Do you think Lily would drive us back to put the screws to the cat if she's lying?"

Paige wrinkled her nose. "No. They'll probably put us in jail for animal cruelty."

"Animal cruelty?" Dewey exclaimed. "That cat is the cruel one. I can't believe she blackmailed us."

"No one is going to believe it. No one can hear her talk but us."

"And supposedly Ellie."

"If that's true," Paige said, "we could get into a lot of trouble if the cat blabs about you being a dragon."

"Let's hope she doesn't." Dewey popped his ring on and turned back into a human. "We only have to get through breakfast. I wonder if Lily knows where we're stopping for lunch."

"Ugh, let the poor woman get through one meal," Paige said, rising and sorting through her duffel bag for a set of clothes.

"She said she's used to it."

Paige shut herself in the bathroom for her morning routine. When she emerged, she found Dewey passed out on the bed. Her heart skipped a beat as she raced to his side. "Dewey? Dewey! Are you okay?"

"Huh, what?" His eyes fluttered open again. "Oh, sorry, fell asleep."

"How can you sleep this much?"

"I'm relaxed here. It's got a nice vibe. This is a great bed and breakfast. Well, wait. It's a great bed. Still waiting to form my opinion on the breakfast part."

"Well, let's go do that. Maybe you can leave them a review while we drive to Midnight Hollow."

"Oh, good idea, Paige," Dewey said as he rose.

They left their bedroom behind and joined the others in the kitchen.

"Breakfast is all ready," Ellie said with a grin. "You can eat here, dining room, or the sun porch. Although, the dog may beg you for bacon."

"I'll bet," Paige said with a smile as she loaded her plate.

Ellie crossed to the counter, uncovering the buttered toast for them. "Did you sleep well?"

"Well enough," Paige said. "I had the last key on my mind, so any insomnia wasn't from your bed."

"That's good to hear."

"Oh, yeah," Dewey said, "I slept great. And this breakfast looks promising."

"I hope you enjoy it," Ellie answered as they settled at the table.

Cassie entered from the sun porch with Cleo in her arms. "Poor kitty."

"What's wrong with her?" Paige asked, her stomach clenching.

Ellie collapsed in her chair with a shrug. "She was sick overnight. Threw up all over my area rug."

Paige's eyes went wide as her lips tugged back in a wince. "Oh, no. Is that normal?"

"She doesn't get sick very often," Ellie answered. "Of course, last night she did, and she wouldn't get off the rug, so cleaning was an entire process."

Paige shot Dewey a guilty glance. "Yikes. Sorry to hear that."

Ellie waved a dismissive hand in the air. "Ah, I'm used to it. That's life with animals."

"I'm sick because you gave me that milkshake," Cleo hissed at her.

Cassie swayed back and forth with the cat. "Poor kitty. I hope you're feeling better."

"It was awful," Cleo said to her. "The redhead gave me ice cream. Dairy makes cats sick. What's wrong with her?"

"Maybe it was something she ate," Paige answered.

"Probably got into something she shouldn't have. She's always begging for some food. Anyway, it's not a tragedy. How far of a drive do you have today?"

"Just a few hours," Cassie answered as she set Cleo down on the floor. "Midnight Hollow isn't too far."

"Will you keep me updated? I'd love to know if you find them all."

"Definitely. What a weird coincidence that you found that key last night." Cassie grabbed another piece of bacon from the plate and bit into it as the cat leapt to her hind legs, pawing at her.

"See what I mean about begging for food?" Ellie asked. "And yeah, although, I'm not surprised. I think that old speakeasy has a lot of secrets."

"I'll bet," Cassie answered as Lily shuffled into the room. "All ready, Mom?"

"Yep. We just need your bags and we'll be set. Damien's got us all packed up."

"Oh, I can run up–"Paige started to stand.

Lily waved her down. "It's fine. We can run up and grab them from your room, and then as soon as you're finished eating, we'll get on the road."

"Great. I can't wait to find this last key. Gosh, I hope it's as easy as the last three have been."

"We really have been hitting it lucky. Someone upstairs must like you," Lily said with a wink. "Now, finish your breakfast, and we'll get on the road and see if we can't find that last key today."

Paige grinned at her as she shoveled more eggs onto her fork. "Sorry to want to race out of here, but– "

"It's okay," Ellie said with a dismissive wave, "I completely understand. I hope you find it."

"Thanks."

They finished their breakfast, said their goodbyes, and piled into the car for the drive to Midnight Hollow.

The time went quickly as the miles passed them by and before long, they were bouncing down a gravel drive toward a house hidden by towering trees.

"Whoa," Paige said as she ducked her head to stare at the sprawling structure. "That's…"

"Creepy," Dewey finished for her.

"It's actually beautiful inside." Lily pulled the car to a stop and threw the shifter into park before she climbed from behind the wheel to greet a dark-haired woman with a shock of gray hair framing her face.

Dewey twisted in his seat, a wince on his face. Before he could speak, the ghost next to Paige uttered one chilling word. "Death."

CHAPTER 16

"*H*uh?" Dewey asked, his features twisting more. "I think...I think she said death," Paige whispered, her eyes flicking to the creepy house in front of them.

"Yeah, that's what I thought." Dewey shifted his gaze to the motionless doll in the backseat. "Now, just what do you mean by that, doll?"

"Easy," Paige said with a shake of her head. "Ri, when you said death..."

"Death, death, death."

A shiver shot down Paige's spine as she grimaced. Outside the car, Lily grinned at the older woman and motioned to car, glancing inside at Dewey and Paige.

"I think we should get out. We're being rude," Paige said as she popped her door open and stepped out.

The wind whipped her hair around as storm clouds gathered on the horizon. "Hi, I'm Paige Turner. Sorry for the delay in getting out."

"It's okay," Lily said. "Ri tends to get vocal around this house."

Paige crinkled her brow, surprised the woman mentioned the ghost sitting in her backseat. "Uhh– "

"It's okay, Althea and Carly are very familiar with spirits. And they know about Ri," Lily answered as Cassie opened the back door and pulled the doll out, reattaching her base.

"Hi, Ri!" A teen bounced out of the house, her dark hair ribboned with pink and purple streaks.

"Carly," the ghost answered.

Paige's eyes went wide as she witnessed the scene. "Wow, she likes you."

"I like Ri. She's pretty cool. Did you know she was a pirate captain? That's awesome for a woman back in her day."

"Cool," Ri answered.

"Yep," Carly said. "You're pretty cool for an old gal."

"Ignore my granddaughter," Althea said, "she thinks anyone over thirty is...what is it you call it? An old?"

"Hey, I'm not an old," Dewey said.

Althea narrowed her eyes at him, a slight smile tugging at her lips. "No, but you are quite unique, aren't you?"

"I'm not...I'm normal," Dewey said with a crinkle of his nose. "Just a normal average, everyday human. Regular old guy. Like Damien here." He thumbed toward the man removing luggage from Cassie's trunk. "Just two regular guys. Nothing weird about us."

"Stop," Paige said through clenched teeth before she grinned nervously at the woman. Something about Althea made her apprehensive. It was like the woman could see right through you. She worried they'd slip up and give away some piece of information that would cost them big.

"It's quite all right. We like different, don't we, Carly?"

"Yep, we do."

"Well, won't you come inside? I have rooms prepared for you in case you'd like to rest for a little after the drive."

"Thanks, Althea. Well, actually, I'm pretty sure Paige and Dewey probably want to get started looking for this key."

"Oh, of course. Carly and I have been discussing it since you called us. I'm not aware of any key, but the house does have hidden spots, so we'll do a thorough search."

"Sounds like most of the places we've been at," Paige said. "Although…we may have a clue."

"A clue? Oh, perfect," Althea answered. "Maybe that'll help."

"Find the pixie, find the key," Paige said.

Damien furrowed his brow at the statement as did Althea. "Hmm, I'm not aware of any pixies, but we certainly will keep our eyes open. Now, I've got a little lunch prepared, why don't you come inside?"

"Oh, lunch," Dewey said, his eyes lighting up. "Yes, please."

"Dewey's our good eater," Lily said with a chuckle as they hauled their bags into the expansive foyer.

Paige studied the portrait hanging on the wall as they entered, her nose wrinkling as the woman's eyes seemed to bore into her.

"I'll have Lester move the bags upstairs," Althea said. "Just leave them here, then follow me to the kitchen."

"Lead the way, sister," Dewey said as he dumped his duffel on the floor and raced behind her.

"Hey," Damien said, sidling up to Paige, "I don't remember anything about a pixie in the clue."

She shook her head. "No, there wasn't. We, uh, stumbled upon it while at the B&B."

"Where?" he whispered.

Paige pressed her lips together and shook her head. "You're not going to believe this, but…the cat and dog can talk."

"Oh. Yeah, I'd believe it. I'm pretty that was the premise of

153

the series. Ellie movies to Salem Falls and learns the animals can talk."

"So, she *can* hear them," Paige murmured. "Good thing she didn't spill the beans about Dewey. She accidentally saw him in true form."

"Yikes. I bet that was…interesting."

"The cat shook us down for a milkshake and burger for the dog. I feel really bad about the whole puke on the carpet situation. Anyway, the cat said find the pixie. Maybe it's bogus, but…keep an eye out."

"Coming from a cat who literally blackmailed you, it could be bogus. The clue said midnight's swallow, but I'm not sure that helps us at all."

"What is a midnight swallow?" Paige asked with a wrinkled nose.

"A pixie," Althea said as she slid a large charcuterie board onto the counter. "You've already said to look for that."

"Oh, well…then we have that information from two sources, so hopefully it's correct."

"Wow, Althea, you really know to put out a spread," Dewey said, grabbing a slice of cheese.

She grinned at him. "And there is some tomato soup on the stove if you'd like a bowl of that with the light lunch. And– "

A boom of thunder rumbled overhead before the lights flickered then went off.

"Oh, darn," Althea said. "Well, that will make things a bit more challenging. And please get soup before it gets cold."

"I keep telling you we need a generator," Carly answered as an older, well-muscled man entered, carrying two lanterns.

"Bah, generators are for wimps," he said. "Hi, I'm Lester."

"Storm," Ri said as she zipped past Althea. "Soup."

"Of course, I'll get you a bowl of soup, dear," Althea answered without skipping a beat. "And some cheese."

"Cheese," Ri repeated.

"This is kind of weird," Paige murmured to Dewey as they filled their plates with crackers, cheeses, and meats.

"And creepy. Now we have to look for a pixie in the dark."

"In a storm."

"In this creepy old house."

"Fire's roaring in the living room if you'd like to eat in there," Lester said. "And I'll rustle up more lanterns if you're intending on searching the house during the storm."

"That would be excellent, Lester," Althea said, balancing Ri's bowl of soup and a plate of cheese for her in her hands. "I believe they would like to search as soon as possible. The matter is quite urgent, if I'm not mistaken."

"Y-yeah," Paige said with a nod. "Sorry, I hope we weren't rude earlier– "

"No, dear," Althea answered, "but I read it on your face. Don't worry, we understand."

Paige offered her a grateful smile as she crossed to collect a bowl of soup.

"Wow, I wonder if she can read on my face that I'm not human?" Dewey whispered.

"I don't know. She's sort of strange," Paige answered as she ladled soup into her bowl. She twisted to find Althea behind her, having already returned from dropping Ri and her food in the living room. "Oh, hi."

"Hello," Althea answered with a soft smile. "I noticed your bracelet earlier while we were outside. Do you mind if I take a closer look?"

"Uh, sure," Paige said, shooting a dubious glance to Dewey as she lifted her wrist.

Althea closed the distance between them, studying each charm with interest before she stepped back. "How interesting. I haven't seen all of those charms before. In particular, the dragon."

"Oh," Paige said with a nervous chuckle, "the dragon is the bane of my existence. It's always catching on things and getting stuck."

"Yes, the little tail has a barb on it."

Paige nodded as she collected her cheese plate before her brow furrowed. "You said you haven't seen *all* of the charms. Have you seen some of them?"

"Oh, yes," she answered with a nod. "Where did you get the bracelet, may I ask?"

"My mother. She left it with me before she disappeared. It's a family heirloom."

"Ah, I figured as much, given your energy."

Paige's features scrunched further. "My energy."

"Yeah, honestly, I don't know what you mean either," Dewey chimed in. "Paige is pretty low energy, if you ask me. She's always tired."

Althea chuckled, scooping a ladleful of tomato soup from the pot and pouring it into a bowl. "Not that sort of energy, young fellow. She has a...magical energy."

Paige's stomach twisted into a knot as her eyes widened. "What?"

"You don't know?" Althea asked. "I assumed if it was handed down, you knew your role."

"Uhhh–"

"Oh, I see," Althea interrupted as Paige's features creased again. "You're keeping it secret. Well, I understand that."

Althea raised her arm, showcasing her own charm bracelet. "See?"

Paige leaned closer, noting similar charms, a few identical like the cat. "You have one, too."

"Similar, a bit different from yours, but it means the same

thing. You are…extraordinary in the world. It means you are magical."

Confusion settled on Paige's features. "Are you?"

"Yes," Althea answered simply with a grin on her face. "Yes, I am. I come from a long line of psychic witches. You are a witch, too, if I'm not mistaken?"

"She is. Wow, you really are psychic," Dewey answered. "Tell me, what number am I thinking of right now?"

Althea eyed him. "That's not exactly how it works, though I'd guess seven."

"Amazing, that is exactly the number I was thinking," Dewey said with a grin.

"Wait, wait, stop with the number guessing. Do you know anything about my background? I…I mean, we figured out the bit about the…" Paige leaned closer, lowering her voice. "Witch stuff. But…I never knew my mother. She disappeared when I was only a few days old. So, I have no idea how any of this works."

"Oh, you poor dear. Well, I can tell you precious little, I'm afraid. Most secrets are kept within families, but it appears you are from an Irish clan, likely with the ability to control animals."

"Amazing," Dewey answered with a grin. "She *can* control animals with that bracelet and some special words."

"Do I have other powers?" Paige asked the woman.

"I imagine so. Likely communicative powers with beasts and possibly even the ability to perform other forms of magic like spells and incantations."

"Wow," Paige answered as she stared down at her bracelet. "I had no idea."

"You're very powerful, I'm certain. I get that energy from you. Though, you'll need practice and training. You'll catch it on your own, but it would be better if someone shared strategies with you."

Paige stared into her soup, her features pinching. "I really hope someone can share strategies with me."

"We'll find the key, darling, don't worry about that." Althea patted her on the arm, giving her a reassuring smile.

"Thanks."

"Now, let's go eat, and then we'll start our search."

Paige and Dewey made their way into the living room, finding comfortable chairs near the fire to settle into as they ate.

With each passing second, Paige grew more agitated about finding the key. She fidgeted after downing her food in record time.

"Oh, boy, Althea, that tomato soup was something else. What's your secret?" Dewey asked.

"No secret, just a standard recipe," she answered. "Now, I'd propose we split up and take the house in sections. Paige has a clue suggesting a pixie may be the ticket to finding the key. I am not aware of any specific pixie representations in this house, but we should all keep our eyes peeled."

Everyone nodded at Althea's words.

"Where would you say it's best for us to start? Mom and I will take a location."

"Well, Carly, Lester and I can peruse the attic. Why don't you two take the upstairs, the rest of the group the downstairs? I'm sorry, it'll be slow-going with the lights out, but I think we'll make some progress."

"Sounds good," Paige said with a nod as she rose. "Can I help with the dishes?"

"Oh, don't worry about those, just set them in the sink, and we'll handle that later." Althea gave them a dismissive wave as she smiled.

They shuffled to the kitchen, dumping everything into the sink before everyone disbanded to search their specified locations.

Paige waved her flashlight around in what happened to be a painting studio. "This is going to be nearly impossible to find in this lighting."

"Hopefully, it'll be obvious," Damien answered. "But did you see all the carvings in the woodwork?"

"Yeah, amazing."

"And difficult. It's so intricate, I'm not sure I'll recognize a pixie within it."

"Right? Or there could be dozens of them," Paige lamented. "We may be searching through hundreds of pixies."

"Gosh, I hope not," Dewey answered, swinging his flashlight across the back wall. "That'll take forever."

"Leave it to the last key to be a pain in the you-know-where," Paige said with a sigh.

"Where?" Dewey asked.

"You know," Paige answered.

"No. Where? Heart? Head? The pain in my head is incredible, right now."

"Never mind," Paige mumbled.

They moved on to a greenhouse space, making a quick search through the plants before they backtracked to search the dining room.

"And then, assuming we find this stupid key," Paige said, "we need to drive back to Hideaway Bay for the Chapter Gate."

"Assuming there isn't one closer," Damien countered.

"How would we know this?" Paige asked.

"We wouldn't. Probably best to just bite the bullet and make the long trek back to Hideaway Bay."

Paige heaved a sigh as she brushed her fingers across the wood chair rail. "Yeah, probably. I'm just...dying to get moving here."

"Oh," Dewey said, his features pinching. "Bad choice of words, Paige."

159

She slumped into a dining room chair, her eyes welling with tears.

"Oh, come on, Paige," Dewey said, patting her on the shoulder. "Think positive. By this time tomorrow, we'll probably be almost back in Hideaway Bay. Then we just need to brave the wilds of Maine, find the serum, and pop back home. Easy."

"From your lips…" Paige forced herself to her feet, her lips still tugging into a deep frown.

They finished their scouring of the dining room before they moved on to the living room, finding it devoid of any pixies.

"I feel sort of bad pawing through their house like this," Paige said as they left the room behind.

"Yeah, but nothing to be done about that," Dewey answered. "I wonder if she's got dinner planned, though."

"You and your stomach," Paige said with a shake of her head. "Well, should we head upstairs and see how the ladies are doing there?"

"I guess. Nothing down here that I saw," Damien answered, mounting the stairs.

Paige followed behind him, shaking her wrist to drop her bracelet down from her forearm. As she took another step up, she stopped, her arm caught.

Dewey plowed into the back of her. "Hey, you need to call your stops, Paige."

"Sorry, I'm caught." She huffed out a breath as she twisted her arm. "The stupid bracelet is stuck on something."

Damien backtracked down the stairs, shining his light on Paige's stuck wrist. "Let me see if I can get you free."

"Thanks."

He squatted down to study the situation.

"It's probably the stupid dragon tail. It's always catching on something," Paige answered.

"Yeah, it is but…"

"What?" Paige asked, her brow furrowing. Her stomach twisted. "Oh no, did it damage the carvings?"

"No," Damien said with a shake of his head. "But it's what the dragon's caught on that's making me pause."

"What is it?" Dewey asked.

Damien flicked his gaze up to them. "A pixie."

CHAPTER 17

*P*aige struggled not to tug against the bracelet, but her heart fluttered at the words. "A pixie? Really? Are you sure?"

"Pretty sure. It's a little sprite-looking girl with wings."

"Could be a fairy."

"I really don't know the different between a fairy and a pixie, but maybe," Damien said. "Still, it's worth looking at closer…just as soon as I free your bracelet. Don't move."

"Right," Paige said, holding her breath as she waited for Damien to try to wriggle it loose. "How did it get this caught?"

"I don't know," he answered. "The tail is wedged between the thing's ankles. I don't want to break the charm or mar the pixie."

"Take your time," Paige answered, her muscles stiff. "But also, hurry up."

With a grimace on his face, Damien slowly shimmied the charm back and forth until it popped free. "Got it."

Paige immediately dropped down to her knees to eye the

carving, her heart speeding up. "Oh, this is promising. I wonder if it'll trigger some hidden space."

"Let's hope," Damien answered as he narrowed his eyes at it. "We should be careful. It's really a delicate carving."

"Yeah, I'd hate to damage it," Paige said.

Dewey pushed closer. "This is no time for delicacy. Twist the gal, and let's see what's cracking?"

Paige screwed up her face at the words. "Are you on drugs?"

"I'm not. But I'd really like to stop being human. It's a real drag and a headache, quite literally."

"Sorry, buddy," Paige said with a pat on his arm. "We'll be careful but go as fast as we can."

Damien eased his fingers around the small carving of the pixie. "I'm trying to find a seam or anything that would indicate whether or not this moves in a specific direction."

"Maybe we ought to just try to gently nudge it," Paige said.

Damien grimaced at it. "Okay, I'll…just…"

He tried a few different grips on the wooden creature before he put gentle pressure on it. "Nothing so far."

"Really give it your all," Dewey answered.

"I'm giving my all. I don't want to break it," Damien shot back.

Paige waved at him to keep quiet.

"Find something?" Cassie asked, shining her light from the top of the stairs.

"Maybe," Damien said. "Hey, maybe you'd be better at this than me. I don't want to break this carving."

"Oh," Cassie said with a grin, "sure. I'd be happy to take the fall for breaking it."

Damien rose and backed away from it. "You've probably got a lighter touch than I do. Plus, you're used to delicate carvings."

"All right. I'll give it a go," Cassie said, passing her flashlight off to him.

As she knelt down to peer at the small carving, a loud whirring noise drew their attention to the top of the stairs.

Ri hovered there, her face lit creepily by the flashlight she held. "Stop."

Cassie held her hands up in the air. "Okay."

"Ri, help."

Paige slow-blinked as the doll rose in the air, hovering for a moment before she floated down the stairs and awkwardly landed next to Cassie.

"Whoa, careful, Ri," Cassie said, steadying the ghost as she teetered on the narrow step.

"Ri, help. Pixie. Wing. Wing."

Cassie's brow furrowed. "Yeah, the pixie has wings."

"Wing. Wing."

Cassie narrowed her eyes before she peered around the doll. "Mom! I need a Ri translation."

Lily appeared at the top of the stairs. "Did you find something?"

"They found a pixie. I was about to try to manipulate it when Ri told me to stop. She keeps repeating herself, which means she's trying to tell me something, but as usual, I can't understand her."

"Do you know how to use the pixie to find the key, Ri?" Lily asked as she descended the stairs.

"Ri, help. Pixie. Wing. Wing."

All eyes focused on Lily as they waited for her to decipher the cryptic message.

"Wing, wing," she repeated. "Does finding the key have something to do with the pixie's wings?"

"Wing. Wing."

Lily rubbed a finger against the intricately carved wood. "Do we move the wings?"

"Pull," Ri said.

"Pull the wings," Cassie said with a nod. "Ahhh, now, I get it. Thanks, Ri."

Paige and Dewey exchanged a glance at the odd situation as Cassie delicately shifted one wing, then the other. A clicking sound echoed in the foyer.

Paige's heart sped up as she grabbed Dewey's arm, her breath hitching. "Did you hear that?"

"Yeah," Damien said with a nod.

Lily shined her beam around the room. "Quick, look around for a panel that opened."

After a few minutes of searching, Paige's light landed on a dark hole in one of the stairs. "Here!"

She hurried to it and knelt down, her fingers trembling. "There's something inside."

"Let's see, Paige," Dewey said, peering over her shoulder.

Paige reached inside, pulling out an unknown object wrapped in fabric. Her heart pounded against her ribs as she carefully unwrapped it. Tears formed in her eyes as she spotted what lay inside. "The key piece!"

"Oh, we did it!" Lily cheered as applause broke out.

"We did. Oh, thank goodness. Now, we have all of the pieces. We can open this safe or whatever it is."

"Yeah, as soon as we get home," Damien answered with a nod.

"I'll go tell the others so they can quit poking around the dusty attic," Lily said as Paige shifted to lean against the railing, pressing the key to her heart.

"So, do you know where this safe is? Should we take you straight there?"

"It's in Aroostook County," Damien said. "I think a friend of ours knows exactly where. If you just take us back to Hideaway Bay, we'll be able to handle it from here."

Cassie's forehead creased at the words. "Hideaway Bay is pretty far from Aroostook County."

"Yeah, it is. But…we got to Hideaway Bay, so, we can get back from Hideaway Bay to Bucksville."

Cassie studied him, her features pinched. "Right."

"I'm sorry, I…"

"No, no," she said with a shake of her head. "I get it. You got there a special way. And you can't tell me how you'll get back, but I'm guess it has something to do with the supernatural."

Damien lifted a shoulder as he shoved his hands into his pockets. "Right."

"Well, we'll get you back to Hideaway Bay then, and say goodbye. And good luck."

"I really would love to visit again," Damien said.

Dewey leaned closer to Paige, his eyebrows wiggling. "Love connection."

"Yeah, that would be great. We'd love to hear how it all turns out. We'll be wondering."

Damien grinned at her. "Cool, yeah. I'll stop by as soon as I can."

"Good enough. Well, we could start our drive back today, but we'll get in pretty late."

"That's okay with me. I'm so sorry, but the sooner we get back, the– "

"Faster you get to save your mom. I get it, which is why I'm willing to drive it straight today." Cassie nodded. "We'll get you back there, I promise."

"Thanks so much. You've both been great," Paige said with a weak smile as Lily, Althea and the others appeared at the top of the stairs.

"So, you've found it," Althea said with a smile.

"Yes," Damien answered. "This little pixie on your railing opens that cubby in your stair."

Althea descended the stairs to study it. "How interesting. Well, I'm so pleased you found everything. Now, will you be staying with us and heading back tomorrow or– "

"We'd really like to leave right away–not because of you. I just– "

"Want to help your mother. Of course you do. Well, I won't keep you, but I do have something I'd like to give you if you don't mind waiting a moment." Althea offered Paige a questioning glance.

"I don't. I think everyone probably needs a few minutes to prepare for the long drive back." Paige shot a questioning glance at the others.

"Absolutely," Lily said. "We'll get on the road as soon as possible, but I think we'll all need a few minutes to use your facilities."

"Queue for the bathroom," Althea said with a chuckle before she climbed the stairs and disappeared into the hallway.

Paige eased onto the step with a shaky sigh. "I can't believe we have them all."

"Now, time to use them."

"And then go home and save my mom." Paige's hands trembled as she considered the moment her mother opened her eyes. Every step they took forward was positive but tinged with the sinking feeling that every moment that passed would mean failure.

Paige snapped her gaze to Lily who waited with them. "And I can't thank you enough for all your help. We'd never have found these without you."

"Oh, I don't think you're giving yourself enough credit," Lily said with a shake of her head. "You would have found them. Maybe not as fast and maybe not without a trip to the slammer, but you'd have found them."

Paige offered a light chuckle at the words before she

nodded. "Yeah, definitely you've made the process faster. And thanks so much for driving us back today."

"Of course," Lily said as Cassie appeared.

"Your turn."

"Thanks," Lily said as she shuffled to the powder room.

Althea returned with Carly, holding a small wooden box.

Paige rose as she descended the stairs to them, thrusting the object forward. "What is this?"

"This is an old music box. Found in the castle that inspired Sleeping Beauty. I thought it appropriate to give to you. It's supposed to have magical properties, though outside of having a pleasant enough tune to lull me to sleep, I haven't found any. Maybe you can."

Paige accepted the wooden box, running her fingers over the ornate inlays. "I can't take this."

"Yes, you can," Althea said. "Carly loves music boxes, but never took to this one. Please take it."

"Yeah, I have an entire collection," the teen added, "but that one's not my vibe."

Paige lifted the lid and tinkling music floated from within. "Thank you. This is…an amazing gift, and I'll always treasure it."

"You are very welcome, Paige Turner." Althea slid a lock of Paige's hair over her shoulder. "Good luck to you. I hope everything turns out well."

"We'll try to send a message back to Lily and Cassie about it. They can pass it along to you."

"I look forward to hearing from them," Althea answered as Lily rejoined them.

"All right, we're ready. Anybody else need to use the bathroom before we head out?"

When everyone had finished, they gathered outside as black clouds pushed away and a new set gathered on the horizon, saying their goodbyes and climbing into the car.

Althea waved them off, her hair blowing wildly in the wind.

Paige rubbed a hand over the music box, her heart pinching as she thought of all the people they'd met on the strange journey who had helped them so much. At least she'd have a reminder of them once she returned to Shadow Harbor.

"Looks like we'll be hitting some rain," Lily said as they pulled from the driveway. "It'll make things a little slower going, but we'll get there."

Paige settled into her seat, her nerves still on edge as the first raindrops pelted the windshield before the deluge started.

They made slow progress until the rain finally cleared.

After a quick stop for dinner, they continued toward Hideaway Bay, arriving around midnight in the small hamlet.

The tires crunched gravel as Lily eased the car into the driveway.

Paige spilled out, her heart thumping harder against her ribs at the prospect of returning to Bucksville.

"Now, do you need a place to stay for tonight or–"Lily asked.

"No," Paige said. "We'll go straight back to Bucksville now. Thank you so much for your help."

After exchanging a hug with the woman, Paige blinked away a few tears and pulled Cassie into a hug, too.

"Goodbye, Paige. And good luck. Get us a message about what happens if you can."

"I will," Paige said with a bob of her head. "Thanks."

She glanced at Damien who said his final goodbyes to both women along with Dewey.

"Ready?" Damien asked.

"Yep," Paige answered with a shaky inhale. "Let's head back."

With a wave at the two women and the ghost, who Cassie had removed from the car, they circled around the house, heading for the beach.

With cellphone flashlights leading the way, they slipped into the beach cave and searched for the Chapter Gate, using it to return to the sea cave near Bucksville.

Outside, the waves crashed against the rocky shore as the sun shone brightly down.

"Wow, I wonder what day it is," Damien asked.

"Let's go see if we can find anyone," Paige said.

Dewey rubbed his hands together. "Let's get into a house so I can be a dragon again. I hate being human."

"Okay, buddy," Paige said as they climbed up to the cliff above.

"Which place do you think they're at?" Dewey asked. "Although either is good. They both have great food."

"You and the food," Paige said with a shake of her head.

"We'll try Alexander's first since we're closer," Damien said, "and if they're not there we'll– "

His voice cut off, and Paige snapped her gaze to him, her brow furrowing. "What is– "

A gasp cut off her words as she stared at the path ahead of them. A massive creature blocked the way. Her eyes rose to take in the tall beast as its tail swishing behind it and enormous wings extended on either side. "W-what the hell is that?"

"Dracopire," Damien answered. "And they are deadly to humans."

CHAPTER 18

"*W*hat now?" Paige asked, her voice shrill with panic as smoke poured from the beast's nostrils.

"Dracopire. A dragon-like vampire. If it even claws you, it can put enough poison in your system to kill you. I know...I died from a Dracopire attack once."

"Huh?" Paige choked out.

"Yep, long story. Anyway, we definitely need to get out of this," Damien said, his arms stretched out to shield them as much as possible.

"Yeah, right. Uhh, can we run?"

"No, they can fly. They'll pick us off easily."

"What are we going to do?" Paige cried.

Dewey tore off his ring, morphing back into his dragon form. "Hey, buddy, you think you're so cool? Look at me. I'm a dragon, too."

The Dracopire drew his scaly chin back to his chest, his yellow eyes narrowing.

Damien shook his head. "Uh, you may not want to taunt him. They're angry."

"Well, so am I. I've got a splitting headache. I'm sick and

tired of being human. If these massive things can stalk around here, then I can be a dragon again."

"Dragon," the Dracopire growled.

"They talk?" Paige's jaw fell open.

"Yeah, they talk. And they– "

"Well, well, well, look what the cat dragged in." Dominique strolled toward them past the Dracopire.

"Why is she not afraid of them?" Paige whispered.

"They're aligned," Damien explained.

"Aligned?" Dominique said with a chuckle. "No. I own them. They do my biding. Now, I– "

Her voice stopped as she stared at Dewey. "What is this?"

"Dragon," the dracopire answered.

"Yeah, I see that, Callun, but dragons aren't real. Plus… he's tiny."

"Teacup," Dewey growled back with his paws curled into tight fists.

Dominique's eyebrows pinched. "No kidding. Wow. You know, you'd look real cute mounted on my mantel."

"Hey," Paige said with wrinkled of her nose. "That's my teacup dragon you're talking about. Step off, lady."

"Or what? Will you wave that ridiculous bracelet at me and shout nonsense again?"

"Leave us alone, Dominique. You know Celine will never let you get away with hurting us."

Dominique doubled over in laughter. "As if she could stop me. I mean, let's get real, huh? Saint Celine barely can keep her life together. But you somehow think she's magically going to save you?"

"She's stopped you countless times before," Damien said with a shake of his head.

"That was before," Dominique answered, her eyes narrowing.

"Dominique, what do you think you're doing?" Marcus asked as he strode toward them.

She raised her eyes toward the sky at the sight of him. "Oh goody, the turncoat."

"I don't think you want to pick this fight with Celine. You know how she feels about Damien."

She stretched her hands to either side. "All the more reason to pick the fight. When did you turn into such a namby-pamby? Oh, right…that girl you married."

"Catherine has nothing to do with this discussion. Take your beastly friend and leave."

"Make me," she said with a raise of her eyebrows.

"If I must." He whipped a fireball into existence from nothing, leaving it floating above his hand.

Paige's eyes went wide at the sight. "Seriously? You have fireballs?"

Marcus lobbed it at Dominique who easily dodged it. "Weak. But I'm not surprised. You've really slipped lately, Marcus."

"I'm giving you a warning. Leave now."

"Or what? You'll throw another wimpy fireball at me? Are you even serious?"

Marcus heaved a sigh, his jaw clenching before he stamped a foot forward and threw his arms out to the sides.

Paige's gaze went skyward as black clouds darkened the horizon and thunder boomed. Lightning tore through the sky, and the ground shook underneath them.

Dominique grinned at his display. "That's super cute, boo, but really ineffective at scaring someone like me. Try again."

A massive burst of blue light arced out of his body, slicing through the air toward her. It smacked into both her and the Dracopire, knocking them both to the ground.

"Run," Marcus said.

Damien grabbed Paige by the hand and tugged her away

from the scene as Dominique leapt to her feet, her nostrils flaring.

"Dewey!" Paige shouted, glancing over her shoulder to find the tiny dragon buzzing through the air behind them.

"I'm coming, Paige!"

"Hurry," Damien shouted as they dodged tree branches in a desperate attempt to escape the battle being waged behind them.

Paige instinctively ducked as a boom split the air. "What is happening? It sounds like the end of the world."

"Just Dominique and Marcus duking it out. It'll die down," Damien said as Alexander's house came into view.

They crossed the clearing and raced inside. Damien slammed the door behind them, flicking the lock.

"Wait, what if Marcus needs to get in?" Dewey asked.

"He can pick locks," Damien said, his head resting against the wood as he gasped for breath.

"D?" Celine appeared at the door leading to the sitting room. "What happened?"

"We got the keys. Dominique and a Dracopire tried to attack us." Damien peeled himself from the door with a sigh.

Celine's features twisted with worry. "What? Are you okay?"

"We're all fine. Marcus stepped in just in time."

"Thank goodness. And you got the keys?"

"We did," Paige said with a nod. "We're ready for the next steps."

Celine sucked in a breath. "All right. We've been researching the location, and we think we have it nailed down. It'll take a bit of hiking to get there."

Dewey huffed out a sigh, his paws curling into fists. "Please tell me it's remote enough that I can stay in dragon form."

Celine chuckled at him. "Aroostook is quite remote, so once we start our trek, you'll probably be fine in dragon form."

Dewey blew out a sigh of relief. "Good."

"Not to be a pain," Paige said, shifting her weight from foot to foot, "but is there any chance we can leave right away?"

Celine offering her a consoling smile. "Absolutely. As soon as Marcus gets back, we'll head out."

"Marcus? But…" Paige's pulse quickened as heat washed over her. "What if… he's…"

"Dominique and Marcus can't defeat each other in a head-to-head battle, don't worry," Celine answered. "They're just getting their frustrations out. It'll die down."

Paige's forehead creased as she recalled the epic battle ensuing as they'd fled the area. "*That's* how they get their frustrations out?"

"We all tend to get our frustrations out that way," Celine answered. "Marcus and I have had some doozies."

"Well, not all of us." Damien waved his hand around in the air. "Some of us are still learning how to conjure fireballs."

"Oh, you can, too?" Paige asked.

"Sometimes. When I'm really scared or upset. And they're tiny. Nothing like Celine or the others."

"You'll get there, D," Celine said with a pat on his shoulder. "Until then, would you like a drink to try to relax?"

"Uh," Paige said, glancing down at the music box still clutched in her hands. "I…"

"Oh, here comes Marcus now," Celine said, her gaze flicking to the glass next to the door. "Good, we'll be able to leave soon."

The tension in Paige's shoulders released a little as she

tried to focus on the task ahead. With any luck, they'd soon have the serum and be able to return home to save her mother. "Oh, good. No offense, but I just want to get this serum and head home."

"I understand. If it was Damien or Gray or anyone in my family, I'd feel the same way."

Paige nodded as the lock disengaged, and Marcus stepped inside.

"I assume things went well with collecting the keys?" he asked, one eyebrow arched high.

"We got them all," Paige said with a grin.

His expression did not change, stuck in an unimpressed stare.

Her smile faded quickly, and she turned more serious. "So, now we just need to find the location to use them."

"A location not easily accessible, though I assume you are willing to battle through," he answered.

"Lead the way." Paige pumped a fist in the air.

"You act ridiculous. Has anyone every told you that? I cannot believe you expect us to believe that we are fictional while you assume you are real."

"Ouch, buddy, that hurt," Dewey said as he landed on Paige's shoulder. "But...did you ever consider that you, too, act ridiculous?"

Marcus's eyebrows raised toward his hairline. "*I* act ridiculous? What a ludicrous statement. Have you ever seen me pump my fist in the air? Or giggle over something inane?"

"No, but you're kind of uptight. I mean, we all knew that from reading the books, but seeing it in person is another thing entirely." Dewey fluttered into the air, buzzing toward Marcus and landing on his shoulder. "Think about it. Is your life really normal?"

Marcus sneered at the tiny dragon perched on him. "My life is quite normal, thank you. I cannot imagine yours is with your asinine running commentary. You clearly are the snarky sidekick."

"You bet I am, bud. I take my role very seriously. I'm snark-tastic," Dewey said with a nod.

Marcus fluttered his eyelashes at the dragon. "Please remove your 'snark-tactic' self from my shoulder, and we will proceed with the serum retrieval. If you can contain yourselves for the endeavor."

Dewey hopped off his shoulder and flew into the air. "Oh, we can. We have contained ourselves for plenty of endeavors. We've beaten werewolves, vampires, pixies, all kinds of things. We're here for it."

Marcus slid his eyes closed. "Your speech makes little sense. Obviously, you are here for the task. It would be impossible for you to complete the task if you were not here for it,"

"No, that's not...never mind. You're not cool enough to understand," Dewey said with a shake of his head.

"Shall we proceed?" Marcus said to Celine.

Dewey landed on his shoulder again and patted him on the head. "Lead the way, Marc."

Marcus heaved a sigh, his features settling into a frown. "Please do not call me that."

"Sorry, 'Cus, nicknames are a thing."

"Let's get this over with, please," Marcus said, shooting a pleading glance at Celine. "I cannot stand much more."

"All right, well, we'll take two cars. You can ride with me, and D, you can take Paige and Dewey."

"Okay," he said with a nod.

They made their way from Alexander's house, crossing to a garage filled with vehicles. Splitting into two groups, they climbed inside two SUVs and settled in. Dewey, still in dragon form, nestled in the backseat, hidden from the windows.

"That Marcus is a real hoot, huh?" he asked as Damien fired the engine.

"Yeah, not really," Damien said, easing the car out of the garage and following Celine down the drive. "He's actually pretty mean sometimes."

"Aw, not really. He just plays at it. You know, the tough-guy act. He's a wounded hero. He's– "

"A jerk who almost ruined Celine's life. He's somewhat tolerable these days, but seriously? The hero worship from you two is…kind of bothersome."

"Don't get your knickers in a twist, Damien. You're pretty popular, too. I like your character, but…Marcus is just…bad-ass."

Damien flicked his gaze in the rear-view mirror, his features pinched. "Gee, thanks."

"No problem, buddy."

Paige stared at her dragon friend, her nose wrinkled. "So, I didn't really read all of the books, so I'm not sure, but…like all my friends like him."

Damien heaved a sigh as he followed Celine's car on the empty road. "I don't know how anyone could really like him. But whatever. Maybe we should discuss a plan on how you could let us know if this works? I'll be curious. And I know Cassie wants to know."

Dewey raised his fleshy eyebrows, a grin spreading across his features. "I can't wait to get home. I have so many ideas for paranormal romance right now, it's ridiculous. Try this on for size…worlds collide as a warlock meets a ghost whisperer and sparks fly."

"What?" Damien screwed up his face. "Are you serious?"

"I'm going to name the characters Damien and Cassie. Ho-ho, and it's going to be a lot of sparks."

Damien glanced in the rearview mirror at him. "No. No, don't write that. Also, don't use my name."

"Save your breath," Paige answered as she studied the pine trees surrounding them. "He wrote a paranormal romance about me and Devon, used my entire name unchanged, and the image on the cover is identical to me."

"Are you serious? This is like…illegal or something."

"Pretty sure it's not," Dewey said. "Most people would be *thrilled* to be in a book."

"Yeah, we'll I'm not. It's kind of weird. Especially a romance."

"Steamy, too," Dewey said with a chuckle. "Ohh, the steam I'll put in."

"Don't write that. Okay, you know what? Forget the plan to let us know what's happening. I don't want to know. Let's just find this serum and send you on your way."

"Just ignore him," Paige said with a wave of her hand. "You'll get used to it. I did. I can't believe it, but I did. And Devon is really into it. He can't wait to read it."

"That's messed up," Damien said with a shake of his head as they turned off the main road onto a small side road. "I think Celine knows the fastest way to get to this spot, so hopefully this won't take long."

In front of them, Celine eased the car off onto the side of the road. They piled out, the scent of pine even stronger than it had been on the Buckley estate.

"We'll have a bit of walking to do," Marcus said. "Would you like to fist pump about that?"

"No way, Marc," Dewey said. "I hate walking. I'll just ride on Paige's shoulder. Or yours. Would you mind?"

"I would. Please do not sit on my shoulder," the man said with a frown etched into his features.

"You can sit on mine," Celine said with a smile.

"Aw, thanks, Celine," Dewey said, landing on her shoulder and patting her head.

Paige crossed her arms as she trudged behind them. "Thanks, buddy. Really feel appreciated back here."

"Oh, Paige, I can ride on your shoulder anytime. When's the next chance I'll get to ride on someone like Celine's shoulder?"

Paige sucked in a breath, trying to steady her nerves as they traipsed through the woods for another thirty minutes until they reached a cave.

"This should be it," Marcus announced as they arrived. "The safe lies within the heart of the cave."

"Heart?" Dewey asked. "Ugh, you're kidding. Couldn't they have put it right at the dang front?"

Marcus raised his eyebrows at the dragon's complaint before he clicked his tongue. "Let's proceed, shall we?"

Dewey fluttered back to land on Paige's shoulder. "Oh, now you want to hang out with me when we're going into the creepy cave, huh?"

"Well, technically, I'd be better off hanging out with Celine in the creepy cave. She's way more bad-ass than you. I mean, not like Drucinda level because she's too nice. But still…those fireballs are…something."

"Then, what did you come back here for?"

"Well, we always do this part together. You know…the big finish. The end run. The triumphant part. We *always* do that together."

A smile spread across Paige's features. "Yeah, we do. And surprisingly we get there, right? We've never been defeated before."

"Nope. We're pretty dang good at this, Paige."

They crept further into the damp cave, the natural light

dying off. Fireballs flared to life in front of them just as Paige thought they should have brought flashlights along.

"Nice that they come with built-in flashlights, huh?" Dewey asked.

"Yeah, that's kind of handy," Paige said as they squeezed through a narrow part of the cave, spilling into a large chamber.

"Here we are," Marcus answered.

Paige wrinkled her nose as she scanned the space. "Where? There is nothing here."

Marcus rolled his eyes at her before he whipped his fireball across the large cavern. It slammed into a portion of the rock wall, lightning radiating across the walls.

Metal glowed hot as they closed the distance between them and the wall.

"Wow," Paige whispered, her voice filled with awe.

"Do you have the keys?"

"Yeah," Paige said with a nod as she pulled them from her pocket, her hands shaking.

"Insert them one by one," Marcus instructed.

Paige bobbed her head as she approached the glowing container. As she inserted the first key, a loud grinding filled the chamber. Paige's gaze rose to the ceiling, worrying about it collapsing. "It's been here for centuries, probably," she whispered to herself as she placed the second key.

Another loud rumbling caused dust to fall onto her head. "Ugh, I'm not loving this. I hope this ceiling holds."

"Just keep placing the keys," Marcus retorted.

Paige's heart thudded harder against her ribs as she slid the third stone wedge into place. The ground under her feet began to rumble. With a wince, she slid the final component into place.

"Ah!" she cried as the rumbling under her feet shook her enough to knock her down.

In front of her, the enchanted safe popped open, a bright light glowing from within. Her breath caught in her throat as she squinted against it.

The ground continued to shake underneath her as she reached toward the open safe, the light searing her eyes. Her fingers touched something icy, but before she could identify it, her world went black.

CHAPTER 19

*P*aige's eyelashes fluttered open but only darkness surrounded her. Her heart hammered against her ribs as she blinked rapidly, struggling to make out anything in the dim light after the bright beam had burned her eyes.

A groan escaped her as she sat up, smacking into something. "Ow."

"Watch it, Paige," Dewey snapped.

"Dewey?" Her heart lifted at the sound of his voice. "Dewey, is that you?"

"Yes, it's me. Who else would you have smacked into when you sat up without warning?"

"Well, I didn't know it was you. It's pitch black in here." She rubbed her head where she'd knocked into him. "Where are we?"

"No idea. I was trying to feel my way around, but…it's pretty dark."

"Hello?" Paige called.

"Paige, I'm right here," Dewey answered.

"Where is everyone else? Where is Damien? Marcus? Celine?"

"Not here, apparently. No one is but us."

Paige climbed to her knees as her eyes began to adjust to the darkness surrounding them. "Damien?"

Her voice echoed off whatever walls surrounded them. "Marcus?"

"Not here, Paige. I'm telling you."

"The ground was shaking like crazy. Did we fall through to another place or something. Are we trapped somewhere away from them?"

"Yeah, and there was that bright light."

"Right. Then I touched something really icy, then blackness."

"Hmm, I didn't touch anything icy," Dewey murmured. "What could– "

"Hello?"

Paige's heart leapt at the sound of a new voice. "Someone. Someone's here! Hello? Hello!"

"Paige?"

Paige recognized Drucinda's British accent. "Drucinda?"

"Drucinda!" Dewey shouted. "Help! We're in here! We're...somewhere!"

"I'm coming," she answered as a new voice entered the mix.

"Paigey? Are you back?" Devon called.

She'd never been so excited to hear Devon's voice. "Devon? Devon!"

Paige rose on shaky legs as light bobbled toward them. She grinned as she spotted the people behind it.

"You found us! We're home!" Dewey cheered.

Drucinda patted the little dragon on the back as he flung his arms around her. "Yes, you are home. And have you been successful?"

"No," Paige said with a shake of her head. "We were just about to open the safe containing the serum and– "

She uncurled her fist, realizing she held something in her hand.

"And?" Drucinda asked. "So, you'll have to go back."

"Wait. What is this?" Paige furrowed her brow as she stared down at the vial in her hand.

"That's the serum," Drucinda answered as she shined the light on the label. "That's what we need, you did it."

Her heart soared. "We did it. We did it!" Her brow furrowed. "How did we do it?"

"I don't know, Paige, but of course, we did," Dewey said as he buzzed over to sit on her shoulder. "We're awesome."

They tried to high-five but missed. "Well, not at that, but still…okay, good. How is my mom?"

"Hanging in there," Drucinda answered as she pocketed the serum vial. "We should get back right away."

"Yes," Paige said with a nod, taking a step toward the woman. Her foot kicked something, and she glanced down at it. "The music box. Oh, I thought I'd left it with Damien."

She bent down to scoop it up, running her hand along the inlaid surface.

"Music box?" Devon asked as he slid an arm around her waist. "I'm glad you're back, Paige. I was so worried."

"Yeah. We had to find these keys to open the safe that held the serum. And we had to go all over to get them. The last set of people who had the keys gave me this music box. It's really pretty, and it's got a lovely song."

"Aw, that's nice," Devon said as they followed Drucinda from the cavern back into the amusement park ride they'd started at.

"So, did you meet Marcus?" Devon asked as they followed the illuminated exit signs to leave the ride.

"We did. He's cool, man," Dewey said with a nod of his head. "You would have liked him."

"I really wish I could have gone. Maybe when all of this is over, we'll take a trip." Devon sucked in an excited breath. "Paige! We could honeymoon there!"

Paige wrinkled her nose as she recalled the hulking Dracopires that roamed around the area surrounding Bucksville. "Uhhh, let's not do that. I mean, we could go there maybe but…it's pretty dangerous there."

"Aww," Devon said with a whine in his voice, "okay, fine. We'll honeymoon somewhere else."

Paige tugged her lips back in a wince, wondering if they should just divorce when the whole thing was finished. "We can talk about it later."

"Okay, sounds good."

Drucinda pushed through the exit door, bright sunshine streaming into the hallway they walked. Dewey slipped his ring on, turning himself into his human form again.

Paige squinted against the light, wondering if the people they'd left behind in Maine realized what had happened to them. Her hands trembled while holding the box as they threaded through the crowd, making their way back to the entrance.

They piled into the car, returning to their plane. As they made the flight home, Paige stared out the window, every second that passed was torture.

Would they make it in time? How long would the serum take to work?

Questions crowded into her mind, and she couldn't answer any of them.

A warm hand slid around her shoulder before another snaked around her waist. "Hey," Devon whispered in her ear. "You look like you're a million miles away."

"I'm however many miles away my mother is from me right now."

"We'll get there soon, babe."

She twisted to eye him as he stroked her hair. "Thanks."

"Of course. You mean a lot to me, Paige. I want to be here for you."

The words crushed her. He'd been so kind to her, and she'd only used him to save her mother. Guilt roiled through her. Her features pinched and tears burned her eyes.

"Paige?" Devon asked, his hand rubbing her back. "You okay?"

She nodded, but it quickly turned into a wag of her head. Guilt mixed with the enormity of the situation she'd just faced along with the upcoming one. All of the uncertainty poured out of her, and a sob escape her. "No."

"What is it?" Devon asked.

Before she could answer, Dewey buzzed from the doorway leading to the back. "What did you do to her, Muscles?"

"I didn't do anything, she just started crying."

"It's not his fault," Paige answered.

Dewey fluttered toward her, landing on the arm of the couch. "Whose fault is it? It's imperative that we place blame appropriately."

"It's just everything," Paige answered. "Will we make it home in time? Will my mom finally wake up? Those people we met who helped us were really kind. Devon is really kind."

"Aw, Paige, I appreciate that. A lot of people think because I'm a vampire, I'm just inherently bad. It's an awful stereotype to live with."

Paige's lower lip trembled as she wrinkled her nose at him. "Yeah, sorry."

"Oh, for heaven's sake," Drucinda said with a sigh as she sauntered into the room. "Again?"

"Huh?" Paige asked with a sniffle.

"All you do is blubber. Honestly. You'll never make it as a librarian. You cry over *everything*."

"Easy, Dru. She's upset over her mom."

Drucinda poured herself a drink. "So am I. I actually knew the woman, yet here I am a pillar of strength."

"You're way cooler than me," Paige answered.

"Obviously. Look, we have the life-saving serum. All we need to do is administer it and wait for her to wake up."

Paige swallowed hard, trying to imagine the moment. "It almost seems surreal."

Dewey patted her on the shoulder. "But soon, it'll be happening."

"And then you'll probably hide in a corner and cry about whether or not Reed will like you." Drucinda rolled her eyes.

"I will not."

"Right. Reed *has* to like her," Dewey countered. "She's her daughter. It's a requirement. Even if Paige is a complete disappointment, Reed has no choice. Even if Paige is the worst possible daughter she could imagine…"

"Okay, Dewey, you're not helping." Paige wiped her tears away as she shook her head.

Her gaze fell on her bracelet. "I wonder if she'll be able to explain anything about this. Althea seemed to know a little."

"Reed didn't know much, but coupled with whatever that woman told you, you may be able to solve it." Drucinda eased onto the loveseat and took another sip of her bourbon. "What did she say?"

"That I had a magical energy, and that I likely came from an Irish clan based on the symbols on my bracelet."

"All of which I've already told you," Dewey reminded them.

"She said I was some form of witch, but she said most secrets were guarded within families."

"And Reed didn't seem to know much." Drucinda wrinkled her nose. "But I'm certain we can figure it out."

"After we save my mom," Paige said with another sniffle.

"Then you both can learn," Drucinda said, offering her a rare half-smile that didn't look like a smirk.

"Right," Paige said as a shudder shook the plane. She glanced around the cabin. "That didn't sound good."

"Relax, Paigey, it's fine," Devon said with a rub of her shoulders. "Planes like to be in the air."

Another tremble of turbulence shook the plane. "Right. Just a little air pocket or something."

"Exactly."

"Well, unless we're going to crash again," Dewey pointed out.

"Why must you say stuff like that?" Paige asked. "Seriously? You're always a downer."

"I am not. But the fact remains that we crashed once before." Dewey crossed his arms and lifted his chin.

"Yeah, exactly, so what are the odds that we'd crash again." Paige let her chin sink into her palm.

Dewey furrowed his thick brow. "Well, that's an interesting question. Normally, I'd say it's pretty low, *but*...we are dealing with you. And you, Paige, are like...accident-prone."

"I may be a little klutzy but I'm not capable of downing planes just by being on them."

The plane shook all over again, rattling the glasses on the drink cart.

"Try again," Dewey said with a shake of his head. "'Cause it looks like maybe you can. Are you using your *magical powers* to do this?"

"What?" Paige cried. "Why in the world would I use magic to down my own plane?"

189

"I don't know. You've been kind of stressed lately. Maybe you have a secret death wish."

Paige screwed up her face, her jaw unhinging. "I just found my mom and am on my way to save her life. Why would I want to screw that up?"

"Maybe you're afraid your mom won't like you, and you'd rather die in a fiery plane crash than face that." Dewey shrugged.

Paige offered him an unimpressed stare. "I'm not using magic to down the plane. It's just a little turb–"

"May want to buckle up back there," the pilot's voice crackled over the intercom. "It's getting pretty rough here."

"That's the same thing they said the last time," Dewey said as he plopped down next to Drucinda and grabbed a seat belt.

"No, it's not," Paige said, buckling her own belt.

"Babe, don't fret," Devon said as he slouched next to her, cool as a cucumber, "we can just bail if we need to."

"Over the ocean. Devon, you can't fly us back to Europe." Paige smacked a palm against her forehead.

He squashed his features at the perceived insult. "Well– "

"Folks," the pilot said, "we're in a spot of trouble up here. We're looking at a crash landing, most likely."

Paige's heart hammered against her ribs. "You're kidding."

"I don't think he has that kind of sense of humor, Paige," Dewey answered as he unbuckled his seat belt and rose into the air. "Stuff me in a bag, someone, and let's get out of here."

"We're *not* going to crash," Paige said with a vehement shake of her head.

"Pretty certain you're wrong about that," Drucinda answered as she rose and peered out the window. "That water is coming at us pretty fast."

"This is what happens when I think positive." Paige dug

her fingernails into her palms, trying to stave off the panic that threatened.

"It's okay, Paige. I'm not going to let you die." Devon patted her shoulder.

"How are you going to stop it? We're literally plunging to the ocean right now!" Paige sank her head into her hands. "Sorry, sorry."

"It's okay, Paige. You're stressed. I get it."

"Why does this keep happening to me? I just wanted to fly home and save my mom."

"You're cursed, that's why," Dewey shouted as he clung to Drucinda. "Save me! I'm not cursed."

"Calm down, little man. We'll figure something out. I'm not about to die in a plane crash."

Paige rose to her feet, struggling to stay steady as the plane shuddered. "Right. Positive thinking."

"No, literally as part-Valkyrie, I won't die. Devon won't either. It's you and Dewey who are at risk here," Drucinda explained.

Paige's heart skipped a beat. She had forgotten she was flying with two immortal creatures while she and Dewey were mortal. Two of them would survive this crash easily. But for her…she glanced out the window as the water rushed toward them. She was facing her own death.

CHAPTER 20

"We need to bail out!" Paige shouted, panic in her voice.

"There's no time for that and it wouldn't help anyway," Drucinda answered. "The best thing we can do is– "

"Prepare for a crash landing, folks," the pilot's voice crackled over the intercom. "We're going to attempt a water landing, but we've barely got control up here. This is going to be rough."

A moan escaped Paige as she wrung her hands. Dewey threw his arms around her as Devon pulled her to the couch and buckled the seat belt around her before he wrapped her tightly in his arms. "It's okay, Paige. I'll protect you."

"Protect me, Beefy!" Dewey shouted as he clung to Devon's t-shirt. "I can't die!"

Drucinda slouched in her seat on the love seat, bracing for the impact.

Paige squeezed her eyes closed, wondering if they'd make a miraculous water landing or if they'd end up in a fiery wreck or worse, submerged under the water in a crumpled heap of a plane.

In the seconds before impact, she wrapped a hand around Devon's, opening her glassy eyes to peer up at him. "Devon–" she started when the plane smashed into the water with a loud bang, but they never stopped moving.

She had expected the water to halt them, but it didn't. They continued to plummet. "What's happening?"

"Must have hit a portal opening in the water," Drucinda shouted as they continued to fall.

"What?"

"Portal!" Drucinda dug her nails into the supple leather as she pushed her feet against the floor. "We could end up anywhere."

"Are you serious?"

"Look on the bright side," Dewey yelled over the roar of the shuddering plane. "We're not dead."

"Right," Paige answered with a bob of her head as she tried to make sense of it. "We're alive and we're– "

"Crash landing imminent," the pilot shouted. "Land crash."

"Land? We were over the ocean." Paige's lips tugged into a taut wince.

"Portal!" Drucinda shouted again, her voice showing her irritation.

Seconds later, trees battered the bottom of the plane before they smashed through them. The plane hit the ground hard, the wheels buckling underneath and sending it sailing forward on its belly as the pilots fought to bring it to a halt.

Silence finally reigned in the cabin as Paige fought to steady her erratic breathing. The lights flickered before they went off, plunging them into near darkness.

"Did we make it?" Dewey's voice finally whispered in the darkness.

"I think so," Paige answered.

A bright light pierced the blackness around them.

"We made it. Let's go find out where we are so we can find a way home." Drucinda, already up, tugged at the door.

"How are you already this prepared to go?" Paige asked as she struggled to stand on her shaky legs.

"It's the Valkyrie in her," Dewey answered, still hanging on Devon as the vampire rose.

"You okay, Paige? We can take a few minutes. Or if you need me to carry you– "

"No, I can walk," she said with a nod. "I'm okay."

"Idiot," Dewey said with a shake of his head. "You should have let him carry you. What kind of heroine are you?"

"An independent one?"

"Hahahaha," Drucinda cackled as she finally kicked the dented door open, revealing a jungle outside. "Hardly. You whine too much to be an independent heroine. If you wanted an independent heroine, the story should have revolved around me. But then, it would be rather boring as I simply dominate everything the entire time with ease."

"I'm not *that* bad," Paige answered. "I get the job done."

"Barely. But I suppose you manage."

"You would write a book called *Somehow I Manage*," Dewey answered.

"Please with the books." Paige approached the door, peering into the dense foliage outside. She listened for any sounds but didn't hear anything until the leaves rustled.

She fell back a step. "Did something just run past?"

"Yes," Drucinda answered. "The question is what and how deadly."

"Any clue to where we are?" Devon asked. "Looks like an earth-like realm."

Drucinda narrowed her eyes before she crouched at the entrance to the plane, studying the soil below them. "Yes, it does. But outside of that, there are no other clues."

Paige gasped again as something red darted through the

green foliage. "There it goes again. It's red. Bright red. Maybe a cardinal."

Drucinda screwed up her face and twisted to stare at Paige. "A cardinal? Are you crazy? There aren't cardinals in a jungle."

"Well, maybe in this realm there are." Paige frowned at the woman as she squatted in the open door. "You don't know everything."

"I know more than you," Drucinda shot back. "That is not a cardinal."

An arrow struck the side of the plane, punctuating her statement.

Drucinda arched an eyebrow at Paige, shooting her a haughty glance. "Do you think the cardinal shot at us?"

"Okay, fine, it's not a cardinal, okay? Are you happy now?" Paige asked.

"Geez, Paige, calm down," Dewey said.

She heaved a sigh, rolling her eyes as she tried to keep her annoyance in check. "Fine, okay. We're all…stressed and upset and– "

"Speak for yourself," Drucinda said as she straightened and yanked the arrow from the plane to study it. "I'm neither stressed nor upset."

Paige's jaw clenched as a warm hand slid around her shoulder. "It's okay if you're stressed and upset, Boo. I'm here for you."

"Thanks," Paige mumbled, still annoyed, but working to cover it. "Okay, suppose we are in another realm– "

"There is no supposing, we are in another realm." Drucinda held up the arrow. "This is a Graggle arrow."

"A what?" Paige asked her nose wrinkling.

Before Drucinda could answer, the red creature darted through the thick leaves again before it emerged in the clearing cut down by their crash.

"What the hell is that?" Paige stumbled back a step, her features aghast.

"Graggle," Dewey answered as Drucinda grabbed the small creature by its scrawny neck and lifted it into the air.

"Graggle?" Paige studied the fluffy red being. "Wait. That's a Fraggle."

Devon chuckled next to her. "No, Paige, that's a Graggle."

Paige poked a finger at the critter kicking its legs as it tugged against Drucinda's grip. "That's a Fraggle. It's Red Fraggle to be specific. I had the doll when I was a kid."

Devon heaved a sigh, shooting a glance at Dewey.

"Paige, yes, there was a rip-off show that painted Graggles as friendly little beings that were kind and sweet, but it was lies. As you can see, real Graggles are mean and nasty. These darn things will bite you rather than look at you."

"Stop fighting me, you little beast," Drucinda growled. "You can't win. I'm far stronger. Now, tell me where your realm gate is."

"NEVER!" the thing shouted in a high-pitched squeal.

"Oh, really?" Drucinda asked before she shook it hard.

"OMG," Paige shouted. "Stop that! You're hurting it."

Drucinda snapped her gaze toward Paige. "Seriously? Would you rather I turned it loose in here?"

"No!" Devon and Dewey shouted in unison.

"I just think that this is...cruel. You're literally beating it up. I feel bad."

"Honestly. This is the problem with pop culture." Drucinda waved a hand toward Paige. "We've raised a generation of adults who fear vampires– "

Devon scoffed as he nodded. "Tell me about it. Paige was totally scared of me for no reason. I wanted nothing more than to love her."

"What? You tried to kill me."

"I didn't try to kill you. We've been over this."

"Whatever," Paige mumbled as she crossed her arms.

"You feared vampires, yet you cherish Graggles. Graggles, of all things. The tiny beasts are menaces. We'll be lucky to make it unscathed to the realm portal with these maniacs running about. But instead, here you are, defending these things because you watched a television show that portrayed them as friendly and cute."

"Fine, okay, fine. They are mean, nasty things, nothing like Red Fraggle or Mokey."

"Mokey is the worst of them. She's awful and does nothing but incite violence."

Paige wrinkled her nose at the description, trying to reconcile the image with what she'd grown up with. "Uh, okay, well…"

"We cannot waste time searching for the portal. They could kill us. Well, you, anyway."

Paige swallowed hard as she stared at the angry face of what had once been her childhood buddy. "Look, Red, just tell us– "

"Shut up, human moron," Red answered.

"Well, that's not very nice. I'm here defending you and your kind, and you insulted me."

"I can't help it you're an idiot," the Graggle shot back.

"Wow. Drucinda wasn't kidding when she said you're nasty. You really are. Okay, fine, shake her again."

"With pleasure." Drucinda smirked as she tightened her grip around the creature's neck.

"Wait, wait!" Red shouted.

Drucinda hesitated as fear flashed in the small creature's eyes.

"Stop!" Paige said, her heart holding hope that the Graggle would help them. "Looks like she may be having a change of heart."

Before anyone could respond, the Graggle slammed a fist

down on Drucinda's wrist and slipped from her grasp. She fell to the floor, using it as a springboard to launch herself toward Paige, teeth bared.

"OMG!" Paige shrieked as the frightening beast careened toward her.

With one swift punch, Devon knocked it to the side. Red smashed into the love seat and slumped to the floor. After a second, she pushed to sit, shaking her head before she scrambled to her feet and raced from the plane.

"Oh, well, that figures. Great work, Paige. Really a bang-up job." Drucinda glared at her.

"I'm sorry. I thought she was going to help us. I thought maybe since I treated her nicely..." She flicked her gaze to Devon, chewing her lower lip. "Thanks for the save."

"Anytime, Paige. No Graggle is going to attack my wife and get away with it."

"Technically, she got away with it," Dewey answered. "She ran off into the jungle, and now we're going to get killed when they swarm our plane."

"No, we are not. We are going to move before they can trap us here."

"Trap us? Really?" Paige questioned as Drucinda rummaged around to find gear for their trek.

"Yes, really. I don't want to be trapped inside here, outmanned and outgunned. If I had more than a knife and a broken arrow, I wouldn't care, but we are severely ill-prepared."

"Any hint of which direction we should go in?" Devon asked.

"None. We may need your beast mode to give us a clue."

Dewey bobbed his head. "Great idea. Devon can fly up and search for the realm entrance, then we'll make a plan for getting to it."

"What does one of these things look like?" Paige asked.

Dewey landed on Paige's shoulder. "A realm entrance? Super easy to spot. Looks like a giant vibrating rainbow."

"Yep, I should have no problem finding it from the air. Just…don't let the Graggles kill me." Devon wrinkled his nose as he shot a pleading glance at Drucinda.

"I'll do my best. Your skin is pretty tough, though, you should be able to fend of at least a few arrows."

"I don't want to fend off a few arrows, Dru. Those could leave a scar."

"Babes love scars, Muscles," Dewey said with a grin.

Devon wrinkled his nose at the dragon. "I'm not ruining my looks over this. Besides, it only matters if Paige digs scars."

Paige lifted her gaze to find him staring at her. "Uhhh, I mean…I'd still…"

He slid his head forward as she stumbled around. "Would you still love me if I wasn't this handsome?"

"Ummm, I mean…"

He let his head fall between his shoulder blades. "I knew it. You wouldn't."

"That's not what I said."

Dewey cracked Paige on the head with a shake of his own. "Nice going, Paige. You ruined your marriage on like the second day."

"It's not the second day, it's the third. Isn't it? And I didn't say anything about if he had scars."

"Okay, let me ask you this. Do you think I'm handsome?" Devon asked, desperation and heat entering his voice.

"Is this really an issue at this moment? I mean, we're being attacked by Graggles, we're stuck in another realm, and we need to get back to save my mom."

Devon smacked a hand against his face as he frowned. "Oh, man, this is worse than I thought. You don't even find me attractive anymore. Look, I'll admit, I haven't been lifting since we got married, but I'll get back to it as soon as we're home."

Paige screwed up her face at his upset.

"Perhaps we ought to—" Drucinda began when Devon cut her off.

"I promise, Paige. I'll get my physique back into top shape, okay?"

Paige stared at him, completely astounded by his words.

"Good, sounds like a plan. Now, let's get you up in the sky—" Drucinda started.

"No!" Devon shouted, cutting her off. "No, not until Paige and I work this out. I can't go up there until I know I have Paige to come back to."

All eyes turned to Paige, and heat rose in her cheeks as she stared at him. "Uhhh, I mean…"

"Get it together, Paige. We need him to get out of this, and you just keep stammering around instead of telling him what he wants to hear."

"I don't want to…I'm trying not to…"

"Lie? Is that it?" Devon asked, his voice breaking. "You don't want to lie to me and say you'll be here when I get back because you won't be. Is it my beast mode that disgusts you? I can only change when you're not around…I can—"

"No, no, it's not that." Paige pressed a hand to her forehead as emotions swirled around inside her, each fighting for dominance. "It's just that…I…"

"Spit it out, for the love of all things holy," Drucinda barked. "I'd like to get going before we are all killed by those mangy muppets."

"I…" Paige raised her gaze to Devon's, her features melting a little at the pleading dancing in his dark eyes. "I will be here for you. I think…I might be in love with you."

His features registered shock as she spoke the words.

"And I wouldn't care if you had a scar because…you're honestly the nicest person I've ever met–"

"Hey!" Dewey protested.

"Next to Dewey who is both mean and snarky, but also nice," she continued. "And I know we said our marriage was fake, but I feel like maybe it shouldn't be."

A grin spread across Devon's face, and he grabbed Paige's hands, squeezing them. "Paige, this is…incredible. Yes, yes, I want to stay married. It's never been fake for me."

"Yeah, I…wanted it to be fake because after growing up alone, I just…have trouble trusting people."

"You can trust me, Paige," he said, pressing her hand against his chest. "I will never betray you."

"Great, perfect. This is lovely. Your marriage is saved." Drucinda whirled a finger in the air. "Now, may we *please* get going."

"Yes," Devon said with an enthusiastic bob of his head. "Yes, I've got to get my wife home to save my mother-in-law."

He wrapped his arm around her, pulling her close to him.

"Wonderful. Let's get on with it, then, shall we?"

"Beast mode, coming right up." Devon kissed Paige hard on the cheek before he morphed into his new form, lumbered to the door and shot up into the sky.

"Whew." Dewey raked his paw across the forehead. "That was close. Good cover with the whole I may love you thing, Paige."

"It wasn't a cover. I really feel that way. I just…have been too afraid to admit it."

Drucinda rolled her eyes. "Honestly, I do not understand you at all."

"What? It's complicated with Devon. We've gone from–"

"Enemies to lovers," Dewey finished. "Popular trope."

"Well…you know what, never mind. This is private between Devon and I."

"Actually, you just made it really public, so I feel like Drucinda and I get to comment as much as we'd like," Dewey answered.

Paige clenched her jaw, wanting to melt into the floor, but before anyone could respond, Devon reappeared in the doorway, shedding his beast form.

"That was fast. I trust you aren't scarred?" Drucinda asked.

"No scars, but also a really big problem."

"The Graggles have surrounded us our deaths are imminent?" Drucinda asked.

Devon shook his head, his features grim. "No. There is no portal. Anywhere."

CHAPTER 21

"What do you mean?" Paige cried, the shock making her knees weak. "Did you miss it?"

Devon stared at her, disappointment floating in his eyes. "No, Paige. I didn't miss it."

Drucinda shook her head. "You couldn't miss it. It would be a massive shimmering rainbow. You would have to be blind to miss it. Take me up."

"Dru, I'm not an idiot."

"I didn't say you were," she answered as she stuffed the knife into her waistband. "But I want to see for myself what we're working with here."

"Fine." Devon morphed into beast mode and waved a clawed hand to Drucinda who crossed to him. He gripped her and flapped his wings, shooting out of the plane and into the air.

"I can't believe this." Paige slapped a hand against her forehead as she sank onto the couch.

"Right?" Dewey fluttered into the air, shaking his head. "I mean, who saw this coming?"

"I know. No portal? How can that be? And how will we get home?"

"Wait." Dewey's brows knitted. "I was talking about the whole…'I'm in love with you, Devon' thing."

Paige screwed up her face as she raised her gaze to the tiny dragon fluttering in the air in front of her. "Are you serious?"

"Yeah. I mean…who saw that coming, right? Like suddenly…you admit you have feelings for Mr. Beefcakes. Although, I knew that all along. I knew you dug his hotness. You kept denying it, but there's no way you couldn't fall for him."

Dewey squashed his features as he rubbed his chin. "Maybe we are fictional characters. This feels like a story arc. I wonder…"

His eyes went wide and his jaw fell open. "No."

"What is it?" Paige asked. "Although, this is ridiculous. We're not fictional."

"Suppose we are. You finally found your mom…you fell in love with Devon…ohhh." His voice warbled as he huffed out a worried sigh.

"What?"

"Paige…this is the series end."

"Okay, so?"

"So? So! Are you kidding me. I can't believe you claim to be a reader. Paige, this is where everything wraps up."

"Right, good. Maybe our lives will stop being a complete mess now."

"Or cease to exist entirely. At least for me."

"How does that make any sense at all?"

"I am the witty side kick. How I was not the star of this book, I still don't know but that appears to be you. Anyway, the witty side kick always…dies."

Paige shook her head. "That's so not true."

"It is true. Somewhere near the end of this story, I'll die a horrible death. You will vow to avenge me as you weep over my limp, broken body. Then you, Devon, and Drucinda will bring down the evil forces, save your mom and live happily ever after. The end scene will be you lighting a candle at a small, flower-filled memorial with a bad picture of me."

"Dewey, I think you're getting ahead of yourself."

"No. No, I'll be…ohhh, I'm going to be Dobby—the movie version. Everyone will cry when I'm dead, but still…the story will just go on thanks to my sacrifice."

He pressed his lips together, tugging them into a frown before he curled his paws into fists. "No. I won't do it."

He flicked this gaze to the sky. "Do you hear me, Nellie Steele? I won't do it! I won't die for the sake of the character coming full circle!"

"Dewey, Dewey," Paige said as she rose and grabbed hold of his shoulders, "you're not going to die. Maybe you're the witty side kick who gets to live like…Watson."

"Watson wasn't the witty one."

"Well, Sherlock lived, too, so…they both lived."

Dewey sucked in a few deep breaths, sliding his eyes closed. "Right. I can live."

He snapped his eyes open. "But let me say this…I will *not* fly in front of any bullets or jump in front of a knife flung at you. None of that. You get shot at, I'm hiding behind you."

"Deal. I don't want you to die either."

"That makes two of us," Dewey said as Drucinda and Devon returned to the plane.

As Devon shed his beast form for his human one, Paige whipped around to face them. "Well?"

"He's right. There's nothing."

Paige's stomach twisted into a knot. "What? How can that be? How did we get in here?"

"I don't know. We can try to track the trajectory of our

plane and see if we can find the portal from there," Drucinda answered.

"Track the trajectory of our plane crash?" Paige asked, her mind whirling. "Are you serious? While the Graggles track us and kill Dewey?"

"Hey!" Dewey shouted. "You said I wasn't going to die."

"Why would Dewey die?" Devon asked, his features squashing with confusion.

"I'm not following it either. He's the least likely to die at the hands of the Graggles because he can fly away from them. They aren't good tree climbers, so he could just avoid them by perching high in a tree."

"But he's the snarky side kick, so he's more likely to die than I am. Or Devon. If this is the series end, no one wants to read that I just said I love Devon and then he dies."

"Ohhh, Drucinda could die," Dewey pointed out. "I mean, she'd be missed but not that much."

"I am not likely to die due to my exceptional skills, little man. And what are you babbling about with his snarky side kick and series ends?"

Paige winced, wrinkling her nose. "We may be fictional characters. In Bucksville, Damien found a book series called Shelving Magic, following the life and trials of a woman named Paige Turner as she starts her new job at the Shadow Harbor Library."

Drucinda stood motionless, her features registering confusion and disbelief. "Have you been sniffing glue? Did you hit your head during the crash?"

"No." Paige shook her head as she motioned toward Drucinda, flicking a glance at Dewey. "You were there. Tell her."

"It's true. On the cover, there was a woman who looked sort of like Paige, although hotter. And a dragon who didn't resemble me at all, but still was close enough to be me,"

Dewey answered. "And the story inside was…strangely familiar."

"Was I in it?" Devon asked.

"I didn't read the entire book, but yeah."

"Wow." He crinkled his brow. "But…I'm likely safe, right? Because…who would kill off the hunky heartthrob, right?"

"Unless it's an ugly cry book," Dewey answered. "If it's an ugly cry book…you're a goner, Dimples."

He tugged his lips into a wince. "Do you think it is? Did it look like that?"

"No, it looked like your standard fare for the supernatural genre, so you may be safe. I'm convinced if someone is going to die it'll be me or Drucinda–"

"Not happening. Look, even if this is true," Drucinda said with a shake of her head, "I won't die. I'm likely the author's favorite."

Paige screwed up her face. "How do you figure that? Wouldn't I be the author's favorite? I'm the main character."

"No, darling, you're the hot mess that she chose to write about. I'm the favorite. The exceptionally entertaining side character who steals the show."

"I'm pretty certain that's me. The snarky side kick who everyone adores," Dewey answered.

"Obviously…I'm in the running here for favorite. I'm hot, hunky, and pretty dang irresistible. And I did win Paige over so…author must like me." Devon puffed out his chest.

"Can we please stop debating this?" Drucinda asked. "Not only is the answer clear, but it's wasting time. The author isn't going to magically get us out of this bind."

"Technically, she is–" Dewey began.

"Stop!" Drucinda shouted. "Please. We have other problems that we must focus on. We are being surrounded by Graggles and have no clear shot out of here."

Paige heaved a sigh. "Fine. So…what should do we? We can't just head out into the jungle and wander aimlessly."

"And we can't stay here, or we'll be killed. It looks like the plane came in from the east, so we'll follow that path." Drucinda tugged her knife from her waistband, readying it for their trek.

"Maybe the pilots saw something," Paige suggested as she crossed to the door. "I can't believe they aren't out here yet."

"The probably bailed out before we crashed," Drucinda answered.

"Bailed out? Really? So, then they're out there in the jungle somewhere. Maybe we should search for them." Paige winced. "Oh, or do you think they're already dead?"

Drucinda slid her eyes closed and shook her head. "I honestly do not understand how you seem to be getting dumber as we go long rather than smarter."

Dewey settled on Paige's shoulder again, patting her head. "Magical bailout. When they saw the portal, they likely bailed and ended up in the ocean in the real world."

"Why didn't they take us with them?" Paige cried. "Maybe they are the author's favorites."

"I'm not certain–" Dewey began.

"Shut up, let's get moving. We need to find this portal and get that serum to Reed." Drucinda heaved a sigh as she hovered in the doorway.

After collecting their things, they followed her out into the jungle.

"These trees are knocked down. We'll go in that direction." Drucinda waved a finger toward a wide swath that appeared to have been sliced down by the incoming plane.

Paige's heart pounded against her ribs as they began their trek into the thick jungle, following the path their plane had made. "It's pretty quiet in here," Paige finally whispered. "Maybe the Graggles– "

An arrow whizzed past, cutting off her words as it rammed into a tree next to her. Her eyes went wide, and her knees wobbled. "Uhh…"

"Graggles!" Drucinda shouted. "Run!"

A wild ululating sounded, closing in on their location and striking fear into Paige's heart.

"Hang on!" she shouted to Dewey as Devon grabbed hold of her hand and pulled her along with him.

"Come on, Paige!"

"Where are we running to?" Paige shouted as she puffed for breath.

Arrows continued to pelt them, landing in trees and on the ground around them.

"Away!" Devon shouted. "I don't want to die."

"OMG," Dewey shrieked. "This is it! This is how I die. An arrow through my heart."

"That's not going to happen," Paige said, determination filling her voice. "We're all getting out of here alive."

Dewey glanced behind them, his eyes going wide. "If you really believe that, you may want to run faster."

"Huh?" Paige twisted, finding a color set of fuzzy characters racing after her. "OMG!"

Before she could react, she was whisked off her feet. She glanced up to find Devon in beast mode, hauling her skyward.

She snapped her gaze forward, finding Drucinda scrambling into a tree. Devon flew to her, landing on a branch near hers.

"We're trapped," she said, eyeing the group amassing below them.

"I can fly around and search for the portal, then fly you there one by one," Devon suggested.

"It may be our only option, but you may run out of steam," Drucinda answered.

"Maybe we should just wait for a bit. They may give up." Paige eyed the group of muppets below them.

"Are you mad?" Drucinda asked. "They are not going to leave. They'll set up a camp at the bottom of this tree and wait for us to die off."

Paige wrinkled her nose. "You're right. We're trapped. Dewey and Devon are our only hope."

"No, no," Dewey said with a shake of his head. "Devon is our only hope. He's the safest of all of us. No one kills off the heartthrob. It's up to Devon."

"I can go," he said with a nod. "I'll find the portal."

With a deep breath, he glanced at Paige before he pulled her closer and planted a kiss on her. "Just in case."

Dewey screwed up his face. "In case of what? She's not going to die. We know this."

Paige shook her head. "We don't know that. I'm just as vulnerable as you are."

Dewey jabbed a claw her way. "Except you're not. You are the main character. If you die, the book just ends. So, that can't happen."

"Maybe it can. Maybe it's an ugly cry book where good doesn't win." Paige shrugged.

"Can we please stop making decisions based on this ridiculous notion that we're not real?" Drucinda said with a huff.

"Fine, you're right. This is silly. We'll all be okay. We're smart and capable– "

"Some of us," Drucinda interrupted.

Paige shot her a warning glance before she continued. "We'll be able to figure this out. We can– "

Her voice cut off as the jungle suddenly became quiet. She wrinkled her nose, peering over the foliage to eye the Graggles that had gathered at the base of the tree.

Her jaw fell open as she spotted nothing but ground. "Where did they go?"

"What?" Drucinda asked.

Paige poked a finger downward. "The Graggles. Where are they? They're gone."

"That's ridiculous. They wouldn't just leave when they have us…" Drucinda sat back on the branch as her brows knitted. "Trapped."

"They're gone. Are they able to camouflage or something?"

"No," Drucinda answered with a shake of her head. "No, they don't have that ability. Why did they leave? This is highly unusual."

"Maybe they decided they couldn't beat us since we have Devon." Paige shrugged. "Maybe they can smell him and know he can fly."

"Hey, I don't smell…except like the rugged scent of dead-wood with hints of citrus and sandalwood."

Paige screwed up her face. "What is this? An Old Spice commercial?"

"It could be…I sent a video to them. I just love Old Spice Timber."

She stared at him, disbelief playing on her features before she shook it away. "Okay, I can't handle that right now. Look, obviously the Graggles left for a reason. Maybe we should capitalize on this opportunity and get out of here without Devon having to fly around and leave us stuck in a tree."

Drucinda peered down to the ground again. "I don't like this."

"They could be lying in wait for us to head back to the ground, then pounce," Dewey answered.

"They could, though I don't see them anywhere. With their colorful fur, you'd think we'd be able to spot at least one of them. But I don't see anything."

Paige sucked in a breath and shook her head. "Look, I think we need to move now. Maybe they are regrouping, bringing backup. We can't wait."

"She has a point," Devon answered. "It's better if we all get to the portal at the same time."

Drucinda scanned the space around them again before she nodded. "All right. We'll give it a try, but...I don't like this at all. What possibly could have frightened the Graggles away from their prey?"

"I don't know, but let's hope this is the break we need," Paige said as Devon morphed back into beast mode and grabbed hold of her.

They descended slowly to the ground while Dewey hovered above them in a slow descent and Drucinda slid down the tree.

As their feet touched the ground, they glanced around warily, wondering if they'd soon be attacked again.

"Looks like they're gone," Paige whispered.

"Yes, but we still don't know why."

"Doesn't matter," Paige answered with a shake of her head. "Let's just keep following the plane's path and hope we find the portal."

With a nod, Drucinda crept forward, her knife at the ready for any threats.

As they pushed through the thick jungle, the ground under them shuddered. Paige froze, glancing around. "Did anyone else feel that?"

"I did," Drucinda answered. "I don't know what it was, but I'd suggest we pick up the pace. I don't like this."

"You've said...many times," Paige answered, annoyance creeping into her voice. "But I really don't see what the big– "

Her eyes went wide as Drucinda tugged back a large leaf. She froze, her head cocking before it slowly tilted to search for the end of the object standing in front of them. "I think I know why the Graggles left," she whispered, her voice breathy.

She twisted around to face them, fear dancing in her eyes. "Run!"

CHAPTER 22

*P*aige's heart hammered against her ribs as she stared at the large stone-like creature that stood in front of them. "What is that thing?"

"Graggle Golem," Dewey informed her.

"What? Like the Golem I befriended?"

"Yes, and no. It's a Golem. It's a lot meaner."

Devon morphed into his beast form again, grabbing Paige and beating his wings hard to fly away from the creature.

Paige glanced over her shoulder, getting glimpses of the stone-like monster as it stormed toward them.

Below them, Drucinda raced in a zigzag pattern, desperately trying to escape the beast.

"Wait, wait, maybe I can tame it," Paige said.

"I don't think Devon wants to chance it if you can't." Dewey clung to Paige as they sailed through the air.

Her eyes went wide as she glanced down at Drucinda. "Drucinda, look out!"

The Golem swiped at her, nearly catching hold of her, but she scurried behind a tree and changed directions.

Paige's lips tugged into a wince. "She's never going to make it.

"I knew it," Dewey shouted as the wind whistled past them during Devon's wild flight. "Drucinda is going to be the sacrifice here. We'll all cry over her body for an emotional catharsis before we finally rally and beat the evil that threatens us."

"No!" Paige shouted. "No, Drucinda can't die."

"Look, if someone has to go, she's the best one. I don't want to die, and you and Devon are safe, so I vote Drucinda," Dewey answered.

Paige shook her head at him before she flicked her gaze downward again. She scanned the ground, unable to find the woman. "Where is she?"

"Probably dead. We'll find her broken body later for our emotional moment."

"Stop saying that." Paige gripped Devon's arm and searched the ground again.

Her eyes rose to the monster racing behind them, expecting to see blood dripping from its stone mouth. Instead, her heart skipped a beat as she spotted Drucinda trapped inside the Golem's stone fingers.

"Let me down, you foul beast!" She pushed against the rocky fingers trapping her before she bit them.

"Wow, she totally just bit into his fingers," Paige said. "I bet that wasn't comfortable. Devon, stop, we have to help her."

He answered with a grunt which she couldn't understand, but he continued to fly away from the Golem.

"Devon, stop. We have to help Drucinda."

"Paige!" Dewey shouted. "Use your bracelet."

"Oh, right. I bet that'll work. Why didn't I think of that?"

"Because the main character is never exceptionally bright. That's what the sidekick is for."

Paige lifted her arm in the air, letting her bracelet catch the light. "Devon, slow down for a second, let's see if this will work."

Devon's wings eased a little despite his grunted response, and Paige twisted to wave the bracelet at the beast. "Stop, you foul beast!"

The Golem's legs continued to move but slowed until he finally froze. Drucinda scrambled to slip from his grip, falling onto the stone thigh below her before she slipped down to the ground. "Thanks."

"Anytime. Now, let's go back toward the portal," Paige said with a nod. "Down, boy."

Devon grunted again.

"Don't give me that," Drucinda said with a shake of her head. "Get down here and change back into your human form. I'm sick of this. I'm not trudging through the jungle alone while you carry her like some sort of princess."

Devon descended to the ground, setting Paige down before he morphed back into his usual form. "She is a princess."

"I don't care. In this jungle, we're all equal. Now, let's go. And keep that bracelet handy in case we need it again."

"Right," Paige said with a nod as she pushed it down her wrist.

Before they could continue their trek along the plane's path of destruction, a humming sounded.

"Oh, now what?" Paige asked, slapping her thighs with her hands. "What sort of creature is it now?"

"Uh, Paige…" Dewey patted her on the head before he poked a claw behind them.

Paige twisted to face a veritable wall of Graggles, all of them murmuring. Her heart pounded against her ribs as she spotted the army of them. "Oh, no. They're going to kill us."

Drucinda narrowed her eyes, taking a step forward.

"Mmm, I don't think so. They'd have done so already. They're in some sort of trance."

"Yeah," Devon agreed. "I can't understand what they're saying."

"I don't speak Graggle either," Drucinda said, "but it seems as though they are…worshipping."

"Worshipping what?" Paige twisted to eye the frozen Golem before she thumbed at it. "Oh, him."

"No, definitely not," Drucinda answered. "He frightened them away."

Paige wrinkled her nose as she searched the area before taking a tentative step forward. The moment she moved toward them, they all bowed their heads.

"Oh, I see," Drucinda said. "It's Paige. Paige is who they are worshipping." She burst into laughter slapping her thighs. "If they only knew."

"Hey," Paige snapped.

"She stopped the Golem. They must think she's magical," Dewey answered.

"I *am* magical, technically." Paige faced the congregation of fuzzy creatures. "Okay, thanks a lot. I appreciate this. Could anyone point us in the direction of the portal thing?"

One Graggle, resembling Mokey, stepped forward. "No. You cannot leave. You stopped the monstie. You must stay. You will protect our village, and we will build you a temple where we can worship. We will feed you from the best meats, endless wine, tend to your every need."

"Sounds good to me," Dewey answered. "Come on, Paige, let's go back to the village."

"No, we can't go to the village. We have to leave this place and save my mom."

"Or we could stay and eat the best meats with endless wine," Dewey answered. "I mean…it feels just as fulfilling as saving your mom's life. Maybe even better because she's one life...but this...this is the lives of an entire village."

"Dewey, no. I don't care how many Graggles I can save, I want to save my mom."

Dewey tugged his lips into a taut frown. "I don't think you're really thinking straight."

She shook her head, her frustration building as she curled her fingers into fists. "Just...okay, that's a very nice offer, Graggles, but...I have to get home and save my mom. So, I can't stay. If you could– "

"We cannot let you leave," Mokey said. "The monsties are a large threat. You must stay and help us."

"Would that I could, but I can't," Paige said with a penitent smile. "I really need to go. I appreciate your offer, though. I've never had someone willing to build me a temple before."

"I could build you a temple," Devon said. "Would that make you happy?"

Paige shook her head at him. "That's a conversation for another time, hon. Let's just focus on getting out of here right now. Anyway, Graggles, thanks and good luck."

Paige took a step away from them when they swarmed her. "Ah! Hey! What the hell?!"

Paige's feet left the ground as several Graggles lifted her up. She toppled over onto her back. Small paws supported her as they carried her through the jungle. "Hey! Put me down. Devon! Drucinda! Help!"

She glanced behind her, noting her entire party being carried by the Graggles.

"Just go with it," Drucinda hissed.

"But– "

"Shut up before we're dead," she growled through clenched teeth.

Paige tugged her lips into a terrified wince as they

continued their awkward trek through the jungle until a village came into sight.

The Graggles chattered in their native tongue as others came to greet them. Paige struggled to try to understand what they were saying but failed.

They were carried to a hut and thrown inside before a door swung shut, trapping them inside.

"When can we expect the food?" Dewey shouted.

They received no response, and Dewey slapped a hand against his forehead. "Seriously? I mean…they promised food. We all heard them, right?"

"Dewey, will you quit with the food?" Paige snapped. "This is serious."

"I know! We were promised wine and endless eats, yet we've been stuffed into a hut…not a temple as promised, a hut with no food."

"I'm a little worried that we're not going to be alive to eat the food," Drucinda said.

"Not if we starve to death *before* they bring it," Dewey answered with a huff.

Drucinda paced the mud floor, shaking her head. "No, not that."

"What is it?" Paige asked.

"They may believe you are a god among women," Drucinda said, poking a finger at Paige, "but we're not."

"Well, I'll just tell them you are my demi-god friends, and we'll be okay."

Drucinda narrowed her eyes. "Possibly not. Have you ever seen the type of behavior where…when they believe a god is inhabiting you, they will…kill you?"

Paige wrinkled her nose. "Why would they harm the person they think is a god?"

"They will probably kill you and try to preserve your

body," Devon answered. "If you're a god, they'll think you'll be fine in spirit."

Paige screwed up her face. "What? Oh, great."

"I'm fairly certain that's what they meant by building you a temple. They will entomb you there."

"What about the food? Why did they offer food?" Paige cried.

Dewey landed on her shoulder bobbing his head. "Now, you're talking. This is the real crux of the matter."

"They will take the food to you and leave it…by your dead body."

Paige slapped a hand against her forehead. "OMG, this is awful. We have to get out of here."

"No kidding," Drucinda said as she eyed the walls. "It shouldn't be difficult. This hut looks fairly rudimentary."

"Right," Paige said with a nod. "Devon could go beast mode and knock it down. Actually, with those muscles, Devon could knock it down in human mode."

"Thanks, babe. I'm flattered you noticed." Devon grinned at her.

"The problem is…we can't make a break for it now. We should wait until dark," Drucinda answered. "Most of them will be asleep except the guards they will inevitably leave near this hut. I should be able to make quick work of them though." She waved the knife in the air.

"Ugh," Paige said with a wrinkled nose. "I just…can't get around killing off the things I loved as a kid."

"Well, get over it fast. I'd like to escape this realm, thank you."

"Yeah, of course. Hey, maybe we'll be able to see the rainbow-y thing better at night. Maybe this little detour is actually a positive thing."

Drucinda narrowed her eyes at Paige. "This is not in any way positive. I don't care if it's easier to see it at night. I'd rather have trudged through the jungle and searched it inch by inch than be stuck here another moment."

"Right," Paige said. "On the upside, at least we still have all our stuff. So, we'll just…wait it out, leave tonight, and be out of here."

She settled onto the floor, leaning against the hut's wall. "May as well relax. We've got a while to wait."

"I'll pace, thank you," Drucinda answered, resuming her back and forth ambling. "How can you be so calm."

"Easy," Dewey answered as he plopped onto the floor next to Paige, "we've been trapped lots of times. We're getting pretty good at it."

Drucinda shook her head at the response.

Time passed slowly as they waited for the sun to set. As twilight lingered, visible through the tiny window on the door, a commotion sounded outside of their hut.

Paige scrambled to her feet. "Uh-oh, what's that?"

"Sounds like a group of them headed our way," Drucinda answered.

Devon peered out the window. "Yep."

"I hope they have food," Dewey added.

The door to the hut burst open and several Graggles entered, their heads bowed and carrying trays heaped with meats, cheeses, and fruits.

"Yesssss," Dewey hissed, pumping his fist.

They left the offerings on the floor in front of Paige, backing away, hunched over in a bow before they slammed the door closed behind them.

"Oh, I'm starving," Paige said as she snagged a slice of cheese and bit into it. "And this is perfect timing because we should fuel up before we head out."

"Dibs on the jerky," Dewey shouted as he buzzed over to peruse the trays.

"We can't eat that," Drucinda said. "It could be poisoned."

Paige grimaced, spitting the cheese into her hand and staring at it.

"It's not poisoned, Dru," Dewey said with a dismissing wave of his hand. "It's fine. Look, the Graggles worked all day to prepare this meal. It would be rude of us not to eat it."

"Would it? It would be rude of us not to die, too, but I'd prefer not to, if it's all the same to you, little man."

Dewey grabbed a grape and sniffed it. "Honestly, it smells fine to me."

"Can you smell all types of poison?"

"No," he admitted with a shrug, "but still…I'm just really hungry, and I'm trying to make the case to eat."

"For you two having been trapped so many times before, you'd think you would learn *not* to eat the food given to you. It's like standard practice."

Paige stared at the feast, her stomach growling. "I really want to eat it. I'm hungry."

"Go ahead. Eat your last meal, friend," Drucinda said with a wave at the food.

Dewey popped a piece of jerky into his mouth. "I'm eating it. It seems fine. And if it's poisoned, I'm going to die almost immediately due to my small size. All we have to do is wait a few minutes to see if I make it."

Dewey swallowed the jerky and grabbed a piece of cheese and some grapes.

Paige narrowed her eyes at him as he munched on the food. Her stomach rumbled as she watched him bite into another piece of a crumbly cheese.

"I am so hungry," she murmured.

"You know, if I'd have already turned you into a vampire, you wouldn't be that hungry," Devon said.

She wrinkled her nose as she glanced at him. "I think I'll pass."

"Just eat, Paige. They're not going to poison us yet." Dewey waved a dismissive hand at her before he popped another grape into his mouth.

"I really hope you're not wrong," Paige said before she bit into a piece of cheese. "Oh, wow, this is good."

"Told you. These Graggles have some good eats. Honestly, if your mom wasn't dying, I'd consider staying here for a while."

"You two are idiots," Drucinda answered as she stalked closer and snatched a few items from the trays, sniffing them before she bit into a piece of jerky.

"But we're not hungry idiots," Dewey said, shooting a finger gun at her. "And look who is joining the idiot brigade."

"I'm hungry," she answered. "And if you two are going to die, I may as well."

"We're not going to die," Dewey assured her. "We maybe too stuffed to move, but we'll be alive."

Drucinda side-eyed him, a frown forming on her lips. "How much are you planning on eating?"

Dewey stared down at the heaping trays before he shot her another glance, his implication that he planned to eat everything clear.

"You're kidding," Drucinda answered with a click of her tongue.

"He isn't," Paige answered, "so grab what you want now because he will literally eat all of this."

Drucinda snagged a few more pieces of the jerky, cheese, and some of the fruit as she shot Dewey a wrinkled-nosed glance.

"Devon? Better get in on this if you want any because Dewey will scarf it all down," Paige said.

Devon stared at the trays. "Do you think the cheese is high in calories?"

"Seriously?" Paige asked. "I mean…it's cheese. It's dairy. It's healthy."

"It's so not. And I'm really watching my weight. I've heard that getting married can lead to weight gain."

Paige chewed the crumbly cheese as she stared up at him. "Are you serious?"

"Yes."

"The jerky's a little salty, so you'll have to up your fluid intake once we're home, but it should be fine," Drucinda said as she glanced out the tiny window at the disappearing sun.

"Right. I'll stick with that, maybe a few pieces of fruit."

"Wow, hubby's judgy," Dewey whispered to Paige. "May want to step away from the cheese."

Paige shot him a glance. "Seriously? We were just in a plane crash. We're eating intermittently as it is and trekking through the jungle. I'll burn it off."

They ate their fill of the food as they waited for the waning light to disappear entirely, plunging the encampment into darkness before they could sneak out.

"All right," Drucinda said when they could barely see their own hands in front of their faces, "let's go."

Paige rose, her knees wobbling underneath her. "Whoa, that walk earlier must have taken it all out of me. I can barely move."

Dewey smacked into her, his wing slapping her in the face.

"Ouch, watch it, Dewey."

"Sorry, my flying is all off. I can't seem to fly straight. Must be the darkness."

Across the room, a loud bang sounded. "Ouch," Devon grumbled.

"What is it?" Drucinda asked.

"I can't walk."

"Me either," Paige answered. "We must have been sitting too long or something."

Drucinda groaned from across the room. "No, that's not it. We've been drugged."

CHAPTER 23

"*D*rugged? What?" Paige stumbled a step to the side. "That's insane. Obviously, we're still alive."

"Yes, and our legs won't work. And I feel quite fuzzy-headed," Drucinda said.

Paige rubbed at her temples. "Yeah, I guess my head feels weird, too."

"My legs feel like rubber," Devon answered in the dark. "Although this isn't as bad as when Dewey drugged me."

"Hey, I saved you, Lover Boy, and don't you forget it."

"I didn't say you didn't, I just said you also got me high as a kite." Devon bumped into Paige before he grabbed hold of her. "Sorry. Okay, wait, I think...I think I can walk."

"We're going to have to try," Drucinda answered. "This is our only shot. Maybe the exercise will get the drugs moving faster."

"Is that a good thing?"

"Well, we want them out of our system. Too bad we don't have any water to help flush them," Drucinda said. "Now, come on. We've got to get out of this hut as quietly as possible."

"Okay," Paige said, awkwardly goose-stepping her way over to the door as Dewey wobbled on her shoulder where he'd managed to land.

"Are we ready?" Drucinda whispered.

"Ready," Paige said with a salute.

"I'm going to kick down the door," Drucinda hissed. A second later, she stumbled backward into Paige, a curse escaping her. "Let me try that again."

"Careful. You're high," Paige reminded her with a giggle.

"Stop giggling, you sound ridiculous."

"Sorry. I just…man, I wish it wasn't dark in here because I would have loved to see you being as awkward as I am."

"You are awkward without drugs. At least I have an excuse."

"Oh, good point. Wait, maybe the drugs make me less awkward. I'll kick down the door."

"Fine, go ahead and try," Drucinda said.

The dark shadow in front of Paige shifted to the side. Paige licked her lips, sucking in a deep breath as she prepared to attempt the feat.

A second later, she lifted her leg and kicked it out. "Ouch," she cried, grabbing hold of her toe and hopping around on one foot. "Didn't work. Didn't work."

As she leapt around in pain, she knocked into Devon. "Hey, watch it, Paige."

He stumbled a step away, crashing into the hut's wall. A second later, it rumbled and shook before it crashed down around them. The thatched roof buried them as the walls splayed out to the sides.

Paige spit out the hay that filled her mouth, rubbing her eyes as she sat up in search of her friends.

"What happened?" Drucinda asked as she scrambled to her feet.

"Devon knocked the entire stupid place down," Paige answered, still spitting the dry roofing from her mouth.

"You crashed into me," he complained as he rose.

"We should get out of here. This will draw attention." Drucinda scanned the darkened huts surrounding them. "Looks like the two guard were knocked out at least."

"That's good," Paige answered as she rose. "Let's...wait... where's Dewey?"

Drucinda arched in eyebrow, her features lit by the pale moonlight. "I haven't seen him. Wasn't he on your shoulder?"

"Yes, and now he's gone." Panic rose in Paige's voice. "Dewey? Dewey!"

"Shh, quiet, stop shouting. You'll have the whole village down on us," Drucinda said with a sharp wave of her hand.

"Well, we need to find him."

"I'm sure he's here, babe," Devon said as he shuffled over to her to squeeze her shoulder.

"But where?"

Paige's stomach twisted into a tight knot. "Oh, no. No."

"What?" Drucinda asked as she kicked around in the hay.

"He's probably...he may have gotten hurt in the collapse. Or worse." She slapped a palm against her forehead. "Oh my goodness, what if he's dead?"

"That's jumping to conclusions, isn't it?" Drucinda retorted.

"Is it?" Paige asked, her voice shrill with panic. "Because Dewey has been convinced he'd be a target, the one to die. The sacrifice that makes people cry. That we'd have to weep over his dead body."

"Will you please stop insisting this is some sort of ridiculous fictional story? It's not. It's real life. Now, look around for him. He's likely just buried under the rubble here."

A lump formed in Paige's throat as she dropped to her knees to dig through the remains of the hut.

As she frantically shoved debris from side to side, a tiny groan sounded on her left. Her heart leapt before it raced, pounding out a frenetic rhythm against her ribs. "Dewey?"

"Did you find him?" Devon asked.

"I heard something over here."

Devon joined her, using his larger hands to shift chunks of the fallen roof and walls aside in search of the little dragon.

Finally, moonlight gleamed off of his teal scales.

"Dewey!" Paige cried. "Dewey, are you okay?"

"Ohhhhh," Dewey moaned, his head lolling from one side to the other.

"Dewey? Are you hurt?"

"Yeah," he moaned. "Paige…it's not good."

Paige's lower lip trembled as tears filled her eyes. "It'll be okay, buddy. We'll carry you to the portal. We'll get you help. You just need to hang in there."

A small cough escaped him before he let his head fall back to the ground with a tiny shake. "No, Paige. No good. I…I don't think I'll make it that far. And I'll only slow you down."

"No," Paige said as tears streamed down her cheeks. "No. No man left behind. We're not leaving you."

Dewey reached a trembling paw toward her. "Paige…save your mom. Do it for me. And…when you and Devon have your first little vampire-ling…name him Dewey, huh?"

Paige fought to stop her lower lip from trembling at the words. Dewey had been right. He'd be the one who didn't make it through their mission. His tiny body couldn't withstand the damage of the hut collapse. How could she say goodbye to her friend?

"Where does it hurt, little man?" Drucinda asked as she dropped to one knee next to him.

"Oh, everywhere," he said. "I would have love to help save

229

your mom, Paige, but…maybe my sacrifice will mean something to future generations."

Drucinda screwed up her face as she stared down at him. "I don't see any blood, or anything broken. Are you quite sure you're in that much pain?"

Dewey slowly nodded, his eyes barely able to stay open.

"He's probably hurt inside." Paige choked out another sob. "His tiny little body couldn't protect him when the roof collapsed."

"The roof is literally made of hay. I'm not sure it could hurt you if it tried," Drucinda answered.

"Well, he's small! Tiny, in fact. When we fell it probably…" She buried her face in her hands as she wept with Devon consoling her.

"Try to be respectful, Dru, she's grieving."

"Uh-huh," Drucinda said with a nod as she rose to her feet. "Well, I suppose then we should be off. We'll leave you here, so we don't have to drag your body through the jungle."

"Of course," Dewey said stoically.

Drucinda reached into her pocket. "Before we go…I've got a bit of jerky left if anyone wants it. May need the energy."

Dewey's eyebrows crinkled as Devon shook his head. "I'm good."

"I can't eat," Paige cried. "I can't think of food right now."

Drucinda shrugged as Dewey raised a claw.

"Uhh, if it's not too much trouble…could I have the jerky…one last meal, you know?"

Drucinda arched an eyebrow. "You want the jerky? You're dying, but your concern is the jerky I have in my pocket."

"Well…I mean, may as well go out with a bang."

"If you want the jerky, fly up and get it."

"Drucinda!" Paige scolded. "I can't believe you. He can't fly."

"Can't he? You want it, little man, come and get it."

Dewey lay on the ground for a second, his eyes narrowing before he struggled to climb to his feet, fluttering his wings.

After another second, he rose slowly into the air. "Wow, it's a miracle! I…I can fly. I'm okay. I'm going to live!"

Drucinda crossed her arms and shook her head. "Just as I suspected."

"What?" Paige sniffled, wiping at her cheeks. "Are you…serious?"

"Paige," Dewey said with a grin, "I'm going to live!"

Paige climbed to her feet, her fingers balled into fists. "Yeah, I can see that. I thought you were dying!"

"So did I," Dewey tried.

"No, you didn't." Paige crossed her arms and shook her head. "You're such a jerk."

"Well, I was…" Dewey lifted one fleshy finger into the moonlight. "Look, I have a scratch. I was afraid I was seriously hurt."

Paige offered him an unimpressed stare.

"Okay, okay. I just…wanted a little attention."

"Your attention could have cost us our chance to escape," Drucinda answered. "Now, perch on her shoulder, and let's go before the entire village is upon us."

"Wait, wait," Dewey said.

"What is it now?" Drucinda asked.

"Do you really have that jerky?"

Drucinda let her head fall back as she let out a muffled groan. "Get on that shoulder."

"No reason to be mean about it," Dewey said as he perched on Paige's shoulder, and they picked their way clear of the debris.

"Anybody remember how to get back to where we were?" Devon asked as they crept through the quiet village streets.

"Why don't you fly up and take a peek around. See if you can spot anything," Drucinda suggested.

Devon winced. "But we should get out of the village first. I don't want anything to happen to Paige."

"Thanks, hon," Paige said with a nod. "I appreciate that. But I'd also appreciate figuring out where to go next."

"Right, on it." Devon gave her a nod before he morphed into beast mode and rocketed into the air.

"I hope he finds something," Paige murmured as they continued to sneak past darkened huts.

"I hope we make it out of here without anyone knowing. These Graggles are a real problem," Drucinda said.

Dewey threw his hands out to the side. "Yeah, well, I was hoping for another piece of jerky, but that didn't happen, so we can't get everything we want."

"Will you stop with the jerky already? We're literally running for our lives *and* Reed's, and you're worried about jerky," Drucinda said.

"Welcome to my world," Paige answered. "And most of the time, we're running for our lives high or half-dead or something else crazy thanks to some mishap."

"Like now? Are you feeling any better?"

"I've gotten used to the weird, wobbly legs, so I'm okay. Dewey's claws digging into me are distracting me from the weirdness."

"I can't help it," Dewey answered, "my legs are wobbly, too. It's all I can do to hang on with your lumbering."

"Lumbering?" Paige asked. "I'm trying my best here to get out of this stupid village before someone kills us...again. In the time since I've known you, I have been almost killed *more* often than I haven't been."

"Oh, so you're blaming me for this?" Dewey asked.

"Well, I'm just saying..."

"Just saying that somehow Dewey attracts trouble. Maybe

it's you. You were klutzy when you came. Maybe you attract trouble to me. Because before you showed up, I lived a quiet life in the library."

"Yeah, stuck there because no one took you out. And now I see why."

"Ohhh, right, because I'm some sort of trouble magnet. Yeah….I'm sure that's the reason."

"Will you two shut up before we get caught?" Drucinda growled.

"We probably will because Dewey attracts trouble."

Dewey's wing smacked her in the face. "Oops."

"You did that on purpose."

"Prove it," he shot back.

Paige curled her fingers into fists, anger brewing inside her as she stomped forward.

Drucinda rubbed her forehead. "I can't wait for Devon to be back. He only acts like a child part of the time."

Paige screwed up her face. "I feel like he acts like a child all of the time."

"Well, he was spoiled simple as a child. That's why."

Paige bobbed her head. "Seems like it. The sun really rises and sets on him, huh?"

"And Luna. Don't think his father doesn't spoil her, too. She gets away with murder."

Paige froze as she processed the comment, her eyes going wide. "Did you hear that?"

"What?" Drucinda crouched, scanning the dirt path in front of them.

"Sounded like whispering," Paige hissed.

They stood still, straining to listen for any sounds that may indicate a threat.

"I don't hear anything," Drucinda answered.

"Me either and my hearing is better than Paige's."

"All right, fine. Let's keep going." Paige shrugged and continued forward.

"I can't believe Devon isn't back yet. What is he doing?" Drucinda asked.

"Maybe he found something, and he's checking it out," Paige offered as another set of whispers hit her ears.

She brushed it off, assuming it was the wind passing through the dense jungle foliage.

"Here's the end of the village up ahead," Drucinda said. "We'll wait outside it for Devon."

"Okay. Maybe he– "

Paige stopped talking, her eyes going wide as torches flared to life. In front of them, stood a wall of Graggles, armed and ready to stop them from leaving the village.

"Uh-oh," Paige answered.

"Well, that was the whispering you heard," Dewey answered. "The Graggles making certain we couldn't escape."

"Right," Paige said with a nod as she wrinkled her nose. "Now what?"

Drucinda shrugged as she shot her a serious glance. "We fight or die."

CHAPTER 24

"*D*ie?" Paige cried. "Wait…no."

Drucinda sneered at the Graggles, widening her stance as she thrust her knife forward.

"Most likely, yes," Dewey said with a nod. "We are vastly outnumbered with limited weapons. Basically, this all hinges on how well Drucinda can fight."

"Well, she can fight really well, I mean she took down all those goblins as a kid."

"Come on, you little muppets," Drucinda said with a wave of her fingers, "let's dance."

"Wow, that was super aggressive," Paige said with a shake of her head. "I would have just said nothing. Why tempt fate?"

"Scare tactic," Dewey said. "I mean…would you attack Drucinda after she said that?"

"I would literally never attack Drucinda, but it doesn't look like that applies to the Graggles. I think they're going to rush her en masse."

The fuzzy creatures formed an attack line fronted by wooden shields.

"Ohh, you should help her," Dewey said.

"What? Why aren't you helping her, too?" Paige asked.

Dewey shrugged. "I'll be there in spirit. I don't want to take a chance with my life."

"Are you kidding me?"

"Paige, you'll be okay. You're the main character."

Paige rolled her eyes. "Fine, go fly into a tree and hide there and Drucinda and I will handle this."

"Well, probably Drucinda will handle it, and you'll just... draw a few off to even the odds for her."

Paige pressed her lips into a thin line as she shot him a glare. Before she could join Drucinda for the fight, a loud whooshing noise descended on them.

Paige glanced skyward, the moon blotted out for a moment as Devon dove down toward the Graggles, still in beast mode.

He barreled through them, knocking them sideways and tossing a few into trees before he rose into the sky again, preparing for another pass.

"Your husband is saving the day," Dewey reported. "Wow, I never expected this of Devon. Good job telling him you loved him at just the right time to turn him into a hero."

"Come on!" Drucinda shouted at them. "Let's make a run for it before they regroup."

Paige rushed forward on wobbly legs, dashing toward the now-open road into the jungle.

"Run, Paige, run!" Dewey wailed.

"I'm running, I'm running," she said, puffing with effort as she pushed her body forward.

A Graggle leapt in front of her, bearing its teeth.

Paige ground to a stop, but Drucinda skirted her, slashing at the creature with her knife before she knocked it aside with a swift fling of her arm.

They continued forward, but the Graggles had started to regroup, forming a new line at the village's entrance.

"Oh, crap," Paige murmured.

Before they reached the line, though, Devon swept down again, knocking the Graggles aside.

A few attempted to leap onto his back but he shook them free before he climbed into the sky again.

They dashed forward through the opening before the stunned Graggles could retaliate, leaving the village behind and racing through the jungle.

Enormous leaves smacked Paige in the face as she tried to put distance between her and the village.

After a few minutes running, Drucinda slowed to a stop. Paige doubled over, gasping for breath as Drucinda merely fixed her ponytail and sucked in a big breath.

"Man, I wish I was part Valkyrie," Paige choked out.

"Everyone does, darling," Drucinda said. "Unfortunately, it's reserved for those of us who are fabulous. Now, where is that husband of yours?"

Paige searched the skies for him. "I don't know. Do you think he could see us from up there?"

"Hard to say. The canopy is fairly dense." Drucinda sent her gaze skyward. "Call out to him."

"No," Paige said with a shake of her head. "That's the stupidest idea I've ever heard. The Graggles will be able to find us."

"A chance we'll have to take," Drucinda answered. "We need to find Devon. Oh, unless you're planning on leaving him behind. You know, the grieving widow bit. You'd stand to inherit quite a bit."

"I'm not leaving him behind, but I'm not going to shout out to him." Paige shook her head before her eyebrows pinched. "Although…there's really no other way for him to find us, is there?"

"Perhaps if I climb a tree and try to reflect something off the moon using Morse Code," Drucinda answered, "though I doubt he'd recognize it. He never did like studying much."

"Still, it might attract his attention. What do we have that will reflect the moon?"

Drucinda raised the knife in the air, blade pointing up. "Best I can do."

She clenched it between her teeth as she mounted a nearby tree and scurried up toward the top before settling onto a branch and using the knife to try to catch the moonlight.

Paige shifted her weight from foot to foot, a shiver snaking down her spine as worry over Devon set in. "Where is he?"

"Probably lost," Dewey answered.

"Well, aren't you a ray of sunshine?" Paige retorted with a shake of her head.

"I am. I could have said dead or captured. I went with the best option: lost."

Paige clicked her tongue, heaving a sigh. A loud crack to her left drew her attention. Her muscles stiffened as her senses stretched to listen for any other disturbances in the jungle.

"Devon?" she whispered, peering into the darkness.

Seconds later, Devon appeared, crashing through the large leaves before he collapsed face first onto the ground.

"Devon!" Paige raced to his side, collapsing to her knees. "Are you okay?"

She rolled him over onto his back, her fingers turning wet and sticky. Her nose wrinkled as she pulled her hand back to peer at her fingers, rubbing them with her thumb.

She gasped as the moonlight revealed blood. "No!"

"Uh, Paige…" Dewey said as he poked a claw at Devon.

She glanced down to find blood dribbling from the corner of his mouth.

"Paige," he choked out, coughing up more blood before he reached toward her.

"OMG," Paige said, her features registering shock as Drucinda's boots hit the ground and pounded toward them.

"What's happened?"

"They got me, Dru. They got me good."

"Is he lying? Is this a Dewey situation?" Drucinda asked.

Paige's head wagged back and forth. "I don't think so. His shirt is soaked in blood."

Paige raised her bloody fingers as proof.

"And he's coughing up blood and sort of acting like he's dying," Dewey added.

Drucinda focused on her friend, her features pinching as she studied him. "How bad is it?"

"Bad, Dru," he answered, his voice gravelly.

"We'll see about that." She grabbed hold of his shoulder, rolling him onto his side.

With her knife, she sliced his shirt open and peered at his wound in the dim moonlight as Devon groaned in pain.

"How does it look?"

"Not good," Drucinda answered, twisting Paige's stomach into a tight knot.

"Well….what should we do? Should we try to get him back to our world or…" Her voice trailed off as she found no other suitable options.

She'd just come to the realization that she may want to spend the rest of her life with him and now it may be too late.

"Oh, no…Devon is the one who's going to die for the cause." Dewey gasped, slapping a paw against his forehead.

Drucinda ignored him as she leaned closer to study the

wound, her eyes narrowing. She pulled the skin apart, sending a stream of blood flowing down his back.

"Ahhhh...should you be doing that? He's bleeding...like a lot," Paige said, her voice shaky.

"I have to assess this. The depth, what– "

"What? What what?" Paige asked when Drucinda's voice cut off.

"I see the problem here," she answered. "This is not great."

"What is it? What's wrong?" Paige inched closer, trying to find what Drucinda found.

"There is a poison arrow tip lodged in this wound." She shook her head as she cursed under her breath. "We need to get this out of him."

"Here? Now?" Paige tried to keep her breathing calm, but it came in ragged gasps.

"We don't have much choice. He's not going to make it to the portal. We're never going to be able to carry him, and our slowed pace will cost us time."

"Well...what are we going to do?"

Drucinda raised her knife, the blade gleaming in the moonlight. "I'm going to perform an emergency surgery to remove this from him. After that, we'll need to cover this with a paste that will suck the poison from his system."

She glanced up at Paige, her features pinching. "Hold him down!"

Paige winced as she shimmied around to place her hands against Devon's shoulders and press down. "Okay."

Drucinda readied her knife, then plunged it into Devon's back. He wailed in pain, squirming and escaping from Paige's grasp.

"I said hold him down, not put your hands on him gently. Hold him."

"Okay, okay," Paige shouted as she slammed her weight

down on top of him, squashing him against the ground with as much force as she could.

"Come on, Paige. You're really dropping the ball here," Dewey answered.

"You're not helping, little man," Drucinda said as she cut into Devon's skin again. "Go gather a few Fiji plants for the paste."

"Right. I'll handle that."

"Be careful," Paige said as she gritted her teeth, sweat beading on her brows from her effort to hold Devon still.

Finally, he went limp, and she heaved out a sigh of relief. "He's out."

"Yep," Drucinda said as she tossed the knife aside and dug into the wound she'd created.

Paige winced as blood oozed from the slit. She curled her fingers into fists as Drucinda grunted with effort.

"Come on," she murmured through gritted teeth. "I can't get it."

"Let me try," Paige said.

Drucinda's jaw unhinged as she stared at Paige. "Are you joking? You?"

"My fingers are slimmer than yours, maybe I can get it."

"Are you saying my fingers are fat?"

"No, just that mine are skeletal and long. Let me try."

Drucinda arched an eyebrow.

"It's his life, Drucinda. Let me try."

Drucinda pulled her fingers from the wound and motioned toward it. "Take your shot."

Paige licked her lips as she stared down at the bloody slit. She winced, her nose wrinkling as her trembling fingers hovered over it.

"Are you going to do it or just think about doing it?"

"I'm doing it. I'm doing it. Just let me…prepare."

"Do it before he dies," Drucinda retorted.

"Okay, okay!" Paige's shrill voice betrayed the panic rising in her. "I just don't want to make things worse."

"It can't get much worse than this. He's dying."

"Right." She sucked in a sharp breath and plunged her fingers into the wound. Warm blood oozed around her skin as she searched blindly for the tip of the arrow. "I feel it."

"Good, now…grab it and pull it out."

"I'm trying." Her nostrils flared as her slimy fingers slipped on the slick metal. "This isn't easy."

"No kidding," Drucinda said.

"Wait…if I can just get under it…" Paige's nose wrinkled as she hooked her finger, digging further into Devon's flesh. "Ughhh…"

Bile rose in her throat, but she tried to concentrate on drawing the tip of the arrow upward. After a few minutes of work, a glint of metal became visible.

"Almost there," Drucinda encouraged, "keep going. Don't lose it now."

Paige forced herself to slow down so she didn't lose her grip on the piece. Finally, she teased it from his wound, raising it triumphantly in the air. "Got it."

"Excellent work, Paige. Excellent work. Let me see it."

Paige dropped it in Drucinda's hand and allowed the woman to study it under the moonlight. "It looks intact. Good. Now, all we need is the Fiji plant."

"Got 'em," Dewey said as he buzzed over, carrying a number of red flowers.

"We need to make a paste with this. We'll have to chew the flowers and spit them out into our hands to form the paste, then spread it into and over the wound," Drucinda instructed.

Dewey stared blankly ahead, pushing the flowers toward Paige. "He's your husband."

"Fine, I'll do it," Paige said with a nod as she snatched a flower. "What's the big deal?"

She shoved the red petals into her mouth and began to chew. A gag escaped her. "OMG, now I see."

"Uh-huh."

"Ugh. Oh, this is awful." She pressed the back of her hand against her lips as she nearly retched again. "It tastes like… vomit mixed with tar."

Drucinda snatched one from Dewey, shoving it in her mouth and chewing with a grimace.

After a few more seconds of chewing, Paige spit hers into her hand.

"Shove it into the wound," Dewey said.

Paige let her tongue loll out of her mouth to ease the taste as she slid the contents from her palm into the slit on Devon's back. "Oh, that's awful, just…terrible."

"Better you than me," Dewey answered as they slathered Devon's back with the concoction.

"How long will this take to work?" Paige asked, still pawing at her tongue to try to alleviate the flavor. "Ugh, is there any water to take this taste away?"

"Where would I get water?" Drucinda asked. "I didn't grab a bottle on the way out of the Graggle village."

"Is there a nearby stream, maybe? I mean, we have to wait for Devon to wake up, right?"

"I saw a stream nearby," Dewey said. "While I was gathering the Fiji plants. I can show you."

"Ugh, yes, please." Paige scrambled to her feet, her hands held to the sides, her fingers dyed red from the flower. "I can wash my hands, too."

"Don't mind me. I'll just stay here with *your* husband," Drucinda grumbled as Dewey buzzed through the air, leading the way to the water.

"How long do you think it'll take for Devon to wake up?"

Paige asked with another grimace as more flavor burst in her mouth. "Wow, this taste just won't quit."

"Oh, yeah, Fiji plants are long lasting, that's for sure," Dewey said as he pushed aside another leaf.

Moonlight sparkled off of a small stream that cut through the jungle. Paige rushed forward, dropping to her knees and waving her hands in the water to clean them before she scooped up some water and slurped it from her palm.

She swished it around before spitting it back out. "Oh, some relief."

Dewey landed on the ground next to her, staring into the water. "Do you think we'll ever make it home?"

"Huh? I hope so," Paige said taking another drink of the water. "Why would you say that?"

"Felt like one of those moments. You know...mid-story, Dewey stares at his reflection in the water, questioning life."

Paige heaved a sigh and shook her head. "You really need to quit thinking of this as a book and just– "

"Just what?" Dewey asked.

Paige's nose crinkled as a strange sensation shot through her body.

"Paige?"

"I feel kind of...weird."

"You're normally weird. How is this different?"

"No, like..." She shot him an incredulous glance. "Strange. Weird. Like something is...wrong with me."

Dewey furrowed his brow. "Wrong with you? As far as I know, Fiji plants aren't poisonous to humans or anything."

Paige rose to her feet, stumbling back a few steps. "Are you sure? I...I don't feel right."

Her head began to pound at the temples, and she doubled over in pain. "Oh, whoa, I don't feel so great."

She squeezed her eyes closed, as heat washed over her, and her skin puckered into goosebumps.

After a second, the sensation passed. "Whew, okay, starting to feel better now."

"Ah, Paige…"

"Yeah?" she asked, her eyes still pinched shut.

"Mmm, not sure how to say this but…"

"What? Honestly, just say it."

Dewey hesitated for a moment before he spoke again. "You've turned into a tiny dragon."

CHAPTER 25

"*W*hat?" Paige asked, her stomach dropping at the words before she snapped her eyes open. "You're jok– "

She stared down at her teal paws, her eyes going wide. "What happened to me?"

Dewey shrugged. "I don't know, but...you're a mirror image of me."

"What?" Paige scrambled to the water to peer into it, her jaw unhinging at the reflection. "OMG. I'm a tiny teal dragon!"

"That's what I said before," Dewey answered. "Do you not listen to me?"

"I did listen. I just didn't believe it. What happened to me? I look like you."

"You improved," Dewey said with a chuckle and a wink.

Paige shot him an unimpressed stare. "That's not funny. How did this happen? Why do I look like you?"

"Just luck, I guess," Dewey answered. "I mean, it could have been worse. You could have morphed into my cousin. He is *ugly*."

"Dewey!" Paige shouted. "I don't care who is ugly. I'm a dragon. I'm a tiny teal dragon."

"Pretty awesome, right? You really hit the jackpot."

"Why? How? Why is this happening?"

Dewey shrugged. "I have no idea. Maybe we should head back to Drucinda and see if she has any ideas."

"I can't go back there like this!"

Dewey's features twisted into a grimace. "What's that supposed to mean? You're embarrassed to be seen as a tiny dragon? Is that it?"

"I'm…no. No, of course not. It's…I'm…I can't explain this to Drucinda is all."

"So what? Most of what happens to you we can't explain. Drucinda will understand. She knows you're weird."

Paige clicked her tongue as she studied her reflection again with a shake of her head. "Fine, fine. We'll go back there."

She rose from her crouch over the water and trudged toward the jungle.

"Ah, Paige, I hate to be rude here, but…with your short legs, it's going to take forever. You should fly."

"I can't fly. I don't–oh wait," Paige flapped her wings and rose into the air. "I can fly!"

"Yeah, and it's so much faster. Come on, let's go."

They buzzed through the jungle back to the clearing where Drucinda sat with a still comatose Devon.

"Have you washed your–" Drucinda's jaw dropped open as she stared at Paige. "What is happening?"

Dewey shrugged. "We don't know. Paige accidentally turned into a dragon. No idea why."

"Yeah," Paige answered, setting her gaze on Drucinda. "I–"

Heat washed over her again and her scales pinched, like the sensation of goosebumps on flesh.

"What is it, Paige?"

"I don't know. I...feel weird again."

Paige landed on the ground, rubbing her eyes as her temples thudded again. "Same as I did before. Maybe I'll– "

"Whoa," Dewey answered as Paige opened her eyes.

She grinned. "Oh, yay, I'm human again."

"Not quite," Dewey answered with a shake of his head."

"What is it?" Paige asked.

Drucinda frowned at her, her features pinched. "Give me my identity back, you thief."

"What?" Paige cried. "What are you talking about?"

"Uh, may want to head back to the river and have a little look-see, Paige," Dewey said. "Now, you look like Drucinda. Like identical to Drucinda.

Paige furrowed her brows. "Really?"

"Stop wrinkling my face," Drucinda said. "Stop looking like me."

"I'm not," Paige answered. "I don't know what's happening. One second I was me, then Dewey, now you."

"Identity theft is not a joke, Paige. Millions of families suffer every year."

A groan came from the ground as Devon fluttered his eyelashes. "Ugh, what happened?"

"You were shot. A poisoned arrowhead lodged in your back, but we dug it out. You've got Fiji paste on your wound to counter the poison," Drucinda explained. "You should be fine."

Devon winced as he pushed up to stand, stumbling back a step while he got his feet under him. His eyebrows shot up as he studied the group. "Whoa. Did you add something to the Fiji paste?"

"No," Drucinda answered, a hand on her hip.

"Dru, there are two of you. And where is Paige?"

"Here," Paige answered.

"Where?" Devon glanced around. "Paige, honey? Where are you?"

"Right here," Paige answered, flinging her hands out.

Drucinda sighed and shook her head. "Paige has stolen my identity."

"I didn't steal–Uh-oh." Paige's eyes went wide as her skin puckered into gooseflesh again. "It's happening again. I can't control it."

"Oh, good, I hope you aren't another version of me." Drucinda crossed her arms as they waited for Paige to morph into her next form.

Devon's jaw dropped open as he stared at her. "Whoa. No way."

"OMG!" Dewey shouted.

"What?" Paige asked. "What now?"

"You…look like Devon."

Paige slapped a palm against her face as she shook her head. "Are you joking?"

"Head back to the water and look if you don't believe me."

Paige held her hands out in front of her, gasping as she stared down at Devon's meaty paws. "No!"

"Oh, uh, wow, this is…I mean, no offense, Paige, but… yeah this isn't cool," Devon said.

Paige shot him an annoyed glance. "Are you serious? I can't control this. I'm just randomly morphing into whatever creature I see last. It's…insane. Why is this happening?"

Dewey rubbed his chin. "Possibly a reaction to the Fiji plant or a combination of the stream water with it. Hard to say with you."

Drucinda shrugged. "Either way, it should wear off."

"But with me in what form? Will I go back to normal?"

"Gosh, I hope so," Devon said, "because…I mean…I can't be married to you like this. I'm just…I like Paige."

"You said for better or for worse," Paige answered, jabbing a finger at him.

Devon crinkled his nose. "Is that really what I look like when I'm mad?"

"Stop obsessing over yourself. We should get a move on to find the–" Drucinda stiffened, glancing behind her. "Shh."

She ripped her knife from her waistband and crouched low before she crept forward into the thick jungle.

A few snarls followed by a muffled yelp sounded before Drucinda returned, holding Red Graggle by her neck. "Look, I found a stray."

Paige eyed the creature. "Maybe she can tell us where the portal is now."

"Never!" Red shouted, grasping at Drucinda's hands as she tried to escape the chokehold.

"No, we'll just tie her to a tree so she can't follow us." Drucinda thrust the knife toward Dewey. "Cut some vines, little man."

"With pleasure," Dewey said with a devilish grin.

"I just...oh great." Paige raised her eyes to the sky as the warmth of morphing shot through her.

It passed after a few seconds, and she shook her head. "I look like a Graggle, don't I?"

Devon arched his eyebrow at her as he stared at her. "Ohh, yep. You do. Well, it's an improvement."

"What? I thought you thought you were good looking."

"I do," Devon answered, "but I don't want to be married to a mirror image of myself."

"Well, now you're not," Paige said as the Graggle in Drucinda's grasp stared at her.

"You really are a god!" Red said. "You are Airia, the goddess of all Graggles."

"Yep, that's me. And I really want you to help me find a

way to the portal. I will bless you infinitely." Paige winced at the lie. Desperate times, though.

"The portal is three clicks to the north."

Paige's features pinched. "Right, thank you. Which way is the north? And what is a click?"

Drucinda shook her head. "I know what that means. But how do we know you aren't lying, you filthy little Graggle?"

"I would never lie to Airia," Red answered. "Airia is known as a vengeful god. If I lie…"

Red shook her head, her features twisting with fear.

"Right," Paige said. "Exactly right. If this is wrong…I will…like…rip your hair out strand by strand and…stuff like that."

Drucinda screwed up her face. "That's the best you could do?"

"No," Paige said with a shake of her head. "That would just be the start."

"And I believe it," Red said solemnly. "Airia is someone to be feared."

"Darn right," Paige said as Dewey returned with several long vines.

"Thank you, little man. Now, I will hold her against the tree, and you wrap her up."

"On it, boss." Dewey wrapped the vine around the Graggle before he buzzed around the tree, wrapping her tighter and tighter with the vine.

He secured it and dusted his hands. "That takes care of that."

"And she's given us the location of the portal," Drucinda answered as she slid the knife back into her waistband. "Let's move."

"Wow," Paige said as they took a few steps away from the trapped Graggle, "these legs are awful."

"Graggles don't have knees," Dewey answered. "You should be able to run like the wind, though."

"I hate to be a pain, but– "

"Oh, for heaven's sake," Drucinda said with a sigh before she lifted Paige onto her hip. "I will carry you like a small child. Is that better?"

"Much," Paige said, her yarn-like red hair flopping as she nodded.

"Wow…so, you've finally done it," Dewey said. "You've managed to hitch a free ride."

"Are you serious?" Paige asked. "You hitch free rides all the time."

Dewey pressed his lips together, stifling a laugh.

"Why are you laughing?"

"I'm sorry…it's just…when you look like that it's hard to take you seriously. I mean…your mouth is…your jaw…it just…sorry."

Paige glared at him.

"I'm sorry, Paige. I just…wow, if you need to stay a Graggle for the rest of your life…I'm not sure we can stay friends."

"Hey," Devon said with a shake of his head, "that's not nice."

"Well…come on, Dimples. How are you going to feel introducing Paige as your wife at parties?"

Devon wrinkled his nose as he glanced at her. "Well, I mean…she's kind of cute. She's like a little doll."

"You do what you want to do," Dewey said. "I'm not introducing the doll as my friend."

"Look, all I need to do is find a new person to emulate. I just haven't found anyone."

"We should find you someone really cool," Dewey said as they continued their hike to the north. "Like blindfold you until we find a really awesome person for you to emulate."

"Ohhh, Madelaine Petsch," Paige said with a nod. "Let's get her. She's like Paige upgraded."

"Upgraded? She's like Paige multiplied by infinity," Dewey said with a nod.

Paige wrinkled her nose. "Hey. She's not *that* far ahead of me."

"Ha, says you. She's a bombshell. Muscles, would you like Madeleine Petsch as your wife."

"I just want Paige back to normal," Devon said.

"Good answer," Drucinda said as she shifted Paige to her other hip. "You are heavier than you look."

"Sorry. It was all that cheese I ate."

They continued through the jungle until a glowing light reached them.

Butterflies fluttered in Paige's stomach as she spotted it. "Please tell me that's not the sun, and it's the stupid portal thing."

"It's the stupid portal thing," Drucinda answered. "Thank heavens."

"Gosh, I really hope this takes us right back home, and we can use this serum on my mom." Paige frowned. "And that it works."

Drucinda ground to a halt as she pushed past a large leaf toward a shimmering rainbow stretching from the ground to the sky. "We're about to find out."

Paige held her breath as Drucinda took another step toward the portal. Would they end up at home or in another nightmare?

CHAPTER 26

They approached the shimmering rainbow, and Paige clung tightly to Drucinda as the colors began to paint their bodies. The light, so bright it stung her eyes, sent warmth radiating through her body.

Her lips tugged back into a deep grimace as they continued through the portal. Goosebumps peppered her arms and legs.

Paige squeezed her eyes closed as they continued forward, warbling noises threatening to make her ear drums bleed.

After a few seconds, the sensation passed, and chilly, damp air swept over her. Her eyes fluttered open, and she pushed up to sit from the cold dirt she lay against.

She stared down at her arms, a smile creeping over her face. "I'm human again. Oh, the portal fixed me."

Paige pressed a hand against her chest as her grin broadened.

She climbed to her feet in the dim light, her hand landing on a cold, rough surface. "We must be in a cave."

"Paige?" Dewey called.

"Yeah, right here."

"Are we home?" he asked.

"I–I don't know. I think so. We're in a cave. Let me try to find my way out."

She ran her fingers along the wall, shuffling forward.

"Ugh," Drucinda groaned in the darkness. "I suddenly feel awful."

"Awful?" Paige asked. "Are you sick? And where is Devon."

"Here," he answered. "Just waking up. I don't feel too bad, but my back is killing me. I really need to get this looked at."

"I'm not sick, I just feel…unfit or something. It's hard to describe. I wonder if I've sustained some sort of ill effects from passing through the portal. I seem to be…swollen or something."

"Like your ankle?" Paige asked, screwing up her face as she inched forward. "I'm looking for a way out now."

"No…it seems to be my entire body. I'm…doughy or something. I don't know."

Paige's forehead creased as a hint of light reached them. Her heart leapt as she spotted it. "Light! I see light!"

"Thank goodness." Dewey buzzed past her toward it. "Oh, yes, it's sunny, too. Oh, please be earth. Please."

Paige picked up the pace behind him, finding it easy to move forward at the faster speed. "That portal didn't hurt me. I feel great."

"Lucky you," Drucinda groaned from behind her.

Paige burst into the bright sunshine behind Dewey, grinning up at it. "This looks like earth."

"Yeah," Dewey agreed as he stared at the trees overhead.

"Oh, I know where we are," Drucinda said from behind them. "This is France. Good, we're home. I can't wait to get back to Reed."

"Me either, I–" Paige twisted to face her, her expression going blank as her eyes widened. "What the hell?"

Drucinda heaved a sigh as she shot her an unimpressed glance. "What is wrong with you?"

Her eyes went wide a second later. "OMG!"

"Why do you look like that?" they shouted at each other.

Devon emerged from the cave, sidling up to Drucinda and planting a kiss on her. "Aw, babe, you're back."

"I'm Paige," Paige said, crossing her arms.

Drucinda wiped at her cheek. "I'm not your babe."

"What?" Devon stared at them, his jaw unhinged.

"What's the problem?" Dewey asked, whipping around to face them.

Both women raised a finger to point at the other. "She stole my body."

Paige pressed her lips together. "That's not true. I didn't do anything. You took my human form."

"I did nothing of the sort. And I don't want *this*." She grimaced down at her body. "Have you *ever* taken a fitness class?"

Paige's jaw dropped open. "Ugh, sorry I didn't train like a ninja since I was six."

"Try since birth," Drucinda said, arching an eyebrow.

"Stop making my face do that. I'm going to get wrinkles," Paige retorted.

Drucinda clicked her tongue. "I think you already have some."

Paige wrinkled her nose at the woman.

"Don't do that with my face."

"I'll do whatever I want to do with your face," Paige said, curling her fingers into fists. "And your body, too. Yeah, I may mountain climb or something."

"Seriously?" Dewey asked. "I can't imagine you mountain climbing."

"The muscle tone she has is incredible. It's just...amazing

how much easier things are with this level of fitness lurking under the surface."

"Give me my body back." Drucinda stamped her foot on the ground.

Paige crossed her arms, lifting her incredibly sculpted chin. "Are you refusing?"

"Looks like she is," Dewey said with a raise of his eyebrows. "And I'm not sure you can do anything about it. Paige could literally kick your butt."

"Paige doesn't know how to fight. My brain does." Drucinda kicked a leg out before she doubled over. "Ow, oh, that was...ohhhh, I pulled something. Definitely pulled something in the leg-groin area. Wow."

"Hey, quit wrecking my body," Paige said.

"You're not pinning that on me. It looks like you've spent the better part of your twenties wrecking your own body."

"Probably all the pizza we eat," Dewey said as he landed on Drucinda's shoulder.

"Hey!" Paige shouted, her fingers curling into fists.

"Oops, sorry." Dewey buzzed over to Paige and landed there. "Hard to keep track of this."

Paige sighed and shook her head. "How could this happen...again?"

"What do you mean again?" Drucinda asked.

"Paige and Dewey swapped bodies a few times when we were realm hopping for the Bronze ring," Devon answered.

Drucinda let her features settled into a frown. "So, in other words, you are a chronic body thief."

"I am not. It just...happens."

"How did you fix it last time?" Drucinda demanded.

"We kept going in and out of the portal until finally we were fixed. It took a few tries, but it finally worked," Dewey informed her.

Drucinda heaved a sigh. "Right, well, that's not an option. That's a one-way portal, and I'd rather not endure several more plane crashes or any more Graggle attacks."

"Me either," Paige said. "So...do we just...accept our new fate?"

Drucinda's nostrils flared as her frown deepened. "No, we do not. There must be some way to fix this. Perhaps my grandmother knows."

"We can call her on our way out of here," Devon suggested as he winced. "I really want to have this shoulder looked at, and we need to get the serum to Reed."

"Dimples is right. We need to keep moving," Dewey said. "Drucinda, you knew where we were. Can you request an evac for us?"

"Of course, though we'll need to climb to the top of that hill to get any reception. We'll call my grandmother while we wait for rescue." Drucinda pointed toward a high crest towering over them.

"All right, let's go." Dewey pumped a fist in the air.

They picked their way through the forest surrounding them, making their way to the hill Drucinda pointed out.

"Ugh. I'm not sure I can make this," Drucinda groaned.

"Really?" Devon asked. "Paige usually makes it."

"I don't understand how." Drucinda pressed against her thighs as they began their climb. "It's like dragging sacks of wheat around."

"It's not that bad," Paige said with a shake of her head from the front of the group.

"For once, we're first," Dewey said.

"Yeah. Don't say anything, but...I understand her point. Climbing this hill is ridiculously easy with these leg muscles. And don't even get me started with the abs."

"Ridiculously sculpted?"

Paige tugged up her shirt as Dewey peered down. "Wow. Those are works of art."

"Yeah, I know. In some ways, I'll be sad to go back to my pitiful, out-of-shape body."

"Don't feel bad, Paige," Dewey said with a pat on her head. "That pitiful, out-of-shape body has saved the world countless times. So, you should feel pretty good about yourself."

"That's true. That's right." Paige nodded. "For all Drucinda's fitness, we've been the ones who have saved the world over and over."

"And…you're a princess, so…"

"Yeah, that's right. Devon likes my out-of-shapeness."

"I don't think that's a word, but still, yeah…you scored on several levels."

Paige pressed her lips together as they continued their ascent. "I just hope I can score on my mom's level. We're so close. It's all I can think about."

"This serum should do the trick."

"If we can get it to her fast enough. This detour isn't exactly what I expected."

"We should be rescued soon," Dewey said as they reached the top of the hill.

Devon tugged his phone from his pocket. "I have signal."

"Good, give that to me," Drucinda said as she snatched it from him. "I'll call Ro."

Paige crossed her arms as she waited for Drucinda to place the rescue request.

Dewey buzzed off her shoulder, landing on the ground and patting the dirt next to him. "May as well get comfortable. We've got a little wait."

Paige stared at the spot for a moment. "I would but… weirdly I don't feel like sitting down. All this muscle tone is really amazing."

"Suit yourself." Dewey shrugged as he lounged against a tree.

"I'm taking that muscle tone back," Drucinda growled as she pressed Devon's phone to her ear again. "Grandmother, I am in desperate need of your help…no…no…no, it does not involve a man."

Drucinda slid her eyes closed and clicked her tongue. "We've been stuck in another realm and only just made it back. In the process of returning to this world, Paige and I somehow how inexplicably swapped bodies."

Drucinda listened for a moment before she nodded. "Yes, I know going back through the portal may do the trick, but that's not possible. This was a one-way portal."

Her eyes rose to the sky before she heaved a sigh. "Right. Yes. All right."

She ended the call and passed the phone back to Devon.

"Well?" Paige asked.

"She'll come out to assess the situation once we're at the hospital. With any luck, she can help us," Drucinda answered.

"I really hope so," Paige said with a sigh.

Drucinda crossed her arms and arched an eyebrow. "Really? Do you? Because you're getting the better end of the bargain here if she can't."

Paige rolled her eyes. "I'm sorry I'm not up to your fitness standards, but I actually like pizza."

"A little too much by the feel of it."

Paige narrowed her eyes. "Are you saying I'm fat?"

"Ladies, ladies," Devon said, stepping between them. "Let's not go there, okay? You're both incredibly attractive women, and both of you are smart and capable, too. Can we all agree to that?"

"I'm smart and capable. Also, hot." Drucinda wrinkled her nose. "Well, I was."

Paige curled her fingers into fists. "You still are! I mean…

wait…I still am. This isn't coming out right. Okay, Devon's right. We're both great in different ways."

"Fine," Drucinda said with a wave of her hand. "If you want to play nice, okay, yes…we all have our strengths. Mine happens to be fitness, yours is pizza consumption."

Paige bobbed her head before she snapped a glare toward Drucinda. "Wait…you know, yes, fine. I excel at eating pizza."

"She does," Dewey said with a nod. "That's definitely a strength of hers."

"Thanks, Dewey. I appreciate your support."

"Anytime," he said with a pat on Paige's head.

The distant sound of a helicopter cut off any further conversation, sending their eyes skyward as they searched for their rescuers.

Within a few minutes, the helicopter came into view. A ladder rolled down toward them, and they scurried up it into the safety of the cabin.

Twenty minutes later, they were touching down at an airport to board another plane.

Paige drummed her fingers against her thigh as the engines revved up. "I really am not looking forward to another plane trip across the pond."

"Let's just hope we don't crash again," Dewey said. "This is getting ridiculous with the plane crashes."

"Tell me about it," Paige said. "I mean, if this is a book, get a new plot device already."

Drucinda settled into the seat next to Dewey. "Don't tempt fate. I'd really like to get back to the hospital and cure your mother. Of course, she'll be highly confused if we're stuck in these bodies."

They settled back for the flight, this time making it safely to their destination.

Paige's stomach twisted into a tight knot as they made the

short trip to the hospital, her heart hammering harder with each mile that passed.

Her legs wobbled under her when they finally slid out of the car and entered the facility, taking the elevator to the top floor.

Rochelle and Ronnie met them as they stepped off.

"Oh, Paige, I'm glad you're back and found that serum." Her gaze fixed on Drucinda.

"Actually," Paige said with a wave. "I'm Paige."

Ronnie's features crinkled as she flicked her gaze between them. "What?"

"There was a mishap when we came back through the realm portal," Dewey explained. "And Paige and Drucinda swapped bodies."

"Oh, a realm swap," Rochelle said with a nod. "Well, it should be fixable."

"Is it?" Drucinda asked. "My grandmother is coming out to assess it. I certainly hope it's fixable."

"Oh, yes. With her expert help, you'll likely be back to normal in no time."

Drucinda breathed a sigh of relief. "Thank heavens. Paige's body leaves something to be desired. I tried to do a kick earlier and managed to pull something. And there is a strange pain in my neck just here. And this elbow seems a bit fiddly."

Paige crinkled her nose. "My elbow isn't fiddly. It's just... you gotta kinda stretch it. Give it a good crack into place."

She extended her arm quickly to demonstrate.

"That's not normal," Drucinda said with a shake of her head.

"Ah, okay, well, maybe we should move forward with the serum for Reed while we wait to sort out the body situation," Ronnie suggested.

"Yes," Paige said, her heart beating faster as she shrugged

the backpack off and dug through it for the serum. "Here it is."

Her hands shook as she passed it to Ronnie.

"It'll be okay, Paige," Ronnie said, squeezing her arm. "Come on. Let's go save your mom."

Paige offered her a slight smile and a nod before they set off down the hall toward Reed's room.

Her mother's heart monitor beeped rhythmically as she lay unmoving in the bed. Tears stung Paige's eyes as she stepped closer. "We got the medicine, Mom."

Her voice shook, and Devon wrapped an arm around her, squeezing her shoulder as Dewey wrapped a paw around her head.

A doctor swept into the room, and Ronnie passed the serum to her.

"All right, we'll administer this directly into the IV. With any luck, we should see some sign of response in a few hours."

After withdrawing the serum from the vial, the doctor injected it into the IV line. All eyes turned to Reed as they waited for any sign of recovery.

Paige wrapped her arms around herself, offering a silent prayer that they'd soon hear good news. But until then… they'd have a long, tedious wait.

CHAPTER 27

$\mathcal{P}$aige wiped her clammy hand against her pant leg before she slid her fingers through her moms again. It had barely been an hour, but so far, there was no change.

Her eyes burned from having already shed tears over not seeing a miraculous recovery. With a lick of her lips, she squeezed her mom's hand. "Come on, Mom. Just open your eyes."

"Paige," Ronnie's voice called softly.

She twisted to find the women in the doorway. "Eyva is here. She'd like to take a look at you both and see if she can get you fixed up."

Paige bobbed her head, her eyes returning to her mother.

"I can sit with her," Ronnie said, patting Paige on the shoulder.

"Thanks. I just...don't want to leave her. I mean, the serum could work at any minute to wake her up and– "

"You don't want her waking up alone. That's fair," Ronnie said. "I won't leave her."

"Thanks, Ronnie." Paige shifted her weight from foot to

foot as her fingers lingered on her mother's. "Probably better if you're here anyway."

"What do you mean?" Ronnie asked.

"She knows you. She'll recognize you. If she wakes up when I'm here…she wouldn't even know me."

Tears filled her eyes as she tried to think of how to explain to her mother that she was her thirty-something daughter.

"Aw, Paige, I think she'll know who you are…oh, well, I mean…after you're not in Drucinda's body. She'll also know Drucinda, so there's an upside to your current situation."

Paige huffed out a weak laugh. "Yeah, true. Except she'd be disappointed that her tough friend wasn't so tough inside anymore."

"I'm sure she's going to love you, Paige," Ronnie said. "She was so excited to have you. It's a shame you lost all that time together."

Paige heaved a sigh. "Well, we can't change it now, but hopefully we'll have a fresh start going forward."

Ronnie nodded as she eased into the chair next to Reed's bed.

"Well, I guess I'll get going and see if I can get my body back."

"Good luck," Ronnie said as Paige shuffled from the room.

Her heart pounded against her ribs as she made her way down to the lab. She knew it was still early, but there had been no sign of change with her mother's condition. Would the serum work?

At least she'd have some time to get swapped back into her real body. She couldn't imagine her mother's confusion waking up to find her daughter trapped inside her best friend's body.

She pushed through the door into the lab with a sigh, finding Drucinda, Eyva, Devon, and Dewey inside.

"There she is," Dewey said from his perch on Eyva's shoulder. "Now we can get to work."

"Yes. Oh, yes, I see, it's a perfect body swap, isn't it?"

"What do you mean?" Paige asked.

"I mean you've retained nothing of your own selves. No lingering eye color or freckles out of place."

"Thankfully," Drucinda answered as she crossed her arms. "My skin is flawless. I don't need it marred with your freckles."

"Oh, don't be a snob, Drucinda," Eyva said with a dismissive wave. "Her freckles are darling."

"Well, they can be darling with her stuck in this body and me in my own."

"All right, all right. Don't get your knickers into a twist, dear. I'll have you patched up in no time."

"Thank heavens. I cannot wait to have my muscle tone back. I've managed to hurt myself simply sitting in a chair."

"Oh, those chairs are killers," Paige answered. "There's no comfortable position."

"I have never had any trouble until now. Apparently, your body isn't accustomed to chairs."

Dewey clapped his paws together, rubbing them. "Now, you tell me what to do, Eyva, and I'll get it done. This is amazing to learn from a master."

"Don't mess it up and turn us into tigers," Paige warned.

Eyva's eyes went wide.

"Yes, he's done it before. Dewey manages to mess up his potions at every turn and do something insane to me like turn me into a puddle or a panther."

Evya chuckled. "Oh, that's incredible. We'll need to swap stories. Once, I turned a young man into a toad. He didn't take kindly to it."

"How's your mom?" Devon asked as Dewey and Eyva set to work on a potion.

"No change," Paige answered with a frown.

"Well, the doctor said it would take a few hours before anything happened, right?"

Paige let her gaze fall to the floor. "Yep. Still...I was hoping for some instantaneous thing to happen like in the movies."

Devon rubbed her arm. "Well, this isn't the movies. Plus, it gives us a chance to get you fixed."

"Yeah, I'm sure that would have been confusing. She wakes up thirty years in the future and finds her best friend in her daughter's body and vice-versa."

"Definitely," Drucinda answered. "I'd rather make this transition as easy as possible for her."

Paige bobbed her head, struggling to control the emotions whirling inside her.

"If it's any consolation," Drucinda said, "I, too, hoped for a miraculous change from the serum."

Paige offered her a weak smile, reaching for her arm to rub it.

"There's no need to get sentimental." Drucinda shrugged her off with a wrinkled nose.

"Sorry, I just...thought maybe we could be friends."

The woman shot her a narrow-eyed glance. "No."

"That's sort of harsh, Dru. I mean...we're friends, *and* you're friends with Paige's mom, so it feels like you two should be friends, too, by extension."

Drucinda arched an eyebrow. "I'll consider it. *After* Reed wakes up."

Paige heaved a sigh, sinking into the plastic chair against the wall. Her forehead creased. "Wow, this chair isn't nearly as uncomfortable in this body as it was in my normal one."

"I told you. There is something wrong with your body. It's…odd."

"There's nothing wrong with Paige's body," Devon answered with a wag of his finger. "That's body-shaming and it's not okay."

"What is this? An after-school special?" Drucinda asked.

"I'm just saying…"

Drucinda rolled her eyes before returning her gaze to Dewey and Eyva as they continued to work.

Dewey poured a heaping cup of purple powder into a green liquid. It exploded, sending a massive cloud into the air.

"Whoops," Eyva said. "I think I meant Delirium powder not Elirium powder. I never can keep those straight."

Paige's stomach twisted into a tight knot as she wondered what problem would befall her with those two creating the solution.

"Please don't mess this up," Drucinda said with a shake of her head. "I want to be normal again. I miss my form."

"Also, I don't want to be turned into something weird like a dog or a squirrel because I'd like to be normal when my mom wakes up."

"No way for that to happen, Paige," Dewey said with a shake of his head. "You're decidedly not normal."

Paige narrowed her eyes at him as Eyva chuckled. "It's not very fun to be normal," she said. "But we'll do our best not to turn you into any creatures."

"Thanks. I really appreciate that."

Devon patted her on the shoulder. "It'll be okay, Paige."

Dewey and Eyva continued their work as Paige drummed her fingers against her thigh, shifting around in seat as the minutes ticked by.

Her heart thudded dully against her ribs as she waited for the serum to be ready.

After twenty minutes, she popped up from her seat and paced the floor.

"You okay, Paige?"

"Yep, just…wondering how my mom is doing."

Devon checked his watch. "Well, probably not awake yet. The doctor said a few hours."

She nodded, her gaze stuck on the floor. "Yeah. Probably."

"This is nearly ready, Paige, so just give us a few more minutes and we'll have you back in your normal body."

"I don't understand how this is going to work," Paige said with a shake of her head. "We're both going to drink this and magically know which body to go into? I mean…should we clear the room so there's no confusion?"

Eyva slapped the counter with a laugh. "No, of course not. There's magic in there to make it work."

"Yeah…I'm not sure I trust magic."

"We put in a sample of your hair. The potion will know then," Eyva explained.

Paige's eyes went wide. "Wait…hair? Are you sure you got mine and Drucinda's? I saw this on Harry Potter once and that's how Hermione got turned into a cat."

Dewey rolled his eyes. "Lies. All lies. Why do you continue to believe this nonsense that you read in books?"

Paige crinkled her nose. "Because it makes just as much sense as believing that a magical potion is going to put me back in my body because of a strand of hair."

"I didn't get cat hair in the stupid potion, okay? It's fine. I didn't get her hair, my hair, or Devon's hair."

"Fine, fine. It's just that…your potion-making skills– "

"Are top-notch," Dewey interrupted with a glare. "Anyone who says otherwise doesn't know what they're talking about."

"Right, of course. You have saved my life before…with a few hiccups, but still…saved my life."

"Those hiccups were not my fault," Dewey shouted, flinging a paw toward her. A giant swath of green goo spattered across her clothes from the spatula he held. "Oops."

Paige shot him an unimpressed stare. "Thanks, Dewey."

"Oh, quiet. Let me finish mixing this so you can both ingest it and be fixed."

Paige grabbed a wad of paper towels and wiped at the mixture. "Sorry, your shirt is stained," she said to Drucinda.

"Please try not to do any more damage to me, will you?" Drucinda shot back.

"Okay, ladies," Dewey said with a grin as he buzzed toward them, "it's ready!"

He held a beaker out to each of them. "Bottoms up."

Paige wrapped her fingers around the glass, her nose wrinkling as she stared at the green goop.

"It's watermelon flavored," Dewey said. "Oh, also, you need to start drinking and finish drinking at precisely the exact same time, or this won't work."

Paige's jaw fell open. "What? That's going to be virtually impossible."

Dewey's lips shook as he tried to hold back a laugh before it burst from him.

Eyva joined in before raising a hand in the air for a high five. "Good one."

Dewey wiped a tear from his cheek before he waved a hand in the air. "Oh, I'm kidding. It doesn't matter. Just drink it and within like two minutes, you'll be back to your normal bodies."

Paige sucked in a deep breath before she clinked her glass against Drucinda's. "To being back in our own bodies."

"Can't happen soon enough." Drucinda pressed the beaker to her lips and chugged down the liquid.

Paige took a few swallows. "Okay, the texture is weird, but the taste isn't bad."

"I told you. I worked hard on that," Dewey said.

She polished off the serum and wiped at her lips. "Okay. Well, anytime now."

Dewey puckered his lips as they waited. Two minutes passed with nothing happening. Paige shifted her weight from foot to foot. "Okay, uhhh, it's been two minutes."

"Patience, Paige." Dewey shot her an irritated glance.

"Well, you said two minutes."

"It was a figure of speech, not an exact measurement." Dewey shook his head at her. "Humans."

"Hey, I can't help it. I'm still learning, but I'm—Whoa." Her lips tugged back into a frown as she reached out to grab onto the edge of the counter.

"What's happening?" Devon asked.

"Ohhhh, I feel…" Paige moaned.

"Like someone is ripping out my insides," Drucinda finished for her. "Uhhhh."

"That's about right," Eyva said. "This is *very* painful."

"Why didn't you warn us?" Drucinda croaked out before she dropped to her knees. "Ohhhh."

"Well, I didn't feel it was necessary," Eyva said. "It had to be done. There is nothing gained by telling you ahead of time so one or both of you could pitch a fit and refuse to drink it."

A pained groan escaped Paige as she hit the floor, too, curling into the fetal position. "Warning would have been nice."

"This is awful," Drucinda cried.

"Reminds me of the time I ate too much Mexican," Paige choked out.

She gritted her teeth as the pain ratcheted higher, blurring her vision.

"Try to breathe through it, Paige," Devon said.

"You breathe through it!" she snapped back.

"Wow, he's going to be really supportive during childbirth," Dewey said.

Eyva crossed her arms and shook her head as Paige writhed on the floor. "You know, in my day, women had their babies with a midwife and a handmaiden. There were no fathers holding their hands and whispering words of encouragement."

"You lived in the Stone Age, Eyva," Dewey said with a shrug. "Today, it's expected. Devon's going to have to step up his support system if he wants to be seen as a really supportive spouse and father."

Devon winced as he knelt next to Paige and rubbed her back, twisting his hands into fists. "Okay, Paige, I'm right here with you. I'm...trying my best to be supportive."

He flicked his gaze to Dewey.

"Better," Dewey said with a nod, "room for improvement."

"Shut up!" Paige shouted as she dug her fingers into her hair. Pain wracked her body as her vision began to darken on the edges.

She sucked in a deep breath, her chest tight. Her head swam, and the room spun. She squeezed her eyes closed before all her senses shut down entirely and she slipped away to unconsciousness.

CHAPTER 28

*P*aige's eyes fluttered open as she sucked in a breath to ease the burning in her lungs. Her vision, blurred and still spinning, couldn't focus. Noises around her warbled instead of making any coherent sense.

She blinked a few times, desperately trying to regain her senses. Blobs flitted around the room as a dull ache formed at her temples.

She groaned, rolling onto her side and squeezing her eyes closed. "Paige?" a garbled voice cut through the din.

"Ugh," she groaned.

She opened her eyes, twisting onto her back. Devon knelt across the room, rubbing Drucinda's back. "It's okay, sweetie. I'm right here with you?"

Paige crinkled her features. "Devon?"

He snapped his gaze to her, his eyebrows shooting up. "Paige?"

"Yeah," she answered as she held her hands in front of her. "Am I back in my body?"

"That you are, Paige," Dewey said with a raise of his chin. "And no ill side effects either."

Devon winced, rising and hurrying over to her. "It's okay, sweetie. I'm right here with you."

"Devon?" Paige's voice called from across the room.

Devon shifted his gaze back to Drucinda. "Wait…"

Dewey gasped, a paw flying up to cover his mouth.

"Ugh, I'm still stuck in Drucinda's body, I guess," second Paige said as she covered her eyes with her hands.

"Uhhhhh…." Dewey snapped his gaze to Eyva, his eyes wide.

"Wait…stop playing games," Paige said. "I'm back in my body. You must be Drucinda."

"I'm not Drucinda," second Paige answered. "I'm Paige."

"You are not," Paige said, scrambling to her feet and poking a finger at Drucinda's form. "I'm Paige. I'm the only Paige."

"Well, I am also Paige, so here we are."

Paige crossed her arms. "Oh, yeah? Prove it. What's my favorite pizza topping?"

"Pepperoni." The second Paige crossed her arms.

"That's too easy. What's my favorite…" Paige rubbed her chin. "Uh…"

"What did I call you that one time we got stuck in the creepy werewolf mansion dungeon and you lost your glasses?" Dewey asked.

"Velma," second Paige answered.

Dewey's jaw flopped open. "OMG. There are two Paige's."

"And no Drucindas," Devon said as he flicked his gaze between them. "So, umm, this is kind of awkward but… which one of you am I married to?"

"Me!" they answered simultaneously.

"Does it matter?" Paige asked. "Why are there two of me and none of Drucinda? Where is Drucinda?"

She glanced around the room in search of some sign of the woman. A cat rubbed against her legs, meowing.

Paige glanced down, her eyes lighting up. "Dickens!"

She scooped up the cat and held it close to her.

"Try again, idiot," the cat answered in a British accent.

Paige stared at the animal. "You can talk now?"

"No, moron, Dickens can't talk. It's me. It's Drucinda."

A boisterous chuckle escaped from Eyva. "Oh, Drucinda. What are you doing inside that kitty's body. Naughty girl, get back into your own."

"If I had a choice, I would have picked my own. Paige is hogging up both. I had no choice but to take over the cat for a time."

"Well…where is Dickens?"

"He's sharing with me, though I'm not exactly giving him much choice. Will you please remove the second Paige so I can flit back over to my own body?"

"Sure thing, Drickens, but the thing is, I don't know how," Dewey answered.

"Did you just refer to us collectively as Drickens?" Drucinda asked.

"I did," Dewey said with a nod.

The cat heaved a sigh, its ears plastered against its head. "Grandmother, do something."

"Would if I could, but I have no idea why she's multiplied." Eyva tapped a finger against her chin. "Fascinating, really. She's literally kept one body and returned to her original one."

"Hmmm," Dewey said. "Maybe it's a ghost left in the other body."

"Oh, could be, yes," Eyva answered.

"You said there are no such things as ghosts," Paige retorted.

"In the traditional sense, no," Dewey answered, "but in this instance, there's a ghost of your soul still stuck in Drucinda."

"We may need to exorcise it out," Eyva proposed.

"Whoa, whoa, that sounds terrible. Don't do that."

"Of course, you'd say that you body hog," Drucinda snapped. "We wouldn't need to if you'd learned to share in kindergarten."

"I know how to share. But this sounds... dangerous. I don't want to end up in the outer ring of Hell after this."

"Mmm, I doubt it would be the outer ring you'd end up in, but there's always hope," Dewey answered. "I haven't done an exorcism before, have you?"

"Oh, many of them, yes," Eyva said with a nod. "We can pull this off if you'll assist me."

"I'd love to," Dewey said with a grin.

"Could you two stop being so giddy over this?" Paige asked. "I'm genuinely afraid of losing a part of myself."

Dewey waved a dismissive paw in the air. "Oh, stop worrying. It's a simple procedure."

"Simple procedure?" Paige cried. "Dewey, you said you had no idea how to do it."

"I don't. But from what I understand it's a simple procedure."

Paige pressed her lips together, shaking her head.

"Just let them do it. I would very much like to return to my body. I've got a strong urge to clean myself, and I'd prefer not to."

Paige patted the cat on the head. "Sorry, Drucinda. I just...don't want anything else bad to happen. And this feels like a disaster. I mean, how did I split in two to begin with?"

"The most likely reason was fear. You were afraid to leave the other body and go to your new one, so you literally tore yourself in half trying to accommodate both things."

Paige wrinkled her nose. "That doesn't sound right. I mean, I'm not *that* much of a scaredy cat."

"Mmm, you're sort of afraid, Paige. You were always afraid of me. And I'm such a nice guy," Devon said.

"You tried to...never mind. Never mind. That's in the past. Okay, proceed. There...how's that for being brave?"

"False bravery is stupidity," Dewey answered, a claw poking in the air.

Paige frowned at him. "Okay, so what do you want? Bravery or stupidity? You can't have both."

"Silence," Eyva said. "You must be quiet so we can proceed with the exorcism."

Paige held up a hand, indicating her compliance as she pressed her lips together. Her stomach twisted into a tight knot, and she chewed her lower lip until it threatened to bleed as Eyva stretched her arms out to the sides.

The woman raised her eyes to the heavens, her features twisting.

Paige winced. "This looks intense."

Eyva returned to her normal posture. "Sorry, just stretching my back."

Paige shifted her weight, her features returning to a disenchanted frown. "I thought that was the start of it."

Devon wrapped an arm around her, squeezing her shoulder. "Try to relax, babe. It should be over soon."

Eyva approached Drucinda's form, eyeing her from head to toe as Paige's heart thudded faster. She sucked in a breath holding it.

Eyva grabbed hold of Drucinda's shoulders and gave her a shake. "Paige's ghost...get out of this body now!"

She raised a hand and slapped Drucinda's body across the cheek. "Now!"

She twisted to Dewey. "Your turn."

He grinned and rubbed his paws together. "Oh, gee. Okay."

"Give her a good slap on the other cheek."

"Oh, leftie. Got it. Okay." Dewey raised his paw and cracked Drucinda's other cheek. "Leave this body now."

A blue-green haze poured from Drucinda's ears, dispersing into the air before it reformed into a tight ball and shot toward Paige, disappearing up her nose.

"Oh," Paige said with a wrinkled nose. "Why is it always up the nose? That is so uncomfortable. Ugh."

She pinched the bridge of her nose, squeezing her eyes closed.

"Oh, good. Yes," Drucinda said as her body sprang to life, her voice matching her form again. "I'm back. Thank heavens."

Paige fluttered her eyelashes, waiting for the burning sensation in her nostrils to die down. "That's it?"

"That's it," Evya said. "I told you…a simple procedure."

"Wow, I thought it would be so much more involved. I mean…when you said exorcism…"

"I didn't mean some sort of Hellbeast," Eyva answered. "Simply a stubborn part of your spirit that needed a bit of coaxing."

"You could have just said that instead of scaring the wits out of me."

"I don't think those were your wits, Paige," Dewey answered.

Paige heaved a sigh as she stroked the cat still in her arms. "Never mind. Let's just…move on. We're finally back to normal, and now maybe we'll have some good news with my mom."

"Should we head back to her room?" Devon asked.

"Yeah," Paige said with a nod. "I'd really like to be there when she wakes up."

Leaving Eyva behind to toy with a few potions, the rest of them headed for Reed's room, finding Ronnie still sitting quietly at her bedside.

"Any change?" Paige asked, her voice low as they crept into the room.

"Not yet," Ronnie answered, giving up her seat to Paige. "Looks like you got everything sorted out on your end?"

"We did. Thanks. I was hoping to find her awake."

"The doctor was in to assess her. She should be in at any moment with the results of her tests. Let's hope it's good news," Ronnie said.

Paige bobbed her head, threading her fingers through Devon's as they awaited the news.

Only the rhythmic beeping of the heart monitor split the silence stretching between them until the doctor shuffled in.

"How do the tests look?" Paige asked, a note of hope filling her voice.

The doctor offered them a sympathetic smile. "I'm very sorry to tell you that…it doesn't look like the serum is working at all."

Paige's chest tightened at the words, her heart plummeting. "What?"

"Perhaps we haven't given it enough time," Drucinda suggested.

The doctor shook her head. "No. If that serum was going to work, we would have at least seen some improvement in her numbers, but…we're actually seeing a decrease."

"The serum made her worse?" Paige asked, choking back a sob.

"No," the doctor answered. "Not worse. She's…deteriorating at the same speed she was before it. The serum has had no effect whatsoever."

Paige's features twisted as tears filled her eyes. Devon rubbed her back as the news sank in around the room.

"So…is there something else we should try?" Paige asked through sobs.

"I'm very sorry to say that at this point...it would take a miracle."

Paige's lower lip trembled as she broke down in tears with Devon doing his best to comfort her. Dewey landed on her shoulder, patting her head. "Really sorry, Paige."

"I know I've given you a lot of information, but at this point, we should talk about comfort measures for her," the doctor said.

Ronnie gave a soft click of her tongue. "Can you give us a minute?"

"Of course," the doctor said with a nod before she excused herself from the room.

Paige struggled to control the sadness threatening to overwhelm her.

Devon continued to rub at her back.

She finally lost the battle, throwing herself over her mother's limp body as she wept. Drucinda flicked a tear away from her cheek, crossing her arms tightly as she chewed her lower lip.

Paige cried until no more tears would come. Across the room, Ronnie whispered to Drucinda and Devon. Her husband bobbed his head before he strode toward her.

Devon leaned closer, brushing a lock of hair away from her face. "Paige, honey, why don't we step outside and get some air."

"No," she sobbed. "I don't want to leave her."

"I know," Devon said. "But I think the doctors need to do some things to make your mom more comfortable. And then we'll come back, okay?"

The words "make her comfortable" brought a fresh round of tears. "How could this happen? How could we find her and then lose her like this?"

Dewey patted Paige's head. "I don't know what to say, Paige. It stinks."

"It does," Devon agreed. "Dewey and I agree on that. It's awful. But...you don't want your mom suffering, right?"

"No," Paige said, covering her face with her hands to steady herself.

She finally pulled them away with a shaky sigh. "Okay, you're right. Let the doctors do whatever they need to do."

Ronnie pressed her lips together as she bobbed her head and stepped to the door. A few minutes later, the doctor entered with a nurse.

She offered Paige a consoling smile again. "So, your mom is currently deteriorating, and we expect that to begin to pick up speed."

Paige sniffed as she rose, her wobbly knees doing less to hold her than Devon's strong arms around her. "So, she's going to go downhill fast?"

"We do expect that to happen, yes. This could be hours from now, it could be days from now. We don't think it'll be much longer than that."

Paige licked her lips, rubbing at her red nose. "Hours to days, right."

"In terms of comfort measures, we'd just like to establish a plan you're comfortable with. Once she begins to deteriorate, would you like us to perform life-saving measures to keep her alive as long as possible, or no?"

Paige's features twisted. "Uhhh, it won't...it won't bring her back, right?" A tear slid down her cheek.

"No," the doctor said. "It won't."

"Okay, then...no." Paige gulped back a sob as Devon rubbed her shoulder.

"Okay, so we'll just need some signatures to process her as a do-not-resuscitate so the care team is aware of that when the time comes. Given that choice, when she begins to slip away, it may be painful. I would recommend we use morphine to make her passing easy."

Paige nodded, swallowing hard, but failing to clear the lump in her throat. "How will we know?"

"We'll know," the doctor said. "We're going to continue to monitor her organ function and vitals. We'll start to see organ shut down, and as soon as we do, we'll begin to administer the morphine."

Paige slid her burning eyes closed as she nodded again. Devon pressed a kiss to the top of her head.

"If you wouldn't mind stepping out to sign the papers…" the doctor prompted.

Paige opened her eyes as Devon guided her from the room to the desk outside. Paige's hand shook as she scrawled her signature across the form, sniffling and wiping at her cheeks.

Devon pulled her into a tight embrace as she finished the last one, and she buried her face in his chest. "I know it hurts, Paige, but you did everything you could."

"I want to sit with her," Paige murmured.

"Of course," Devon said with a nod. "I'll stay with you, too."

"Thanks." She threaded her fingers through his, and they headed back into her mother's room. Drucinda vacated the chair by the bed.

"If you want to sit there, it's okay," Paige said.

Drucinda shook her head. "No, it's your mum, you should sit with her."

Paige gave her a shaky smile as she crossed to her backpack on the windowsill.

"I've got some tissues here if you need more," Drucinda offered.

"No, I…I want to play this music box that I got from Althea. I thought maybe somehow it would comfort her." Paige's shoulders slumped. "It's probably stupid."

"No," Drucinda answered. "No, it's not. I think that's a lovely idea, Paige. I'm sure Reed would like it very much."

Paige tugged the wooden box from within the bag and shuffled to the bedside table, setting it on top and opening the lid.

Tinkling music filled the air as Paige sank into the chair and took her mother's cool hand into hers.

Paige studied Reed's face, peaceful at the moment, as she settled in to watch her mother die.

CHAPTER 29

*D*evon's hand swiping across her back did little to comfort her as Paige counted her mother's heart beats, wondering which one would be the last.

As she sat back in her seat, using another tissue to wipe away her tears, the doctor quietly slid into the room.

"We're just going to grab some blood to see where we're at, okay? Did you want to step out?"

"No," Paige said with a wave of her hand. "No, I'll be okay, go ahead."

The doctor bobbed her head as she slid a needle into Reed's elbow and drew out two vials of blood.

"How long until you have the results?"

"Shouldn't be long, and I'll let you know as soon as we have them where we're at."

"Thanks," Paige said with a nod.

The music box's song died down, and she reached to wind it again. "Do you think she's getting close?"

"We'll know soon, Paige," Devon said with a pat on her shoulder.

Paige flicked her gaze to Dewey. "You're probably starving."

He offered her a weak grin. "I couldn't eat. I'd like to stay to support you."

"Wow," she said with a chuckle mixed with a sob, "you turning down food. What has the world come to?"

"Right?" he asked with a weak laugh.

Silence stretched between them as the heart monitor continued to beep rhythmically. Paige chewed on her thumbnail as she waited for the test results, wondering if it would be time or if they'd have another few hours of a reprieve from it.

Finally, footsteps approached the room, and Paige's heart ramped up, thudding against her ribs.

The doctor entered the room, flipping through the papers in the file.

Paige held her breath, waiting for the results.

"How does it look, doctor?" Devon asked.

The doctor's brow furrowed, and she licked her lips. "Ahh…"

Paige's gut twisted, and she pressed her teeth together to stop her lower lip from trembling. "It's time, isn't it?"

"Uh, no, I'm very sorry to have given you that impression. It's…just…I'd like to repeat the test. Something is off with these results."

"Off?" Drucinda asked.

The doctor bobbed her head. "Yes. Off. These numbers… well, they've improved and there is no way that should be happening."

Paige's eyes widened. "Improved? Could the serum be working?"

"The serum has already left her system. There's no evidence of it in her bloodstream. That's what's even more puzzling. She had no reaction to it, but now...well, inexplicably, she is improving."

Paige glanced at her mother, her eyebrows furrowing.

"So, I'd like to repeat the test, so we have a clear idea of what's happening here."

"Yes, of course," Paige said with a bob of her head. "Yes, please do it."

The doctor set the chart aside and proceeded with another blood sample collection.

As she left the room, Paige let her gaze scan the others. "Well, do you think there's any hope?"

"Miracles do happen, Paige," Ronnie said with a nod. "So, let's hope the doctor comes back with good news."

Devon rubbed her shoulder. "Yeah, we're all hoping for that."

"But...you think it's just a flawed test," she said, studying the doubt in his eyes.

"No, no," Devon said with a shake of his head. "Let's just wait and see."

Paige paced the length of the room as they waited for the second test results to come back. After another thirty minutes, the doctor strolled back into the room.

"Well? Did this one show anything different?" Paige asked, breathless.

"No," the doctor answered. "No, it was the same. Actually, that's not true. She was even more improved than she had been before. At this point...I'd say there may be a chance that she wakes up."

"What would be the reasoning for the about face?" Drucinda asked.

The doctor shrugged, her eyelashes fluttering. "I...don't know. This is highly unexpected and unusual. There's no reason her numbers should be improving. But we'll check back in a few hours and see where we're at."

Paige chewed her lower lip as she stared at her mother. "Are you trying to come back to us?"

They spent the next several hours pacing, taking turns at Reed's bedside, and finally ordering food to keep them sustained. As they ate, the doctor reappeared, taking another vial of blood for tests.

When she returned, her features were pinched. "This time she's had a bit of a setback. Not much, but she has slid backward again."

Paige's shoulders slumped as she set her takeout container aside. "Come on, Mom. You've got to fight."

"So, could the last set of numbers have been a rally before...you know?" Drucinda asked.

The doctor sucked in a breath. "It could have been her body's last ditch effort to climb out of this. We'll keep monitoring her to see."

Paige eased into the chair next to her mother, sliding her hand around Reed's. "Come on, Mom. You can pull out of this."

"Keep talking to her, Paige. Maybe she hears you. Maybe that's what she's responding to."

Paige's forehead creased. "Maybe she likes the music box."

With a sniffle, Paige rose and twisted the knob, allowing the lilting music to fill the air again.

The tinkling sound continued to play until the doctor returned for the next blood draw.

"Does it look like she has more color in her cheeks?" Paige asked as they waited for the results.

"Maybe," Dewey answered. "Could be a little rosier."

Drucinda shifted her weight. "Hard to say. Let's hope the test results show a clear direction."

The doctor strode into the room with the printouts in hand. "Well, we have another improvement. A big one, this time. I have no idea what's causing this, but it looks like we're trending in the positive direction."

Paige's heart filled with hope at the news. "Come on, Mom. You can do this."

Ronnie shuffled over to the bedside table, glancing at the music box. "Where did you get this?"

"Oh, uh, from a woman named Althea. She gave it to me and said her granddaughter didn't care for it."

Ronnie lifted it, studying it before she glanced at the bottom side, gasping.

"What is it?" Drucinda asked.

Ronnie flashed the underside of the music box at them, her finger tapping a red stamp.

"Is that…"

"Wow," Devon said, running a hand through his hair.

"What? What am I missing?" Paige asked.

Dewey's jaw fell open as he poked a claw at it. "That, my dear Paige, is a Harmonia Enchanted music box."

"Okay?" she asked.

Dewey's shoulders slumped as he shook his head. "Sometimes, Paige, sometimes."

"It's a brand of magical music boxes crafted by Edwin Harmonia, a master of weaving magic and music," Drucinda answered. "His music boxes can do everything from soothe a broken heart to…"

"Heal someone," Devon said.

"Heal someone?" Paige repeated, her eyes going wide as they fell onto her mother. "Do you think…"

"It certainly explains the numbers," Drucinda answered.

Ronnie twisted the screw and set the music box on the table. "Which means we need to keep this playing. It's healing her."

Paige's heart skipped a beat at the words. "Really?"

"We can only hope," Ronnie answered. "Let's hope this is the miracle we've been waiting for."

Paige wrapped her arms around her midriff as she stared at her mother, hope filling her heart again, though it was tempered with a twinge of disbelief.

After everything they'd been through, would a magical music box, one given to her by chance, really be the answer to her prayers?

"Wow, we really hit it lucky with that lady giving us that music box, huh?" Dewey said. "I mean, what are the odds?"

"Well, if we're book characters–" Devon said.

"Please stop with that nonsense," Drucinda answered with a sigh and a shake of her head.

"What?" Ronnie asked, her nose crinkling.

Paige slid into the chair next to her mother's bed as the music box tinkled along. "Dewey thinks we're all characters in a book. Like our lives are controlled by some puppeteer author."

Ronnie furrowed her brow. "Why do you think that, Dewey?"

"Because when we went into the Shadow Slayers book, one of the characters had a book with a cover that eerily resembled Paige with a tiny teal dragon perched on her shoulder that looked nothing like me, but close enough, if you know what I mean."

He fluttered into the air. "A quick glance through the first few chapters painted a picture frighteningly similar to the circumstances under which Paige and I first met."

Ronnie's lips parted as she stared at Dewey. "I don't know what to say about this. I don't feel like a book character."

"Well, that's the thing…neither do the Shadow Slayers. They insist they are real. They balk at the very notion that they are merely puppets in a show," Dewey said.

"Huh," Ronnie muttered. "That's...well, we'll look into it. See if we can find a creator portal or something."

Paige wrinkled her nose. "Really? You actually believe this?"

"No," Ronnie said with a chuckle and a shake of her head. "No, but...I mean, anything is possible."

Paige let her gaze fall on the music box. "I guess we just traveled into fictional worlds and brought back a magical music box, so who knows."

Her fingers curled into fists. "But if this is true...I mean... how dare this woman manipulate our lives like this."

Devon's hands fell onto her shoulders, giving them a quick rub. "I don't know. I'm kind of happy with the result."

"Of course, you are, Lover Boy. You were the roguish hero that all the women are swooning over."

Devon offered him a dimpled grin. "That's sort of awesome if it's true."

"If we're book characters, Paige is the quirky, klutzy yet lovable main character, I, of course, am the snarky, wise, lovable, awesome, show-stealing side kick. Devon is the hunky love interest, and Drucinda is– "

"I'd argue I'm the show-stealing...wait, I'm not a sidekick. I'm just the show-stealer period."

"Show-stealing? I mean maybe I'm just...the show."

The others in the room exchanged glances before they burst into laughter.

Dewey fluttered over and settled onto her shoulder, patting her on the head. "It's okay, Paige. But that's definitely not the truth."

Paige shifted in her seat, her features pinched. "Whatever."

"Oh, come on, Paige. I'm sure people like you, too. But... some of us just...are built to be the stars."

"Oh, really? Then why didn't Nellie write you as the main character? Or Drucinda?"

"The books wouldn't have been nearly as entertaining without all your stupidity, that's why. She's probably a comedy writer."

"So, you're admitting that I'm more entertaining than you," Paige answered.

"Obviously not. If she wrote about me, they would be taut, gripping thrillers, though my uncanny ability to excel at everything may have made it a bit dull."

Drucinda waved a hand in the air. "Picture it. Would cliffhangers even work in a chapter end? Drucinda facing certain death? Readers would laugh. Drucinda would never face certain death. She'd easily battle her way out. Therefore, the thrillers wouldn't be quite as thrilling."

"But you," she continued, "well, readers definitely would turn pages to see if you're going to live because there's a good chance you'd die."

"Well, I'm still living."

"Thanks to Nellie's good graces," Dewey answered. "Let's hope she likes your mom, too."

Paige heaved a sigh as Ronnie spoke. "Let's put a moratorium on the 'we're book characters' discussion and file it away for later. We should focus our energy on Reed."

"Right," Dewey said with a nod. "Definitely."

"How long until the next check?" Drucinda asked.

Ronnie glanced at her watch. "Should be within the hour."

They waited, tension filling the room, until the doctor drew more blood for another check. When she returned, she stepped into the room, grinning. "Things are looking good. With the progress she's making, I…I don't want to get your hopes up too high, but I'd expect to see her wake up in a few hours."

Paige grabbed Devon's hand, squeezing it as her heart thudded against her ribs.

"That's great news," Ronnie said with a grin. "We'll keep our fingers crossed."

"We really can't explain it but– "

Ronnie held up a finger with a grin. "I think we can."

She skirted around Paige's chair and held up the music box. "This is a Harmonia music box. This could be healing her."

The doctor's jaw unhinged as she leaned forward to study it. "It well could be. If she does awaken, would you mind if we took a closer look at that music box? It could be very useful."

"Of course," Ronnie said, sliding it back onto the table. "But for now…it stays right here."

The doctor nodded. "Let's hope it continues to help her."

As the doctor left the room, Paige twisted back to her mother, grabbing her hand. "Come on, Mom, just a little more fight."

She rubbed her arm for encouragement as her muscles tensed. Every breath her mother took was one step closer to her waking.

They waited for over an hour before Paige gasped. "I think she moved. I think she moved her finger."

"I'll grab the doctor," Ronnie said, hurrying from the room.

Paige's heart hammered out a frenetic beat against her ribs as she stared expectantly at her mother, hoping to see some change.

The heart monitor ratcheted up, the spikes coming faster and faster.

Paige rose from her seat, her hand clutching Reed's. "Mom?"

Paige glanced at the monitor again, wishing the doctor

would arrive soon. She wasn't certain the latest developments were good news or not.

"Reed?" Drucinda asked. "Are you trying to come back. Open your eyes, darling."

Drucinda stroked Reed's red hair as she clutched her other hand.

Seconds later, Reed's eyelids slowly slid open. She stared at the ceiling unmoving as Paige's heart skipped a beat. Was her mother finally awake?

CHAPTER 30

"*M*om?" Paige whispered, trying to hold back tears as her mother lay staring at the ceiling but virtually unresponsive in every other way.

"Reed?" Drucinda said. "Darling, can you hear us?"

Reed's eyes finally shifted to the side, following Drucinda's voice. Her features pinched as she focused on the Valkyrie's face. "Dru?"

Drucinda broke into a teary-eyed smile as she nodded. "It's me, yep."

Reed huffed out a breath, her own eyes turning glassy as she stared at her. "I'm awake. I'm alive."

"Yes, you are both, darling. And it was hard fought." Drucinda sniffled, wiping a tear away quickly.

"Did you rescue me?" Reed asked, her voice shaky.

Paige bit into her lower lip, trying to hold back a sob. Her mother had finally awoken, but she latched immediately on to her best friend. Of course, she had no idea who Paige even was. She had no reason to be excited to see her. She didn't even know her.

She tried to take solace in the fact that her mother was

awake, and that she was talking. And also, that she seemed comforted by having her friend, Drucinda, at her side.

Paige took a step back, suddenly wanting to be anywhere but there when Drucinda answered Reed's question.

"No, darling, I didn't. That credit goes to someone very special. Someone I think you'll want to meet."

"Ronnie?" Reed questioned, her eyes searching Drucinda's face.

Drucinda shook her head, motioning toward Paige. "No, darling. Your daughter, Paige."

Reed's gaze shifted, her forehead pinching as she focused on Paige.

Paige pressed her lips together, raising a shaky hand in a wave. "Hi."

Reed's jaw hung open as she stared at her, her features pinching. "Paige? My baby!"

She reached for her, an exclamation of surprise and relief escaping her as she pulled Paige closer, hugging her tightly. "Oh, my little baby."

"Your little baby is all grown up, darling. And she's turned out to be quite a woman. She's not only single-handedly fought off werewolves, but she's also fought so very hard to find you and bring you home."

"And also to find a cure for your twilight trance," Devon added, clapping Paige on the shoulder as she rose and wiped at her wet cheeks.

"Devon?" Reed asked, her eyes wide as she spotted him.

"Hey, Reed. It's really good to see you awake."

Reed shifted in the bed, struggling to sit up.

"What do you need?" Drucinda asked.

"To sit up. And to know what Devon LeBlanc is doing in a library-owned hospital facility." She glanced at Drucinda. "Oh, please don't tell me you married him."

Paige tugged her lips into a wince, her nose wrinkling.

"Not me, darling. I am and always will be a free agent."
Drucinda used the buttons to raise the bed before adjusting
Reed's pillow.

"Then…"

Devon gave her a dimpled grin. "Mom."

"What?!" Reed's heart rate shout through the roof as she
glanced at Paige, slapping a palm against her wrist. "How did
this happen? Drucinda, how could you let this happen? You
let my child marry Dominic Durand's son!"

"Wow, that ramped up quickly," Dewey said as he landed
on Paige's shoulder. "Look, lady, no one made Paige do
anything. Devon very cleverly manipulated the entire situation so Paige would marry him but because he's rich, it's
okay."

Reed furrowed her brows as she stared at him. "Who are
you?"

"Dewey Decimael, Paige's archivist."

"You're a librarian?" Reed asked. "And what do you mean
because he's rich, it's okay?"

Dewey slid his eyes sideways. "If he's rich, manipulation
is romance. If he's poor, it's a psychological thriller. Everyone
knows this."

Reed screwed up her face as the doctor rushed into the
room, her eyes wide.

"You're awake."

"Yes, but it seems like I'm too late to have prevented
tragedy."

"That's a little much. I really love Paige," Devon said.

"Maybe another time," Paige said to him.

"Definitely another time," the doctor answered. "Would
you mind clearing out while we examine her?"

"Must we?" Drucinda asked.

"I'm afraid so. I know it's very hard since she's just woken up, but we really do want to ensure her health and be certain she stays this way."

Paige's lower lip trembled as she considered leaving the room.

"Come on, Paige," Devon said softly, gently tugging her back. "Let's let the doctor's do their work so we can get back in here."

She pressed her lips together, trying to hold back the tears forming as she nodded and allowed him to lead her from the room.

They shuffled into the hall, and Devon wrapped her in his arms, but she remained stiff.

Ronnie approached them, her face questioning.

"She's awake and talking," Drucinda said.

"And disappointed in me," Paige answered with a sob.

"What?" Ronnie asked.

"No, darling. She's just…still trying to get acclimated to what's going on. She's missed over thirty years of your life," Drucinda said with a rub of Paige's shoulder.

"Yeah, she'll totally get over it once she realizes you're a rich princess," Dewey said with a pat on Paige's head.

Paige's features melted, and she covered her face with her hands.

"Reed was a little…surprised at Paige's choice in husband's," Drucinda explained.

"Ohhhh," Ronnie murmured with a lift of her chin. "Things when Reed went missing were really different, Paige. She'll come around."

Paige chewed her lower lip, offering them a bob of her head.

"You have to remember that she's been out of the world for decades. She doesn't know what's happened recently. It will take time."

"She seemed happy to see you," Paige said to Drucinda.

"Of course, she was. We were best friends. She was happier to see you, though. Her little baby that she never got a chance to raise."

"I feel like a disappointment to her."

"No," everyone hurried to say.

"Paige, look at how far you've come. You're a successful librarian. You're a princess. You have the best partner ever. And...you're about to be the main character in a best-selling paranormal romance, so...you've really made it," Dewey said.

Paige laughed a little through her tears. "Yeah, you're right. You're the best part of me."

"Yeah," Dewey said with a nod. "She ought to be proud of you for partnering with me alone."

The doctor exited from Reed's room a moment later, making notes on the chart. "So, everything looks good on the initial exam. We're going to run a battery of tests on her starting with blood work. But for now, you can visit with her. She may nod off a few times, though, don't be alarmed."

Paige sucked in a shaky breath as she nodded. "Okay, thanks for the warning. I'll probably panic the first time she falls asleep."

"I know," the doctor said with a nod. "But her body has been through a lot, and she needs rest. We'll continue to monitor her, though I don't see her slipping back into a coma anytime soon."

"Thanks, doctor," Ronnie said.

"Well, should we all head back in?" Paige asked. "I'm sure she wants to see everyone."

"I'm certain she wants to see you, but I'd like to go in," Drucinda said as Ronnie nodded.

"For a little while, if you don't mind, Paige," Ronnie added.

"Mind? I don't mind at all. I want her to see all of her old friends. I think it will be good for her. Comforting."

"Paige, I can wait out here if you prefer. I don't want to upset your mom or you."

"That may be…" Paige glanced up at him, her mind racing with all of the details of how he'd helped her find her mother and save her. She'd told him she loved him. Was it fair to exclude him now?

She shook her head. "No. No, you played a big role in my mom being found and recovering. And we're married. She'll have to accept that."

He offered her a soft smile. "Yeah, but she doesn't need it shoved in her face right now. I'm totally fine hanging out in the waiting room."

"Just to be clear," Dewey said, "I am not cool waiting in the waiting room and would like to head inside whether your mom likes it or not. Just because she's been in a magical coma doesn't make her any more special than anyone else."

Paige furrowed her brow. "Uh, okay, yeah, you can go in. And Devon, you can go in, too. Like I said, you were a huge part of finding her, and I think she needs to know that."

Devon's smile broadened as he wrapped his arm around her. "Okay. And thanks. I'd really rather support you than be stuck in the waiting room."

"Okay, with that settled, let's head in. Also, maybe order a snack. Your mom is probably hungry, and so am I."

Paige chuckled as he buzzed toward the door. "Okay, buddy. We'll get you a snack."

They followed Paige to the room. She poked her head in with a tentative smile. "Hi, Mom, how are you feeling?"

"Like a pin cushion," she said as she stared at the bruises on her arms from the blood draws. "But happy to be alive."

"We're very happy about that too," Ronnie said with a tentative grin.

"Ronnie!" Reed answered, breaking into a wide smile as she stretched her arms toward the woman.

Ronnie skirted past Paige to hug Reed. "Oh, it's so good to see you alive and awake."

"I never thought I'd make it back."

"What did happen?" Drucinda asked.

"Maybe we shouldn't push her," Paige said.

Reed glanced at Paige, her eyes falling on Devon's arm around Paige. "It may be best that this be kept in a stricter confidence, but I should give someone a statement before it's too late."

"Too late?" Ronnie asked.

"I hope it's not too late. I really need some breadsticks or something. I'm fading fast," Dewey said.

"We'll get you some food, bud," Paige said.

"I don't think she means too late to eat," Ronnie answered with a frown.

"I don't. There is something big going on, and I don't have all the details but...we need to stop it before it changes the world forever," Reed warned.

"Changes the world forever?" Paige repeated.

Reed's eyes fixed on her before they slid toward Devon. "I can't say now. I can't..."

"Okay, wait. I'm sorry, but...Mom, I feel really bad saying this given that we basically just met but Devon has been a big part of making sure we found you and saved your life. You wouldn't be here if it hadn't been for him stepping up. And I think it's really unfair that you're judging him based on decades-old information."

"Devon LeBlanc comes from a dangerous family who will use whatever methods they can to dominate the supernatural food chain. On top of that, he's a notorious playboy."

"Hey," Devon said with a shake of his head, "I may be popular with the ladies but I'm *not* a playboy, and I'm definitely true blue to Paige."

"Devon's right, Reed. Plus, a lot has changed since you've

been gone. The Durands are still dominating things, but better them than whatever has been going on with Higgins."

Reed shook her head. "Drucinda, you have never understood. Coming from the family you've been born into, your views have always differed from mine."

Drucinda crossed her arms. "With all due respect, friend, you have been out of the game for over thirty years."

"And the Durands haven't morphed into good people."

"The Durands are the only reason you're here," Drucinda shot back. "Devon, whom you are so quick to judge, has protected your daughter at every turn and provided her with the means to find you. Dominic gave her a soul compass when she married Devon."

"Look, Mom–" Devon said.

"Please, don't," Reed answered with a shake of her head. "That's…just Reed is fine. I mean…you delivered my baby on the side of the road, so Mom sounds strange."

Reed's eyes fell to her lap. "And then you married her. Oh…wow."

"We've already had this conversation, Reed," Dewey said. "We even speculated that Devon could be Paige's dad. It got super weird from there, but…since he's not, it's all okay."

Reed wrinkled her nose at him. "And you're Paige's partner, right?"

"That's me. Dewey. Partner extraordinaire. Paige and I have been through some situations, let me tell you." Dewey chuckled as he patted Paige on the head. "And if you think she's awkward now…you should have seen her with her glasses before Eyva fixed her vision."

"Paige was cute in glasses, come on, man," Devon answered.

"Please stop talking," Paige said with a shake of her head.

"I'm sorry," Drucinda interjected. "This conversation has gone well off topic. Can we get back to the whole world-changing bit? You know...the thing we have to stop before it's too late?"

"Right," Paige said, her stomach churning again. "If there's something that's a threat, we should address it. And Devon can be trusted."

"Paige is right," Ronnie said. "Devon's been working with the library. Anything you tell me is probably going to get to his ears anyway. Paige trusts him, Drucinda trusts him, I trust him."

"Dewey also trusts him. Why was Dewey left out of that equation?" Dewey asked.

"Well...she doesn't know you. She knows us."

"She doesn't *really* know Paige," Dewey argued with a shrug.

Ronnie shot him a wide-eyed glance. "Look, anyway, if there's something happening, we need to know."

Reed's skin turned ashen, fear dancing in her eyes. "Higgins has been amassing artifacts for decades, stealing them from the library. He's...experimented. Joining them together, tearing them apart, you name it. He used my magic to do it– magic I didn't even know I had in me."

Reed raised her glassy eyes to scan over the others in the room. "He's building a new magic system. One that will be undefeatable. One that will end the world as we know it and allow him to be the supreme ruler over everyone."

The words hung heavy in the air as Paige's lips parted, her eyes widening. Had they finally met a problem they couldn't solve?

CHAPTER 31

"*U*ndefeatable magic system?" Paige's stomach twisted into a tight knot even though she didn't understand the words entirely. "What does that mean?"

Drucinda arched an eyebrow. "Are you serious? It's pretty obvious. It's a system that cannot be defeated."

"Yeah, but...like how?" Paige asked.

"I think it's a relevant question," Ronnie said with a shrug. "I mean, the more we know about this the more we can try to tackle it."

"Higgins stumbled upon an ancient tome, one that talked about magic that we had never seen. He managed to reverse engineer one of the artifacts by combining several of the things in our archive."

"So," Dewey said as he buzzed into the air, "he, for example, combined a...MagnoPro with a duplicating mirror to create multiple massive beasts?"

Reed poked a finger at him. "That's the idea, yes, only on a much more grandiose level."

Drucinda's features pinched. "And how is it that he is still alive, by the way. We saw him die."

Reed hung her head, chewing her lower lip. "I'm afraid that's my fault."

Paige arched an eyebrow. "What do you mean?"

"He had a deadly form of cancer. After he died, we…used some of my magic combined with an artifact to resurrect him. It also gave him multiple magical powers. I…I shouldn't have done it but…I had no choice."

"No one is blaming you, Reed. These people staged your murder, kidnapped you, and held you hostage for decades," Ronnie said. "It's not your fault."

"I feel so guilty. Why did I go to that warehouse?"

"What was there, by the way? I followed you but…outside of blood, there was nothing."

"Liches. Two of them. They're part of the cabal."

"Liches?" Devon choked out. "The Liches have partnered with Higgins?"

Reed bobbed her head.

Devon stiffened next to Paige, his jaw tightening. "I need to call my dad."

"Whoa, no," Reed shouted, her heart monitor beeping faster.

"Easy, Reed," Ronnie said, patting her arm. "Try not to get upset."

"I am upset! I didn't share this information so Devon could feed it to his father."

"Hey, my father can be a powerful ally in this. And it sounds like we need all the allies we can get."

"We don't need those type of allies. We'll be beholden to them when this is over which puts us in just as bad of a position as if Higgins takes over the world." Reed's features pinched.

Paige frowned, her mind trying to wrap around the entire scenario. Her reunion with her mother hadn't been what she'd expected. Within hours of waking up, she'd hated her husband and then told them the world was likely about to end.

Now, chaos ensued as arguments broke out about how to handle the tricky situation.

"Okay, Devon, can you hold off for a little while before you speak with your father as a courtesy to the library," Ronnie said. "I need to do a little digging on my end."

"Please be careful, Ronnie," Reed answered. "If you tip them off…"

"I know," Ronnie said with a nod. "We could end up worse off than we are right now."

Drucinda cocked her hip, crossing her arms. "I disagree with all of this. First, I think we should allow Devon to inform his father. The Durand's can be powerful allies in this, and we may need them. Second, I don't believe we should do any digging. We need to strike."

"While I disagree with your first statement, Drucinda has a point about striking immediately. The longer this goes on, the less chance we have of being successful in destroying what they've built."

Ronnie wrinkled her brow. "Well, do we have any idea where to strike? That's the question. We know so very little."

"They have a stronghold they've retreated to. I don't know the exact location, but I believe it's somewhere in the…"

Dewey clasped his paws together. "Please don't say a cold place, please don't say a cold place, please don't say a cold place."

"Artic."

"Noooooo!" Dewey shouted as he flung his arms to the sides.

"I've still got your tiny snowsuit, little man. You'll be fine." Drucinda shifted her gaze to Ronnie. "That's the digging we need to do. Find the location where Higgins is holed up. And we'll destroy it."

"Wait, how are we going to destroy it?"

"Magic bomb," Drucinda said with a shrug.

"I'm not so sure about that, Dru," Reed said with a shake of her head. "He's created magic we've never seen before. A magic bomb could release things into the world that we don't want."

"We can't possibly retrieve all of the assets and defeat Higgins and his merry band of Lichs," Drucinda said. "We need to go big."

"I agree about going big, but...magic bombs are messy."

"So, in other words, we need the properties of both a containment bomb and a magic bomb," Dewey said. "We need to destroy everything then rapidly suck up any traces of magic into a container to be archived."

"That would be a fantastic idea," Ronnie said with a bob of her head. "If that existed."

"I'll invent it," Dewey said. "I can do it. You track down where this little hideout is. I'll invent a magical containment bomb."

Reed arched an eyebrow. "Just like that?"

"Just like that," Dewey said with a nod.

Ronnie lifted her chin. "Dewey created a cure for a day-walking vampire beast mark wound. We won Best Library Team last year."

"Ronnie!" Reed grinned at her. "Congratulations! And Dewey, that sounds...wait...why did Paige need cured from a beast mark."

Her smile faded as she focused on Devon.

"Dimples over here may or may not have marked her early on before he fell in love with her, and accidentally almost killed her," Dewey answered.

"You nearly killed my daughter, and now you married

her?" Reed's voice turned shrill as she balled her fingers into fists.

"Yeah. And it's the subject of my first paranormal romance trilogy," Dewey said. "You can read all about it starting February fourteenth!"

"No way, dude," Devon said, his eyes wide. "Oh, I've got to preorder this. I can't wait."

"No, don't…Mom, don't read that. Dewey used our names and our likenesses but…the story is nothing like what he wrote. There was no…please don't read a steamy romance about me and Devon."

Drucinda rolled her eyes. "Get over it, Paige, there will be thousands of us reading all those steamy details. But the important thing is for us to find Higgins and destroy this magic system. Now, little man, you go start on the bomb with Paige. Ronnie and I will try to find Higgins's lair. Devon, put your father on high alert. If we fail, we'll need him and his entire network."

Devon nodded as he pulled his phone from his pocket and strode from the room.

"I don't like this," Reed answered.

"I know, but this is a good plan," Ronnie said. "You lie back and try to rest, okay? We'll keep you updated."

Paige crossed to her mother, taking her hand. "Mom, we'll fix this, okay?"

Reed reached for her cheek, cupping it. "Oh, Paige…when you were born, I wanted so many things for you…I feel like I've failed you."

"No," Paige said, her features scrunching. "No, you didn't fail me. Look…"

She forced a grin onto her face. "I'm a librarian. It's like… the world pushed me exactly where I needed to go anyway."

"I just…every day that I spent in captivity, I wondered about you, dreamed about you, lamented the life we'd lost. I could have raised you in the library, taught you so many things."

"Stopped her from marrying Devon, but then would we have as great of a story on our hands?" Dewey asked.

"I, uh, I think we'd have a better one, but that's just me."

"The beef cake isn't that bad," Dewey said as he landed on the mattress next to Reed. "Give him a chance. And Paige, too. Wait until you see what she can achieve. You'll be amazed. Your daughter is pretty great."

Reed offered Paige a glassy-eyed grin. "I'm so proud of you, Paige. I just…wish I'd raised you."

"Me too. But hopefully we'll be able to spend lots of time together now. After we defeat the evil guy looking to take over the world, of course."

Reed chuckled, a tear escaping to her cheek. "Of course."

"We'd better get going. I have a lot to learn about these bombs. I'll check soon," Paige said, reluctantly letting go of her mother's hand.

Reed bobbed her head as she settled back into the pillow. "I look forward to it."

Paige backed from the room, her stomach tightening as she turned her back on her mother. Every step she took away from her made her nervous. What if she fell back into the coma? What if she disappeared again?

"Paige?" Dewey asked softly.

"Sorry, just…it's hard walking away from her after everything that's happened."

"Oh, right, that, yeah."

"What did you think it was?" Paige asked, her features scrunched.

"Hunger. I'm pretty hungry."

Paige's shoulders slumped. "Okay, we'll get you some food."

"I think you need some, too, Paige. It shouldn't be that hard to walk."

"What?" She shook her head. "No, not…it's hard to leave my mom in that hospital room because I'm afraid I'll go back, and she won't be there.'

"Well, I mean, they may take her for tests…"

Paige slapped a palm against her forehead. "No, I mean… she'll be gone. Like dead or…missing again."

"Ohhh, this is irrational fear, I see."

"Yes, Dewey," she answered, her tone unimpressed, "irrational fear. Which I am totally entitled to after what happened."

"Sure, of course you are. But could you possibly have it *after* we've invented a new bomb because I really need you to focus."

Paige heaved a sigh as she drummed her fingers against the counter. "Okay, fine. You have my full attention."

"Good, start reading up on these bombs so you can help me with my tests. I'm going to begin formulation on a few options, and we'll see what happens."

"Why is that so frightening to me?"

Dewey squashed his eyebrows together. "No idea. Can't come up with a reason. Now, grab the RP and get a feel for these things."

Paige nodded as she slid the device off of the counter and shuffled to the chair. A quick search of containment bombs revealed that, unlike their more violent counterparts, simply created a vacuum that sucked all the magic inside of it.

Paige flicked her eyebrows up. *Easy enough.*

She may have to read more about how it pulls the magic inside effectively to contain it, but she moved on to study the magic bomb. These seemed to range from relatively mundane things that sent out tiny spurts of magic into the air that quickly fizzled to massively violent explosions that would destroy virtually everything in their paths and could spew magic into the air, sending it out untethered into the world to latch onto anything.

It was widely believed that many artifacts were created this way.

"Hmm, interesting," Paige murmured.

"What is?" Dewey asked, glancing at her through a pair of safety googles.

"This magic bomb that has been responsible for some artifact creation."

"Oh, yeah obviously. I mean, it's not the only way artifacts are created, but it is a way. We need to make sure we don't do that."

"Yeah, with this new sort of magic, we don't want it getting out at all. It's sort of scary."

"Sort of? It's terrifying. A new magical landscape? And Higgins at the helm? No thanks. Now, have you done your research? I'd like to run some ideas past you."

Paige rose and crossed to him. "I have, but I don't see how this is going to work. One literally sucks things in while the other pushes energy out to destroy things. How can we do both?"

"Well, here's my idea...first, we blow it all to smithereens. Massive explosion that just wipes out everything in its path. *Then*, we quickly reverse course and collect it all up with a containment bomb."

"Oh, that's actually...a really simple, but brilliant solution," Paige said with a nod, her features turning impressed.

Dewey puffed out his chest. "Right? Brilliantly simple, that's me."

The grin slipped from his face. "No wait...that's...I'm brilliant, let's leave it at that."

"Okay," Paige said with a grin. "Now, how do we do this?"

"Well, that's what I don't know. I mean, in theory this is

fantastic, but in practice…well, we're going to need to figure out how we can ensure we've blown everything sky high but also reach one hundred percent containment. If even a speck of this new magic is left, it could spell trouble for us."

"So, maybe…we do like a bomb with a big radius, but then, a containment bomb with a bigger radius," Paige suggested.

"I like it. Let's see if we can do it."

"Wait, how will we know?"

"Simple," Dewey said, motioning toward a setup tucked behind a massive piece of glass. "We can test it inside here. We'll do it on the small scale, then extrapolate our results."

"Oh, got it. Well, this should be easy then."

"Yeah, seems almost too easy," Dewey answered as he began gathering materials from the shelves. "Then again…we *are* geniuses, so maybe it's just easy for us."

"Also, we're sort of new to the game and that kind of energy can really change things. You know, you get stuck in a mindset after so long, and you don't think of fresh ideas."

"Exactly," Dewey answered, measuring out a variety of powders and liquids. "There's a reason we're the best library team."

Paige shot a finger gun at him with a wink. "Yep and looking to take that title again."

"Heck yeah!" Dewey said as he put together the materials he'd mixed into a plastic container with a wick.

"Okay, now I've made this for a blow radius on the first bomb of about three feet, and on the second four."

"Let's see how she does."

Paige donned a pair of googles as Dewey delivered the device to the test area. He set a few bits of pretend magic loose in the chamber along with some fake artifacts.

"Light fire and get away," he said as he lit the wick and buzzed backward to join Paige.

They waited with bated breath. The wick burned down to nothing. Then nothing happened.

"What the he– "

The bomb suddenly blew violently inside the test chamber. Paige ducked instinctively, keeping her eyes trained on the bits of artifact fluttering in the air.

Seconds later, they began being pulled back into the tube that had housed the bomb.

"Come on, come on," Dewey said. "Shoot!"

A few blobs of magic and bits of artifact still floated in the chamber after the bomb finished.

"Second radius of five?" Paige suggested.

"At least. I'm thinking we do six just to be safe."

"Is there any harm in going bigger?"

"Not from my perspective," Dewey said.

He built a second bomb, and after three tests they were satisfied that they'd achieved the desired effect and would leave no magic traces in the atmosphere.

Dewey peeled off his goggles. "Well, we solved that pretty easily. Now, all we need to do is get to the lair and set it off."

Paige raised her hand in the air, seeking a high five. "Yep. Bad guy's lair…here we come."

Dewey slapped a paw against her palm, and both their eyes went wide. "We did it!" Paige exclaimed.

"Yep, we did," Dewey said with a nod. "Because we're awesome. All we had to do was solve this problem and suddenly, we're awesome."

"Yeah! Let's go back and check on my mom and see if the others completed their task."

"Okay," Dewey said, landing on her shoulder.

They traversed the hospital's halls back to Reed's room, finding her asleep.

Paige tiptoed back into the hall as the Drucinda, Ronnie, and Devon approached.

"Well?" Drucinda asked as Paige pressed a finger to her lips.

"She's asleep. We managed to create the bomb. Did you find the lair?"

Drucinda screwed up her face. "Lair?"

Paige crossed her arms, her features unimpressed. "What do you want me to call it? The place where the bad guys are?"

"How about the target?" Drucinda arched an eyebrow.

"Oh, right, that's…good. Umm, so have you found the target?"

"Yes, we have," Ronnie said with a nod. "Smack dab in the center of the Arctic. We're prepping the plane and your gear."

"Any luck with the bomb?" Drucinda asked.

"We're ready to roll," Dewey said. "We successfully tested it thrice. Now, I just need the rough specs of the la–target, and we can extrapolate the bomb to be large enough."

"I've got the rough size…let me warn you, it's big."

"No problem for my bomb. Trust me, Ronnie…we've got Best Library Team in the bag again this year." Dewey patted her on the shoulder.

"All right. I'll email you the specs, you build the bomb, Drucinda will get you to the spot– "

"And we'll handle the rest," Dewey said, raising his chin.

"Yep…with any luck in a matter of hours…Higgins and his evil plan will be wiped off the face of this Earth." Paige grinned, confidence swelling in her. They were about to defeat the bad guys once and for all. What could go wrong?

CHAPTER 32

Snow pelted them, covering them in a thick blanket as they trudged along. Paige's boots sank with every step, and she wrangled herself free with her walking sticks.

"Remind me why we couldn't take the Cats closer?" she shouted over the whipping wind as she stopped to catch her breath.

In his thermal suit and perched on her shoulder, Dewey glanced at her through his snow goggles. "Because the rumbling would alert the people in the lair."

"You mean the target?" Paige asked.

"Right, that."

"Thank goodness Devon is carrying the bomb," Paige said with a shake of her head. "Ugh."

"Is there a problem?" Drucinda shouted from several feet in front of them.

"No!" Paige called back with a wave of her thickly gloved hand.

"Onward," Dewey said.

"We should have brought a dog sled. This is the worst."

"You should have kept Drucinda's body for this," Dewey answered.

"Oh, yes," Paige said as she let her head fall back. "Why didn't I think ahead?"

"Really. I mean, this would have been a cake walk."

"It really was so nice. I should work out more."

"And eat less breadsticks," Dewey added.

"Or I could just struggle every time we have to trudge through a snowstorm in the Arctic which isn't that many times so…payoff really isn't worth it."

"I agree. I'd never give up the breadsticks."

Paige wrinkled her nose. "I hope Devon doesn't expect me to work out with him."

"Oh yeah, you married a hot, beefy guy."

"I did. I really hope my mom takes to him eventually." Paige heaved a sigh, shaking her head as she recalled her mother's reaction to her marriage.

"It's got to be weird for her," Dewey countered. "I mean… the last she saw Devon, he was delivering you after being called away from his playboy life by his good friend, Drucinda…Ohhhhhh."

"What?" Paige asked.

"Oh wow. Oh my gosh. Oh, I really wish I would have brought my voice recorder."

"What is it?"

Dewey patted her on the head. "Well…I was thinking… Your mom said Devon was a notorious playboy. But I wonder if…delivering you changed him in some way. Like suddenly, he was thrust into Dad mode. His playboy tendencies faded because he'd been given a new purpose, a new sense of self."

Paige squashed her features. "Oh, that's…kind of messed up. Like I changed Devon's life when he delivered me because he felt like a dad relationship, and then we got married."

"Walk faster, catch up with Devon...I've got to know if this is true."

"No, I don't want to know. I'm...disgusted."

"Come on, Paige." Dewey shimmied around on her shoulder before he cupped his paws around his mouth. "Devon! Devon!"

The man twisted to eye them before he trudged back to them. "You okay? Paige? Do you need a rest?"

"No, I don't need a rest. Just...walk away from us."

"Huh?" Devon screwed up his face.

"Listen, Muscles, I have a question for you," Dewey said.

"Okay," Devon answered as they continued forward through the blizzard.

"Would you say that delivering Paige changed your life."

He tugged his lips into a smirk. "Well, obviously, since I married her."

"Ugh," Paige groaned.

"No," Dewey said with a shake of his head. "Is delivering Paige the moment that made you give up your playboy ways and want to settle down?"

"Oh, uh, no. I mean, I wasn't ever really *that* much of a playboy. I just...lots of women threw themselves at me because I'm a prince. It comes with the territory. But, you know, mostly I liked to hang out with Drucinda and play-fight and stuff."

"Wow, just wow," Dewey answered. "I mean...look at you, the playboy prince with a heart of gold."

Devon shot him a dimpled grin. "I like that. Hey, can you use that in the advertising for our book?"

"Oh-ho, yes, I can, buddy. All the ladies love a bad boy with a heart of gold. We'll make a mint."

"I am so glad this is working out for you both. Meanwhile, my reputation is ruined." Paige rolled her eyes.

"Aw, come on, Paige. It's not. Everyone is just going to know that you're…easily wooed by power, money, and washboard abs."

Paige heaved a sigh, her lungs hurting from the cold weather. "You know what, I don't even care. Whatever. Let's just end this stupid thing with Higgins and focus on getting back to our future. My mom is alive, I've got my dream job…"

"You've got your dream husband," Devon said with a grin.

Paige pressed her lips together. "Fine, okay, yes, you're a good husband."

Devon slid an arm around her shoulders. "Aw, Paige, that's the nicest thing you've ever said to me."

"Love is in the air," Dewey said. "And soon, so will my bomb. Now, let's get moving so we can finish this."

They continued their trek, finally approaching a lone igloo in the middle of the frozen tundra.

"Wow, that's the lair?" Paige asked as they huddled a distance away, glancing through night vision binoculars at it.

"It's underground. It spreads out underneath that igloo. We must enter there and search for the archive to blow it. Devon and I will handle the guards at the entrance. Once we're inside, you two find the archive and set off the bomb. We will find Higgins and destroy him."

"What about the Liches?" Paige asked.

"They'll fall in line when they don't have another option," Drucinda answered as she stowed the binoculars in her backpack.

"Should we go with you? In case you need an assist with the guards?" Paige asked.

Drucinda chuckled, shooting Devon an amused glance. "Are you quite serious?"

"Well, I mean…we've fought off werewolves and all kinds of stuff, actually. So…"

"Barely," Drucinda answered. "I'm certain we'll be fine."

"Okay, fine. I'm not going to fight you on it. Just…hurry up. I'm cold."

Drucinda rolled her eyes as she rose. "Let's go, Devon. Your bride is cold."

"I'll warm you up later," he said with a cheeky grin before he stood.

Paige and Dewey waited as they crept forward and disappeared into the igloo. "I can't decide if I feel upset over being sidelined or glad."

"Oh, I'm glad. Definitely. We can't fight worth anything. I mean…we can scrap a little…protect ourselves, but as far as a strategic strike to take down a set of guards. Nah."

"Good point, let them do the heavy lifting."

"Yeah, we need to do the smart work. Like set off our bomb that is going to save the world *and* win us Best Library Team second year running."

"Heck yeah," Paige said, raising her hand for a high five.

They connected for a second time, and Dewey gave her a thumbs up. "We're getting good at that."

"I know. Because we're awesome."

They chuckled together before a light flashed in the distance at the entrance of the igloo.

"There's our signal," Paige said as she rose, hurrying through the snow toward it.

"Almost there," Dewey said. "And then we'll end this once and for all."

"Can't wait."

They reached the entrance, ducking inside to find Devon tying up the second guard. He shifted the backpack with the bomb off his back and handed it to Paige.

"All right, you two, go set that bomb," Drucinda said as

she used one of the guard's badges to open the heavy metal door.

A long set of dark stairs stretched in front of them. Paige frowned. "Ugh, they couldn't have put in an elevator?"

"Maybe you ought to try a workout sometime, darling," Drucinda answered before she disappeared down them.

"Just take your time, Paige. And if you run into any trouble…"

She tapped her radio. "I'll call."

He grinned at her before he descended the stairs.

Paige grabbed hold of the metal railing as she started her descent. "Why are there so many stairs?"

"Beats me. Higgins is sort of strange though."

They finally spilled into a series of hallways. Paige slid her gaze down one hall, then the next. "So, which way?"

"Hmmm, right, left, or straight?" Dewey said. "Which way would the archive be? And please don't ask the question about if you were an archive because– "

"I know, I know. I can't be an archive." She heaved a sigh and shrugged. "Let's go left."

Paige took a step in that direction.

"Wait, why?" Dewey asked.

"Why not?"

"Well…traditionally, most people would suggest right, or straight. But you suggested left."

"Well, I just…I figured we'd start here and work our way around."

Dewey rubbed his chin. "Why not start right and work our way around."

"Then we'd be going counterclockwise, but in my version, we go clockwise."

"Hmm." Dewey narrows his eyes. "That's a valid point. Okay, we'll go left."

Paige huffed out a breath as she entered the hall and

traversed past a few doors that appeared to house laboratories.

"Those must be his spaces for creating the new magic," Dewey said. "Oh, what beautiful facilities. If I wasn't firmly team library, I'd defect."

"Dewey!" Paige shouted. "You can't go over to the dark side because they have nice labs."

"I can…I bet they also have cookies, too."

She clicked her tongue, rolling her eyes as she wandered further down the hall to a set of double doors at the end. "Oh, this could be the jackpot."

"Could be. It would make sense if they put the archives at the end of the hall from the labs."

"Yeah," Paige said with a grin as she pushed the crash bar to open the doors. "Look at us picking the right way for once, huh?"

"It's all coming together for us, Paige." Dewey raised his eyebrows, an excited expression on his face.

"I know. All we need to do is set off this bomb, and we're on easy street."

Dewey threw his head back with a laugh. "Yep. Smooth sailing from here on out."

"Oh, it's going to be so nice. Just normal asset retrievals!"

"Can you imagine?" Dewey asked as they wandered further into the darkened space filled with shelving units. "Just run out and get a haunted necklace or something."

Paige slapped her thighs with a laugh. "Kids' stuff."

"Child's play," Dewey answered.

Paige bobbed her head. "We're going to be bored because we'd literally saved the world so many times that this will just be mundane."

"I know," Dewey answered. "But we can invent stuff to challenge ourselves. Like we invented this bomb. Clearly, we're smart."

"Geniuses," Paige said with a nod.

"Exactly," Dewey agreed. "So, we'll be able to be the leaders in inventing new technologies and ways to counterbalance the magic in the world."

"It's going to be so nice." Paige glanced overhead. "Do you think this is the center of the room?"

"Mmm, looks close enough to me. Let's drop the bomb and get this over with."

Paige dropped to one knee, shifting the backpack off her back and onto the cold floor. "You brought a lighter, right?"

Dewey's face went blank, his eyes going wide.

"Dewey!" Paige said, her voice sharp and shrill.

A grin spread across his face. "Kidding." He unzipped a pocket in his snowsuit and pulled out a lighter. "See."

Paige pressed a hand against her chest, breathing a sigh of relief. "Don't scare me like that. That's the exact kind of stuff we normally do to screw up."

"You forget," Dewey said, poking a finger at her, "we're not screw-ups anymore."

"Oh, right. We're awesome now."

"Yep."

Paige set the bomb on the floor, the wick pointing in the air. "Okay…all we need to do is light it and this entire nightmare is over."

Dewey stared down at the homemade magic containment bomb. "Yep."

He shoved the lighter toward Paige. "You do the honors. You deserve it."

She pressed a hand against her heart. "Aww, thanks, Dewey."

With a deep breath, she tightened her fingers around the lighter, her mind racing. After a second, she flicked the light to life. The flame danced, and she eyed it for a second before she lowered it to the wick.

"Burn, baby, burn," Paige whispered as the flame lit the wick.

"Time to leave!" Dewey shouted.

Paige flung the backpack onto her back and raced away from the bomb, aiming for the double doors that would lead to the hall.

They made it to the door. Paige glanced back over her shoulder one last time before she tugged it open.

They escaped into the hall, grinning at each other as Paige made her way back toward the entrance.

After a few steps, she glanced over her shoulder again, her features pinching. "Is it...eerily quiet in here?"

Dewey rubbed his chin. "Yeah...sort of. Although, maybe it's fine. Maybe those doors are soundproof or something."

"Yeah, that's probably it," Paige said, facing front again as she continued toward the exit. "Although...maybe...maybe we should check. Just be sure it destroyed everything and sucked up all the magic."

"Wouldn't hurt to peek in the doors, I guess," Dewey said.

Paige whipped around and hurried back to the double doors. She pressed her ear against them before she shook her head. "Nothing. I hear nothing."

"Just crack it open a little. The whirlwind is pretty strong, so we don't want to get caught."

Paige nodded as she inched the door back. A second later, she tugged it open fully. "Nothing. Nothing happened. Should we go in there?"

"Well, we have time if it didn't go off. I mean, first it destroys the magic, then it sucks it in, so we can safely get out in time before the vortex happens."

"Maybe something happened to the wick," Paige suggested as she snaked her way toward the middle of the room.

As they rounded one of the shelves, she spotted the bomb with no active fire burning down its wick.

"Well, there we are. The wick must not have worked."

"I brought an extra," Dewey said. "We'll just feed it in and relight it."

"Nice," Paige said as she approached it. "Now, we're starting to use our brains."

As Paige approached the bomb, it began to rumble. She furrowed her brow before glancing at Dewey. "Uh…"

"Is that…"

Paige's heart skipped a beat, her eyes widening. "It's going to blow!"

"Run!" Dewey shouted.

Paige spun her heel and raced back toward the door.

"Don't worry, it destroys magic first, then sucks it in, so we'll make it easily."

Paige nodded as she continued to race toward the exit. A loud explosion sounded behind her, and she clapped her hands over her ears, her feet still propelling her forward.

She continued running but found herself not moving. Then, she began to slide backward. "Uhhh."

"Oh, shoot," Dewey said as he clung to Paige.

"What?"

"The stupid bomb is sucking in the magic, *then* destroying it!" Dewey cried.

"What?!" Paige glanced over her shoulder with a frightened expression. "OMG. We're going to get sucked right into it!"

CHAPTER 33

*P*aige reached for one of the shelves as items flew
off of it and grabbed hold.

"Hang on, Paige!" Dewey said as he clung to her. "We've
got to ride this out."

"What was it you said about smooth sailing?" she asked as
her feet lifted off the ground.

"I didn't," he shouted over the din. "I said easy street."

She clenched her teeth. "Same difference."

"Not really. One is a solid surface, the other is liquid.
Completely different mediums."

With a growl, she shook her head. "It doesn't matter. How
are we going to survive this? I can't hang on that much
longer and the bomb isn't even close to finishing."

"Dig deep, Paige!" Dewey shouted. "We can't die now! We
just learned to high five!"

She clenched her teeth, her fingers struggling to hang on
to the shelf as the bomb worked to suck in all of the dark
magic surrounding them.

With her eyes squeezed closed, she focused all of her

energy on surviving the cyclone that threatened to obliterate them from the earth.

"I'm…not…going…to…make…it!" She ground her teeth together, her fingers beginning to slip.

"Just a few more seconds, Paige! It's nearly done!"

Her lips tugged into a tight grimace, her muscles shaking from the tension to hang on.

Finally, the strain pulling against her lessened. Her feet brushed against the ground again. As the last of the whipping wind died down, she sucked in deep breaths, collapsing to the floor with her muscles quivering. "Oh, that was…intense. I can't even right now."

"Well, you may want to try," Dewey answered. "Because that bomb…it's about to blow again."

"What?" Paige cried as she snapped her eyes open and stared down at it.

The pipe, now blackened at the edges, rattled around on the floor like it would blow at any minute.

"Yeah, it must have reacted with some of the dark magic or something. I don't know, but I can't be responsible for what's about to happen."

"What do you mean you can't be responsible? You are responsible. You're definitely responsible!"

"Geez, Paige," Dewey said with a frown, "way to pile on the guilt. Look, how was I to know that whatever Higgins invented was going to do this. Anyway, this is no time to argue. We have to get out of here."

Paige scrambled to her feet, her muscles screaming as she pushed them to move.

Dewey landed on her shoulder again, clinging to her. "Run!"

"I'm trying. I can barely move after all that tension."

"That was on your arms, not your legs. Those should still be good."

Paige shot him an angry glance as she stumbled her way to the double doors.

"Better call Devon and Drucinda, too."

"Do you think you can handle something? I'm busy trying to run away to save our lives." She thrust the radio toward him.

"Right," Dewey said as he grabbed it and pressed the button. "Hey guys, Dewey here."

"Skip the small talk and tell them to get out!" Paige screamed as she barreled down the hall.

"Oh, right, okay." He pressed the button again. "Hey, you should get out of here ASAP because the bomb is malfunctioning and I'm pretty certain it's about to blow this place sky high, so...you know wrap up what you're doing and leave."

Paige ripped the radio from his fingers with a shake of her head. "Devon, Drucinda. Get out now. This whole place is going to blow."

"Wow," Dewey said as Paige reached the intersection with the other halls. "That was really succinct."

"We're already outside," Drucinda answered. "Moving away from the facility now."

Paige screwed up her face. "How are they already outside? Why is she so good at everything?"

"I don't know, but I kind of wish you had her body right now because it feels like you're running really slowly and we're not going to make it."

"Oh, am I?" Paige asked as she tried to push her rubbery legs faster toward the stairs. "Am I running *really slowly*? Maybe get off my shoulder and fly out if I'm going to slow for you."

"No, I mean...I'll stick with you, but...feels like there could be more effort on your part."

"Shut up, Dewey!" Paige growled as she reached the steps

and pushed her weary limbs to climb up.

"Sure is a lot of stairs. Don't know what will happen if we're on the stairs when that bomb blows…"

"I'm going as fast as I can." She panted for breath as she pushed herself to continue without stopping for a break.

By the time she reached the top, her knees threatened to buckle, and her lungs hurt from wheezing for breath. She stumbled forward through the door into the igloo and dove through the exit into the cold snow beyond.

She pushed herself to trudge further from the igloo.

"Keep going, Paige. We want to be as far away from this place as we can when the bomb bl– "

His words cut off as a rumbling shook the earth before fire spewed from it. The force of the explosion knocked her from her feet, slamming her into the blanket of snow.

She groaned as the forces from the explosion waned, struggled to push up to stand in the snowbank.

"Whew, just made it," Dewey said with a swipe of his brow. "Good thing I pushed you."

"Yeah, good thing," Paige said with a groan as she climbed to her feet and brushed the packed snow from her snowsuit.

"Where are Devon and Drucinda? I'd like to get back and report our success," Dewey said.

A light blinked in the distance, signaling to them.

"There," Paige said with a heavy sigh. "Oh, let's hope they were able to do what they needed to do, and this is over."

"Only one way to find out," Dewey said.

After another second of rest, Paige trudged forward through the snow toward the others. As she approached, she spotted a third figure with them.

"Is that…"

"Higgins," Dewey answered with a bob of his head. "They took him out of there."

Paige closed the distance between them, her features tugged into a frown as she eyed the man. "Why is he here?"

"Because," Drucinda answered, "he ought to face what he's done. He should be tried and convicted."

"Oh, yeah, good call," Paige said with a bob of her head. "He should have to pay for what he's done."

"Let's get him back to Shadow Harbor. I know more than one person who will love to see you face the consequences of your actions, Higgins," Drucinda said as she shoved him forward.

He sneered at her but before he could answer, she smacked him across the face, knocking him to the ground. "That was for kidnapping my best friend."

She cracked him again, sending him sprawling on his side into the snow. "That was for keeping her for thirty years."

He pulled himself up to sit on his haunches when she knocked him down again. "That was robbing Paige of her mother."

Drucinda's voice turned more frenzied as she raised her hand to strike again.

Devon grabbed hold of her arm, pinning it behind her back. "Easy, Dru, easy."

"Sorry," she said, her chest heaving for air. "Got carried away."

"Let's just take him back to Shadow Harbor and let him be tried for the criminal he is," Paige recommended.

Drucinda yanked her arm from Devon's grasp with a nod. "You're right. It's over now. Let's finish this."

* * *

Three months later

. . .

328

Paige bounced down the stairs into the archives as Dewey buzzed across space, the RP in his hand.

"Have you seen the news?" he asked with a grin.

He flashed the screen toward her, and she read the headline. *Higgins sentenced to life without possibility of parole.*

A grin crossed her features. "So, it's over."

"It's over, Paige. He's done. Higgins is going to jail for a very, very long time."

"Good," Drucinda answered as she sauntered from between the shelves. "He ought to be fed to the wolves after what he did, but at least he'll have a very long time to think about it."

Paige offered her a nod with a tight-lipped smile as her mother appeared behind Drucinda. "Hi, Mom. How are you feeling?"

"Pretty good. I see we have a new mission alert over there."

Paige slid her eyes sideways as the door slammed at the top of the stairs.

A second later, Devon slid his arm around her. "Hey, babe, new mission?"

"Looks like it." Paige wandered to the ticker and pulled the tape from it.

"What do we got?" Dewey asked.

She glanced up, her gaze scanning all of the faces in the room. "Red level. Special request of the new Shadow Harbor Library Team. What do you think? Go for it or pass it to the Grand?"

"Go for it," the others answered at once.

"Darn right," Dewey added. "We're the best library team out there. This mission is ours."

Paige sucked in a breath. "Okay. Looks like this is the first mission in a new era."

"And what an era it will be," Dewey answered as he landed on her shoulder, his paw raised for a high-five.

She slapped her hand in the air, missing his paw entirely. "Yeah, it's going to be the same as before, isn't it?"

"Probably," he answered.

"But," she said, "we'll get through it. We always do."

And with the help of her husband, mother, and new best friend, Drucinda, they would take the magical world by storm.

The End
That's it for Paige and Dewey!

Want to read more fantasy?
Read *Shadows of the Past*

A haunting melody. A whisper of magic. Can she withstand the dangerous pull of a supernatural abyss?

Josie Benson's nights are plagued by nightmares so vivid they blur the lines of reality. When a centuries-old music box surfaces on her doorstep, playing a tune that echoes in the darkest corners of her subconscious, her life spirals into a chilling mystery–one with life-changing potential. Inside the box lies a ruby necklace, hinting at otherworldly secrets buried in the shadows of her past.

Guided by an enigmatic stranger and cryptic visions, Josie is thrust into a maze of hidden truths buried along the rugged Maine coastline. But his presence weaves a tapestry of danger, entangled with a legacy that could reshape her world.

Each clue Josie uncovers draws her deeper into a realm of

ancient magic, supernatural mysteries, and lurking danger. And when she's confronted by a supernatural foe with a malevolent agenda, Josie must unravel her mysterious past and confront an unknown future.

If you love mortals meets immortals and strong female heroines, you'll love Book 1 of Nellie H. Steele's Shadow Slayers series.

Click HERE to get your copy now!

Let's keep in touch! Join my newsletter and receive five free books!

ABOUT THE AUTHOR

Award-winning author Nellie H. Steele writes in as many genres as she reads, ranging from mystery to fantasy and allowing readers to escape reality and enter enchanting worlds filled with unique, lovable characters.

Addicted to books since she could read, Nellie escaped to fictional worlds like the ones created by Carolyn Keene or Victoria Holt long before she decided to put pen to paper and create her own realities.

When she's not spinning a cozy mystery tale, building a new realm in a contemporary fantasy, or writing another action-adventure car chase, you can find her shuffling through her Noah's Ark of rescue animals or enjoying a hot cuppa (that's tea for most Americans.)

Join her Facebook Readers' Group here!

OTHER SERIES BY NELLIE H. STEELE

Cozy Mystery Series

Cate Kensie Mysteries
Lily & Cassie by the Sea Mysteries
Pearl Party Mysteries
Middle Age is Murder Cozy Mysteries
Whispers of Witchcraft

Supernatural Suspense/Urban Fantasy

Shadow Slayers Stories
Duchess of Blackmoore Mysteries
Shelving Magic

Adventure

Maggie Edwards Adventures
Clif & Ri on the Sea

Made in the USA
Las Vegas, NV
14 October 2024